THE
LIBRARIANS
AND THE
POT OF GOLD

THE
LIBRARIANS
AND THE
POT OF GOLD

GREG COX

TOR

A TOM DOHERTY ASSOCIATES BOOK
NEW YORK

THE LIBRARIANS AND THE POT OF GOLD

A Tor Book
Published by Tom Doherty Associates
175 Fifth Avenue
New York, NY 10010

www.tor-forge.com

The Library of Congress Cataloging-in-Publication Data
is available upon request.

ISBN 978-0-7653-8410-2 (hardcover)
ISBN 978-0-7653-8411-9 (trade paperback)
ISBN 978-0-7653-8412-6 (ebook)

First Edition: October 2018

Printed in the United States of America

0 9 8 7 6 5 4 3 2 1

To public libraries everywhere

THE
LIBRARIANS
AND THE
POT OF GOLD

1

A ring of standing stones crowned the summit of a rocky mountain on the rugged west coast of Erin, overlooking the island-spotted bay thousands of feet below. Although spring was drawing nigh, the night was cool and damp. A gibbous moon cast its chilly radiance upon the looming, rough-hewn stones, which had watched mutely over the lonely mountaintop for millennia.

Lady Sibella was less patient.

She stood at the center of the ring before an equally primeval stone altar. A dark silk robe, of the finest quality, shielded her from the cool vernal winds blowing off the ocean. A scowl marred her pale, aristocratic features, whose gleaming skin seemed almost iridescent in the moonlight. Lustrous black hair was coiled atop her head in the style of a lady of means. Long, sinuous fingers toyed with an exquisitely crafted bronze dagger with a hilt shaped like a striking serpent. The dagger was an emblem of her authority, passed down from one generation of leaders to another by an ancient, clandestine order whose tireless pursuit of magic and power was destined to someday transform the world.

The Serpent Brotherhood.

"I grow weary of waiting," she announced, her accent that of a wellborn Briton. "The appointed hour has come and gone. The little man tests my forbearance."

Two warriors accompanied her, to guard her person and to carry out her wishes, sanguinary or otherwise. One was a Greek mercenary, the other a disgraced Roman legionnaire. The latter had his short sword drawn, the better to defend her, while the former held a bundle wrapped in a plain lamb-skin blanket. A mewling sound escaped the bundle, which was cradled in the mercenary's brawny arms. Sibella's stomach grumbled at the sound, reminding her that she had not dined in hours.

"Perhaps he has been delayed, milady," the Roman said. His clean-shaven face bore a snake tattoo on one cheek.

"Not for much longer, I hope." She tapped her foot against the stony ground. "My time is valuable . . . and my nature none too forgiving."

She gazed past the standing stones at the sleeping woods and pastures beyond the eastern slope of the mountain. Only a few pathetic farms and hovels could be glimpsed in the distance, the smoke from their pungent turf fires rising up from thatched huts cowering behind crude walls of rock or timber. Ireland was a backward, barbaric isle, far from the comforts of civilization; a land of barely literate savages, so far removed from the affairs of the greater world that even Rome had left it untouched. Sibella had journeyed a long way, crossing the Irish Sea, to reach this benighted isle. She hoped the voyage was worth it.

"And if he does not come?" the Greek asked.

Ice entered Sibella's voice. Her finger tested the point of her ophidian dagger.

"Then he will learn not to trifle with his betters." A rustling in the brush reached her ears. She raised her voice, calling out to the shadows outside the stone ring. "If you can hear me, show yourself at once, before I do something you will almost certainly regret."

At first, none answered, but then a voice responded in the peculiar Gaelic tongue of the isle.

"No need for threat. Here I be, as agreed."

A diminutive figure detached himself from the shadows at the base of one of the standing stones. No more than two feet tall, the newcomer was the size of a child, but had the appearance of a man in his forties, right down to his bushy red beard. His cocked hat, jacket, and breeches were forest green, while brass buckles adorned his belt and shoes. Tiny fingers gripped a shillelagh of proportional size. The sturdy blackthorn walking stick was topped by a bulbous knob, making it useful as a cudgel as well.

"Took you long enough, sprite," Sibella said. "Or is punctuality not deemed a virtue among your kind?"

"'Twas no easy task you set for me," the leprechaun said, bristling at her tone. He glanced anxiously over his shoulder as though fearful that he was being pursued. "But I've brought what ye asked for."

"I should hope so," Sibella said. "Show me."

"As ye wish."

There was a ripple in the air before him, as of a glamour being cast aside, and a sizable pot of gold was revealed before the leprechaun. A king's ransom in golden coins was piled within the antique bronze pot, which was adorned with the interlocking spirals and triskeles so beloved by Celtic artisans. The embossed image of a pagan god presided over one panel, Sibella observed. The coins themselves gleamed in the moonlight, as though freshly minted. The warriors flanking Sibella gasped out loud. She could practically smell the avarice surging through their veins, not that she could blame her men for their reaction. A fortune in gold was enough to awe any mortal.

"Yesss." Sibella's slitted yellow eyes widened at the sight of the treasure that was finally within her grasp. Her icy heart beat a little faster. "Fetch it!" she eagerly ordered the Roman. "I must have it!"

"Be not so hasty!" the leprechaun objected. With a wave of his shillelagh, he banished the pot and its gleaming contents, so that it vanished from sight. "What of yer end of the bargain?"

Sibella scowled, unhappy at the delay but willing to put up with the inconvenience if it meant securing the pot with a minimum of bother. She nodded grudgingly at the Greek, who stepped forward and laid his bundle on the sacrificial altar before her. Looking grateful to be rid of his unmanly burden, he unwrapped the swaddling to expose its squirming contents: a baby girl no more than a month old.

A look of distaste crossed Sibella's face. She had little use for children, except perhaps as appetizers. Her stomach grumbled once more.

"Ah, ye poor motherless babe," the leprechaun murmured. "Let me spirit ye away from this wretched place!"

Now it was the leprechaun's turn to start forward eagerly, but Sibella scraped the blade of her dagger against the stone altar to get his attention. He froze in place as she raised the knife above the defenseless infant.

"Who is being hasty now?" she said mockingly. Her free hand caressed the top of the ancient altar, her fingertips traced the winding grooves and drains carved into the stone by artisans of ages past. "Did you know that this mountain, known to the rustics hereabouts as Cruachan Aigle, has long been sacred to the fierce god Crom—and before that to even darker, more voracious deities? This plump little morsel would hardly be the first innocent to be sacrificed upon this venerable stone, let alone the first to perish at my hand."

"She-devil!" The leprechaun flushed with anger. "What kind of woman are ye to threaten a helpless babe?"

"I assure you I am quite cold-blooded . . . literally." She let the sharpened blade of her ceremonial dagger catch the moonlight. "And the Serpent Brotherhood is hardly known for its benevolence."

"That it's not," the leprechaun muttered darkly. Conceding defeat, he lifted the glamour hiding the pot so that the gold glittered brightly once more. "Very well then. Take your treasure, much good may it do ye."

"Oh, you have no idea what plans I have for this divine prize," she gloated. "Nor does the world beyond this pitiful island. My ambitions are immensely bigger than you, little man!"

At her bidding, the Roman sheathed his sword and strode forward to claim the pot. Grunting beneath the weight of the gold, he placed it on the altar next to the mortal child, who had begun to whimper annoyingly.

Sibella ignored the infant, her gaze fixed only on the treasure before her.

"At last," she exulted. "After so much time and trouble . . ."

"Crow over yer spoils later," the leprechaun said, frowning. "I've paid yer ransom. Now give me the child."

Sibella laughed out loud.

"Why should I, sprite?" She placed the blade against the baby's throat. "I still have the upper hand here, not you." She chuckled at his naiveté. "Are all the denizens of this absurd little island so trusting? Or has sentiment simply gotten the better of your judgment?"

The shocked look on the leprechaun's face was almost worth the arduous journey she had endured to reach this moment. The brutal reality of his situation struck him with the force of a battering ram.

"But . . . but I gave ye what ye asked for!"

"What I ask for and what I take are often two very different propositions." She looked the dismayed leprechaun over, assessing him as she might a promising piece of livestock. "For all your foolishness, you may prove valuable to me. The Brotherhood is about nothing if not putting magic to good use. It would be a pity to let a creature such as you go to waste."

The blood drained from the leprechaun's previously ruddy face. "You mean to enslave me?"

"Very good. It seems you have a working brain, after all." She turned to the Greek. "Bind him with silver so that he can't escape."

The sprite backed away fearfully. "You cannot do this. I won't allow it!"

"You would prefer I sate my hunger on this tasty tidbit?" She licked her lips in expectation, a forked tongue briefly on display. "I confess, all this tiresome haggling has left me quite famished. . . ."

"Fiend!" The leprechaun shook his shillelagh at her. "Ye're not human, ye're not!"

"Not entirely," she admitted, "but look who's talking." A smirk lifted her lips. "So then, will you save yourself . . . or the infant?"

"Curse ye," the leprechaun said. "Ye know that's no choice

at all." His shillelagh slipped from his fingers, falling to the ground. "Get on with it then. Proceed with your deviltry."

The Roman circled around the sprite and bound his wrists behind his back with a coil of flexible silver wire. The precious metal would not only restrain the leprechaun physically; it would also prevent him from attempting any magical trickery for as long as the silver bound him.

"Do what ye will with me," he said, wincing. "Just spare the babe, for mercy's sake."

"Mercy?" Sibella laughed. "You really are a credulous old fool." The baby started crying, its strident wails grating on the noblewoman's nerves. Sibella ran her hand over the pagan altar once more. "Now that I think of it, it would be rude not to leave some offering at this place. Perhaps a sacrifice is indeed in order, as a courtesy to the old gods. . . ."

She raised the dagger, her mouth watering in anticipation.

"Courtesy?" a familiar voice challenged her. "You always did have a peculiar sense of manners."

A man clad in simple traveling clothes stepped out from behind one of the standing stones across from the altar. His clean-shaven face was youthful in appearance, while his keen gray eyes and thoughtful expression hinted at his scholarly nature. Sandy-blond hair was in need of a comb. A British accent marked him as a stranger to these shores, although Sibella already knew that. Venom all but dripped from her tongue as she recognized him.

"Librarian."

Erasmus emerged from cover, judging that the time for concealment had passed. That Lady Sibella had no intention of sparing the nameless infant was hardly unexpected, yet he had bided his time on the off chance that the exchange between Sibella and the leprechaun would proceed smoothly, thereby removing the baby from jeopardy. It was clear, however, that he could not wait any longer to confront Sibella and her minions, not if he hoped to save the child.

"Milady," he addressed her. "You're a long ways from your usual haunts."

"Travel has its rewards," she replied. "And dare I ask how you came to find me here, at such an inconvenient juncture?"

Erasmus shrugged. "You did your best to conceal your movements, but I managed to intercept a missive to your agents in Byzantium, informing them of your journeys. My compliments, by the way, on the ingeniously devious cipher you employed to protect your message from prying eyes; it took me the better part of a day to crack it."

"A pity it wasn't more challenging," Sibella said acidly.

"Next time employ a dead language somewhat more obscure than ancient Egyptian. Perhaps Akkadian or pre-Adamic," Erasmus said. "From there it was a simple matter to see through the relatively transparent alias you used to book passage to Ireland and to follow you to these famously verdant shores, where your trail was child's play to pick up . . . once we won the trust of various observant locals." He kept talking, to distract Sibella from her innocent hostage. "If it's any consolation, you may flatter yourself that you and your entourage are hardly inconspicuous, even when traveling incognito. There was bound to be talk among the native population of a highborn lady, of foreign extraction, passing through these parts, in suspicious proximity to certain pagan ruins—which, I could hardly fail to notice, happened to be located at the junction of several active ley lines."

In truth, that was the abbreviated version. Catching up

with the elusive Serpent had taken considerable effort, a fair amount of luck, and the help of an invaluable local guide.

"How doggedly persistent of you," Sibella observed. "But you said 'we' before." She looked past Erasmus at the looming monoliths behind him. "May I assume that the redoubtable Deidre is joining us as well?"

"You assume correctly, witch." A Pictwoman, of Amazonian proportions, stepped out from behind another standing stone. Her skin dyed blue by woad, she wore a belted wool tunic and leather boots. Intricate tattoos painted her arms and face. Braided brown hair framed her features, while her hands gripped a hardwood staff capped with iron ferrules at both ends. Her voice held the burr of the distant Highlands from which she hailed. "Now step away from that child before I forget that I'm a Guardian, not an assassin."

"And who is going to make me?" Sibella said, flanked by her formidable bodyguards, whom Erasmus recognized from previous clashes with the Brotherhood. Their weapons already drawn, the burly warriors glowered at the intruders like attack dogs on a leash, awaiting only their mistress's command to charge into battle against her enemies. Sibella sneered at Deidre. "You two alone?"

"Not alone," a new voice declared. "The righteous are never truly alone."

An older man, wearing a monk's brown robe, joined Erasmus and Deidre. A tonsured cranium testified to his faith and his calling. His weathered, sun-baked features bespoke years spent toiling in the countryside, first as a slave and then as a missionary. More than forty years on Earth had laced his light brown beard with spreading strands of gray. The Good Book hung from his belt in lieu of a weapon. Callused knuckles gripped the handle of a plain iron bell.

"And you are?" Sibella asked.

"Call me Padraic," he said. "And you contaminate this precious land with your unholy presence."

He rang his bell, the clear, clean chimes reverberating across the mountaintop—and having an immediate effect on Sibella. The dagger dropped from her fingers as, screaming in agony, she threw her hands over her ears.

"Silence him!" she shrieked at the men. "Make it stop!"

Unleashed, the warriors charged at Padraic, who kept ringing his blessed bell at the stricken Serpent. Erasmus glanced urgently at his Guardian.

"Deidre?"

"Leave them to me," she answered. Determination was written on her face, which showed no sign of fear. The painted warrior-woman had proven herself in raids and battle above Hadrian's Wall before being recruited by the Library to defend Erasmus's body and soul. "See to the child."

My thoughts exactly, he thought. With Sibella distressed for the moment, he seized the opportunity to dash to the altar and snatch the frightened infant. His gaze briefly fell upon the glittering pot of gold also resting upon the altar, but his priorities were clear. Keeping Sibella from her prize would have to wait; rescuing the baby was paramount. Cradling the child in his arms, he hurried it away from the altar and out of Sibella's reach.

"There, there," he cooed, attempting to soothe the babe. "I have you."

He was all too aware, however, that the danger was far from past. Looking to his allies, he saw that Deidre was already engaged in battle with Sibella's guards, fighting to keep them from reaching Padraic, who had in turn gone to the aid of the

captured leprechaun. Erasmus watched anxiously as Deidre
wielded her weapon like the seasoned warrior she was, de-
flecting the men's attacks with the flame-hardened oak shaft
while striking high and low with both ends of it. Profane
curses, in both Greek and Latin, sprayed from the guards' lips
as they battled to get past her defenses. The Roman swung
his short sword, more properly known as a *gladius*, while the
Greek wielded a battle-axe.

The staff spun in the Guardian's hands like a thing alive,
yet Erasmus knew that no magic was imbued in the weapon;
the only wizardry was Deidre's own superlative fighting skills,
which had kept both her and Erasmus alive through many a
perilous quest on behalf of the Library. As always, he was
struck by the way she combined both grace and ferocity in
one remarkable personage, even as he feared for her safety
against two such formidable opponents. These were no mere
ruffians, he knew. The Serpent Brotherhood employed only
the best and most ruthless of killers.

Fight well, Deidre, he urged her silently. *More than one life
may depend on your valor.*

He yearned to assist her with what meager martial prow-
ess he had acquired over the course of their adventures, but
he could scarcely enter into the fray while shielding a baby in
his arms, which left Deidre on her own against their foes,
unless there was some way to tip the scales in their favor.

"Unbind me!" the leprechaun beseeched Padraic over the
din of battle and Lady Sibella's screams of torment. "Let me
loose, I beg ye!"

If the ringing of the missionary's bell afflicted the leprechaun, the little man gave no sign of it. Erasmus suspected
that was because the *aes sidhe* were neither good nor evil by

nature, but simply otherworldly. At worst, the bell probably
did no more than irritate the leprechaun, like nails scraping
against a slate.

"Take heart." Padraic employed his free hand to unwind the
silver wire binding the leprechaun's wrists together, while still
ringing the bell with his other hand. "We'll see you free ere
long."

As a youth, Erasmus knew, Padraic had been captured by
pirates and sold into slavery, spending many years in bond-
age before finally escaping to freedom. Small wonder that
he could not stand by and let another suffer a similar fate, not
even an ungodly member of the Fair Folk.

"Thank ye kindly, Father," the leprechaun said, "but make
haste! That viper of a woman is not so easily foiled! Her wicked-
ness knows no bounds!"

"You preach to the converted, my small friend," Padraic
said. Working one-handed slowed Padraic, but his deft fingers
soon freed the leprechaun, who sprang forward the instant he
was rid of his bindings. He snatched up his shillelagh from
where it had fallen before.

"Och, that's more like it, so!"

A sharp yelp from Deidre yanked Erasmus's attention back
toward her battle with Sibella's men. A glancing blow from
the Roman's sword had sliced her shoulder, drawing blood.
Snarling, she drove the head of her staff into the man's foot,
then drove its opposite end into the Greek's gut, buying herself a moment's respite. From what Erasmus could see, her
wound appeared to be a minor one, but it attested to the odds
against her. Her opponents came at her from both sides, forcing her to whirl like a top to keep them at bay and away from
Padraic and his bell. Erasmus took scant comfort in the fact
that, caught up in the heat of battle, the furious warriors now

seemed more intent on slaying Deidre than getting past her. Few victories were worth losing his Guardian.

"What's the matter?" Deidre taunted them. "Is one woman too much for the two of you?"

Sweat drenched her face, reminding Erasmus that her strength was not inexhaustible. Outnumbered as she was, and by two able soldiers, it was only a matter of time before one of the guards landed a decisive blow. Already they had her on the defensive.

He couldn't let her fight this battle alone!

Burdened by the baby, Erasmus looked about frantically. Was there anyplace he could safely stow the child long enough to go to Deidre's aid?

A small hand tugged on his trousers. He glanced down to find the leprechaun at his side, the sprite's head barely level with the Librarian's knee.

"Ho, Librarian!" The little man offered up his shillelagh. "Trade ye for the babe?"

Erasmus hesitated for only a heartbeat. Although the leprechaun's obvious concern for this particular child remained a mystery, the Librarian had witnessed enough to know that the baby girl would be far safer in the leprechaun's hands than left to the untender mercies of the Serpents. His decision was an easy one.

"Take good care of her," Erasmus said, handing over the infant.

"Ye have my solemn word on it." The leprechaun surrendered his shillelagh in return. "Now then, that brave lady needs ye!"

Erasmus needed no urging to go to Deidre's aid. Gripping the sturdy cudgel, which looked much smaller in his own fist, he turned back to the battle just in time to see the Roman lunging at Deidre from behind while she was busy warding off a furious head-on assault by the Greek, who let out a bloodcurdling war cry as he hacked and slashed furiously at Deidre's defenses, demanding all her concentration and leaving her vulnerable to the Roman's cowardly attack. Deidre was probably the finest warrior Erasmus had ever known, but even she didn't have eyes in the back of her head or an extra pair of arms to fight with, unlike that slavering tomb guardian they'd encountered in Samarkand a few years ago.

That had been one for the annals. . . .

But now was not the time for reminiscences of exploits past. With nary a moment to waste, Erasmus sprang forward, swinging the shillelagh like a club, and delivered a resounding blow to the back of the Roman's skull, just seconds before the man would have run Deidre through with his sword. The blow staggered the soldier, dropping him to his knees, if only for the moment. Erasmus gasped in relief, not wanting to think about how close he had come to losing Deidre. His arm throbbed from the impact, while his heart stampeded wildly in his chest. He was a scholar, not a soldier, but sometimes, he had learned, a stout stick proved handier than a citation.

At least in the short term.

"He who strikes from behind is felled from behind," he quipped. "If that's not an adage, it should be."

"Nicely done, Librarian," Deidre compliment him, as though she *did* have eyes in the back of her head. "We'll make a gladiator of you yet."

"That strikes me as a fine waste of a decent education!"

"Suit yourself," she replied. "My job's just to keep your overstuffed skull in one piece!"

No longer besieged from afore and behind, she faced off against the Greek, but before she could regain the offensive, a lucky blow from the Greek's axe splintered Deidre's staff, cleaving it in twain. Deidre was left holding the severed halves of the broken staff.

"What now, wench?" he chortled, pausing to savor his victory.

"Look sharp," she replied. "I believe you owe me a weapon."

With a flick of her wrist, she reversed her grip on the fragment of staff in her left hand and flung it at the Greek like a missile. The ironclad end of the stick struck the man squarely between the eyes, causing him to reel backward, waving his axe wildly. A second throw sent the remaining half of the staff smashing into the man's shoulder, numbing his arm. Bellowing in pain, he lost his grip on the axe, which went tumbling through the air—and into Deidre's waiting hand.

"That will do," she said.

And all at once, Erasmus noted, the tide of battle seemed to turn in their favor. He brained the kneeling Roman with the shillelagh once more before the stunned soldier could clamber back onto his feet, and the disarmed Greek was teetering unsteadily, an ugly bruise forming where the thrown missile had caught him unawares. Both warriors were in a sorry state, while Lady Sibella—

"Erasmus!" Padraic shouted. "Watch out!"

Without warning, Sibella sprang at him like a striking cobra. Blood trickled from her ears, which may have finally been deafened by the holy pealing of Padraic's bell, so that she could no longer hear the ringing. Seizing Erasmus from behind, impossibly wrapping her lower body around him like the coils of a python, she opened her jaws wider than humanly possible, exposing a pair of curved serpentine fangs that were literally dripping with venom. Hissing in Erasmus's ears, her forked tongue flicking out from between her lips, she arched her head back, only seconds away from sinking her fangs into the Librarian's neck.

"Let that good man be!" Padraic commanded her. "I have another blessing for you!"

Rushing to the rescue, he flung the contents of a simple brass flask at Lady Sibella's demonically distorted countenance. Holy water splattered against her face, burning her like acid. Hissing in torment, steam rising from her seared skin, she reared her head back, away from Erasmus, who had also been doused by the water, albeit with considerably less dramatic results. Blinking the water away from his eyes, he saw Deidre racing toward him, swinging her captured axe.

"Erasmus!" she shouted. "Duck!"

He complied just in time to hear the axe whistle above his head right before it liberated Sibella's head from her body. He heard the severed head land with a disquieting thunk atop the altar.

A gift for Crom?

Sibella's headless corpus released him, falling limply to the ground. Gulping, Erasmus reached up to check his throat, simply to confirm that he'd escaped the Serpent's fatal bite. He averted his eyes from the altar, where Sibella's vicious jaws snapped spasmodically for a few endless seconds before finally falling still forever. Slitted eyes glazed over.

Padraic crossed himself. Deidre's response was characteristically blunter.

"Should have done that long ago," she said before turning toward the vanquished bodyguards, who suddenly found themselves obsolete. She grinned wolfishly at the dumbfounded men. "Who's next?"

Shaken by their mistress's abrupt demise, the guards turned tail and ran. Scrambling out of the rock ring, they fled into the night, half-running, half-tumbling down the steep, gravelly slope of the mountain. Crashes and curses and the rattle of dislodged scree marked their headlong exodus.

"Begone, servants of darkness!" Padraic shouted after them, ringing his bell to speed them on their way. "Depart this emerald isle and never return!"

It dawned on Erasmus that he had lost track of the leprechaun in the tumult. Glancing around the summit, he found no trace of the little man, who seemed to have vanished along with the nameless infant.

Nor were they the only things missing.

"The pot of gold!" Deidre realized belatedly. "It's gone."

"So it is," Erasmus confirmed. All that remained of the leprechaun was the miniature shillelagh he had bestowed upon Erasmus in exchange for the imperiled child. "It would appear our wee friend absconded with both the baby and the gold while we three were otherwise occupied."

"'Tis the way of the little folk," Padraic said. "Look away for a moment and you'll find yourself empty-handed."

Erasmus considered the events of the night. "I wonder why Lady Sibella craved that leprechaun's gold so ardently."

"Beyond the obvious?" Deidre asked.

"The Serpent Brotherhood has accumulated several fortunes over the centuries, so I can't imagine she came so far just to refill their coffers." Erasmus stroked his chin thoughtfully. "She had to be after more than mere treasure."

"Perhaps it was *magic* gold she was after?" Deidre suggested.

"Quite possibly." Erasmus made a mental note to thoroughly research faerie gold and its potential applications once he was comfortably ensconced back at the Library. "For the time being, however, I suppose we should count our blessings and call this a victory. Not only did we save an innocent child and keep the gold out of Sibella's hands, but we also drove the Serpent Brotherhood from Ireland, perhaps forever."

"From your lips to heaven's ears," Padraic said.

"And we could not have succeeded without your generous assistance," Erasmus told the missionary. "We were fortunate to have you as our guide and companion on this quest."

"You're a good man," Deidre agreed. "A veritable saint."

"A saint?" Padraic chuckled at the notion. "Someday, perhaps, God willing, but not just yet. I'm simply a humble missionary."

"Right," Deidre said sarcastically. She cocked her thumb at Erasmus. "And this one is just a simple librarian."

The sky began to lighten in the west, out over the ocean, bringing the promise of a new day after a long and hazardous night. Although anxious to return with Deidre to the Library, albeit empty-handed, Erasmus couldn't but wonder what had become of the leprechaun—and the unknown child whose life they'd saved tonight.

But that, perhaps, was a mystery for another day.

2

"So the Phantom of the Opera was for real?" Ezekiel Jones boggled at the notion as he and Jake Stone made their way down a murky underground corridor. The dapper young Librarian shook his head in disbelief. An Australian accent tinged his remark. "You'd think that, by now, this wouldn't surprise me, but I'm starting to wonder if *anything* is just a story."

"You heard what Jenkins said," Jake Stone said gruffly. A backpack hung from his broad shoulders. A flannel shirt, jeans, and work boots combated the dank atmosphere of the age-old tunnel. "Gaston Leroux, who wrote the original book, was a celebrated investigative journalist back in the day, and his so-called novel was actually based on eyewitness testimony and written records he unearthed while looking into certain real-life events that had taken place at the Paris Opera . . . and beneath it."

Stone glanced up at a vaulted stone ceiling. A world-class expert on the history of art and architecture, albeit under a number of pseudonyms, he took a moment to contemplate the historic edifice towering above them.

The Palais Garnier was the largest opera house in the world, seventeen stories tall and a full three acres across. Located in the heart of Paris's 9th arrondissement, it had taken nearly fifteen years to build back in the late nineteenth century, its construction occasionally interrupted by wars, riots, and revolutions. At one point, it had even been turned into an armory and makeshift prison, its vast basements and subterranean catacombs converted to dungeons housing many an unfortunate prisoner of war. These gloomy subterranean chambers had witnessed ghastly scenes of torture and execution even before the Phantom had famously haunted them. If the dank stone walls could talk, they might well moan and groan instead.

Stone repressed a shudder as he and Ezekiel made their way down a dimly lit stone ramp leading into the lower reaches of the Opera House's fifth basement. These dismal cellars were a far cry from the opulent Belle Epoque elegance several stories above them, which the Librarians had visited briefly not too long ago. Dirty water trickled down the damp granite walls. Cobwebs infested the corners of the ceiling. Rats scurried at the Librarians' approach, their beady eyes reflecting the flashlight beams from the men's phones. Stone and Ezekiel relied on the beams to navigate the sprawling labyrinth, whose pervasive shadows had once sheltered the infamous Phantom—and might well be doing so again.

"So how come we got stuck spelunking down in the cellars," Ezekiel griped, "while Baird and Cassandra get to snoop around upstairs where all the lights and glitz are?"

"Because I know historical buildings," Stone said, "and you know how to break into hidden treasure vaults. If anybody is going to locate the secret hiding place of Phantom's long-lost masterpiece, it's you and me." His brown eyes took in the authentic nineteenth-century architecture; despite the urgency of their mission, the expert in him appreciated the opportunity to explore the Opera House's sprawling subbasements. "While Baird and Cassie try to find out what the competition is up to."

Rumor had it that the only copy of the Phantom's legendary concerto, *Don Juan Triumphant*, was still concealed somewhere in the depths of the Opera House. Not even the Library had a copy, despite its extensive collection of rare (and often literally mythical) musical compositions. Nor had Jenkins, the Library's venerable caretaker, been able to say for certain that a copy of the Phantom's masterwork had survived, or even that it had ever truly existed at all. Still, the fabled concerto remained the most likely target of whomever (or whatever) was rumored to be once more haunting the Opera.

"Well, when you put it that way." Ezekiel grinned impishly, soaking up the implied vote of confidence. As Stone well knew, the only thing the cocky thief liked better than demonstrating his talents was having them recognized by others. "No dusty old sheet music can hide from Ezekiel Jones." He grudgingly tossed a bone to Stone. "And associates."

"Assuming we get to it first," Stone said, having no reason to believe that they weren't the only ones prowling these cellars recently. "And don't run into any opposition."

Ezekiel's arm started to droop as it held out the phone in front of him.

"Watch it," Stone said. "You need to keep your arm up, at the level of your eyes, just like Jenkins warned us."

"Right, right," Ezekiel said skeptically, "so the Phantom can't strangle us with his spooky noose. . . ."

"The Punjab lasso." Stone kept his own right arm carefully

aloft, as instructed. "Which was the Phantom's weapon of choice back in his heyday."

"Sure, but, even if the Phantom was for real, that was over a century ago, right? And he was just a psycho stalker with a thing for sopranos, not some sort of immortal like Prospero or Dulaque." Ezekiel frowned at the memory of those notably ageless foes. "You don't really think he's still alive . . . and back up to his old tricks?"

"Better safe than sorry." Stone reached over and raised his friend's arm. "What with some of the stories going around upstairs."

Ghost stories, to be exact.

————

"So what's this about the Opera House being haunted?" Colonel Eve Baird asked. "Again, I mean."

She had been surprised to discover that the Paris Opera had its own library. The Bibliotheque-Musee de l'Opera National de Paris was a combined museum and library dedicated to preserving and cataloging the long history of the Paris Opera and its myriad productions. Its voluminous archives contained hundreds of thousands of books, musical scores, libretti, set and costume designs, correspondence, posters, programs, scale models, and even some three thousand pieces of antique costume jewelry. Housed in a domed pavilion on the west side of the theater, the library paled in comparison to *the* Library, but was still pretty impressive in its own right. Towering oak shelves lined the walls, with the rarer volumes protected by wire screens. Framed paintings of dancers and divas decorated any available wall space. An ornate crystal chandelier hung over the elegant reading room on the second floor of the library, where Baird and her companion, Cassandra Cillian, were currently interviewing the director of the library, while posing as, well, librarians.

"Sheer foolishness," Monsieur Claudel assured her, dismissing the reports with a wave of his hand. He was a slight, middle-aged man distinguished by spectacles and a receding hairline. "Nothing more than idle rumors fed by overactive imaginations. The Phantom is just a legend, kept alive by Hollywood and the musical theater."

Baird was grateful for the man's impeccable English. A statuesque blonde in casual attire, she had picked up a smattering of French, along with several other languages, during her stint as a counterterrorism operative for NATO, but it was easier to converse in English, and she suspected that Cassandra felt the same way. Her partner-in-sleuthing was a math and science whiz, not an expert linguist.

"Is that so?" Cassandra asked. The petite redhead had donned a jaunty beret for this excursion to Gay Paree. "Word is that a mysterious masked figure has been glimpsed prowling around the opera in recent weeks, appearing and disappearing like a ghost."

"This is an opera house, mademoiselle. Masks and costumes are nearly as ubiquitous as superstitious performers. Why, there's a new production of *Faust* debuting tonight even as we speak, complete with any number of sinister demons and disguises." Dramatic music, coming from the Opera's main auditorium, could even now be heard faintly in the background, although Claudel had no trouble speaking over it. "Who knows? Perhaps these rumors you mention are nothing more than a publicity stunt to get people talking about the Opera?"

Baird wasn't buying it. The Clipping Book back at the Library would not have alerted them to the recent spate of ghost sightings unless there was an actual situation that required the Librarians' attention. And her gut told her that Claudel wasn't being entirely forthcoming. She'd taken part in enough inter- rogations to know when somebody was holding out on her.

"Too bad," she said. "Here I was hoping that maybe you had some inside scoop on the stories you could share with us." She gave him a conspiratorial wink. "Just between us librarians?"

"Well . . ."

I knew it, Baird thought. She leaned forward, as though hanging on his every word. She was not above playing to the Frenchman's ego if it got him talking. "Yes?"

Claudel glanced around furtively and lowered his voice, even though there was no one around to listen in, or at least so it seemed.

"It was probably nothing, but there was one night, not too long ago, when I was working late and briefly thought I saw a cloaked intruder rifling through one of the archives, but when I flicked on the lights, nobody was there." He chuckled weakly. "My own imagination playing tricks on me, no doubt."

"Or not," Baird said. "Can you show us where exactly this went down?"

Claudel gave her a quizzical look. "Why exactly are you so interested?"

"What can I say?" Baird said. "I can never resist a good ghost story."

"And we're big Andrew Lloyd Webber fans," Cassandra lied. "You don't want to know how many times we've seen the musical. So, pretty please?"

"If you insist," Claudel agreed. "Although I fear you're wasting your time on such nonsense. Are you quite sure you wouldn't prefer to review our current exhibit on the illustri- ous history of the *Opera-Comique?*"

"Maybe another time," Baird said. "Indulge us."

Claudel shrugged. "Far be it from me to refuse such lovely colleagues."

"*Merci*," Baird said.

"It was over this way." Playing tour guide, he led them toward a nearby row of bookcases. The cases stretched all the way up to the ceiling, requiring a rolling ladder to reach the upper shelves. "This particular archive houses records and memorabilia from the late 1800s."

Cassandra's eyes lit up. "That's roughly when Leroux's 'novel' is set."

"Surely a coincidence, mademoiselle," Claudel insisted. "As you say, that was just a novel. . . ."

"Can't always judge a book by its label," Baird said. She contemplated the looming shelves, which were practically overflowing with bound librettos, scrapbooks, playbills, periodicals, posters, and random theatrical ephemera dating back to the *previous* previous century. "Do you recall," she asked Claudel, "what exactly the intruder was looking at?"

"*Apparent* intruder," he said, shaking his head. "As I said, I caught only a glimpse of a shadowy figure, who was nowhere to been seen when the lights came on. My weary eyes must have simply deceived me."

"I wouldn't sell your eyes short just yet," Baird said, unconvinced. She turned to Cassandra. "What about you, Red? Anything suspicious leap out at you?"

"Let me take a closer look," the other woman said.

Cassandra closed her eyes, then opened them again. She raised her hands and swept them gracefully through the air as she surveyed her surroundings as only she could. Cassandra's unique mind and senses had always bordered on the magical, and all the more so since a risky brain operation had

removed the life-threatening tumor that had previously inhib-
ited her special abilities. Her fingers traced diagrams and
flowcharts in the air that only she could see, as though ex-
ploring a virtual version of the archives around them.

"Sorting by date, category, obscurity, relevance, allowing
for attrition and institutional drift," she murmured softly to
herself. "Filing, organization, shelving, alphabetization *à la
française* . . ."

Baird couldn't see what Cassandra saw, but she knew that
the brilliant Librarian could find patterns—and deviations
from a pattern—that nobody else could even recognize. For
Cassandra, the world was an endless series of real-life-story
problems that she had a definite knack for solving. If anyone
could zero in on a telltale clue here, it would be her.

"There!" Cassandra pointed at a particular shelf of dusty
books, secured behind a locked metal grille. "One of those
volumes is missing."

"You can't be serious," Claudel scoffed. "No offense, mademoiselle, but I know these archives better than anyone
alive, and I see nothing amiss. You can hardly expect me to
believe that—"

"Trust her on this," Baird said, interrupting him. "She has
an eye for this sort of thing."

"More like a brain," Cassandra corrected, "but the eyes
helped."

Baird brushed by the dumbfounded director to investigate
the shelf in question. "You're going to need my key," Claudel
began.

"Not necessary." Baird tried the latch, and the protective
grille swung open easily. "Looks like somebody's already
picked the lock."

The Phantom?

She and Cassandra exchanged a concerned glance before Baird took a closer look at the exposed volumes, which appeared to be a collection of scrapbooks containing correspondence and newspaper clippings from the second half of the nineteenth century. Most of the volumes looked as though they hadn't been consulted in years, but, sure enough, there was a narrow gap in the collection, indicating a missing volume, covering the year 1881. Squinting at the gap, Baird made out a black paper envelope resting on its side.

"Somebody left us a note," she observed.

Claudel's jaw dropped. Cassandra, more accustomed to unusual discoveries in unlikely places, simply waited expectantly as Baird procured the envelope and examined it. The black paper had caused the letter to blend in with the shadows unless one looked closely enough. Inside was a handwritten note, inscribed in bloodred ink, which she read aloud:

> *My apologies for borrowing this precious volume outside of normal business hours. Rest assured that it will be of great aid to my research.*
>
> *Your Most Humble and Obedient Servant,*
> *O.G.*

Claudel gasped. "*Non.* This must be a joke."

"O.G.?" Baird asked.

Cassandra supplied the explanation.

"Opera Ghost."

———

An underground lake lay before the spelunking Librarians. Stygian black waters, never touched by the sun, stretched like an immense liquid shadow beneath the crouching stone ceiling of the Opera House's deepest, darkest subcellar. The water lapped softly against a set of low stone steps leading down into the lake. Ezekiel didn't want to think about what might be swimming below the inky surface of the subterranean reservoir.

"This lake's been here for more than a hundred and fifty years," Stone exposited. "When they first started constructing the Opera House back in 1862, the excavation kept filling with water from an underground stream, so the architects added an immense concrete cistern to the foundation to help stabilize the building. A clever solution, actually, providing ballast as well as containing the excess groundwater."

Ezekiel took his word for it. Old buildings and blueprints were Stone's specialty.

"I'm guessing we're not turning back," Ezekiel said, sighing. Given a choice, he'd have preferred a luxurious hot tub in a swanky hotel to a dismal black lagoon five levels underground. But being a Librarian wasn't always glamorous, even if you were a master thief and international man of mystery.

"Not a chance." Stone swept his flashlight beam across the lake. "Look over there."

The light from the phone fell upon a small white gondola docked at the opposite side of the lake, in front of a moldering brick wall. The elegant craft looked better suited to a Venetian gondola than to a dank underground cistern, but there it was regardless. The boat was empty at the moment, which begged the question of who had oared it across the lake—and where he, she, or they were now.

"Looks like someone's already been this way," Ezekiel said.

"Yep." Stone shucked off his backpack. "Good thing we came prepared."

He removed a collapsed inflatable raft from the pack. It

took a few moments to pump the raft full of air, but it beat swimming across the deep, dark pool. "Kinda figured we'd need this," Stone said. "In most versions of the story, the Phantom's lair is across the lake."

"Good thinking," Ezekiel said. "All aboard?"

The men clambered into the raft and pushed off from the shore. Ezekiel let Stone handle the rowing, since the roughneck Librarian liked that kind of outdoorsy stuff; Ezekiel chose to save his energy for tasks better suited to his talents.

Like cracking safes or breaking and entering.

"Keep it up," he encouraged Stone. "We're making good time."

"What do you mean 'we'?" Stone grumbled.

"I'm navigating," Ezekiel said. "And keeping watch."

"Watching for what, exactly?"

"I'll let you know when I see—"

Something splashed in the darkness to one side of the raft. Startled, Ezekiel swung his flashlight beam toward the noise, but found only some circular ripples in the water, left behind by whatever had briefly broken the surface. Ezekiel gulped as his heartbeat settled down. His mouth went dry, but he wasn't remotely tempted to take a sip from the stagnant lake.

"What was that?" Stone asked.

"A fish or a lizard or something?" Ezekiel said, crossing his fingers. He knew from personal experience that the alligators in Manhattan's sewer system were no urban myth; he hoped Paris had a better handle on reptile control. "There are no sharks in the story, right??"

"No," Stone said. "But didn't the Phantom used to drown unwelcome visitors in this very lake?"

"You tell me, mate. It's not like I know that old yarn."

Stone eyed him incredulously. "You don't know *The Phantom of the Opera?*"

"From where? A creaky old French novel? A silent movie? A sappy Broadway musical?" Ezekiel scoffed at the very notion. "Don't be ridiculous. That's all old media."

He knew the basics: a mad genius "haunting" the Opera House and obsessing over some cute Parisian babe with nice pipes. But that was pretty much the extent of his knowledge. Just because he was a Librarian didn't mean that he had a headful of musty old "classics" from before he was born.

That was what Jenkins was for.

"Just row faster, okay?"

Stone muttered something under his breath, but took Ezekiel's advice.

In no time at all, they arrived at the far end of the lake, which, by all appearances, was a dead end. The white gondola was tied up at a low stone wharf facing a moldy brick wall that *seemed* to block any further progress, but Ezekiel knew from experience that appearances could be deceptive, especially where lost artifacts and relics were concerned.

"What do you think?" he said as they managed to disembark from the raft without tumbling into the drink. "A secret passage or trapdoor?"

Stone nodded. "Legend has it that Erik, the Phantom, was one of the original architects and builders of the Opera House, and that he took advantage of that opportunity to install various concealed doorways and passages that he used to come and go throughout the Opera undetected, as well as to spy on the goings-on there. He's also supposed to have constructed a private lair here in cellars hidden somewhere between the thick double walls constructed to contain the lake."

"So the whole 'ghost' business was just trickery?" Ezekiel said. "Like on *Scooby-Doo?*"

"In theory," Stone said. "Which is why our magic detectors aren't going to do us any good here."

Among the Librarians' resources were unique handheld sensors that, under the right circumstances, could detect mystical energy the way a Geiger counter detected radiation. They came in useful sometimes for locating and identifying magical objects and entities in the field.

"No worries, mate," Ezekiel said confidently. "I've got this."

He examined the dank brick wall by the light of his phone. A slimy layer of mildew coated most of the bricks, much to his disgust, except for one brick off to one side and just above eye level. A closer inspection revealed smears in the slime that might have been made by fingers pressing down on the brick.

"Bingo."

Smirking, he reached up and pushed on the brick. His grin broadened as a concealed lever shifted with a satisfying click. A door-sized section of the wall rotated to reveal an entrance to a darkened chamber beyond.

"*Voila!*" Ezekiel gestured toward the door. "*Après vous?*"

"Your accent sucks," Stone said, "but good work, man. Let's see what you found here."

They cautiously stepped through the secret door, wary of potential ambushes or booby traps, and suddenly found themselves in a very different environment. Hidden behind the dungeon-like walls of the cellars was a once-opulent suite whose former elegance was still evident despite more than a century of decay and disuse. Tattered silk and satin draperies, in faded hues of black and scarlet, hung on neatly painted walls. Antique pieces of furniture, exquisitely carved and upholstered, displayed their fine lines and quality construction even through thick layers of dust and cobwebs. Ezekiel gulped at the sight of an open coffin occupying an ornate bier, where saner people would have put a comfy bed or sofa. Peering into the coffin, he was relieved to find it empty, except for some plush red cushions and pillows. A man-sized depression in the cushions suggested that the casket had been occupied at some point.

"Okay, what's the deal with the coffin?" Ezekiel asked. "Please tell me that the Phantom wasn't actually a vampire, 'cause I am so over vampires."

"Not that I know of," Stone said with a shrug. "Maybe he was just kind of morbid? The guy did live underground while posing as a ghost." He swept his flashlight beam around the spooky boudoir. "Hey, get a load of this."

Hanging on the wall above a carved wooden mantelpiece was a framed portrait of a beautiful blond woman with delicate features and soulful blue eyes. Her pristine white gown looked more like a theatrical costume than everyday wear, even way, way back in the day; Ezekiel assumed she was cosplaying a character from some famous old opera he'd never heard of. An offstage spotlight gave her an almost angelic radiance, while her wistful expression conveyed both innocence and a trace of melancholy. Ezekiel turned his back on the coffin to fully contemplate the painting.

"So that's her?" he said. "The bird the Phantom had the hots for?"

"Can't imagine it's anyone else," Stone said. "Christine Daae. The Phantom's protégé and obsession." He took a moment to admire the artwork. "Nice brushwork, very reminiscent of Degas, which puts it more or less in the same era as the Phantom and Christine. You can see the influence of early

French Impressionism, particularly in the looseness of the brushstrokes and the play of light and color." He leaned in closer, squinting at the bottom of the canvas. "You see a signature?"

"Enough with the art appreciation." Ezekiel stepped up to the portrait. His eyes narrowed suspiciously as he observed that, unlike the rest of the furnishings, the painting had been carefully dusted—by someone who cared? And was it just his imagination or was the painting hanging slightly askew? "You seeing what I'm seeing?"

Stone glanced at him. "Which is?"

"I have a hunch." Ezekiel couldn't resist drawing out the suspense. "Let's peek behind this valentine."

Working together, they took down the painting, exposing a hidden niche built into the wall. Ezekiel was disappointed but not surprised to find the cubbyhole empty.

"Called it," he said. "Want to bet this is where the Phantom hid that long-lost music we're looking for?"

"Makes sense," Stone agreed. "He stored his masterpiece behind a portrait of his greatest love. Kinda romantic, actually."

"In a creepy, crying-out-for-a-restraining-order way," Ezekiel said.

He groped inside the niche, confirming that it was empty. Whoever had left the gondola outside was clearly one step ahead of them, even if that whoever had taken the time and care to dust off the portrait and put it back where it belonged.

"No sheet music here," he said. "Somebody's beaten us to the prize."

Organ music suddenly blared throughout the underground lair, coming from somewhere way too nearby. The booming notes bounced off Ezekiel's eardrums.

"You think?" Stone said.

Leaving the empty niche behind, they followed the music through a curtained doorway into an adjacent chamber dominated by a large, old-fashioned pipe organ. A caped figure in evening dress sat before the organ, his back to the Librarians, as he pounded away at the keyboard. A silver candelabra, resting atop the organ's hefty wooden console, illuminated the chamber. Shifting shadows seemed to dance along with the unearthly music emanating from the organ. Squinting in the flickering candlelight, Ezekiel made out the title on the yellowed sheet music propped up on a rack before the mystery organist's eyes. Dramatic black strokes, rendered with a flourish, proudly named the composition.

Don Juan Triumphant.

Apparently that part of the story was not a myth either. Jenkins would be pleased to learn that, assuming the team could actually acquire the Phantom's legendary magnum opus for the Library. Ezekiel guessed that their music-loving competitor might have his own ideas on that score. Wouldn't be the first time a long-lost treasure fell into the wrong hands first.

The Librarians' arrival did not go unnoticed. Without missing a note, the organist glanced back over his shoulder at the intruders. A white porcelain mask covered the upper half of the man's face, exposing only his lower jaw and chin. A chill ran down Ezekiel's spine as he wondered what kind of gruesome visage lurked behind the mask. Could this really be the actual Phantom of the Opera?

He sure looked the part.

"Bonjour!" the Phantom said, turning his masked face back toward the music. His mellifluous voice was far from monstrous. *"Qui vient?"*

"And good day to you," Stone replied in English. "Sorry to interrupt your little underground recital."

"Kind of stuffy for my tastes," Ezekiel added. "I don't suppose you take requests?"

"I'm afraid this is a private concert," the Phantom said, switching to English. Annoyance colored his voice, along with his cultured Gallic accent. "And you would be?"

"We're . . . Librarians," Stone said.

"Then you're in the wrong place. The Opera Library is several levels above us."

"No problem," Stone said, thinking of Baird and Cassandra. "We've got that covered." He stepped toward the figure at the organ. "So who are you . . . really? And what do you want with that music?"

The Phantom scowled below his mask. "This is a concert, not an interrogation, and you'll forgive me if I prefer a *captive* audience."

A gloved finger stabbed an ebony key—and a trapdoor opened up beneath the Librarians.

Ezekiel yelped as he and Stone plummeted through the dark, landing hard on a sandy floor several feet below the trapdoor, which snapped shut behind them. The impact knocked Ezekiel's breath out, and it took him a moment to recover. Groaning, he sat up and tried to look around, but saw only blackness. No trace of light invaded wherever it was they had landed.

"Stone?" he called out.

"Over here," Stone answered, close enough that his voice made Ezekiel jump. "In one piece, I think."

"Me, too." Ezekiel tested his limbs experimentally; nothing seemed to be fractured, although he was probably going to be black-and-blue tomorrow, assuming they saw tomorrow. "Where are we?"

"Nowhere good," Stone predicted.

Ezekiel groped for his phone, hoping that it hadn't been shattered by the fall. Just as he located it, however, the lights came on, bright enough to hurt his eyes. Blinking, he scoped out the scene.

Mirrored walls surrounded them on all sides, reflecting the fierce light, which seemed to come from everywhere and nowhere. Multiple reflections of themselves gaped back at them, and those reflections were captured by mirrors across from mirrors, multiplying them to infinity. A blazing sun was painted on the high, six-sided ceiling, while a deep carpet of glittering white sand conveyed the illusion that the Librarians (and their mirror images) were trapped in an endless, sun-bleached desert.

"Great," Ezekiel muttered. Wincing, he clambered to his feet. "A bloody hall of mirrors."

"More like a torture chamber." Stone stood up and wiped the sand from his jeans. "Straight out of the story."

"Not a story," a disembodied voice interrupted. "History!"

The Phantom's voice echoed off the walls of the chamber. The lights dimmed slightly and the Librarians' reflections were replaced by a view of the Phantom seated at his organ. Snarling in anger, Stone lunged at their adversary, only to bounce off a tall glass wall.

"Save your strength," Ezekiel advised him. "It's all done with mirrors . . . literally."

In fact, the Phantom surrounded them on all sides, his image somehow reflected from the music room one level up, so that he appeared to be facing them even as he faced the organ.

Ezekiel glimpsed the rest of the gloomy chamber behind the (presumably) villainous virtuoso.

"Neat trick," Stone conceded, scowling. He looked faintly embarrassed for having fallen for it, but Ezekiel resisted the temptation to tease him about it.

Maybe later, he thought. *After we get out of this.*

"Erik was a master of tricks and illusions," the Phantom proclaimed, "as well as many other skills and disciplines, from music to architecture. Indeed, this very chamber is a superb example of his ingenuity; you should take a moment to admire it, gentlemen. He based it on an elaborate torture chamber he had previously devised for the Shah's palace in bygone Persia, before a cruel reversal of fortune forced Erik to seek a new life in Paris, albeit here in the shadows, hidden away from the shallow judgments and prejudices of mankind, who failed to truly appreciate his genius."

Ezekiel shrugged. "Or maybe he was just crazy?"

"No!" the Phantom said vehemently. "He was misunderstood, scorned, maligned! Driven to madness by an uncaring world that could not see the brilliant mind—and wounded heart—behind his accursed ugliness. He should be revered as a genius, not reviled as a monster!"

That *this* Phantom kept referring to Erik in the third person was not lost on Ezekiel. "So?" he asked. "What's it to you?"

"I am Erik's direct descendant and rightful heir! The living legacy of the all-consuming passion that inspired his greatest masterpiece!"

It took Ezekiel a moment to process that. "Wait. Is he saying that the Phantom and that Christine chick . . . ?"

"Guess Leroux cleaned things up a bit," Stone said. "Perhaps to protect Christine's reputation?"

Ezekiel wasn't too scandalized. "Well, this *is* France. . . ."

"Theirs was a forbidden love that defied convention . . . and ended in despair. But I will make the world pay for the wrongs done to my illustrious forebear and his name, by carrying out his ultimate revenge!"

He returned to his music, pounding away at the keyboard with a vengeance, even as the music grew steadily louder and more violent. At the same time, the light bouncing off the mirrors got noticeably brighter . . . and hotter.

Much hotter.

————

"'Opera Ghost'?" Baird repeated.

"It's from the book," Cassandra explained. "It's how the Phantom signed his notes."

"Like this one." Baird held up the missive they had found in the Opera library. "But are we actually dealing with the honest-to-goodness Phantom of the Opera?"

"It's possible," Cassandra said. "Could be he's a Fictional sprung from the pages of his book."

"Or maybe just a Phantom wannabe who is copying the original?"

"That works, too," Cassandra said. "Or maybe the book was based on a real person who is still around, like with Dorian Gray? Impossible to say at this point."

Poor Monsieur Claudel looked completely nonplussed by both their conversation and their discovery. "*Pardon,*" he entreated, briefly falling back on his native tongue, "what kind of librarians are you, precisely?"

Technically, Baird was a Guardian, not a Librarian, but that was more than the perplexed director needed to know.

"The kind that's got a bad feeling about this," she said,

wondering what sort of craziness they were in for this time. Unfortunately, her familiarity with *The Phantom of the Opera* was limited to fuzzy memories of seeing some old movie version or another; about all she remembered was the Phantom's mask getting ripped off, exposing his monstrous features, and a giant crystal chandelier crashing down on the audience during a performance at the Opera House.

That was the problem with traveling instantaneously via a Magic Door. There were never any long plane flights on which you could fully study up on the mission. If they'd had to fly from Portland to Paris, she could have read the damn novel on the trip.

Then again, that's what she had a team of Librarians for.

"I'm almost afraid to ask," she said to Claudel, "but you don't still have a great big chandelier these days . . . do you?"

"But of course, mademoiselle. One of the finest and most impressive in all of Paris."

"Of course it is."

Cassandra frowned, clearly following Baird's chain of thought. "You don't think . . . ?"

"I hope not," Baird said, "but it pays to anticipate the worst."

She glanced nervously up at the smaller chandelier over their heads, just in time to see it sway ominously back and forth. Seconds later, a heavy book tumbled off the open shelf and crashed loudly to the floor.

"Okay, what's happening?" She backed away from the swinging lamp, just to be safe. "Tell me it's just the music from onstage shaking things up."

"I wish I could." Cassandra placed her palm up against a wall. Worry creased her brow. "But, no, this is something different. There's a peculiar vibration—strange, discordant— coming from somewhere. And it's building in intensity. . . ."

Baird didn't like the sound of this. "What kind of vibration?"

"Give me a second."

Baird watched tensely as Cassandra's super-brain switched into high gear again. As before, Baird couldn't see anything herself, but she could imagine the luminous graphs and equations manifesting before Cassandra's wide eyes as the rapt Librarian gestured like a maestro conducting an orchestra, shifting her hallucinatory images around in order to examine them from every angle.

"What—what's wrong with her?" Claudel asked, somehow managing to stammer in fluent English, which was something of a feat.

"Not one thing," Baird said. "Not anymore."

There had been a time when Cassandra's singular abilities had overwhelmed her, when she couldn't always process all the brilliant perceptions flooding her mind, but that was before she'd found her calling as a Librarian. Now she controlled her gift, not the other way around. Baird didn't have to worry about Cassandra getting lost in her own brain anymore.

Good thing, Baird thought, *since I'm guessing we're in enough trouble right now.*

Cassandra gasped, the sharp intake of breath putting Baird on full alert.

"Oh, no," the Librarian whispered. "This is not good."

"What is it?" Baird demanded. "Spit it out, Red."

It took Cassandra a moment to come down from her heightened state of awareness. Taking a deep breath, she lowered her arms and focused her gaze back on Baird, who could tell from the other woman's expression that bad news was on its way.

"The vibration, the one I'm feeling, it's setting up a resonant frequency within the Opera House that's amplifying the building's own natural vibrations. If it keeps building like this, steadily increasing the amplitude of the oscillations on an atomic level, the resonance effect could conceivably threaten the structural integrity of the entire building."

For once, Baird thought she understood the theory. "The way enough marching footsteps, moving in the same rhythm, can cause a bridge to collapse?"

As a soldier, she had been trained to break stride when marching across bridges for that very reason.

"Exactly!" Cassandra said. "Once the vibrational energy exceeds the building's load level, the Opera House will shake itself apart!"

"Crap!" Baird swore. "Any idea where these bad vibrations are coming from?"

"I'm not sure," Cassandra said. "Maybe from somewhere below?"

Baird put the pieces together. "The cellars. The Phantom's old stomping grounds." She hastily fished her phone from her pocket. "We need to alert the guys. Let them know what's up."

"Maybe they're already on top of this?" Cassandra said hopefully.

"Or under it." Baird glared in frustration at her phone. "Damn. I can't get through to them."

"Spooky underground lairs tend to have inadequate Wi-Fi," Cassandra said. "In my experience, that is."

Baird remembered running into the same problem while buried alive beneath the Mountains of Madness. She'd needed Morse code and a cursed Tibetan gong to get out of that one.

"No luck." She put the phone away before turning to Claudel. "You heard what she said. We need to evacuate the Opera House immediately."

Claudel balked at the idea. "On whose authority? A pair of ghost-hunting American librarians?"

"*The* Librarians," Baird insisted, even as she realized that there was no time to go over his head. Even if she could reach the proper officials in time, what was she supposed to tell them? That the Phantom of the Opera was about to bring the house down in a big way? Yeah, that was going to go over well.

"Let me guess," Cassandra said. "We're on our own?"

"So what else is new?"

A drastic tactic occurred to her. Glancing around, she hastily located a convenient fire alarm and lunged toward it. Claudel gasped in alarm as he grasped her intention.

"No, mademoiselle! You mustn't! There is a performance under way!"

"Sorry, *mon ami*. But *Faust* is going to have to take a rain check."

Triggering the alarm wouldn't nab the Phantom or save the Opera House, but hopefully it would clear the building before it fell down and went boom, assuming they couldn't find a way to cut off the dangerous vibrations at their source. Bracing herself for an ear-piercing siren, she pulled down on the lever.

Nothing happened.

"The alarm!" Cassandra exclaimed. "It's not working!"

The Phantom's work? Baird suspected as much. The Opera Ghost must have sabotaged the alarm system as part of his sinister agenda.

"Damn it," she muttered. "I hate it when the bad guys plan ahead. That's supposed to be *my* specialty."

"So now what?" Cassandra asked.

A rhythmic creaking noise drew Baird's gaze upward once

more. The chandelier was rocking even more wildly now. Cracks appeared in the ceiling where it was mounted. A jolt of adrenaline shot through Baird's veins.

"Watch out!" she shouted to the others.

The swinging chandelier tore itself loose from the ceiling, crashing down onto the floor. Baird dived out of the way to avoid being hit by the flying fixture, even as Cassandra yanked Claudel out of the line of fire.

"Everyone okay?" she called to them.

"We're fine," Cassandra reported, letting go of the shaken director. "But that's just the beginning. The tremors are only warming up."

More books toppled from the shelves, but Baird had bigger concerns.

Just like the Opera House had a much bigger chandelier . . .

————

The blazing light and heat put the "torture" in "torture chamber," and the deafening organ music wasn't helping any. Between the oven-like temperature and the Phantom's impassioned playing, Stone could barely think.

"I liked this better when it was a *silent* movie," he muttered.

"What?" Ezekiel said, his hands over his ears. He shouted over the increasingly manic strains of *Don Juan Triumphant*. His face gleamed with perspiration.

"Never mind."

Sweating like a legionnaire in a Roman bathhouse, Stone searched for a way out. Presumably there was a secret exit hidden behind the mirrors somewhere, but he couldn't find it. Tearing off his flannel shirt, he wrapped the fabric around his fists and tried to smash the mirrors, in part to kill the merciless light and heat reflecting off them, but the original Phantom had apparently anticipated this response on the part of his prisoners—the mirrors were unbreakable. Shielding his eyes with his hand, Stone squinted up at the ceiling where the trapdoor had been, but it was too high to reach even if the blinding glare hadn't made it impossible to locate.

He glanced over at Ezekiel, who was trying to call for help on his phone. Jenkins couldn't open a Magic Door to the torture chamber if there was no door in sight, but maybe Baird and Cassandra could come to their rescue?

"No luck!" Ezekiel shouted over the music. "No signal!"

Figures, Stone thought. *This is a dungeon, not a coffee shop.*

Sweat dripped down his face, tasting salty upon his parched lips. He found himself pining for the murky water of the lagoon or even the moisture seeping down the grimy stone walls of the cellar earlier. The oppressive heat rippled the air above the sandy floor, almost as though they were genuinely stranded beneath the harsh sun of some forbidding desert. He started digging through the sand in search of a way out. Maybe another trapdoor buried under the sand?

"What are you doing?" Ezekiel asked, putting down his phone.

"You got a better idea?"

Ezekiel opened his mouth as though to supply one, but his usual cocky attitude evaporated in the heat. "I got nothing," he admitted, then started tunneling through the sand as well.

To be honest, Stone wasn't sure if this was an actual strategy or if their brains were just baking, but he kept digging away, if only to try to escape the faux sunlight beating down on them, not to mention the relentless sonic assault of the Phantom's organ. He wondered how many victims had lost their minds in this torture chamber back when the original Phantom had called these underground dungeons home. He vaguely recalled something about thirst-crazed captives hanging themselves to escape the agonizing heat. . . .

But those prisoners weren't Librarians, he thought. *We don't give up even when the odds are against us.*

"Hang on!" Ezekiel shouted hoarsely. "I think I found something!"

Stone scurried over to where his friend was frantically scooping handfuls of hot sand away from what turned out to be a closed ebony box buried under the sand. Ezekiel tugged on the box, which didn't budge—it was mounted to the floor at the very center of the torture chamber. The men exchanged a look before Ezekiel popped open the lid of the box to reveal two carved jade insects resting atop a velvet cushion.

A grasshopper and a scorpion, to be exact.

"What the heck?" Ezekiel said, sounding disappointed by the box's contents. "Just what we need: a pair of creepy-crawly knickknacks!"

He reached for the grasshopper, perhaps to throw it away in frustration.

"Wait!" Stone grabbed Ezekiel's wrist. "Don't touch them!" His mouth and throat felt as dry as the Sahara, but he mustered enough spit to speak. "There was something like this in the book. It was a booby-trap thing: if you turned the right insect, you were saved, but if you chose the wrong one, you were dead."

"Okay," Ezekiel said. "So which was which, the grasshopper or the scorpion?"

"I'm not sure." Stone ransacked his memory, but his brain was moving about as well as a car with an overheated engine.

His synapses were stalled along the side of the road, waiting for a tow truck. "I'm trying to remember but it's so damn hot . . . and that music! I can barely hear myself think!"

"Tell me about it." Ezekiel took out his phone again. "Just give me a moment to download the book onto my . . ." His voice trailed off as he realized the flaw in that plan. "Oh right. No bars."

Stone chuckled. "Doesn't matter. You just reminded me of something." He reached back and extracted a dog-eared paperback copy of a novel from his rear pocket. "I grabbed this from the Library when we were prepping for the mission."

The look on Ezekiel's face was priceless. Stone spared a minute to rub it in.

"Think about this the next time you rag me about preferring 'dead-tree' books." He snickered as he flipped through pages. "Sometimes the old ways are still the best ways."

"Less gloating, more reading, mate," Ezekiel replied. "And I'd appreciate it if you didn't share this with Jenkins. You just know he'd get his lecture on about it."

"No promises."

Sweaty fingers stained the pages as Stone searched for the crucial passage. To his relief, Leroux was an old-school author who gave each chapter a title of its own, so Stone could flip straight to "Chapter XXV: The Scorpion or the Grasshopper: Which?"

"Thank God for the table of contents," Stone said, which, it occurred to him, was probably one of the most Librarian-y things he had ever uttered. Even still, it felt like a small eternity before his bleary eyes managed to extract the vital info from Leroux's florid prose. "Here it is! Turn the scorpion to live, turn the grasshopper and it's *adieu*, sweet world."

He reached for the jade scorpion, but Ezekiel restrained him.

"Not so fast!" the worried thief said. "How do we know that Leroux got it right? He left out the part about the Phantom knocking up Christine, didn't he?"

Ezekiel had a point. They had no idea how much Leroux might have fictionalized the true story when penning his so-called novel. And there did seem to be some discrepancies between the book and what they had already stumbled onto here in the Phantom's old domain, not that Stone wanted to dwell on that at the moment. Trusting the book too far could cost him and Ezekiel their lives—and allow this new Phantom to carry out his fiendish scheme, whatever it might be. Stone contemplated the battered paperback in his hand. How much was fiction? How much was fact?

And what other options did they have right at the moment?

"If there's one thing I've learned in this job," he said, "it's that there's more truth in old stories than anyone could ever guess." He looked to Ezekiel, not wanting to make this choice without consulting his cohort. "You cool with this?"

Ezekiel nodded. "We're Librarians. Live by the book, die by the book . . . even a ridiculous dead-tree one."

Stone took a deep breath and rotated the scorpion.

Ancient gears creaked as one of the mirrored walls pivoted sideways, creating a route out of the torture chamber. A chill breeze invaded the dungeon, tantalizing the men with the promise of escape from the heat.

"Score one for old-school investigative journalism." Stone scrambled for the exit, with Ezekiel right on his heels. "Let's get the hell out of here."

A dank, gloomy stairwell waited beyond the exit. The

beckoning shadows came as a blessed relief as the men rushed up the steps to confront the Phantom, who was still pounding away at his keyboard. The music itself was growing steadily wilder and more sinister, as melancholy longing gave way to madness and menace. Threatening notes and chords began to drown out the romantic heights of the earlier sections, sending a chill down Stone's spine. Without really understanding why, he knew in his gut that they didn't want to let the new Phantom keep on playing, not if they wanted to stop him from avenging his infamous ancestor.

"That's enough!" Stone rasped, loud enough to be heard over the music. Fists clenched, he stalked toward the Phantom, ready to kick some masquerading butt if he had to. "I don't know exactly what you're up to, but this opera is over. The fat lady has sung!"

"What he said," Ezekiel added, while fumbling with his phone. "Good news: I'm finally getting some bars now that we're out of the oven."

"Not really the time, man," Stone said.

The Phantom was undeterred, despite being outnumbered by two very sweaty and pissed-off Librarians.

"Keep back!" he warned. A gloved finger hovered over yet another ebony key. "One more step and I'll bring the chandelier down!"

Ezekiel glanced anxiously at the ceiling. "What chandelier?"

"Not here." Stone froze in place. He knew exactly which chandelier the Phantom was talking about. "The big one . . . over the auditorium upstairs."

Stone recalled that a gala performance was under way above. Could the Phantom really drop the giant chandelier on the audience by striking the right key on the organ? Stone had no idea, but he wasn't about to call the Phantom's bluff, not with innocent lives at stake. Frustrated, he glanced over at Ezekiel, and was annoyed to see his partner still messing with his phone.

"Seriously, dude? You're checking your signal now?"

Ezekiel shrugged.

"Got to stay connected."

————

Cassandra and Baird sprinted up a spiral staircase, racing to secure the great chandelier before it was too late. They could hear *Faust* being performed loudly onstage as they left the public areas of the Opera House behind, venturing into backstage areas frequented only by the cast and crew. The compulsively analytical part of Cassandra's brain couldn't help picking apart the soaring octaves and chords, the same way she might break down a complex mathematical equation. There was a lot to digest in the music, and some catchy melodies, too. Too bad there wasn't time to take in the show.

"You sure this is the right way?" Baird asked.

Cassandra tapped her noggin. "Magic brain, remember?"

She had hastily surveyed a map of the Opera House in the library downstairs before bidding adieu to poor, baffled Monsieur Claudel. Cassandra was not the serious student of architecture that Stone was, but she had a photographic memory and a gift for grasping designs and patterns. That was all she needed to navigate the sprawling Opera House with confidence.

In theory, at least.

"*Halte!*" a security guard ordered as they reached an upper landing. He held up his palm like a traffic cop. "You are not allowed here."

"Sorry, pal," Baird said, "but we don't have time to debate this."

A judo flip laid the unlucky guard flat on his back, the wind knocked out of him. Cassandra gave him an apologetic look as she stepped over his stunned form.

"Trust us, we know what we're doing."

Or so she hoped.

A rapid dash up another flight of stairs led them to a cupola directly above the auditorium, which was now used for dance lessons and rehearsals. To their relief, it was vacant at the moment. A wall-sized mirror reminded Cassandra of the way the Phantom lured Christine through a dressing-room mirror in the musical. A long barre was mounted to the wall across from the mirror. A hardwood floor awaited the tortured toes of the ballerinas, some of whom were probably downstairs waiting for their cues. Baird slammed the door behind Cassandra and herself to keep them from being interrupted.

"There should be a trapdoor in the floor that they use to raise and lower the chandelier for maintenance," Cassandra said, panting after rushing up the stairs. She pointed at approximately the right spot. "Over there somewhere."

"I'm on it," Baird said.

The athletic Guardian wasn't even winded, despite their rapid ascent up the stairs. Cassandra envied her friend's physical fitness and made a mental note to up her own exercise regime. Being a Librarian required a surprising amount of running and jumping, at least if you wanted to survive the job. She couldn't always count on her Guardian to handle the more physical challenges.

"Here we go!" Baird dragged a dance mat out of the way to expose a pair of hinged doorways on each side of the massive steel brace supporting the chandelier. Grabbing a handle, she tugged one of the double doors open, the well-oiled hinges making nary a squeak compared with the opera being loudly and enthusiastically performed many feet below—beneath an immense crystal chandelier that more than lived up to its hype. At least seven tons of bronze and crystal hung on a chain high above the unsuspecting heads of the audience, whose attention was fixed on the lavish spectacle playing out onstage. More than two thousand people occupied the huge audi- torium, sumptuously decorated in red and gold beneath a brightly colored ceiling mural. Intent on *Faust*, no one in the audience noticed the two women staring down through the opening above the chandelier. Cassandra wasn't sure if that was a good thing or not.

"Just our luck," Baird said. "It's a packed house."

Cassandra placed her palm against the brace. Just as she feared, the hazardous vibration had increased dramatically in the time it had taken them to sprint up the stairs. It was only a matter of time before the chandelier shook loose from its mooring—with the entire Opera House collapsing not long after. Shaking her head in dismay, she confirmed the diagnosis to Baird.

"This chandelier is heading for a fall . . . just like in the story."

"Great. Another unnecessary remake," Baird grumbled. "How much time do we have to rewrite the script?"

Cassandra started to do the math, but was interrupted by a chime from her phone. Her eyes widened as she read the text.

"It's from Ezekiel," she told Baird. "They've run into the Phantom, who is threatening to drop the chandelier by re- mote control!"

"Can he do that?" Baird asked urgently.

"It's a slight update on his M.O., but certainly in character." Cassandra leaned out over the trapdoor to take a closer look at the chandelier. Was there something going on there beyond the impending resonance disaster? Raising her hands before her, she kicked her brain into a higher gear, the better to analyze and observe. "Let me see what I can see."

Synesthesia scrambled her senses as her world came into sharper focus, showing her the complicated equations and geometry underlying everything around her. The swelling music flashed in all the colors of the rainbow, with the altos and sopranos and tenors at the brighter end of the spectrum and the basses and tenors at the darker end, while the orchestra added its own complementary hues. Flutes and piccolos streaked the music with brilliant shades of crimson and scarlet, the highest notes ascending into infrared even as the deep, dark colors of the bassoons and kettledrums edged into ultraviolet. She smelled the brilliant sets and costumes, and the glittering, prismatic shine of the crystal chandelier tasted like rock candy on her tongue. Studying the chandelier, absorbing its lines and symmetry, she constructed a glowing, hallucinatory model of it in the empty air before her eyes. Her hands manipulated the image, which only she could see, rotating it along the x, y, and z axes so she could examine it from every angle, looking for any detail that didn't belong . . . such as maybe that odd little bump where the chain met the top of the chandelier? The one that marred the chandelier's otherwise perfect symmetry?

"There!" Cassandra waved away the virtual chandelier, letting her senses ramp down to everyday levels, and plucked a pair of opera glasses from her purse. She had packed the glasses on the off chance she might be able to take in the show, but now she used them to zero in on the actual chandelier and that one incongruous flaw—which proved to be a tiny metal box with a blinking red light on it. Pointing urgently, she handed the magnifying goggles over to Baird. "Please tell me that's not a miniature explosive device."

"Wish I could, Red," Baird said, confirming the worst, "but that's exactly what it is. Guess our Phantom is determined to replay the chandelier scene one way or another. Want to bet that charge is rigged to snap the chain holding the big lamp up?"

Footsteps sounded outside the rehearsal room.

"Great," Baird said sarcastically. "We've got company on the way. You keep them out of my hair while I deal with this."

"Deal with it how?" Cassandra asked, making a beeline for the door.

"How else?" Baird said. "The hard way."

———

Wood scraped against wood as Cassandra shoved an antique wardrobe up against the door to the chamber, barring the entrance just in time. Fists pounded on the other side of the door. Angry voices, shouting in French, demanded admittance. Baird sighed and rolled her eyes.

You deck one security guard, she thought, *and everyone wants to make a federal case out of it.*

But the upset locals could wait; Baird had a bomb to defuse. Seeing no other option, she dropped through the trapdoor and shimmied down the heavy-duty metal chain until she reached the top of the chandelier, which swayed slightly beneath her feet. Baird hoped her added weight wasn't making a dire situation even worse.

"I knew I should have skipped that extra slice of cheesecake last night."

She could feel the massive chandelier tremble from the pernicious vibration working its way up from the cellars. Despite her precarious perch, she was relieved to see that the explosive charge was pretty standard-issue, as opposed to some exotic magical talisman. She had defused similar gadgets plenty of times during her career in counterterrorism, albeit never while suspended above an audience of rapt Parisian culture-lovers. She could disarm this device in her sleep.

Assuming the chandelier didn't come crashing down first.

"Time?" she called out to Cassandra.

"Kind of busy right now." The wardrobe scraped across the floor. "Just . . . hurry."

Baird heard Cassandra straining and shoving to keep the door to the rehearsal room closed. Baird appreciated the effort, but knew that the petite Librarian couldn't keep the Opera security goons out for long. Cassandra was fighting a losing battle.

Too bad the guys weren't on hand to help with the heavy lifting.

Focus, Baird told herself. *One problem at a time.*

Fully aware the Phantom could conceivably trigger the device at any moment, Baird got to work. With her favorite Swiss Army knife, she deftly pried open the casing on the device to expose its innards. No arcane knowledge or ancient lore was required to locate the detonator; if anything, Baird experienced a peculiar sense of nostalgia as she confidently cut the blue wire, rendering the device inert. The blinking red light went out.

Just like old times, she thought.

Not that they were out of the woods yet. She could feel

the chandelier quivering beneath her. If Cassandra's math was on target—and it always was—the entire Opera House was on borrowed time.

Unless Stone and Ezekiel could cut off the vibration at its source.

————

Stone found himself in an old-fashioned standoff, afraid to call the Phantom's bluff. He knew full well how large and heavy the grand chandelier over the auditorium was. If there was even a chance that the Phantom could drop it on the audience by pressing a single black key, they had to take the masked madman's threat seriously.

"Keep back," the Phantom repeated as he resumed his concert. "But do feel free to enjoy the music. I am literally playing to bring the house down!"

Don Juan Triumphant blared from the pipe organ. The music shook the underground sanctuary, causing dust to sprinkle down from the ancient masonry. Stone's eyes widened in alarm as he grasped the Phantom's ultimate ambition.

"The music! The vibrations!" Stone recalled an article he had once written, under one of his many aliases, on the dangers of mechanical resonance with regards to high-rise construction projects, going all the way back to the Tower of Babel. "You're trying to trigger a structural collapse!"

"Not trying . . . succeeding!" the Phantom corrected him. "There is no possibility of failure. *Don Juan Triumphant* is more than just Erik's masterpiece; it was composed to be his ultimate revenge against the world above, held in reserve until this very moment!"

The music grew wilder and more thunderous, building toward its apocalyptic crescendo. Stone started forward to drag the Phantom away from the organ, then hesitated as he remembered the chandelier, hanging like the Sword of Damocles over the vulnerable operagoers in the auditorium.

"A thorny dilemma, isn't it, Librarian?" the Phantom taunted. "Do you dare risk my wrath by attempting to interfere? Are you truly willing to sacrifice innocent lives to prevent an even grander, more glorious catastrophe?"

"Shut your mouth," Stone snarled, his fists clenched at his sides. He couldn't just stand by and let the Phantom keep playing, but what about the chandelier? He turned desperately to Ezekiel, who was still glued to his phone. "Help me out here, man. What are we supposed to do?"

Ezekiel smirked. "No worries. Just got a text from Cassandra. The chandelier's staying put . . . for now."

"Hang on!" Stone couldn't believe his ears. "Are you saying—?"

"Baird took care of it. We're good to go."

That was all Stone needed to hear. He lunged at the Phantom, who stabbed an ebony key with one finger. "Fools. You brought this on yourself . . . and on the innocent souls you just condemned to death!"

Stone kept on coming. Down here in the depths, there was no way to tell whether the chandelier was falling or not, but Stone trusted his teammates. If Cassandra said that Baird had things under control upstairs, he believed it without question.

Which meant that the Phantom was about to get whupped.

"Show's over, dude. Get your hands off that keyboard!"

"No! Keep away from me!" The Phantom jumped to his feet to evade the furious Librarian, knocking over the bench in front of the organ. He hastily snatched up the precious sheet music, clutching it to his chest. Stone caught hold of the Phantom's black cape, determined not to let him get away, but the Phantom shrugged off the cape and flung it back at Stone, briefly snaring the Librarian in its folds. "Damn your souls!" the foiled Phantom cursed. "You've ruined everything . . . for now!"

"Forget it!" Stone yanked the cape off him and tossed it aside. "That concerto is coming with us!"

"Never! Erik's legacy belongs to me, his rightful heir!"

The Phantom snatched the silver candelabra from atop the organ and hurled it at Stone, who ducked to avoid being nailed by it. Trailing sparks, the candelabra whooshed past Stone to crash to the floor at Ezekiel's feet.

"Whoa!" the thief protested. "Watch where you're throwing things!"

Darkness fell over the chamber as the candles sputtered out, leaving only the glow from Ezekiel's phone. In the dim light, Stone saw the Phantom shove his way past Ezekiel, knocking the other Librarian to the floor, as the masked lunatic fled down a staircase into the lower depths of the underground lair. Stone took off after the Phantom, knowing that no building in Paris—or the world—was safe as long as the obsessed madman possessed the Phantom's malignant magnum opus.

"We can't let him get away!" Stone shouted raggedly, his voice still raw from his ordeal in the torture chamber. "Not with *Don Juan*!"

Activating the beam from his own phone, Stone dashed down the winding stone steps after the Phantom. He burst through a stone archway into a long, sepulchral corridor. His beam swept the forgotten catacomb before him, searching for the masked fugitive, who was no longer in view. Stone swore under his breath, frustrated to have lost sight of his quarry. Who knew how many secret doors and escape routes were hidden in this subterranean abode? He had to catch up with the Phantom quickly, before the fiend could slip away with the deadly concerto.

"C'mon, c'mon," Stone said. "Where are you?"

A silken snake wrapped around his throat, cutting off his breath.

The Punjab lasso, Stone realized too late. In his haste, he had forgotten to keep his arm raised in self-defense. Glancing up, he saw the Phantom glaring down at him from a trapdoor in the ceiling, clutching the other end of the noose with both hands. Crazed blue eyes blazed behind the Phantom's trademark mask as the fiend cackled maniacally.

"American meddler! Meet the fate of all who cross the Phantom of the Opera!"

The strangler's cord bit into Stone's neck, choking him. He tried to pry the noose away from his throat, but his desperate fingers could not get between the slippery silk and his skin. A ragged croak escaped his lips as his feet lifted off the floor, leaving him dangling in the air like a condemned man meeting his end upon the gallows. His lungs gasped for air even as the lasso tightened around his throat, depriving him of oxygen. Darkness encroached on his vision, adding to the shadows already surrounding him, as he fought to keep from passing out.

Never thought it would end this way, he thought, *far beneath one of the world's great buildings.* . . .

"Uh-uh." Ezekiel sauntered into the catacomb. "Cut him loose, mate."

"You dare to dictate to me in my own domain! Flee, so that the world may know that the Phantom lives again—and that his vengeance cannot be delayed for long!"

"I don't know about that," Ezekiel said with a smirk. "Missing something?"

He held up a loose page of the concerto, flaunting it before the Phantom, whose shocked eyes and dropped jaw betrayed his dismay despite his porcelain mask. The rope holding up Stone slipped slightly in his grasp.

"No!" the Phantom gasped. "How . . . ?"

"Did I mention I was a thief?" Ezekiel's voice took on a harder edge as he gripped the top of the music with both hands, poised to rip the purloined sheet from the top down. "Let my friend go—now—or the music of the night is confetti!"

"Stop, I command you! That's Erik's masterpiece, the enduring culmination of his genius!"

"More of a pop fan myself." Ezekiel began tearing the sheet, just a fraction of an inch. "Going, going . . ."

"Wait!" the Phantom cried out in panic. "You mustn't . . . !"

He let go of the lasso, dropping Stone to the floor. The choking Librarian barely noticed the impact; all that mattered was that the taut noose had slackened around his neck. Gasping for breath, he tugged the silk cord loose. Hungry lungs sucked in heaping mouthfuls of air.

"You okay, mate?" Ezekiel asked.

"Better than a few seconds ago," Stone rasped. "Thanks, man."

"For what? Lifting a stray sheet of music during that confusion upstairs?" Ezekiel feigned modesty. "Please. That was child's play." He grinned at Stone. "You're welcome, though."

Stone massaged his throat. "Would've helped if you'd told me, before I got myself strung up."

"Like you really gave me a chance," Ezekiel replied. "Besides, *somebody* had to chase after the bad guy, and you looked like you were definitely in the mood to give this poseur a well-deserved beat-down. Who was I to get in your way?"

"Well, next time . . ."

Their banter was too much for the distraught Phantom, who peered down anxiously from the ceiling.

"Please!" the masked musician interrupted. "I did what you asked—I spared your comrade." He reached desperately for the missing page of *Don Juan Triumphant*. "Now give me that sheet. It's my inheritance. It belongs to me!"

Ezekiel shook his head. "Nothing doing, mate. Pretty sure you forfeited your claim with that whole attempted mass-murder thing." He brandished the stolen sheet, tantalizing the Phantom by keeping it just out of reach. "Here's how it's going to work. You're going to hand over the rest of the music and we'll make sure that it ends up safely tucked away in the world's most secure library, preserved for posterity, or this page is lost to history forever."

"You wouldn't dare!" the Phantom raged.

"You don't think so?" Ezekiel turned toward Stone. "You tell him, Stone. Would I or wouldn't I?"

"Oh, he'd totally dare," Stone confirmed. "Trust me on this. He has no sense of history, no respect for fine art and music, whatsoever. Drives me nuts sometimes." Stone climbed shakily to his feet. "If I were you, I'd take his threat seriously . . . if you really care about preserving Erik's master-work."

To be honest, Stone had no idea whether he was feeding the Phantom a load of bull or not. Would Ezekiel really shred a priceless artistic treasure to teach the Phantom a lesson? Stone wouldn't put it past him, but still . . .

"Curse you both!" The Phantom shook his fist angrily. Spittle sprayed from his lips. "This was none of your business!"

"Pretty sure it was, mate," Ezekiel said. "So what's it going to be? Immortality . . . or the wastebasket?"

Bloody murder flared in the Phantom's eyes, but then his shoulders slumped in defeat.

"I . . . I surrender."

"Good call." Ezekiel held out an open palm. "Hand it over."

With the dexterity of a gymnast, the Phantom dropped down from the ceiling and dolefully turned the remainder of *Don Juan Triumphant* over to Ezekiel. The fight seemed to have left the defeated "ghost," but, not taking any chances, Stone tied the man's hands behind his back with his silk lasso. He drew the cord tight, and none too gently. He hadn't forgotten the torture chamber, nor the countless innocent lives this Phantom had put in jeopardy.

"So now what do we do with him?" Ezekiel asked.

"Baird still has connections with NATO and Interpol," Stone reminded him. "Let them sort it out . . . but first, let's find out what's hiding behind this mask."

Morbid curiosity compelled Stone to reach for the Phantom's mask. He braced himself for whatever deformed, disfigured visage lurked behind the featureless disguise. Perhaps a face like a living skull, as in the original novel and movie? Or scarred by acid, as in the remakes?

What he *wasn't* expecting was for the face beneath the mask to be . . .

Handsome?

The face of a male model or pop star glared sullenly at the Librarians. Flawless skin, unblemished in any way, adorned perfect cheekbones and chiseled features that gave Michelangelo's *David* a run for his money.

"Huh?" Ezekiel said. "Is it just me or does he look more like the Phantom of the Boy Band?"

Flaxen hair and blue eyes reminded Stone of the portrait in the original Phantom's macabre boudoir.

"Guess he takes after his great-great-grandmother."

3

"Any word from Flynn?" Baird asked.

Jenkins looked up from polishing the long-lost arms of the *Venus de Milo*, which tended to get a bit cranky if they were neglected for too long. Although the arms usually resided in the Library's Greco-Roman gallery, the ageless caretaker had them propped up at his personal workstation a few yards away from Baird's usually neatly organized desk, which had an annoying tendency to clutter itself when she wasn't looking. The ground-floor office of the Library's Portland Annex currently served as the Librarians' base of operations and anchor to this physical plane of reality. Adjacent doorways and corridors led into the Library proper, which was infinitely larger than the institutional-looking gray building housing the Annex. Polished wooden bookcases, crammed with volumes both useful and arcane, lined the walls of the office, while an old-school card catalog ran alongside the sweeping staircase leading up to the mezzanine. Antique cabinets and sideboards, framed maps and scrolls, and an eclectic assortment of vintage knickknacks and curios, including an old-time radio and a genuine nineteenth-century bowie knife, gave the

Annex a cozy, timeless feel that Baird had come to appreciate over the last few years. It was more than just her work-
place. It was a sanctuary.

"I'm afraid not, Colonel," Jenkins answered. A distinguished, silver-haired gentleman in a conservative gray suit, who
only appeared to be in his sixties, he had been tending to the
Annex for far longer than you might guess just by looking at
him. The Library was, Baird suspected, the closest thing
he'd had to a home since the fall of a certain bright and shining
kingdom a long, long time ago. "But that's to be expected,"
he continued. "The Lemurian conclave was always going to
take a good while, leaving Mister Carsen effectively incom-
municado for the duration."

Flynn Carsen, the most experienced Librarian still on
active duty, had been called away to serve as an impartial
arbiter at some delicate deep-sea treaty negotiations between various feuding clans of mer-people. And the fact that
"mer-people," complete with gills and scales, were actually a
thing still boggled Baird's mind occasionally.

"Given the frequently rancorous relations between the
parties involved, most notably the displaced tribes of Mu and
Ys," Jenkins elaborated, "I rather suspect that Mister Carsen
has his hands full at the bottom of the Marianas Trench . . .
for a few more days, at least."

"I know, I know," Baird said with a sigh. She and Flynn were
more than just Librarian and Guardian, so she was understandably impatient for his return. A framed photo on her desk
reminded her of his boyish good looks. "Flynn said he would
be back when he was back."

"An accurate assessment," Jenkins judged. "You wouldn't
think that water-breathers could be so long-winded, yet simply

reciting the genealogies of the various breeding populations can take forever. . . ."

Despite Jenkins's jaded tone, Baird couldn't help worrying a little.

"But this is just a diplomatic thing, right? There's no real danger involved?"

Jenkins shrugged. "It's been said that diplomacy is nothing but warfare concealed."

Baird thought she recognized the quote. "Von Clausewitz?"

"*Star Trek*," he corrected her. "Nonetheless, this is hardly Mister Carsen's first conclave. I'm quite confident that he's staying afloat, metaphorically speaking, despite being more than thirty thousand feet beneath the waves." His voice softened in an obvious attempt to reassure her. "Chances are, the greatest perils he's facing are an excess of seaweed salad and overheated oratory."

"Thanks, Jenkins. I guess I'll just have to wait for him to come sloshing back onto dry land." She contemplated, without much enthusiasm, the overdue filing and correspondence on her desk. "Too bad we don't have a case to occupy me in the meantime."

"It's not too late to join Game Night," Cassandra called out to her from the nearby conference table, where she and the other Librarians were relaxing with a hard-fought game of Trivial Pursuit. The long oak table rested at the center of the office, atop the compass design embedded in the floor. "You could be my partner."

"Hey, no fair," Ezekiel protested, his face still deeply tanned from his recent stint in the Phantom's torture oven. "We're not doing teams. This is strictly one-on-one-on-one."

Stone rolled the dice and moved his plastic playing piece

around the board. "And it's not as though you're exactly hurting for wedges, Cassie," he said before swiveling in his seat to address Baird. "Not that you're not welcome to join in on your own. We can even spot you a wedge or two, since we've got a head start on you."

"Thanks," Baird said, appreciating the offer. "But I bet I can catch up with all three of you without any concessions. I may not be an actual Librarian, but I've picked up a thing or two in my travels."

"Not doubting that one bit," Stone said amiably.

Baird wandered over to check out the game. Scanning the board, she was amused to see that the Librarians' gameplay reflected their individual specialties. No surprise, Cassandra was cleaning up on the Math and Science questions, Stone already had his Art and History wedges, while Ezekiel had aced the Entertainment and Leisure categories. All three Librarians had mastered Geography, which was to be expected given all the globetrotting they did on a regular basis, although Baird doubted that there were too many Geography questions concerning Shangri-La, El Dorado, or the Bermuda Triangle.

"Maybe we can do girls against boys," Cassandra persisted, still pushing the teams idea. "Come on, please, I'm never going to get the Sports wedge on my own. . . ."

There was something to be said, Baird reflected, for putting together a well-balanced squad whose members' strengths and weaknesses complemented one another's. She was about to throw in with Cassandra when the Clipping Book interrupted the game by thumping loudly on its book stand at the other end of the table. As though blown by a mystic wind, its pages flipped of their own accord to a formerly blank page that now displayed a pasted newspaper clipping that hadn't been there only moments before.

"Never mind, people," Baird said. "Looks like we're back on the clock."

The Clipping Book, which was a large leather-bound scrapbook of the sort that newspaper archives employed back in the predigital era, was the Library's preferred means of alerting the Librarians to developing situations requiring their attention. These typically involved outbreaks of freaky occurrences caused by dangerous magical knowledge, relics, and/or entities that had not yet been safely filed away in the Library. In many ways, the job was much like Baird's former career in NATO; the only difference was that, these days, the potential weapons of mass destruction tended to involve ancient myths and sorcery.

"Ooh," Cassandra enthused, visibly excited as ever by the prospect of a new case. Possibly even more than any of her compatriots, being a Librarian had brought purpose and excitement into her life. "Where do you think it's sending us now?"

"Not another glorified sewer, I hope," Ezekiel said. "If you ask me, I think we're overdue for an all-expenses-paid trip to Hawaii or Monte Carlo."

Stone shot him a warning look. "Don't jinx us, dude."

Game Night already forgotten, Baird and her team hurried to inspect the Clipping Book, as did Jenkins, who carefully locked Venus's notoriously roving arms in an antique mahogany armory before joining the others. Baird didn't waste time speculating about what the enchanted scrapbook had in store for them this time, not when the tantalizing newspaper clipping was now pasted in the book right before their eyes:

IRON-AGE MONUMENT VANDALIZED

COUNTY MAYO—A weathered stone monolith, which
had stood for more than a thousand years on a remote island in Clew Bay, was finally toppled by unknown parties who left the site in ruins. Authorities have no leads
regarding the identity of the vandals or their motives and
are asking the public for assistance. The monument, one
of many scattered throughout Ireland, is believed by historians to date back to the fifth century at least.

"Ireland?" Cassandra said, sounding thrilled. "We're going
to Ireland?"

"Okay, I can live with that," Ezekiel said, "as long as we
don't get stuck out in the sticks the whole time, dodging cow
poop."

"Lots of intriguing sites and history in Ireland," Stone
observed, "going all the way back to the Neolithic era. The
Celts, the Vikings, the Normans . . . they've all left their mark
on the island's art, language, and architecture." He scowled
as he reread the article, absorbing the whole story. "Damn
it, I hate hearing about stuff like this, priceless landmarks
wrecked without any consideration for their historical or cul-
tural significance. What kind of loser trashes a genuine piece
of history?"

Baird understood his indignation, but guessed that the
Clipping Book would not have been triggered by a simple, if
inexcusable, act of vandalism. There had to be more to the
story, a mystical angle worth alerting the Librarians to.

"Someone looking for something they shouldn't?" she wondered. "Or out to unleash something? Or with a *very* old score
to settle?"

She had been associated with the Library long enough to

know that there could be any number of possible reasons for
desecrating an ancient monument, few of them good. She reviewed the news article, which had apparently been imported
from *The Irish Times*, before consulting Jenkins.

"Any thoughts or convenient exposition?" she asked the immortal caretaker, who possibly knew more about history's most
obscure magical nooks and crannies than anyone else alive.
"There anything we should know about this particular location or monolith?"

"Not that I immediately recall, Colonel." He peered over
her shoulder at the clipping. "As correctly noted in the article, Ireland is well-supplied with a generous assortment of
age-old menhirs, dolmens, henges, barrows, raths, and other
stubbornly durable remnants of times long past. You can find
them in bogs, pastures, hills, caves, and elsewhere, many of
them still quite far from the beaten path. The unlucky stone
in question is but one of many."

"Oh well," Baird said, disappointed. "Figured it couldn't
hurt to ask, although I suppose I should be relieved that you're
not immediately sounding a pre-apocalypse alarm. This news
isn't raising any obvious red flags we should know about?"

"Believe me, Colonel, if toppling this monument opened
up one of the Seven Seals, you would be the first to know."
He strolled over to a bookshelf and started leafing through a
heavy tome on some related topic. "Further research may
yield some light on the matter, of course, though it may take
a fair amount of digging."

Baird could believe it. The Library's records stretched all
the way back to Alexander the Great—and then some. Not
even Jenkins could be expected to have instant recall of every
ancient scroll, journal, or illuminated manuscript tucked away
in the Library's ever-expanding collection.

"Roger that," she said. "You hit the books while the rest of us head out to examine the scene of the crime. With any luck, we'll find some clues pointing us to whatever the Library is worried about."

Not for the first time, she wished the Library could provide more guidance than just provocative newspaper clippings, like perhaps a detailed military-style briefing, complete with maps, backup plans, rules of engagement, and a decent amount of actionable intel, but that was not how it worked. The Library, in its enigmatic wisdom, simply let them know when there was a fire that needed to be put out; it was up to her team to find the fire, figure out its source, and bring it under control before too many innocent people got scorched.

Good thing she had three bona fide geniuses on the case.

"All right, people," she said, glancing at her wristwatch. Ireland was seven time zones away, so it was late afternoon there. "Gear up and get ready. Let's hit the road at ten-forty hours, ten minutes from now."

"Sounds like a plan," Stone said, as the Librarians scrambled to prepare for the expedition ahead. Nobody bothered to put the board game away. "Hibernia, here we come."

Getting to Ireland in a timely fashion was easy enough. A Magic Door, which could conceivably connect with any other door on the planet, made crossing the globe as simple as stepping through a doorway, assuming Jenkins got the coordinates right. In theory, they would be setting foot on the Auld Sod before sunset, local time.

And then?

The strategist in Baird liked to plan ahead, but being a Guardian had taught her that no scenario was too unlikely where magic was concerned. Anything could happen—and probably would—so how did you anticipate the impossible?

She was still working on that.

"Good luck, Colonel," Jenkins said.

"The Luck of the Irish?" she quipped.

Jenkins frowned. "A peculiarly inapt expression, if you ask me. With all due respect to fabled Eire and its people, Ireland's tumultuous history contains more than its fair share of invasions, conquests, famines, plagues, and strife. Quite frankly, I'm not certain I would be doing you and your charges a favor by wishing you luck of that sort."

Baird sighed.

"You know, Jenkins, we really need to work on your pep talks."

4

※ *Inishclogh, off the coast of Ireland* ※

An ancient portal tomb, consisting of a horizontal granite slab resting atop two mammoth standing stones, sat in the middle of an open green pasture beneath a cloudy sky. Once, thousands of years ago, the tomb would have been buried beneath a mound of smaller stones and earth, but time and the elements had gradually exposed it to view, so that it resembled the homemade table of some mythical giant. Despite its descriptive label, however, the tomb had not been employed as a portal for millennia.

Until today.

A brilliant white light flashed beneath the capstone, briefly filling in the open space between the vertical supports, and Cassandra and the others stumbled through the doorway onto the damp, grassy expanse beyond. As always, she missed a step as she crossed from the Annex to elsewhere; even after more than three years of Librarian-ing, she still couldn't step through the Magic Door without it throwing off her stride for a few paces. Maybe because of the rotation of the Earth?

Or perhaps it was simply that crossing untold miles in a single step was always going to be a tad disorienting.

One minute they'd been in the Annex, bidding good-
bye to Jenkins as he programmed the Door using an ornate
globe of the world that was magically linked to the large,
frosted-glass double doors. The usual white glow had filled
the doorway, letting them know they were ready for departure, and here they were: on a small island off the west coast
of Ireland, more than four thousand miles away from Portland.

It was early March and the weather was still a bit nippy, so
Cassandra was glad that she had put on a toasty sweater and
leggings before heading out into the field. The rest of the team
had dressed for the season as well; jackets, sweaters, and boots
were the order of the day. Glancing up at the overcast sky,
Cassandra wondered if they should have brought an umbrella
as well.

The white light blinked out behind them. Stone turned
around to admire the unusual threshold they had just crossed
over.

"Using a Neolithic dolmen as an actual portal," he said
appreciatively. "I got to hand it to Jenkins. That's pretty
slick."

Cassandra could see where that would impress Stone in
particular, considering his interests, but she also thought that,
as doorways went, the looming megalithic ruins were a whole
lot cooler than stepping out of an unoccupied broom closet or
an outhouse, which had been known to be the case when
their options were particularly limited. She scanned the rugged countryside surrounding them, seeing nothing but grass,
boulders, fields, and a few low stone walls carving up the landscape. Purple thistles added a trace of color to endless green-
ery. Birds cawed overhead.

"I don't get it." Ezekiel gave the huge stone table a baffled look. "Those oversized building blocks don't look all that trashed to me, aside from a few thousand years of wear and tear."

"Wrong monument," Cassandra explained. "This was just the closest 'doorway' in the vicinity." Despite the cloud cover, she managed to orient herself from the approximate position of the sun and pointed to the northwest. "The monolith we're looking for is that way."

Baird doubled-checked their bearings by consulting the GPS on her phone. "About seven klicks from here."

"Seven-point-four-nine," Cassandra said. "To be exact."

"I stand corrected," Baird said, smiling. "Let's get hiking." She adjusted her watch to local time. "We're burning daylight."

Leaving the portal behind, they set out across the fields, which they appeared to have pretty much to themselves, aside from the native flora and fauna. According to Wikipedia, this particular island, one of more than three hundred in Clew Bay, was sparsely inhabited, with only a few isolated farms and villages here and there. Low rock walls, intended to keep herds of sheep or cattle from straying, proved easy enough to clamber over, even where a convenient stile could not be found. The brisk exercise helped Cassandra keep warm.

"So how come there wasn't a parking lot, visitor center, and gift shop back at that old tomb back there?" Ezekiel asked. "Seems like a waste of a perfectly good tourist attraction."

"Like Jenkins said," Stone said, "Ireland is littered with old monuments and ruins and archeological digs, some of them more famous—and convenient to get to—than others. The big-name sites, like Newgrange or Blarney Castle, get the long lines of tourists, but you can still find the remains of a forgotten ring fort or Viking settlement tucked away in a pasture somewhere, far from any main roads or highways." He contemplated their isolated surroundings. "Frankly, I gotta wonder how long it took before some wandering farmer or birdwatcher noticed that this old monolith had been disturbed."

"Not too long, I hope," Baird said. "We're already playing catch-up here."

A longish hike brought them to their destination, which turned out to be atop a high cliff looking out over the bay separating the island from the mainland. Taking in the view, Cassandra noted a conical gray mountain rising up from the coast of Ireland, far across the waves. Her weary legs were grateful that, if nothing else, they hadn't had to hike up the side of a mountain to get where they were going. She doubted there were any convenient doorways at the summit.

"Bingo," Baird said, calling Cassandra away from the view. "We've reached ground zero."

Sure enough, a huge granite monolith, which had once risen at least twelve feet above the ground, was now lying on its side, crushing the grass and soil beneath it. A gaping pit in the earth indicated where the monument had stood before being uprooted. Cassandra peered down into the pit, which was deeper than she expected.

"That's odd," she commented.

"What is?" Baird asked.

"This hole. It's deeper than it ought to be." Geometry sang to her and variables smelled like pistachios as luminous equations briefly manifested before her eyes. By her calculations, taking into account the estimated size and mass of the monolith, as well as its center of gravity, the depth of the pit needed to be only about one-third its total height, assuming a ninety-degree angle and reasonable margin for error, but that wasn't what she was seeing with her regular vision. "I just ran the math, and the foundation of the monolith didn't need to be buried nearly so deep. There's an extra six feet or so that I can't account for."

Stone squatted down beside the pit and looked it over himself. Besides being a student of architecture, he had also worked laying oil pipelines in Oklahoma before being recruited by the Library, so he knew all about construction issues involving big holes in the ground.

"You're right about that, Cassie. Just eyeballing it, I'd say that somebody excavated the ground beneath the monolith, digging to at least two yards below where the foundation used to be." He glanced over at the fallen stone. "We can verify that by measuring how much of that pillar was originally underground, but I'd stake a couple of my degrees that this pit goes deeper than that—on purpose."

"Which means something was buried beneath the rock." Ezekiel's eyes lit up at the prospect of hidden treasure. "Something valuable?"

"Or dangerous," Baird said grimly. "Magically dangerous."

"But did they find what they were looking for?" Stone wondered aloud. "Or were they looking in the wrong place?"

"I doubt the Clipping Book would have notified us if this was a wild-goose chase." She winced at the memory of a recent *Mother* Goose Chase, but pushed the thought aside; that was a whole other adventure. "My money's on a buried magic artifact or grimoire or something."

"Let's find out," Cassandra said, rescuing her favorite magical spectrometer from her pocket. The handheld device was about the size of a handheld calculator and had a nifty digital display; it wasn't as cool-looking and steampunky as the model that looked like an eggbeater, but it was easier to carry and not nearly so conspicuous to operate . . . not that there were any nosy bystanders around at the moment. "In theory, we should be able to pick up any residual traces of serious magic."

She scanned the pit from above, grateful that the device's range was such that she didn't have to climb or be lowered into the hole. She was not claustrophobic, technically, but after being stuck at the bottom of a cursed wishing well that one time in Budapest, she was in no hurry to relive the experience. The spectrometer chirped to indicate that it was working. Her eyes widened as she squinted at the readout.

"Okay, I didn't see that coming," she said.

"Let me guess," Baird said. "The readings are off the chart."

Cassandra shook her head. "Just the opposite. There's the usual ambient mystical energy, like background radiation, that you find pretty much everywhere these days, now that wild magic has returned to the world, but nothing more than that. I'm not picking up any spikes at all." Turning away from the pit, she scanned the surrounding terrain as well. "In fact, we don't seem to be anywhere near an active ley line."

Ley lines were like natural currents or jet streams carrying concentrated magical energy around the globe. Many of them had been dead or dormant in the modern era, until the Serpent Brotherhood had reactivated them a few years ago, resulting in a serious uptick of magical crises requiring the Librarians' attention. Cassandra almost took it for granted these days that any major outbreaks would take place on or around the juncture of two or more ley lines.

"That doesn't make any sense," Stone said, scratching his head. "Ancient monuments—obelisks, rock rings, temples, and such—are almost always erected at sacred sites believed to have special mystical qualities, which usually means that they're on top of a ley line or two." He shot a questioning look at Cassandra. "You sure that gadget's not on the fritz?"

She handed him the detector so he could inspect it himself. "I can always check the charts back at the Library, but—"

"No worries," Ezekiel said. "I've got an app for that."

Stone spun toward him, taken aback. "You've what?"

"I put together a digital version of those old maps weeks ago." Ezekiel took out his phone and tapped on an icon resembling the globe at the Annex. "Because this *is* the twenty-first century, after all."

"Points for initiative, Jones." Baird nodded in approval. "So what's the verdict?"

Ezekiel consulted his device. "Cassie's on the money. There's a ley line running under that portal we used before, a few miles away, but right here is a dead zone where magic is concerned. It's almost as though somebody deliberately went out of their way to put that big rock far away from any magical hot spots."

Stone scowled. "That's not how it works."

"Unless," Baird said, "they buried something that needed to be kept away from magic, just to be safe."

"That's a . . . disturbingly plausible theory," Cassandra said, "since it suggests that this was something that was *supposed* to stay buried forever."

"But we still have too many blanks and question marks," Baird said, counting them off on her fingers. "Who buried the something? Who is looking for the something? Did they find the something? And what the heck is the something anyway?"

"*If* there even is a something," Cassandra pointed out, "which we still don't know for sure." She turned her attention away from the pit to the toppled monolith. "What does the monument itself tell us?"

"Good question," Baird said. "Stone?"

He was the resident expert on, well, old stones, so Cassandra and the others held back while he examined the monolith. He thought aloud as he circled the stone, surveying it with his well-trained eye.

"There's no evidence of any other standing stones, past or present, so this was probably a solitary monolith, not part of a henge or rock ring. The terminology gets a bit blurry here, with a certain degree of overlap between monoliths, megaliths, and menhirs, but it seems this monument has always stood alone." He got down on his knees to inspect what had been the top of the monument before the stone fell over. A triumphant grin suggested that he had made a breakthrough.

"Hot damn," he blurted. "Take a look at that."

The others hurried forward to find out what he'd found. "What is it?" Cassandra asked, dying of curiosity.

"I found part of an inscription . . . in ogham!"

Blank looks greeted his declaration, prompting him to elaborate.

"Ireland's first written alphabet. See these hatch marks along the edge?" He indicated what looked to Cassandra like random slashes cut into the stone. "Ogham consists of series of strokes along or across a vertical line, like branches on a tree or musical notes on a staff. Some strokes are at right angles, some are diagonal, and they can be larger or smaller or various combinations thereof. It was originally cut into tree trunks or planks of wood, but by the fourth century it could be found on stone monuments throughout Ireland. As far as we know, it was the first attempt to write down the spoken tongue of ancient Erin, which we now refer to as Primitive Irish."

His face and voice grew more animated as he warmed to the topic. Cassandra had often thought that Stone was a born teacher and would have made an excellent college professor, if fate (and the Library) had not had other plans. His obvious enthusiasm for the subject matter was infectious.

"Attempt by who?" Baird asked.

"Funny you should ask that," Stone said, as though addressing a favorite student. "The origins of ogham are lost to history and the subject of ongoing debate. Some say it was devised by the druids, others by early Christian missionaries looking for a way to translate the native tongue into the written word. Legend, on the other hand, holds that ogham was gifted to the Irish people by the Tuatha Dé Danann themselves."

"The who?" Cassandra asked.

"You've never heard of the Tuatha Dé Danann?" Stone looked at her with what looked like genuine surprise. "Cillian . . . that's a good old Irish name. I just kinda assumed you knew this stuff."

"The name is Irish, but I'm a New York girl," she said, a little sheepishly. She felt vaguely embarrassed that Jake Stone from Oklahoma knew more about her ancestral heritage than she did. "I mean, sure, I'm of Irish descent, I guess, but that's about as far as it goes, I'm afraid. . . ."

"No big deal," Stone said. "Didn't mean to put you on the spot."

Ezekiel helped her out by getting back to the point. "So who are these Tuatha dudes?"

"The gods and goddesses of pagan Ireland, later demoted to faerie royalty or bygone heroes after the coming of Christianity, depending on who was retelling the old stories. They're said to have retreated to a mystical 'Otherworld' beyond the mortal plane, but are credited with inventing ogham back in the day." Stone carefully brushed off a portion of the inscription, clearing away some accumulated dirt and mud. "Needless to say, most reputable scholars don't regard ancient myths and legends as all that factual, but . . ."

"We Librarians know better than to dismiss them," Cassandra said, finishing his thought. She smiled wryly. "Being chased though a labyrinth by a minotaur will do that."

"Not to mention fighting the Egyptian god of chaos," Ezekiel added. "And trolls, and werewolves . . ."

"In any event," Baird said, "can you read ogham?"

"Kinda, sorta." Stone made a so-so gesture with his hand. "But there's a problem."

Baird sighed. "Of course there is."

"Ogham is written along the *sides* of monuments, using the edges as the vertical staff, not on their faces. You start at the bottom of the left-hand side of the stone, work your way along the top, and go back down the right side if necessary. Problem is, with the stone flat on the ground like this, instead of erect, there's no way to read most of the inscription without raising the whole thing off the ground. All I can make out is the portion written along the top."

"Which says?" Baird pressed him.

Stone shrugged. "'Do Not Disturb,' basically."

"Well, that's not ominous at all." Baird glanced back at the gaping pit. "So how do we read the rest of the inscription?"

Cassandra contemplated the massive stone. By her estimate, it had to be at least five tons. "That's going to be a challenge."

"Maybe if all four of us try to lift it?" Baird said uncertainly. "Or just shove it over onto one side?"

"Do I look like the Incredible Hulk?" Ezekiel eyed the heavy stone dubiously. "And does the Library's health plan cover hernias and slipped disks?"

"We have a health plan?" Cassandra asked.

"Focus, people," Baird said. "How did folks lift these things back in the old days?"

"Brute force and slave labor?" Ezekiel suggested.

"Neither of which we have at our disposal right now." Baird looked hopefully at the nearest authority of primitive construction techniques. "Stone?"

"That's another thorny issue. Historians and engineers, amateur and otherwise, are still arguing about how, say, Stonehenge or the pyramids were erected using primitive tools and manpower." Cassandra could practically see the wheels turning in his brain as he took apart the problem. "Possibly there's something that could be rigged up involving fulcrums and counterweights, or maybe some sort of block-and-pulley system . . . ?"

"Or a lever," Cassandra contributed. "A *really*, really long lever."

"All of that sounds pretty elaborate and time-consuming," Baird said, "and we don't really have time to round up a lot of equipment, let alone a work crew. Let's not forget, the somebodies who dug up the something already have a jump on us. Who knows what they could be up to at this very minute. Isn't there any faster way to lift this humongous paperweight?"

"Who says we have to lift it?" Ezekiel said. "Why not just go under it?"

All eyes turned toward him. "Under it?" Cassandra asked.

"Sure," he said. "When pulling a heist, the easiest way to

get at something is often from below. If I had a dime for every time I tunneled under some immovable barrier . . . well, I would still want to rob things, but I'd also have more dimes than I'd know what to do with."

"But if you tunnel under the stone to check out the writing, won't it come crashing down and squash you?" Grisly images of Ezekiel pancaked beneath a five-ton monolith forced their way into her brain without an invitation. She cringed beneath her warm, woolly sweater. "I'm still liking the lever idea."

"I'll be fine," Ezekiel insisted. "The writing is along the edges of the stone, right? So all we need to do is dig a shallow gully or ditch around the perimeter of the stone, leaving the bulk of it still supported by the ground underneath it. Then I wiggle under the edge, snap some pics of the inscription, and, with any luck, we find out what exactly was not supposed to be disturbed." He glanced down at his clothes. "Mind you, the Library is going to owe me some new threads if I have to play earthworm in the dirt."

Cassandra was still worried. She looked to see if Baird and Stone were okay with this.

"Could work," Stone conceded. "The hash marks *are* on the very edge of the sides, so we can leave the bottom face of the monolith supported by solid ground. We'll just have to be careful not to dig too far under one side or another, so we don't risk it tipping." He sighed. "Counterweights would be cooler and more authentic, though."

"Not really the point right now," Baird said. Cool eyes assessed Ezekiel. "You really up for this, Jones?"

He flashed a cocky grin. "Remind me to tell you how I got into Al Capone's *real* vault one time. Now *that* was a tight squeeze!"

Stone paced along one side of the monolith, then another. "Still going to require some hard labor," he commented.

"Better get at it then, mate." Ezekiel smirked at the others. "Anybody bring a shovel?"

5

"'*Here lieth the bones of that foul serpent which once infested our shores. Let no hand disturb these unholy remains, on peril of your soul,*'" Jenkins recited. "Or words to that effect."

The entirety of the inscription was now transcribed onto a whiteboard mounted in the office across from the conference table. Marker in hand, Jenkins stood before the board while the Librarians and their Guardian listened intently to his translation, courtesy of the snapshots taken by Ezekiel at the site in Ireland. The dire, if cryptic, warning struck the immortal caretaker as definite cause for concern.

"I managed most of that," Stone muttered, "more or less."

"Which was impressive in its own right," Jenkins assured him. "Ogham is an extremely odd and obsolete alphabet; people who can accurately translate it in the field are even rarer today than people who know how to use apostrophes and semicolons properly. Even my ogham is rusty, and I'm old enough to remember when it was trendy."

"It was a team effort all around," Baird stressed. "So now that we have the inscription, what do we think it means?"

Jenkins admired Baird's ability to stay on point. Beyond

keeping the Librarians' bodies and souls in one piece, she also excelled at corralling her occasionally distractible charges and getting them to function like a well-oiled machine.

Well, semi-oiled at least.

"The bones of a foul serpent?" Ezekiel echoed. He had showered and changed into fresh clothes after returning to the Library bedecked in dirt and grime. "Who'd want to dig up something like that?"

"Maybe it's not a literal serpent," Cassandra suggested. "I mean, there aren't any actual serpents in Ireland, are there?"

"Not since Saint Patrick," Stone joked.

Jenkins stiffened as though he had just been bitten by a snake. There was an ominous hiss at the back of his mind as a long-slumbering memory stirred and began to uncoil, prodded by the Librarian's flippant remark. He wheeled about in response. "What did you just say, Mister Stone?"

The intensity of his query seemed to catch Stone off guard. "Um, I made a crack about Saint Patrick, since, you know, he supposedly drove the snakes out of Ireland."

"Of course!" Jenkins smacked his forehead, figuratively kicking himself for not making the connection earlier. Granted, his memory was almost as overstuffed as the Annex itself, and the annals of the Librarians' long history were voluminous in their own right, but the clues had been right there in front of him. "Not snakes," he said gravely. "Serpents . . . as in the Serpent Brotherhood."

Gasps and stricken expressions greeted his invocation of that infamous name. Jenkins judged that to be an entirely appropriate response. The Serpent Brotherhood had been the Librarians' archenemies for longer than even he had walked the Earth; unlike the Library, which was dedicated to keeping magic safely contained, the Brotherhood saw magic as a power to be used to impose their will on the world—and to shape the course of history as they saw fit. Moreover, they were utterly ruthless when it came to achieving their ends, as too many past Librarians had discovered, to their sorrow.

"Those jerks again?" Ezekiel said. "I thought we were done with them."

"If only, Mister Jones," Jenkins replied with the dour solemnity of an undertaker. "It's true that the Brotherhood have been keeping a low profile since you and your associates successfully thwarted them a few years ago, but this would hardly be the first time—or the fifty-first—the Brotherhood made a comeback, possibly under new leadership."

A pang stabbed his eternally beating heart as he recalled the downfall of the Brotherhood's most recent mastermind. Dulaque, as he was known in this century, had let his misguided ambitions turn him into a villain, not to mention a mortal threat to the very fabric of reality, but Jenkins still mourned the man Dulaque had once been—and wished that there had been another way to stop him.

"Back up," Baird said. "What makes you think the 'serpent' in the inscription refers to the Serpent Brotherhood?"

"A long-ago chapter in the Library's history that, alas, slipped my mind until now," Jenkins said. The pieces were finally coming together, adding credence to his theory, but he appreciated Baird's insistence on reviewing the evidence at hand. "I will need to retrieve the relevant documents from the archives, but I seem to recall that there was an incident in Ireland, back in the fifth century, when the Librarian of the time—Erasmus, I believe he was called—sent the Serpent Brotherhood packing . . . with the aid of a certain Christian missionary whom history would remember as 'Patricus.'"

"Patricus . . . Saint Patrick?" Cassandra reacted much as she had upon discovering that Santa Claus was not a myth: with wide-eyed surprise and delight. "Are you saying that the whole story about Saint Patrick driving the snakes out of Ireland had to do with a Librarian . . . and the Serpent Brotherhood?"

"That is precisely what I'm saying, Miss Cillian. There have never been any actual snakes in Ireland; being cold-blooded, they were unable to cross over from the mainland during the Ice Age, and the sea has cut them off from Ireland to this day." The real story was slightly more complicated than that, involving a Pre-Diluvian pact between rival totem spirits, but Jenkins chose to avoid any unnecessary tangents. "But the Serpent Brotherhood *did* make their way to Ireland more than fifteen hundred years ago, only to be repelled by a Librarian and his allies, including the future Saint Patrick."

"Fifteen hundred years ago," Stone observed. "That's about right for the ogham stone. Or at least it's within the right window for inscribing a monument in ogham."

"Nor is that the only telling point of fact," Jenkins said, as another portion of the puzzle fitted into place. He pulled a world atlas from a bookshelf and opened it to a detailed map of Ireland and its environs. A magnifying glass, retrieved from his work area, helped him locate a small dot in the blue water to the left of Ireland, amidst many other similar dots of varying sizes. His finger pointed out the dot that mattered. "This is the small, inconspicuous island you just returned from. Tell me—during that excursion, were you perhaps able to glimpse a large gray mountain on the other side of the bay?"

"Yes!" Cassandra raised her hand in the air like an overeager schoolgirl dying to be called upon by the teacher. "I did see that! A big, cone-shaped mountain way over on the mainland."

Jenkins nodded, unsurprised. His finger shifted to the mountain marked on the map, about an inch to the right.

"That would be Croagh Patrick, loosely translated 'Patrick's Stack,'" Jenkins said. "Legend has it that it's where Patrick famously banished the snakes . . . or Serpents . . . somewhere around 441 A.D."

"Whoa," Stone said.

"Whoa indeed, Mister Stone." Jenkins left the atlas open for their inspection. "That the uprooted monument bearing that worrisome inscription just happens to be within sight of Croagh Patrick is unlikely to be a coincidence, particularly given the Clipping Book's interest in alerting us to the matter."

Baird glanced briefly at the map before rendering judgment.

"Okay, I'm sold," she stated. "I've launched missions on flimsier evidence, and if there's even a possibility that the Brotherhood is back, we need to assume the worst." She looked at Jenkins with a steely expression that reminded him of a Crusader girding himself for battle. "What else do you recall about this business with Saint Patrick way back when?"

"Nothing personally, I'm afraid. The fifth century was . . . tumultuous."

Painful memories rose unbidden from the vaults of his memory: a sundered Round Table, a fallen king, a quest, a grail, a witch, a father's grievous sin. . . .

"I was otherwise occupied at the time." He pushed the old sorrows back down into their dungeon. "As a result, whatever I know about that bygone incident is what I've run across in my studies of the archives, and the finer points of that particular episode elude me. It will be necessary to unearth the original records to give us a fuller picture of what actually transpired in 441."

"Understood," Baird said. "Well, this is a library, so there was bound to be some research involved. I assume we can count on you to help with the homework?"

"Consider me already on it, Colonel."

"Thanks, Jenkins. The more info we can gather about that earlier incident, the better we may be able to anticipate what we're up against." A pensive look came over her face. "Any chance you remember what exactly the Serpents were after back in the day?"

Jenkins paused to rifle through centuries of study and contemplation, flipping through his recollections like the pages of an encyclopedia. Now that he knew where to look, the story was starting to come back to him. . . .

"If memory serves, Colonel, it was a pot of gold."

"Yes!" Ezekiel enthused. "Now we're talking. I'll take a pot of gold over some old bones any day."

"Don't take this matter lightly," Jenkins said sternly, employing his most cautionary tone. He swept his gaze over the all-too-fragile mortals seated around the table. "I'm certain I don't have to remind any of you just how merciless and resourceful the Serpent Brotherhood can be. If they have indeed resurfaced, countless innocents may be in extreme jeopardy. As of this moment, determining their whereabouts and objective is our first and only priority. Nothing can be allowed to distract us."

Which made it the worst possible moment for the doorbell to ring.

6

"The doorbell?" Stone said. "There's something we don't hear very often."

The Annex building, which was tucked away under the southern end of a towering suspension bridge spanning the Willamette River, was not open to the public. Aside from the occasional invaders, including the Serpent Brotherhood, intent on pillaging the Library, Stone couldn't immediately recall any visitors dropping by unannounced, unless you counted a couple of determined Girl Scouts hawking cookies.

Who in the world?

"The Serpents?" Baird said warily, jumping to her feet. "Back for revenge?"

Stone doubted it. "Politely ringing the doorbell isn't exactly their style. They're sneakier than that."

Cassandra winced slightly. The last time the Brotherhood had infiltrated the Library, they had done so by promising her a cure for her brain tumor. That was years ago, and she had since redeemed herself many times over, but Stone feared his comment had hit a nerve, even if he hadn't intended to bring up that past betrayal. He made a mental note to watch his words a little more carefully for Cassandra's sake. It had taken a while for her to regain his trust, but she had it now—in spades.

The bell chimed again, demanding their attention.

"Jenkins?" Baird prompted.

"Yes, Colonel," Jenkins huffed, clearly displeased by the interruption. He crossed the office to where a velvet cloth was draped over a tall piece of furniture. He whipped off the cloth to reveal the standing, wood-framed mirror that served as the supernatural equivalent of a closed-circuit security monitor. A wave of Jenkins's hand activated it, so that instead of displaying his reflection, the magic mirror offered a view of the scene outside the building, where a distraught-looking young woman was leaning on the bell by the Annex's front entrance.

Her short red hair, in a pageboy do, was only a shade darker than Cassandra's. Freckles embellished her fair complexion, while a rumpled windbreaker and faded jeans protected her from the elements. One thing was for sure: she didn't look like a Girl Scout. Stone didn't recognize her.

"Anybody we know?" he asked.

A chorus of nopes went around the table. Stone glanced at Jenkins, who was the only one of them who actually lived at the Annex. "Friend of yours?"

"Not by appearances," the caretaker said. "Most of my social contacts have long since departed this vale of tears. Present company excluded."

The bell kept ringing as the woman in the mirror stabbed the button urgently. Her restless eyes searched the lifeless utilitarian façade for any sign of habitation. Desperation was written all over her face.

"She looks like she's upset," Cassandra said with concern. "Maybe she's in trouble?"

Stone had to agree. This was no casual visit; the stranger really wanted somebody to let her in. Her mouth was open wide, her lips moving, but no sound emerged from the glass— or penetrated the solid front door. Stone wished he could read lips as well as he did ogham.

"Can we get some audio?" he asked.

"If you insist." Jenkins stepped away from the mirror and switched on a vintage Cathedral-style radio from the 1930s sitting next to a Tiffany lamp on a stained walnut sideboard. A female voice emerged from the radio, in synch with the image in the mirror. Despite a slightly tinny quality, it was easy enough to make out her words:

"Hello? Is anyone home? Can you hear me?"

The anxiety in her voice could be heard even through the geriatric speakers. Stone shared a worried look with the others. Whatever the stranger wanted, it sounded serious.

"Please!" she entreated, just outside the door. "I need your help. I need . . . the Librarians!"

That got their attention in a big way, as if her unexpected arrival wasn't surprising enough. The existence of the Librarians was largely a secret, known only to wizards, dragons, djinn, secret societies, clandestine government organizations, and, okay, a few ordinary people whom the Librarians had pulled from the fire over the years. The Library's phone number was unlisted, nor could it be found on Twitter or Facebook. The Portland Public Library System did not have borrowing privileges.

"Whoa," Ezekiel said. "So *not* a Jehovah's Witness then."

"And here for a reason, I'm guessing." Stone got up from the table and started for the door. "Let's find out what's up."

"Absolutely not," Jenkins protested. He stepped between Stone and the door to obstruct him. "We do *not* take walk-ins."

"But you heard her," Stone said, not backing down. "She needs our help."

"Your chivalrous instincts do you credit," Jenkins said, "but the Library is one of the most secure sites on the planet for a reason. We are a repository for countless dangerous books and relics, as well as more priceless, irreplaceable items than the Smithsonian, the Library of Congress, the Louvre, the Tower of London, and eBay combined. We do not let random strangers stroll in as though this is the neighborhood Starbucks."

Baird spoke up. "I hate to say it, but he has a point."

"So what are we supposed to do?" Stone asked. "Pretend we're not home and hope she goes away?"

Jenkins didn't budge. "You'd be surprised how effective that strategy is."

Giving up on the doorbell, their mysterious visitor started pounding on the door with her fists. The blows echoed across the office.

"I don't think she's giving up anytime soon," Ezekiel said.

"But the Librarians are all about helping people." Cassandra flinched at every knock. The woman's distress clearly tugged on her heart. "Aren't we?"

"The Librarians are about protecting the world from magic and vice versa," Jenkins clarified. "Need I remind you that we have larger matters on our plate? Namely, a resurgent Serpent Brotherhood?"

"But shouldn't we at least hear her out?" Cassandra asked. "Looking for the Serpents can wait for a minute."

"Can it?" Jenkins asked.

A clap of thunder signaled the arrival of an afternoon storm. It started raining outside, yet the woman refused to turn away from the door and seek shelter elsewhere. The sudden squall turned into a downpour, drenching her.

"Please!" she shouted via the radio. "I have no one else to turn to. It's a matter of life or death . . . I think!"

"The hell with it," Stone decided. "I'm opening that door. Anybody got a problem with that?"

"More like serious reservations," Jenkins said, stepping aside. "But the decision is up to you and your associates."

Despite his (extreme) seniority, Jenkins was only the caretaker, not a Librarian. Stone figured it was his call unless one of the others objected.

"Just keep an eye on her," Baird insisted "Remember, she's a security risk until proven otherwise."

Ezekiel didn't look worried. "She's just one soaked bird. I think we can handle her."

"Have you forgotten Morgan Le Fay?" Baird said. "Or Lamia, or the Queen of Hearts?"

Ezekiel gulped. "Never mind."

"Do it," Cassandra urged Stone. "Don't leave her out there any longer."

Stone took that as a consensus. Striding past Jenkins, he yanked open the front door. A drenched redhead gasped in surprise and/or relief. Wide green eyes gaped at him.

"Oh, thank heavens," she said. "Are you . . . a Librarian?"

"Maybe," he answered. "How can I help you?"

7

"My name is Bridget O'Neill and I didn't know where else to go."

A blanket was draped over her shoulders as she sat at the end of the conference table, sipping a cup of hot tea that Jenkins had procured for her, his objections to her presence not eliminating his manners apparently. She glanced around the office, taking in its eclectic décor, before turning back toward Stone and the others.

"So you're really the Librarians?"

"Guilty as charged," Baird said. The cat was obviously out of the bag, so Stone figured Baird didn't want to waste time playing games. "But can I ask how it is that you know about the Library?"

"A friend of a friend works for DOSA—the Department of Statistical Anomalies—so when I found myself desperately in need of help with . . . a very unusual situation . . . they quietly pointed me in your direction. Said there were some people in Portland who might be able to help me."

"What friend of a friend, precisely?" Jenkins asked, sounding rather like a prosecutor interrogating a witness on the stand.

"Oh, I can't possibly betray that confidence," Bridget replied. "It was strictly off the record. 'You didn't hear it from me,' that kind of thing. The last thing I want to do is get anybody in trouble after they went out on a limb for me."

Jenkins frowned. "I see," he said suspiciously.

Stone bought her story, though. DOSA was a top-secret government organization that definitely knew plenty about the Library. Not too long ago, a small army of DOSA personnel had temporarily occupied the Library before finally handing control of the place back to Stone and the others. DOSA's operations and files were super-hush-hush, but, with that many people involved, some info was bound to leak out eventually. Stone could readily imagine an anonymous DOSA agent steering Bridget toward the Annex, if only on the Q.T.

"You're protecting your sources," Stone said. "I get that."

Jenkins did not press the point. "Please proceed with your story, Miss O'Neill."

"All right." She gripped the teacup with both hands. "Anyway, all I really heard was that there were some unusual 'Librarians' who specialized in . . . situations like mine. It sounded ridiculous at first, but . . . I was grasping at straws, so I hopped on a plane to Portland and . . . here I am." Her voice cracked. "Please, I've come all the way from Chicago. You've got to help me. If not . . . I don't know what I'm going to do."

Her desperation was obvious, not just in her voice, but in the lengths she had apparently gone to in hopes of finding help with her as yet unspecified problem. Stone had to wonder what strange, presumably supernatural dilemma had brought her to their door.

"What exactly is your situation?" Baird asked.

Bridget took a deep breath, and a bracing sip of tea, before getting down to brass tacks. "You're going to think I'm insane. . . ."

"Trust me," Stone said. "'Insane' doesn't begin to describe most of the stuff we deal with on a regular basis."

"What about a banshee?"

If she was expecting them to react with shock or disbelief, she was mistaken, but her announcement both intrigued and concerned Stone. He had no doubt that banshees were real, but he had never personally dealt with one. This was new, potentially dangerous territory. From what he knew of them, banshees were not exactly good news.

More like harbingers of death.

"Oh dear," Jenkins said. A look of pity crossed his face, which Stone knew could not possibly bode well.

First Saint Patrick, now a banshee, Stone noted. Just a coincidence, or was there a reason that all roads seemed to be leading to and from Ireland at the moment? Come to think of it, Saint Patrick's Day was only days away. . . .

"You believe me?" Bridget sounded both surprised and relieved.

"No reason to doubt you," Stone said. "Why don't you tell us the whole story?"

"Okay, you asked for it." She took another sip of tea before diving in. "It started small, to be honest. I'd be awakened in the middle of the night by this weird wailing noise coming from somewhere outside. It was annoying and, yeah, a little creepy, but I didn't think much of it at first. I figured it was just the wind or a distant car alarm or something, so I would just roll over and try to get back to sleep, but, as time went by, the wailing started sounding louder and closer, almost like it was closing in on me." She shuddered under the blanket. "I live above my pub, on the second floor, and one night when I couldn't stand it anymore, I went to the window and saw a woman crying in the alley behind the building. I called 911, thinking she might be in trouble, but when the police arrived she wasn't there anymore . . . and it turned out that none of my neighbors had reported any disturbances. It was like only I could hear her."

She paused for a moment, remembering.

"That was when I started to wonder whether I was losing my mind, and it just kept getting worse. Night after night, but not every night, she was out there, wailing beneath my window. *If* it was the same woman, that is. She was almost always dressed in gray, but some nights she looked different than on others. . . ."

"Let me guess," Stone said. "Sometimes she was young, sometimes she was older and more matronly, and sometimes she looked like a withered old hag."

Bridget nodded. "Exactly."

"Maiden, mother, crone," Stone said. "The triple aspect of the goddess. It's a common motif, particularly in Celtic art and mythology."

"Quite right, Mister Stone," Jenkins confirmed. "And the banshee is indeed known to take those three guises, among others." He looked like he was tempted to exposit more, but restrained himself—for the moment. "Please continue, Miss O'Neill."

She went on with her story. "After I struck out with the police that one night I got so desperate that I tried confronting her . . . them . . . her . . . myself, but it was no use. By the time I ran downstairs to the alley, she was gone. But I could still hear the wailing all night long."

Thus explaining the heavy shadows under her eyes, Stone

reflected. He wondered when she'd last gotten a decent night's sleep.

"Finally, one night the wailing was louder than ever, unbearably so. I got up to go to the window again, to scream at her to shut up, no matter what the neighbors thought, and . . . she was right there."

"Down in the alley?" Baird asked.

"No, *right outside my window*. Staring into my bedroom, hovering in the air . . . like a ghost."

"Or a banshee," Stone said.

Bridget nodded, trembling at the memory. "That's when I knew—or finally admitted—that this was nothing natural, and that I needed help outside the ordinary . . . from someone like the Librarians."

She sat back in the chair, awaiting their reaction.

"So what do you think? Am I crazy or not?"

Stressed, yes, Stone thought. *Insane, no.* He wasn't getting a tinfoil-hat vibe from Bridget. "I'm not an expert on banshees," he said, "but you don't seem crazy to me."

"Me either," Cassandra said. "You're having a sane reaction to an insane situation."

"Me three," Ezekiel added. "Who wouldn't be worried by some sort of ghostly Debbie Downer getting all emo on them?"

Baird appeared to be taking Bridget seriously, too. "Speaking of experts," she asked Jenkins, "what can you tell us about banshees?"

Bowing to the inevitable, Jenkins went into lecture mode, which was pretty much second nature to him by now. Exposition was his comfort zone.

"Banshees," he began, "are Irish spirits whose keening foretells the coming of death. Although somewhat ghostly in nature, they are actually a variety of fairy. Indeed the word 'banshee' derives from the Gaelic *bean-sidhe*, which, roughly translated, means 'woman of the fairy.' Traditionally, they cry for members of certain venerable Irish families—including, I'm afraid, the O'Neills." He cast a distinctly sympathetic look at Bridget. "I should stress that the banshee's cry can be an omen of impending doom *or* merely a warning of same, allowing for a chance at averting it. There's some wiggle room there, depending."

"Depending on what?" Bridget asked tensely.

"Just depending," Jenkins said. "It's not an exact science."

"But a banshee isn't actually dangerous in her own right?" Baird asked. "They don't attack or kill people?"

"That is correct," Jenkins said. "They are harbingers, not avatars of death. At worst, a banshee's cry heralds the coming of the *Coiste Bodhar*, a death-coach that carries off the newly dead to whatever awaits them beyond this life. The *Coiste Bodhar*, let it be noted, is said to be driven by the Dullahan, a headless coachmen who, once summoned, never returns empty-handed."

Bridget paled. She clutched her chest with one hand, nearly spilling the tea. "Never?"

"Not once the death-coach has come for you," Jenkins stated soberly. His voice was both gentle but direct, not unlike a physician delivering a terminal diagnosis. "Forgive me for asking, Miss O'Neill, but have you any reason to fear that your life may be in jeopardy, aside from the possible manifestations of a banshee?"

She hesitated briefly before answering. "I had a heart attack about a year ago, right out of the blue. Turns out I had a congenital heart defect that went undetected my whole life until . . ." Her voice trailed off as her hand came away from her chest. "I've had surgery since, to correct the defect, but there were complications and, well, nothing's guaranteed." She struggled to maintain her composure. "So you can understand why this banshee business is so disturbing to me . . . beyond the whole scary, supernatural thing."

"Oh, I can understand," Cassandra said. "Believe me."

"We all can," Stone said.

Bridget put down her tea and looked expectantly at the Librarians and their Guardian. "That's my story, as sad and bizarre as it sounds. What now? Can you help me or not?"

Stone pondered her question. It seemed to him that there were three vital questions still to be answered: Was there really a banshee haunting Bridget, what exactly did it mean, and was there anything they could do about it?

"Give us a few minutes to discuss your case," he said, reluctant to answer on behalf of the others without consulting them. "In private."

After she'd left the room, Jenkins said, "I'm not unsympathetic to the young lady's plight, but the Serpent Brotherhood *must* remain our top priority. We cannot allow our efforts and attention to be divided while the Brotherhood is out there, up to heaven knows what kind of ambitious, possibly apocalyptic deviltry. Need I remind you that the last time we clashed with the Serpents, they very nearly unraveled the fabric of time and space?"

Unwilling to leave their visitor unattended in any part of the Library, Jenkins had provided Bridget with an umbrella and asked her to step outdoors while the team conferred. Stone had thought that was a bit extreme, but then again, it wasn't like they had a secure reception area.

"But you heard Bridget," Cassandra protested. "Her life is in danger. We have to save her!"

"Sadly, it may be that she is beyond saving," Jenkins said. "If the banshee is indeed foretelling her demise, it could simply be that her time is almost upon her . . . of perfectly natural causes. A tragedy, to be certain, but fate is not always kind."

"No!" Cassandra said vehemently. "I'm sorry, Jenkins, but I was told the same thing for years, regarding my tumor, and I let myself believe it for too long. There's always hope, even if it's only a slim one. We can't just give up on her. I'm *not* going to give up on her."

Stone agreed with her. "You said that sometimes the banshee's wail is only a warning," he pointed out to Jenkins, "not necessarily a death sentence."

"That is correct," Jenkins conceded, "but how many other lives might be lost if we divert our attention away from the Serpent Brotherhood?"

"I worry about that, too," Baird said. "The Clipping Book alerted us to that toppled monolith, and whatever was buried beneath it, for a reason. That's the case the Library wants us focused on right now."

"Excuse me," Ezekiel piped up. "Ireland . . . Saint Patrick . . . banshees—am I the only one seeing the connection here? Who says this isn't the same case, just coming at us from different directions?"

Stone considered the possibility. The fact that they seemed up to their ears in Irish folklore had not escaped his notice, but it was hard to see an obvious link between the "serpent's bones" in Ireland and a haunting in Chicago.

"What you are saying?" Stone asked. "That Bridget is mixed up with the Serpent Brotherhood somehow?"

"I don't have a clue, mate," Ezekiel said, "but what's with all the Irish stuff all of a sudden? We really think that's a coincidence?"

"Could be," Cassandra said. "We've run across various items from Greek mythology over the years, on unrelated cases. Maybe we were just overdue for a spike in Irish magic instead . . . as a matter of statistics."

"Or maybe there's a connection we're not seeing yet," Baird said. "I'm not a big believer in coincidences when it comes to possible enemy action."

"Coincidence," Jenkins agreed, "is often merely a failure to see the proverbial forest for the trees, but that still leaves us with the question of where best to direct our efforts—toward the unknown object uncovered at the monolith or toward Miss O'Neill's predicament?"

"Why can't we look into both?" Ezekiel said. "I mean, it's not as though there's only one Librarian anymore. What's the point of having a whole team of us if we can't cover more than one base at a time?"

Good question, Stone thought.

8

The next morning, before they split up, Jenkins had more history to impart.

A leather-bound codex, which he'd retrieved from the archives, lay open on his desk as he addressed Cassandra and the others. Bridget had been dispatched via Uber back to her hotel room in the city with the promise that the Librarians would be in touch shortly, once they formulated their plan of action regarding her situation. Cassandra hoped the banshee would leave Bridget alone until they could get their act together. She knew what it was like to wait helplessly for death to arrive, never really knowing when the Grim Reaper was scheduled to drop by. That had been Cassandra's life, too, for far too many years.

"What do you have for us, Jenkins?" Baird asked.

"Background, Colonel." He looked up from the dusty tome, which he had handled carefully, using blue latex gloves. "Thankfully, I managed to locate the appropriate annals without too much difficulty and, having reviewed them, now possess a somewhat fuller picture of what transpired in Ireland nearly sixteen hundred years ago."

"Good work," Baird said. "Let us have it."

"By all means," he said. "Quite an intriguing account, actually."

Cassandra listened intently as, with his characteristic gravity, Jenkins explained how way back in 441 A.D., a Librarian named Erasmus, along with his Guardian and the future Saint Patrick, had stopped the Serpent Brotherhood from making off with a leprechaun's pot of gold and sacrificing a defenseless baby. The confrontation, which had indeed taken place on Croagh Patrick, had apparently ended in the defeat of the Brotherhood—and the decapitation of their leader, a certain Lady Sibella.

"Whoa. They chopped off her head?" Ezekiel reacted. "Guess those old-school Guardians didn't mess around."

"It was a simpler time," Jenkins replied with a hint of nostalgia in his voice. A former knight of the Round Table, he had probably beheaded a few miscreants in his time. Or so Cassandra assumed.

"'The bones of the foul serpent,'" Stone said, referencing the inscription on the vandalized monolith. "The grave of this Sibella woman?"

"Possibly," Jenkins said. "The site on the island was just across the bay from the mountain. Lady Sibella's remains could have been easily transported there by boat."

"And buried in the middle of nowhere," Baird said, "away from any ley lines."

"But why would the modern-day Serpent Brotherhood want Sibella's bones anyway?" Cassandra asked.

"That remains to be determined," Jenkins said, "although, knowing the Brotherhood, I doubt that it was simply to rebury the remains with honors elsewhere. We must assume some darker purpose."

"Maybe there was something buried with her?" Stone speculated.

"Forget the bones," Ezekiel said, adding somewhat predictably, "what happened to the pot of gold?"

"Alas, the fate of the pot has been lost to history, along with the name of the leprechaun who absconded with both the gold *and* the anonymous infant."

Cassandra shuddered when she recalled what, according to the records, had nearly happened to the baby. Sacrificing an innocent child was vicious even for the Serpent Brotherhood.

"About that baby," she said. "Do we have any idea who she was or what happened to her afterward?"

"I'm afraid not," Jenkins said, "although she is surely dust by now, unlike the leprechaun, who may well still be roaming the earth and thus able to provide some firsthand insights into this matter . . . provided we can determine his identity and current address." He gently closed the tome on his desk. "I do have contacts among the Fair Folk who might be able to assist us in our inquiries, so perhaps a brief fact-finding expedition may be in order."

Cassandra's ears perked up. "You're going back to Ireland? To meet with some actual leprechauns?"

"No need to go all the way to the Emerald Isle," Jenkins replied. "As it happens, there's a thriving leprechaun colony right here in Portland."

"You're kidding me," Stone said. "Portland, Oregon, has leprechauns?"

"You didn't know that?" Jenkins appeared bemused. "I thought that was common knowledge."

Cassandra couldn't tell whether he was pulling Stone's leg

or not. Jenkins's sense of humor could be dryer than the Kalahari sometimes.

"Can I go with?" she asked. "I've never been to a leprechaun colony, which seems a shame given that I'm Irish-American and all."

He regarded her curiously. "To explore your ancestral roots?"

"Something like that," she said.

To tell the truth, she was still bothered by how little she apparently knew about where her family came from, generations ago. She had never given her Irish heritage much thought before, perhaps because she had always been more fixated on her terminal lack of a future. But now that she had a tomorrow, maybe she finally had time to look backward—and get in touch with her Irish ancestry?

"Far be it from me to discourage such a worthy endeavor," Jenkins said. "I would be grateful for your company."

"Count me in, too," Ezekiel said. "I'm not Irish, but I'm up for visiting the local leprechauns . . . just to be neighborly."

"And help yourself to their gold?" Jenkins scoffed at the notion. "Please credit me with a little common sense. Mixing a trickster-thief such as yourself with an enclave of Little People is just asking for trouble." He shook his head. "Might I suggest that you join Mister Stone and Colonel Baird in hunting for the banshee instead, while Miss Cillian and I pursue this other avenue of investigation?"

Ezekiel frowned. "Hold on. How come Cassandra got a green light?"

"So you *weren't* thinking about the leprechauns' gold?" Stone asked. "At all?"

"Well, maybe a little," Ezekiel admitted, "but—"

"Give it up, Jones," Baird said decisively. "You're the one

who suggested that we split up to cover more ground, and I'm going to let Jenkins make this call, since these are his contacts." Baird held up a hand to silence any further objections. "You're coming with Stone and me, so I can keep an eye on you . . . for everybody's sake."

"Thank you, Colonel," Jenkins said. "The Little People are not to be trifled with . . . or pilfered from."

"Just find out what you can," Baird said. "I want to know what old business we might be dealing with here."

"You and me both, Colonel."

9

Lady Sibella's skull occupied a position of honor in a glass display case in an elegant penthouse apartment. Carefully cleaned and polished, it sat atop a lightweight aluminum carrying case holding the remainder of the bones exhumed in Ireland. An impressive pair of long, curved fangs enhanced the relic's death's-head grin.

Max Lambton admired the fangs. The late Sibella had embodied the Serpent Brotherhood more literally than most. He could respect that.

He ran his tongue over his own flawless white teeth, which were less apropos, but perfect nonetheless. Everything about Max was perfect, from his smoothly shaved cranium, neatly trimmed goatee, and tailored bespoke suit to his impeccably manicured nails, which he absently filed as he contemplated Sibella's recovered remains. A slender Englishman in his early thirties, of aristocratic mien and bearing, he appreciated the sense of history conveyed by the relic. Lady Sibella may have fallen, as had various other Serpent leaders over the ages, but the Brotherhood continued. He was proud to be carrying on its illustrious traditions by filling the void left by the fall of Dulaque.

My hour has come round at last, he thought. Now he merely needed to cement his position as the future of the Brotherhood, despite the existence of a few rivals also jockeying for the top spot, by scoring a major victory—and defeating the Library once and for all.

But first he had to find a certain pot of gold.

"Is it time?" he asked.

"Almost," Coral Marsh replied. "We're ready to go."

Max turned away from the display case to inspect the preparations. A large map of North America was laid out atop a stylish chrome-and-glass table. A balcony window faced east, awaiting the dawn, if perhaps not as eagerly as Coral.

"Sunrise is scheduled for exactly 7:08," she reported. Dyed pink hair, the color of cotton candy, tried too hard to display her individuality, at least as far as Max was concerned. Unlike Max, she had hardly dressed for the occasion, having merely thrown on a baggy sweater and jeans that looked as though they had never been ironed. Wire-rim glasses perched upon her nose. Copper earrings, fashioned to resemble coiled serpents, signaled her allegiance to the Brotherhood, as did the silver Ouroboros on Max's ring finger. A transparent crystal prism, no more than six inches long, dangled from a chain around her neck.

Short and round and overcaffeinated, she was practically percolating with excitement as the critical moment approached. She sipped from one of the noxious energy drinks she seemed to live on. Although it was still early morning, Max guessed that it wasn't her first. He preferred a strong cup of black coffee himself.

From freshly ground Sumatran beans, of course.

"A shame we have to do this at such an ungodly hour," he observed, repressing a yawn. He had been up late trading on various precious metal and rare coin exchanges. Until he secured full control of the Brotherhood, he had only limited access to its vast treasuries, forcing him to rely on additional income streams for the time being.

"But it's the only way," she insisted, her Midwestern accent marking her as an American. "It has to be the first ray of daylight, or the crack of noon, when the sun is highest in the sky, or the last light of day, or the whole procedure is compromised. It's not just a matter of simple optics; dawn and noon and dusk have mystic significance that, coupled with the fundamental principles of applied astrological symbolism, is essential to producing the desired effect due to—"

"Yes, yes, I understand all that," Max interrupted, hoping to head off another lengthy exegesis on the finer points of the magical science involved. Coral's enthusiasm for her work could be exhausting sometimes. "You've explained that before."

Many times, he added silently.

"Sorry," she said sheepishly. She shuffled her feet and looked down at the floor. "I guess I'm still psyched that we're able to pull this off."

"As well you should be," he said, giving credit where it was due. "Not everyone could do what you have done: create an all-new magical artifact for our use."

He was quite sincere in his praise. Most objects of power, such as Aladdin's Lamp or the Golden Fleece, dated back to antiquity. To forge a new such item, without any history, was a considerable accomplishment indeed.

"Thanks!" she chirped, looking up from the floor. "Although, of course, I couldn't have done it if the Brotherhood hadn't reactivated the ley lines a few years ago, and let wild magic back into the world."

"You're welcome," he said, although that had been Dulaque's doing, prior to his ignominious defeat at the hands of the Librarians. "And that's only the beginning. Before we're done, the Library will be ours and no longer able to hide magic away from the world. We're going to change the world, Coral; and, speaking of which . . ."

"Right!" She removed the chain holding the crystal prism, which was her most prized possession. She handled the prism carefully to avoid smudging its polished sides. "Here we go."

The sky was starting to lighten outside, presaging the dawn. Max dimmed the lights in the penthouse and removed a felt-tip marker from his suit pocket. Coral claimed a plastic spray bottle from a counter and misted the air above the map with water taken from a sacred pool in Killarney; as Max understood it, the dispersed water vapor was not essential but helped to facilitate the divination process.

Whatever gets the job done, he thought.

Coral got in place, holding up the crystal between the balcony window and the map table. Despite having witnessed this procedure several times before, Max held his breath until a single ray of sunshine passed through a prism, refracting into a brightly colored rainbow that arced above the table before coming to rest at one specific spot on the map. Marker in hand, Max sprung forward to mark the exact location of the end of the rainbow, where a leprechaun's pot of gold could be found.

Somewhere in Pennsylvania, he noted.

"Did you get it?" Coral asked. "Did it work?"

"As ever," he assured her. "Your brilliant creation does not disappoint."

"Great!" She lowered the prism, even as the enchanted rainbow lost definition and clarity, fading away into the morning light. She rushed over to the map to see where the prism had directed them this time, but couldn't wait for the answer. "Where are we going?"

Max peered at the map.

"Pittsburgh," he reported.

"Really?" She sounded slightly disappointed. "I was hoping for Vegas or New Orleans or something."

"Mission first, tourism later," he reminded her. "We're on a quest, not a sightseeing expedition."

"Of course." She looked duly chastened. "Eyes on the prize, I understand that."

"I know you do."

A private jet waited to take them wherever they needed to go. Max had no doubt that another pot of gold awaited them in Pittsburgh; Coral's ingenious prism had not steered them wrong yet. And this evening, at dusk, they could apply the prism to a detailed map of the city and thereby zero in even more precisely on the gold's location.

"But will it be *the* Pot?" he wondered aloud.

Although the faerie gold they'd plundered so far had helped to finance this current operation, Max was after one particular Pot—the very one that Lady Sibella had tried and failed to obtain more than fifteen hundred years ago.

"There's no way of telling," Coral admitted, "but we're getting closer. I know we are!"

It was Coral, in fact, who had unearthed the full story of Lady Sibella and her plans for the Pot from the Brotherhood's top-secret archives, and who'd brought that tantalizing intelligence to Max. A first-rate historian and occultist, Coral would have probably made a fine Librarian had she not been recruited by the Brotherhood instead. Max had headhunted her himself.

"No doubt." He dearly hoped that they would find their ultimate prize in Pittsburgh, but was fully prepared to keep hunting for however long it took, no matter how many leprechauns they had to track down first. They had started in Ireland, naturally, before venturing farther afield. In retrospect, however, they possibly should've started searching in America first, given how many of the Irish had immigrated to the New World since the days of Lady Sibella; as Max understood it, there were actually more people of Irish descent in America than there were in Ireland these days, so perhaps that applied to leprechauns as well? Fifteen hundred years was more than time enough for a certain leprechaun to relocate to the States. "Rest assured, we'll find the right pot eventually."

"Yes!" Coral enthused, her eyes gleaming behind her spectacles. She carefully hung the precious crystal back around her neck. "And then we'll finally be able to rid the world of want!"

"Naturally," he assured his invaluable, if overly idealistic, associate. Max's own designs were somewhat less humanitarian in nature, but Coral played a vital role in his campaign, at least for the present, so he was not about to disillusion her. "Just as the original Serpent dared humanity to taste the fruit of knowledge, to boldly seize their own destiny, so shall we lead the world into a glorious new age of magic and miracles."

And power, he amended.

He looked over at Lady Sibella's fleshless remains. Her fanged skull seemed to grin in anticipation.

Soon, he promised. *Very soon.*

10

❋ *The Annex* ❋

"I thought we were going to see the leprechauns?" Cassandra said.

"So we are," Jenkins replied as he escorted her through the byzantine byways of the Library. It was a bewildering maze of halls and galleries, holding everything from Penelope's unfinished tapestry to Prufrock's intimidating peach, yet Jenkins navigated the sprawling Library with ease. "But we need to go properly prepared."

The Library's Hibernian Wing, which was devoted to Irish history and mythology, was one of many subsections comprising the Library's vast and all but unfathomable entirety, including the Large Collections Annex and the Theoretical Animals Wing. Even after three years and change, there were parts of the Library that Cassandra had barely explored. She wasn't entirely sure she had ever visited the Hibernian Wing before.

Some Cillian I am, she thought guiltily. *I suck at being Irish.*

A newfound determination to better appreciate her heritage prompted her to scope out the surprisingly sizable collection as she followed Jenkins into the wing. Along with shelf after shelf of books on Ireland, from Ireland, and by Irish authors, poets, and playwrights, various other relics and artifacts were also on display, including a gorgeously illuminated manuscript that rivaled the celebrated Book of Kells, a three-faced stone idol, a weathered Celtic cross, a fiddle, a bog mummy, a humble iron bell, an oil painting of a cattle raid, a bottle of Guinness and . . . a potato?

"Wow!" she exclaimed, trying to take it all in. "I had no idea the Irish collection would be so . . . extensive."

"Not for nothing is Erin known as the Land of Saints and Scholars," Jenkins commented. He gestured at the packed rows of books. "Its contributions to literature alone warranted its own dedicated wing of the Library."

Cassandra scanned the bookshelves. A serpentine design embossed on the spine of one volume caught her eye and she pulled it from the shelf. Inspecting the book, she read the type of the front cover aloud:

"*The Lair of the White Worm* by Bram Stoker."

"Born and raised in Dublin," Jenkins informed her. "One of his lesser works, to be frank, but not nearly as fictional as generally believed."

She flipped open the book, revealing an interior illustration depicting a sinuous creature that was part snake, part woman. Reptilian eyes peered malevolently from a classically beautiful face. A forked tongue escaped smirking lips.

"Not sure I needed to know that," Cassandra said.

With a shudder, she snapped the book shut and returned it to the shelf. Heading deeper into the wing, she came upon another intriguing item: an ordinary-looking rock, about the size of a brick, resting under a glass dome atop a velvet cushion as though it were one of the Crown Jewels. That the rock occupied a position of honor within the collection piqued Cassandra's curiosity.

"What's so special about this rock?" she asked.

Jenkins paused to answer her. "That, Miss Cillian, is the *actual* Blarney Stone, as opposed to the one that throngs of tourists kiss every day in hopes of obtaining the fabled gift of the gab." He grimaced in distaste. "You can understand, no doubt, why we keep the real Stone under lock and key. The last thing the world needs is more silver-tongued charmers who can talk others into anything."

I can see that, Cassandra thought.

Catching up with him, she found Jenkins looking over a flowerpot resting atop a windowsill. Sunlight filtered in through a green stained-glassed window, while a simple tin watering can sat nearby on a small end table. Sprigs of fresh green clover sprouted from the soil in the pot. At first, Cassandra thought that the sprigs were merely shamrocks, but then she looked more closely.

"Wait," she said. "Are those all . . . ?"

"Four-leaf clovers," he confirmed. "I cultivate a small crop for just such occasions."

Using a miniature pair of gardening shears, he clipped off two of the sprigs, one for each of them. He affixed one to his lapel as a boutonniere, then turned toward Cassandra.

"If I may?"

"Go ahead," she said. "I mean, please do."

He deftly threaded the stem of the second clover through a buttonhole on her sweater, making Cassandra feel as though they were going to the prom. (Not that she would know, having had to skip her prom for medical reasons.) She blushed slightly.

"Is this a formal occasion?" she joked. "Or are we just hoping to blend in with the leprechauns?"

"Think of it as a passport," he explained, "not to mention a prudent precaution. A genuine four-leaf clover, worn on your person, allows one to see through any glamours or illusions cast by the Fair Folk."

That Jenkins thought such a measure necessary worried Cassandra. "Is that something to be concerned about?" Pretty much everything she knew about leprechauns came from Lucky Charms commercials and an old Disney movie, but she had never gotten the impression that they were particularly dangerous. "Are leprechauns friendly or not?"

"Depends on their moods, which can be mercurial," Jenkins said. "Leprechauns are more mischievous than malevolent by and large, yet they can be capricious and prone to trickery, so it pays to be on your guard when dealing with them. As a poet once sagely wrote: *'Up the airy mountain, Down the rushy glen, We daren't go a-hunting, For fear of little men.'*"

11

Mill Ends Park was officially the smallest city park in the world, being nothing more than a small circle of shrubbery, only two feet in diameter, in the middle of a concrete traffic median on a public street. According to Jenkins, it was also the largest leprechaun colony west of Ireland and had been formally recognized as such ever since Saint Patrick's Day, 1948, some seventy years ago. Tiny Irish flags and doll furniture, situated around the minuscule "park," suggested that Portlanders were still going along with the gag—or what they *thought* was a gag.

"This is it?" Cassandra said, underwhelmed.

She and Jenkins loitered in the traffic median on SW Naito Parkway, not far from the riverfront. Fog and drizzle had chased any other pedestrians indoors, even as cars and trucks drove past the pair on both sides of the parkway. The fog helped conceal them from view, but they had to watch out for spray from vehicles driving through puddles and potholes. A dank chill penetrated Cassandra's bones; she was having second thoughts about tagging along on this trip.

"Don't be deceived by appearances," Jenkins advised her.

"This whimsical curiosity is merely the gateway to our ultimate destination: a faerie Otherworld that is home to a sizable
contingent of expatriate leprechauns who emigrated to the
Pacific Northwest decades ago, at least as time is reckoned on
the mortal plane. Time tends to pass at a slower rate where the
Fair Folk are concerned, so I suggest that we don't linger any
longer than necessary."

Cassandra grasped the concept, but hoped their visit
wouldn't be too much of a rush trip. How often did you get
to visit a whole tribe of leprechauns for real?

"So what's next?" she asked.

"We need only pass through the portal," he said confidently,
"after properly requesting admission, naturally."

Glancing around to make certain that they were unob-
served, he produced a flask from beneath his jacket and spilled
a splash of Irish whiskey onto the base of the park, accompany-
ing the 80-proof libation with an incantation in what Cassandra assumed was flawless Gaelic:

"Deontas duinn bealach isteach le do thoi!"

She envied the ease with which the peculiar syllables rolled
off his tongue. Why, he even managed a proper Irish brogue.

Is everyone better at being Irish than I am?

The ritual complete, Jenkins put away the flask and stepped
toward the park expectantly.

Nothing happened.

Cassandra wasn't quite sure what was *supposed* to occur,
but nothing resembling a gateway appeared. The shrub remained a shrub, and she and Jenkins remained stuck in the
median in the cold, clammy fog.

"Maybe they're not home?" she suggested.

"Unlikely," Jenkins said, frowning, "but they *are* showing
a surprising lack of hospitality." He heaved a weary sigh. "I

would have preferred a less pushy approach, but if they insist. . . ."

He stamped on the concrete ring surrounding the bush, as though to demand the leprechauns' attention. His voice took on a sterner tone, like a cop presenting a warrant.

"Attend to my words. By the authority invested in me as a duly recognized representative of the Library, per the Seelie Accords and the Investiture of Myrddin, I hereby demand admission to the realm beyond and below."

Again, nothing happened.

"I think they're closed for business," Cassandra said, disappointed. "Maybe if we come back later?"

"By treaty, they cannot deny us access." Concern furrowed Jenkins's brow. "That they are continuing to do so is . . . disturbing." He turned to Cassandra. "It is fortunate that you accompanied me on this mission."

"Me?" she said. "Why is that?"

"Because you are a daughter of Eire *and* a Librarian, which carries more weight than you might imagine in this context." He reached out and took her hand. "Kindly repeat after me: In the name of Danu, Lugh, and the High Kings of Tara . . ."

Cassandra trusted him enough to follow his instructions without asking for more information. "In the name of Danu, Lugh, and the High Kings of Tara . . ."

". . . Open wide your gate."

". . . Open wide your gate. Yikes!"

She had barely finished reciting the words when a sudden wave of vertigo left her so light-headed that it took her a moment to realize that both she and Jenkins were *shrinking* at a precipitous rate. The dinky little cypress tree at the center of the park suddenly loomed as tall as a redwood, even as a hole opened in a knothole at its base, sucking them in like a whirlpool. She lost her grip on Jenkins's hand as they plunged through the portal, sliding feetfirst down a long, winding tube worthy of an amusement park.

"That's more like it," Jenkins said.

The high-speed plunge lasted only a few seconds, but still left Cassandra breathless. To be honest, she had been expecting something more like the Magic Door. . . .

A golden glow appeared at the bottom of the slide. Cassandra braced herself for impact, but somehow ended up landing on her bottom onto something soft and spongy.

"Oof!"

Jenkins, on the other hand, landed nimbly on his feet, as though he'd done this many times before. He chivalrously offered her a hand up.

"Well done, Miss Cillian," he said, which took some of the sting out of her awkward landing. "Your Irish blood tipped the scales, it seems."

"Any time," she said. "Although it would be nice if it stopped rushing through my veins quite so quickly!"

Back on her feet, she gaped at their new surroundings, which appeared to be some vast underground cavern or burrow. A gentle glow magically suffused the cave, bringing light and warmth to a large grotto at the base of the slide. Glittering veins of gold and crystal sparkled throughout the walls, while a high ceiling kept the burrow from feeling cramped. Archways and side corridors led off in all directions; lively fiddle music came from somewhere just around the corner. Mushrooms the size of furniture sprouted from the thick green moss carpeting the floor of the cavern. A rich, earthy smell like freshly turned soil permeated the air. All in all, the leprechaun colony felt cozier and toastier than the misty city street . . . directly above them.

"Are we actually under Portland?" she asked Jenkins.

"In a manner of speaking, but we have been translated to another realm as well."

"Got it," she said. "Kind of like the way the Library exists outside ordinary time and space."

"Precisely. We are beneath the city, but just one step removed from the more prosaic version of reality."

Which explains the notable absence of sewers and utility tunnels, she thought. *Works for me.*

Their arrival had not gone unnoticed. A crowd of people, clad in old-timey clothing in various shades of green, gawked back at Cassandra, who was puzzled, and a trifle disappointed, that the leprechauns—if indeed that was what they were—all seemed to be of more or less normal height. She had expected the Little People to be, well, littler.

"Galeas!"

A hearty voice greeted Jenkins as a single leprechaun approached them through the crowd, which parted to let him pass. He was a stocky, solidly built fellow, seemingly in his mid-thirties, with bushy red sideburns and a ruddy complexion. His right hand held a rustic clay pipe, while a golden torc upon his brow signaled his authority, as did the deference of the other onlookers. He wore a waistcoat over a vest that had decorative shamrocks printed on the fabric. Brass buttons and buckles shone as though newly polished. A broad smile put Cassandra at ease.

"A thousand and one welcomes, good knight!"

"Really?" Jenkins groused. "Our initial reception seemed rather less than welcoming."

The other man's smile grew more forced. "Ye must forgive us, sir knight. Alas, recent circumstances prevent us from being as hospitable as we would prefer."

"What circumstances?" Jenkins pressed.

"All in good time," the man promised. "But first I believe introductions are in order." He smiled at Cassandra. "Who might this lovely colleen be?"

Ever the gentleman, Jenkins surrendered to etiquette.

"Allow me to introduce Miss Cassandra Cillian, a Librarian of some distinction." He gestured at their beaming host. "Miss Cillian, please make the acquaintance of Connall MacDonagh, the high chieftain of Mill Ends."

"A pleasure to meet ye, fair lady," MacDonagh said, laying on the charm along with a lilting accent. "'Tis clear the beauty of our beloved Ireland has graced ye as well. Ye're a veritable Rose of Tralee, ye are."

"Thank you," Cassandra said, wondering if she was supposed to curtsy or something. She was eye to eye with MacDonagh, for he was pretty much her height. "I have to admit, you're taller than I expected . . . for a leprechaun, I mean."

She hoped she hadn't spoken out of turn, but MacDonagh merely laughed out loud before responding, "This is yer first visit to Otherworld, I take it?"

"Size, along with time, is variable between planes," Jenkins explained. "Passing through the portal brought us into scale with the leprechauns, although they tend to lose some altitude going the other way."

"The better to hide from avaricious humans," MacDonagh said with a chuckle. "Present company excluded, of course."

"Your gold is safe from us," Jenkins assured him, making Cassandra glad that Ezekiel hadn't tagged along after all. "Nor are we in pursuit of wishes."

"Glad I am to hear it," MacDonagh said. "But what does bring ye here, Galeas?"

"I go by 'Jenkins' these days," the former knight replied, "and I'm afraid that this is far from a social call. Miss Cillian and I are here on Library business, in hope that you and your people can assist us in a matter of some urgency."

MacDonagh's smile gave way to a more sober expression. "I feared as much. But perhaps this is a conversation to be had somewhere a tad more private?"

He tilted his head at the growing crowd of curious leprechauns come to inspect the new arrivals. Cassandra got the impression that the Mill Ends colony didn't get a lot of visitors from the mortal world. Gazing back at them, she saw that some looked more human than others. Pointed ears gave a few of them a more elfin appearance, while gossamer-like wings fluttered from the shoulders of several of the female sprites, making them look more like storybook fairies than your traditional Irish leprechauns. Was there such a thing as female leprechauns? Cassandra assumed there was . . . although maybe they were more properly pixies or nixies or something? It dawned on Cassandra that she was a bit fuzzy when it came to faerie taxonomy.

"By all means," Jenkins agreed. "We don't need an audience."

MacDonagh gestured toward a waiting tunnel. "This way then, if ye please."

They followed him to a smaller grotto that appeared to serve as MacDonagh's private study. Bookshelves shaped from the very walls of the cavern held an assortment of leather-bound tomes as well as a handful of parchment scrolls. A roaring fire in a sturdy stone hearth helped dispel the last trace of Portland's dampness and chill from Cassandra's person. MacDonagh took possession of a high-back wooden chair that looked distinctly thronelike, while Jenkins and

Cassandra made themselves comfortable in smaller seats on the opposite side of an antique desk. A jug sat atop it, which MacDonagh uncorked and offered to his guests.

"Care for a nip of poteen? Ye'll not taste finer anywhere this side of Dublin."

"No, thank you." Jenkins shot Cassandra a cautionary look. "I will abstain . . . and so will Miss Cillian."

MacDonagh withdrew the jug. "You've gotten suspicious in your old age, sir knight."

"Which is no doubt how I've survived so long," Jenkins replied. "And let it be noted that my knightly days are far behind me."

"Are they truly? I wonder," MacDonagh said. "Ye still haven't told me what quest brings youse to my door."

"Nor have you explained," Jenkins observed, "the difficulties we encountered gaining admission to your realm."

"Ah, that," MacDonagh said ruefully. "I suppose I do owe youse an explanation. The plain truth is that we are all a bit on edge due to some unpleasant goings-on back in the Auld Sod."

"What sort of unpleasantness?" Cassandra asked.

"Murder, good lady, and robbery to boot," he said gravely. "Word has reached us of our brothers across the sea being cruelly slain for their treasure troves. So youse can understand why our gates are more tightly barred than is customary."

"Somebody is killing leprechauns?" Cassandra said, appalled. "For their pots of gold?"

"Just so." MacDonagh held up four stubby fingers. "At least four of our brethren, from County Cork to Donegal, have been found murdered, their pots absconded with by parties unknown."

Cassandra and Jenkins exchanged a look. She could tell

that the parallels with that long-ago incident on Croagh Patrick were not lost on him either.

"That is troubling," Jenkins said, "but I fear that these dire tidings may relate to the purpose of our own visit. We have reason to suspect that the Serpent Brotherhood has resurfaced, and that their current activities may be related to an occasion many centuries ago when the Brotherhood went to great lengths to obtain an unknown leprechaun's pot of gold, only to be foiled by a Librarian and his allies."

MacDonagh's eyes widened at the mention of the Brotherhood, whom he was obviously familiar with. He listened attentively as Jenkins succinctly informed him of the events of 441 A.D., as well as of the far more recent disturbance at the monolith. He did not, Cassandra noted, mention Bridget O'Neill and her banshee problem, perhaps to avoid confusing matters.

Probably a good call, she thought.

"So ye think that the attacks today may trace back to that earlier deviltry, ages past?" MacDonagh asked finally, after Jenkins was finished. "And that the Serpents are behind it all?"

"We cannot rule out that possibility," Jenkins stated, "which is why anything more we can learn about that past incident, and the individual leprechaun involved, may be of great help, not just to our own investigation but also perhaps to identifying and halting whoever is attacking your kinsmen back in Ireland."

For herself, Cassandra felt certain that the Brotherhood were responsible. That leprechauns were being killed for their gold at the same time somebody was literally digging into that similar incident of fifteen hundred years ago felt like a pattern to her, even if she wasn't quite sure where Bridget's banshee fit in . . . yet.

"What can you tell us about the leprechauns who were murdered?" Cassandra asked, trying to think like a detective. "Did they have anything in common?"

"Mind you, this is all taking place back in the Old World," MacDonagh said, "so I cannot claim to be intimately acquainted with the particulars or personages, but me understanding, from conferring with me counterparts overseas, is that the victims were all solitary sorts who dwelt by themselves and preferred their own company to that of others. I fear their unsociable habits and dispositions made them more tempting targets."

Cassandra could see that. "Loners and hermits, in other words."

"Indeed," MacDonagh said, nodding. "As opposed to those of us who dwell together for both safety and the pleasure of good fellowship."

Cassandra wondered if the unnamed leprechaun on Croagh Patrick had been a loner as well. "I don't suppose you know who that leprechaun was, who ran afoul of the Brotherhood back in the fifth century?"

MacDonagh shook his head. "From what ye say, 'twas long ago and far away, and 'tis not a tale I have ever heard before. Whoever this fellow was, he must have kept his own counsel and never shared the story. His name may well be lost to memory."

"Perhaps not," Jenkins said. "With your permission, I would like to peruse your annals, particularly your global census records, going back to the fifth century at least. The Library's records are comprehensive, but there are still holes that your archives may be able to fill in, to provide a more complete picture of that earlier incident."

MacDonagh frowned. "Ye ask much. Our history is our own, and not always to be shared with outsiders."

"Even if it means possibly catching the killer?" Cassandra asked. "And preventing the Serpent Brotherhood from stealing another leprechaun's gold?"

"Ye make a good case," MacDonagh conceded after a moment's thought. "Very well. In the spirit of amity and for our mutual welfare, youse may consult our annals. And let us wish that yer studious efforts will be of benefit to all concerned."

"Wishes are your province," Jenkins said dryly, "but, on behalf of the Library, we appreciate your cooperation."

"As well ye should," MacDonagh said, his tone lighter now that the decision had been made. "And yet, I suspect ye have a long, dreary task before youse, poring through countless dry and brittle pages. Surely the young lady would prefer to enjoy our hospitality instead, to savor the music and merriment of the world below?"

Cassandra wasn't sure how to respond. There was something distinctly patronizing about MacDonagh's suggestion—she was a Librarian, not some flighty young thing—and she knew she ought to be irked by it, and yet . . . it *would* be a shame to spend her whole time in Otherworld chained to a desk, digging through lots of dusty old tomes. She could do that back at the Library.

"Jenkins?"

"Go," he said generously. "Enjoy yourself."

"Are you sure?" Cassandra asked, not wanting to stick him with all the work while she took in the sights.

"Unless you are fluent in ancient Gaelic and Brythonic, I am probably better suited to this task. You have already contributed significantly to this expedition; I will not begrudge you this opportunity . . . although if I may have a word first?"

He took her aside and lowered his voice so that only she could hear.

"By all means, indulge your curiosity, but the usual rules for visiting faerie realms apply: accept no gifts, food, or drink unless it is certain that there are no conditions attached. Many is the mortal who became a prisoner of faerie hospitality, so keep your wits about you."

Cassandra appreciated his concern. She checked to make sure her protective four-leaf clover was still in place.

"Don't worry," she said. "This isn't my first field trip to another dimension. I'll be careful."

"I know you will be." Jenkins said. "Which is why I'm comfortable letting you out of my sight . . . unlike certain other Librarians I might name."

Stepping away from Cassandra, he turned to address MacDonagh.

"Now then, about those census reports . . ."

While Jenkins got down to business, Cassandra took off to explore the burrow. Wandering wide-eyed through the seemingly endless caverns, while being gawked at in turn by passing leprechauns, she was struck again by how warm and cozy the underground dwelling was compared with most of the spooky caves and catacombs she'd visited as a Librarian. Mill Ends was more like an extended hobbit-hole than a mummy's tomb.

The sound of music and laughter, echoing through the winding corridors, drew her onward until she reached the largest grotto she'd seen so far: an enormous chamber the size of a ballroom, where a raucous celebration was already under way. Scores of leprechauns filled the chamber, dancing a jig to the lively fiddle music Cassandra had been hearing ever since she'd first arrived in Otherworld. A red-capped fiddler, poised atop a towering toadstool, provided the music as the other leprechauns hopped and stepped with abandon, so light on their feet that they often seemed to defy gravity. Winged fairies whirled through the air overhead, faster and faster as the tempo kept increasing. Cassandra clapped in delight, her feet tapping along with the music as though literally enchanted. She had no idea what the occasion was and didn't really care. For all she knew, this was just an ordinary night at Mill Ends.

That's it, she thought. *I'm definitely signing up for an Irish dancing class once this case is over.*

The music somehow grew louder and even more enticing. She was just about to join in the festivities when one particular dancer, who was maybe a wee bit taller than the others, made eye contact with her. Curly red hair, tumbling down past the dancer's shoulders, framed a familiar, freckled face that Cassandra suddenly recognized.

"Bridget?"

12

※ *Chicago* ※

The Pot O' Gold was a traditional Irish pub in downtown Chicago. Numerous bottles of spirits were stacked neatly in front of a long, frosted mirror across from a polished mahogany bar. Brass taps gleamed beneath hanging lamps with translucent green shades. Framed newspaper clippings, celebrating various World Cup victories, adorned the wood-paneled walls, along with autographed photos of minor celebrities. A list of appetizers was scrawled on a chalkboard propped up behind the door, while empty stools, chairs, and booths awaited thirsty patrons. It was early morning, so the pub wasn't open for business yet, but Baird got a positive vibe from the place. It struck her as the sort of authentic neighborhood watering hole that she wouldn't have minded frequenting even if she weren't investigating an alleged banshee haunting.

"Nice place," she said.

"Thanks," Bridget said. "It's been in my family for generations now, ever since my great-granddad came over from the Old Country. Family legend has it that some lucky gold coins, bestowed on my ancestors by a friendly leprechaun, provided the funds to launch the pub back in the day."

The Magic Door had deposited the Librarians and their new "client" at the pub by way of the tavern's rear entrance. Baird had momentarily balked at revealing the Door's existence to a civilian, but had concluded that the whole magic Library thing was pretty much out of the bag already, so it hadn't been worth wasting several hours flying from Portland to Chicago just to avoid showing the Door to Bridget, who, to her credit, had been merely reasonably flabbergasted as she'd stepped through the magical shortcut.

"A leprechaun?" Baird echoed.

"Gold?" Ezekiel said almost simultaneously.

Stone shot Baird a look, obviously making the same connection she had. The Serpent Brotherhood had been after a leprechaun's gold way back in the fifth century. No way was this a coincidence.

"That's right," Bridget replied. "In fact, the last of the original coins is supposedly on display right here."

She called their attention to a single gold coin embedded in the top of the bar beneath a thick sheet of glass. A plaque provided the inspiration for the pub's name:

"Actual gold coin straight from a leprechaun's Pot O' Gold."

"To tell the truth," Bridget said, "I'd always figured the story behind the coin to be pure blarney, but then, when the medical bills started piling up, threatening to bankrupt both me and the pub, several more gold coins showed up on the bar one morning, right out of the blue."

"And you have no idea where the coins came from?" Baird asked.

"Not a clue." Bridget dusted off the glass with a rag. "But I can tell you this: I would have almost surely lost the pub if that gold hadn't shown up when it did, so who knows? Maybe there is a leprechaun looking out for me . . . along with a banshee foretelling my doom."

"About that," Baird said. "What's the timing there? What came first, the gold or the banshee?"

Bridget thought about it. "Now that you mention it, the banshee thing started not long after I cashed in the gold coins to pay my hospital bills. Do you think there's a connection?"

"Follow the money," Baird said, speaking from experience. "Maybe spending the coins attracted the banshee somehow, not unlike the way I used to track laundered money back to black-market arms dealers and terrorists."

"Right!" Ezekiel said. "Or the way that marked bills can get you in trouble when you finally try spending them. Not that this ever happened to me, mind you."

"Uh-huh," Stone said skeptically.

An odd thought occurred to Baird. "So where do leprechauns get their gold in the first place?"

She expected Stone to answer, but Bridget spoke up first.

"Nobody really knows. There are lots of conflicting stories and legends. Some say the gold is stolen from Viking hoards buried beneath the earth. Others say they earn the money as cobblers, making and repairing shoes for the other fairies, who wear theirs out by dancing, or that they earn it as fiddlers, playing for the revels of fairy kings and queens. And some say the gold comes from long-forgotten mines and treasure troves dating all the way back to the misty days of legend, when ancient gods and goddesses reigned over Ireland."

Ezekiel eyed her suspiciously. "You seem to know an awful lot about this stuff."

"I own a pub called the Pot O' Gold," she pointed out, "and

I'm being haunted by a banshee. So, yeah, I'm up on my Irish folklore."

"Okay," he conceded. "Fair dinkum."

Baird considered the gold coin and Bridget's story. Leprechauns and their pots of gold were apparently a real thing, so she had no reason to doubt any of this, even if the connection to the banshee—and the Serpent Brotherhood—remained fuzzy. She turned to her team for answers.

"Okay, Librarians. Put those big brains of yours to work. What's to be learned here?"

Stone inspected the coin through the protective glass.

"Not quite sure what to make of this," he admitted. "Conventional wisdom is that the Irish didn't start striking their own coinage until the Normans showed up in the twelfth century, well after that business with the Serpent Brotherhood back in Saint Patrick's time. Whatever coins made it to Ireland before then would have been Greek or Roman or British or Viking, depending, and valued more for their precious metal than for their monetary value, but the design on *this* coin is unmistakably Celtic."

The face of the coin boasted an embossed portrait of a bearded god or king whose crown sported the interlocking spirals associated with traditional Celtic art. Twin braids hung from the icon's bushy beard, while his raised hands held smaller, mortal figures aloft. Mythical beasts of some sort capered along the circumference of the coin. Baird examined the portrait as she might have a mug shot.

"Any idea who that's supposed to be?"

"Possibly one of the Tuatha Dé Danann?" Stone said. "That would be my best guess, although I'm going to want to look it up to be sure."

Baird recalled that the Tuatha Dé Danann were the gods

of pagan Ireland. "Maybe Jenkins can help out with that," she suggested. "Heck, he may have seen plenty of coins like this back in his Round Table days. Probably used them to pay for lunch during the Dark Ages."

"Not like this," Stone said. "This is a rarity . . . if it's for real."

"Only one way to find out." Ezekiel unclipped a handheld magic detector from his belt. "Good thing I came prepared."

Easing Stone aside, he scanned the coin with the gadget. Baird peered over his shoulder as the digital display started ticking upward into the green zone. It beeped as loudly as a Geiger counter.

"And we have a winner," Ezekiel said. "That coin is definitely giving off some serious magical emanations."

Baird nodded. "Which means it really could have come straight from a leprechaun's pot."

But what did that have to do with the banshee?

13

※ *Otherworld* ※

"Bridget?"

Cassandra made her way across the crowded grotto, weaving through the bouncing leprechauns until she reached the other redhead, who was still merrily dancing a jig to the fiddler's music. Familiar green eyes regarded Cassandra with curiosity—and not a trace of recognition.

"Do I know ye?"

Cassandra scrutinized the dancer. Up close, the resemblance was even more striking. The woman's hair was longer and curlier than Cassandra remembered, her accent more Irish than American, and her clothing more traditional, but there was no mistaking that face, which was the same one Cassandra had first viewed via the magic mirror back at the Annex.

"Bridget O'Neill? From Chicago?"

"Simply Brigid," the woman said, not missing a step of her dance. "And where be Chicago?"

Not the same person, Cassandra realized. Brigid, not Bridget, but a dead ringer for the other Bridget nonetheless. Cassandra found herself hopping back and forth from one leg to another, in her best attempt at a jig, as she pondered this new mystery, which had to be another piece of a larger puzzle.

"My name is Cassandra . . . and I think we need to talk."

Brigid looked intrigued. "About what, pray tell?"

"Another Bridget, who looks just like you."

Surprise showed on Brigid's porcelain features. "Now that sounds like a tale worth hearing." She stopped dancing and took Cassandra's hand. "Come with me."

She led Cassandra to a quiet alcove at the edge of the grotto, where Brigid took a seat atop a mushroom the size of a barstool. Cassandra awkwardly situated herself atop another overgrown fungus, which felt a bit like being perched on an elevated beanbag chair. The mushroom swayed slightly beneath her weight, but Cassandra tried not to let that distract her.

"That's better," she said. "Not that it wasn't nice dancing with you, of course, but I have so many questions . . ."

"Is it true what they say?" Brigid asked. "That ye're from above, the mortal world?"

"That's right, and in that world I met another Bridget, who could be your twin."

Brigid regarded Cassandra with fascination. "How is that possible?"

"That's what I want to know." She looked Brigid over as closely as she could without giving her the wrong idea. No pointed ears or gossamer wings presented themselves. This new Brigid appeared just as human as the one being haunted by a banshee back in the real world; but, as Jenkins had pointed out not too long ago, appearances could be deceiving. "You're not a leprechaun, are you?"

"I am not, but the Fair Folk have given me a home since I was a mere babe in arms, or so I am told," she said with a chuckle. "I can't remember that far back myself."

"How far back?" Cassandra asked.

"Heaven only knows," Brigid said, seemingly unconcerned. "Long enough to grow up, I suppose."

Cassandra recalled Jenkins saying that time passed differently here, so there was no telling how long that might be in relation to the mortal world. The lack of precision annoyed the mathematician in Cassandra. There really ought to be some sort of formula for converting faerie time to mortal time.

"But how did you come to live among the leprechauns?"

"I was an orphan, they say," Brigid answered, "lost and alone until the Folk took me in and gave me a home, here below." A wistful sigh escaped her lips. "Make no mistake: I'm forever grateful for their kindness, but sometimes I wonder about the world I came from. Tell me more of it, please, for I confess I am fierce curious."

Cassandra didn't know where to begin, let alone how to figure out the connection between Brigid and Bridget. Were they simply distant relations with a strong family resemblance, or was there more to it? She remembered what Jenkins had said earlier about coincidences sometimes being anything but. Cassandra felt positive that she had stumbled onto another piece of the puzzle.

Now she just needed to find the pattern.

14

Appropriately enough, the tiny shop was located below ground level. A short flight of concrete steps led down from the city sidewalk to the front entrance of the business, which was identified by a quaintly old-fashioned sign in the shape of a boot which read:

COBBLER
BOOTS & SHOES REPAIR

Max was amused to note that the toe of the boot curved upward in a distinctly elfin fashion. A sly joke on the part of the proprietor or an unintentional admission? In either event, he felt confident that the prism had led him to the right place. Leprechauns were traditionally cobblers, after all.

"After me," he instructed his bodyguard.

Owens nodded. A tight black T-shirt strained to contain his prodigious pectorals, which owed as much to steroids as to weight lifting. A python was shaved into the back of his close-cropped blond hair. His thick neck would have given a hangman pause. A man of few words and even less personality, the hulking bodybuilder took "laconic" to the extreme; Max wasn't sure he'd ever heard the man utter more than five words in succession. Not that it mattered—Owens was around to provide muscle, not conversation.

Descending the steps, they entered the shop to find a cramped, cluttered space smelling of glue, polish, and shoe leather. Examples of the cobbler's craft were displayed on tables near the front of the shop: shoes and boots mostly, but also a handful of purses, handbags, and belts, all lovingly maintained and/or restored. Brown-paper parcels bearing handwritten tags filled rows of shelves behind the front counter, waiting to be picked up by customers who had dropped off their worn footwear to be mended. Wooden shoe stretchers of various sizes hung from a rack. Framed documents testified that the shop's proprietor, one "Seamus Kincaid," was certified in orthotics, prosthetics, and pedorthics.

The sound of tapping came from a workshop somewhere in the back. Max visualized the cobbler nailing a new sole onto an old shoe.

Classic, he thought. *If a tad clichéd.*

A bell over the door announced their arrival. The tapping halted and the cobbler emerged from the back of the shop. Kincaid appeared mortal enough; he was an older fellow with a fringe of receding gray hair who might have been on the verge of retirement. He wore an apron and a visor and was still carrying a hammer in one hand. He was not quite short enough to be called dwarfish, but small enough to invite the question. Max wondered idly if the cobbler was wearing lifts.

"Can I help you gentlemen?" Kincaid asked from behind the counter. A trace of an Irish brogue suggested that he had indeed emigrated from the Old Country at some point, along with so many of his countrymen. "We'll be closing shortly, but I can always squeeze in one last customer."

"How very accommodating of you."

Max discreetly cased the establishment while browsing. A quick survey confirmed that no other customers were present, and he sincerely doubted that there were any other workers in the back. Cobblers tended to be solitary sorts and to run one-man operations, which made things ever so much easier. Max paused to admire a pair of high-quality riding boots that had been restored to pristine condition. The leather was supple, the stitching impeccable, the repairs so effective that it was all but impossible to tell how old the boots actually were—they might have been three years old or thirty. Max approved; if there was one thing the Serpent Brotherhood had taught him, it was that even the oldest and most neglected items could be restored to their former glory and power, at least by someone who knew what he was doing.

"Exquisite work," he observed.

"Thank you." Kincaid placed his hammer down on the counter. "I've been at this trade a long time."

"Oh, I'm quite certain of that."

A hint of menace in Max's tone, along with the looming presence of Owens, put the cobbler on guard. Kincaid's eyes narrowed warily and his gaze darted to the hammer lying within easy reach. Max caught the cobbler's sideways glance, and Kincaid noticed Max noticing, much to Max's amusement. He savored the unspoken tension as well as the cobbler's growing uneasiness.

Kincaid swallowed hard. "As I said, we'll be closing up soon. . . ."

"Excellent," Max declared. "So we won't be disturbed then."

He nodded at Owens, who casually flipped over the "Open/Closed" sign hanging by the entrance to better ensure their privacy. Kincaid's eyes widened in alarm. Now certain he was in danger, the cobbler reached for the hammer, but Max was faster. His gloved hand shot forward as swiftly as a striking serpent and seized Kincaid's wrist.

"Consider yourself caught, little man."

Kincaid feigned ignorance. "I don't know what you mean. If it's money you're after—"

"Please, don't waste my time dissembling." Max kept his gaze on the cobbler as he issued a curt command to Owens. "Bind him."

The bodyguard grunted in assent and removed a pair of custom-made, solid-silver handcuffs from his rear pocket. Crossing the shop, he stepped behind the counter and approached Kincaid, who panicked at the sight of the silver cuffs.

"No! You can't! I won't allow it!"

He tried to yank his arm free, but Max maintained an iron grip on the cobbler's wrist—even as the man abruptly transformed into a huge black bear. Standing erect upon its hind legs, the bear roared ferociously at Max. Bone-crunching jaws displayed a mouthful of razor-sharp teeth. Hot breath and drool sprayed Max's face as he suddenly found himself gripping the bear's bristling, black foreleg. A massive paw clawed at the counter, gouging the woodwork.

Or so it appeared.

The illusion was impressive enough that even Owens backed away from the snarling "bear," but Max was not fooled. Steeling himself against the frightening sight and sound and stench of the beast, he kept his eyes fixed on his prisoner and did not let go of the captured limb. The cobbler's startling transformation merely confirmed that Kincaid was no mere mortal.

"A grisly glamour," Max quipped, "or do I mean 'grizzly'?"

The bear growled angrily at his insolence before transforming, in the blink of an eye, into a gigantic striped snake instead. Rising up like a cobra, the monstrous serpent hissed at Max while flaunting its fangs. A forked tongue flicked out. The bear's arm turned into a scaly length of coil that writhed and twisted in Max's grip, trying to wriggle free.

"Is this supposed to scare me?" Max laughed out loud. His Ouroboros ring gleamed on his finger as he tightened his grip on the serpent. "You really have no idea who you're dealing with, do you?"

Owens kept his distance, no doubt baffled as to how to put handcuffs on a snake. Perplexity undermined his typically stony expression. Max decided this pantomime had gone on long enough.

"No more tricks." He twisted the snake as he would a man's wrist, causing the reptile to hiss and spit in fury. Losing patience, Max snatched up the hammer with his free hand and raised it over the trapped coil. "I dislike getting my hands dirty, but I'm not above more direct means of persuasion if required."

And this, he reflected, was why he left Coral behind on these excursions. As formidable as her brain was, she lacked the stomach for such measures.

"I'm counting," he said. "Three, two, one . . ."

"All right, all right!" The snake instantly turned back into Kincaid. "I yield!"

"A wise decision." Max maintained his hold on the man's wrist. The bear's illusory spittle vanished from his face and clothing, just as Max had expected. "What good's a cobbler with a shattered hand?"

No longer deterred by a giant bear or snake, Owens carried out Max's order. None too gently, he clamped a silver cuff on the cobbler's other wrist. Max smiled as he heard the restraint click into place.

The effect of the silver was instantaneous. The leprechaun's true form was finally revealed. His ears tapered to a point. He shrunk in size so that he hung from the countertop, his feet dangling in the air. His clothes, including his apron, turned various shades of green. Years fell away from the cobbler's wizened features, so that he now appeared no more than forty or so.

That's more like it, Max thought.

"Blast ye!" Kincaid railed. Even his brogue and dialect had transformed, becoming more pronounced than before. "Unhand me!"

Max ignored the sprite's vituperations. He gestured to Owens, who lifted the squirming leprechaun up onto the counter. With Kincaid now bound by silver, Max was free to release the captured wrist so that Owens could cuff both of the leprechaun's hands behind his back. The bodyguard's own beefy paws rested heavily on Kincaid's shoulders, holding the prisoner in place. Kincaid winced at the rough handling and glared balefully at Max.

"Let me guess," he said. "'Tis wishes ye want?"

Tempting, Max thought, *but far too risky*. He wasn't the scholar Coral was, but he knew that magic wishes, be they granted by fairies, devils, djinn, or a mummified monkey's paw, almost invariably backfired on the wisher, no matter how carefully the wish was phrased. Max considered himself cleverer than most, but he was also smart enough to recognize the very real dangers of hubris. He had no desire to outsmart himself.

"Keep your wishes," he said. "Where is your pot of gold?"

The frowning leprechaun looked unhappier still. "I should've known. Ye're as greedy as the rest of yer kind."

"Says the pint-sized miser sitting on a hoard of gold." An edge crept into Max's voice as he toyed with the hammer. "You know the rules, little man. Don't make this any more unpleasant than it has to be."

Kincaid proved shrewd enough to know when he was at a disadvantage. "So be it," he said bitterly. "Let me down from here and I'll show youse."

Max nodded at Owens, who set the leprechaun down on the floor behind the counter. The silver handcuffs rendered the leprechaun powerless, but Owens kept close to Kincaid anyway, just in case the sprite foolishly tried to make a break for it. Max hoped the cobber knew better.

"No tricks," he reminded the leprechaun. "We're wise to your ways."

"Have no fear on that account," Kincaid replied. "I want this over and done with even more than ye do. Losing me gold's a small price to be rid of youse!"

"An equitable arrangement," Max agreed. "Shall we proceed?"

Kincaid led them into the back room, which was equipped with a sewing machine, motorized grinders, a tidy work-bench, and generous stockpiles of replacement heels, buckles, zippers, and soles. Glass cupboards held an assortment of brushes and daubers. In one corner, a wooden barrel was filled to overflowing with random scraps of leather that Max assumed had been salvaged from shoes and boots and purses deemed beyond repair. Glancing around, he didn't see anything resembling a pot of gold, but this did not concern him. He hardly expected the leprechaun's treasure to be in plain sight.

Now that *would be suspicious*, he thought. "Show me."

"As ye wish, ye divil."

There was a shimmer in the air, like a mirage fading in or out, and the scrap barrel was replaced by a large black cooking pot filled to the brim with gleaming gold coins and jewelry. Most people would have been transfixed by the miraculous sight, overcome with greed and excitement.

"Damn it all," Max muttered, disappointed.

It was a genuine pot of gold to be sure, piled high with enough precious metal to cover his operating costs for some time. Coral's magic prism had once again led them straight to a mythical fortune beyond any ordinary individual's dreams.

But it was not *the* Pot.

We'll have to keep looking, he realized, sighing wearily. *It's only a matter of time.*

In the meantime, waste not, want not. Max strode forward to claim the pot, hefting it effortlessly by the handle. Ordinarily, a pot of gold would be too heavy for the average mortal to lift easily, but magic made a difference where a leprechaun's pot was concerned. Helpful enchantments ensured that such pots were light enough to be transported by even the littlest of Little People.

Handy, that, Max thought.

Disappointed but determined, he headed out with the gold. A limo waited outside to take him to the airfield where his private jet awaited. Already he was thinking ahead, wondering where the prism would send them next.

"Curse ye for taking me gold!" Kincaid spat at his back. "May it bring ye no happiness!"

"Happiness?" Max said. "I was thinking more along the lines of compound interest."

Only one loose end remained to be attended to. He placed the hammer down on the workbench for Owens.

"You know what to do," he instructed.

The bodyguard grunted.

Kincaid's face went pale. "But . . . but I gave youse me gold!"

True enough, Max thought, but he could not afford to leave any witnesses behind while he was still searching for the Pot. Until he achieved his objective, he preferred to keep a very low profile. The last thing he needed, at this delicate stage in his endeavors, was to attract undue attention from third parties such as the Seelie Court, the Unreal Conclave . . . or the Librarians.

"Don't take too long," he told Owens. "We have places to go."

He helped himself to that fine pair of boots on his way out.

15

"Jenkins! I've got somebody you have to meet."

Dragging Brigid behind her, Cassandra barged into the colony's archives in search of Jenkins. A green-clad sentry was posted outside the entrance, possibly to ensure that Jenkins didn't walk off with any rare tomes, but the guard let the two women rush right into the chamber beyond, where she was surprised to find Jenkins seated in front of . . . a computer?

Shelves of oldish-looking books and parchments lined the walls of a quiet, well-lit space that resembled the main reading room back at the Library, but Jenkins himself was manning the keyboard of a very modern computer terminal. Cassandra blinked at the sight, momentarily taken aback.

"A computer . . . in Mill Ends?"

"This is 2018," MacDonagh commented. The chief leprechaun was settled in a plush wingback chair nearby, puffing on his pipe. "Did ye think we don't keep up with the times?"

"And I'm hardly a dinosaur when it comes to new information technologies," Jenkins observed as he downloaded a file onto a convenient thumb drive, "even if I do predate punch cards and magnetic tape by a considerable margin."

"I . . . I didn't mean to imply otherwise," Cassandra said. "It's just that computers never seemed your style."

"The right tool for the right job, Miss Cillian. I had no desire to transcribe centuries of census records by hand." Looking away from the computer, Jenkins belatedly noticed Brigid. His eyes widened as he "recognized" her, in a manner of speaking. "And this would be . . . ?"

"'Brigid,'" Cassandra explained, "as opposed to 'Bridget.'" She quickly related how she had come across Brigid and what little she had learned of the woman's history. "It's not just me, right? She does look just like the other Bridget?"

"To a striking degree," he confirmed. "You are by no means mistaken."

"I knew it!" she said. "So what's the explanation?"

"A few theories come to mind." Jenkins eyed Brigid speculatively. "Tell me, are you familiar with the concept of changelings . . . ?"

Before he could elaborate, an agitated leprechaun dashed into the archives. "Sir!" he addressed MacDonagh. "Forgive the interruption, but I bring dire tidings!"

MacDonagh sprang to his feet. "Tell me."

The messenger glanced warily at Cassandra and Jenkins, then whispered his news into MacDonagh's ear. The elfin chieftain stiffened in shock. His ruddy face went pale.

"You don't say?" he gasped. "'Tis worse than I feared!"

Cassandra didn't like the sound of this. "What is it? What's the matter?"

"Another murder?" Jenkins guessed. "Another pot of gold stolen?"

MacDonagh nodded grimly. "Just that, and no longer distantly across the ocean. Word has come of another such atrocity . . . in Pittsburgh, no less!"

"Pittsburgh?" Cassandra was stunned by the news. "Here in America?"

"The very same, which is far too close for comfort." Mac-Donagh reacted immediately to the news, firing off orders to his subordinates. "Seal all gates! Double the guards and enhance all glamours and defenses! Let none leave or enter until the danger is passed!"

Let none leave?

"Hold on!" Cassandra said. "You don't mean us, do you?"

"My apologies, good lady, but I can take no chances where the safety of my domain is concerned. Mill Ends must be locked up tight for the duration, so I'm afraid ye and yer distinguished escort shall have to remain our guests for a wee bit longer than anticipated."

Jenkins rose from his seat to confront MacDonagh. "Prisoners, you mean."

"Honored guests," MacDonagh maintained. "Unless ye choose to press the issue, which would be ill-advised on your part."

The sentry from out in the hall stepped into the doorway, his fist gripping a sturdy shillelagh. The messenger dug in his heels beside MacDonagh as well, glowering sternly at Cassandra and Jenkins. The message was obvious if unspoken: the visiting humans were already outnumbered, and that wasn't even counting the entire colony of leprechauns in the burrow beyond. Cassandra found herself regretting that they weren't small enough to drop-kick—and that Baird wasn't around to kick some leprechaun butt.

"But, sir," Brigid protested, "they wish only to return to their own world."

"Keep your peace, foundling," MacDonagh admonished her. "My decision is final." He stepped toward Cassandra and Jenkins and held out his palm. "Your talismans, please."

Jenkins coldly swept his gaze over MacDonagh and his men, as though weighing the odds, before grudgingly removing the four-leaf clover from his lapel and surrendering it to MacDonagh, who took Cassandra's sprig as well.

"Is he confiscating our passports?" she asked.

"More or less," Jenkins said, "while taking away our ability to see through whatever illusions might be concealing the exits."

"'Tis exactly so." MacDonagh tucked the clovers in his vest pocket for safekeeping. "Neither ye nor anyone one will be able to find their way in or out of Mill Ends until the danger is passed." He offered them a conciliatory smile. "But please don't feel too inconvenienced. Fitting quarters will be prepared for youse, and ye may count on us to make yer stay as comfortable as possible."

Cassandra wasn't feeling it.

"For how long?" she demanded.

A pained smile greeted her query. "No longer than necessary."

"By mortal standards, that could be a *very* long time," Jenkins said, discreetly pocketing the thumb drive on which he had downloaded the leprechauns' records. "And I'm afraid we don't have years to spare, let alone centuries."

Cassandra did a double take. "Did you say *centuries*?"

"Again, my apologies," MacDonagh said. "'Tis a pity, but there's nothing to be done."

We'll see about that, Cassandra thought.

Visiting Otherworld was one thing, but dancing a jig for a

century or two was not on her bucket list. The Library was waiting for her, along with the rest of her life.

"I'm so sorry," Brigid said. "Ye should have never come here."

"Would you believe I volunteered?"

16

The Pot O' Gold was doing good business. Plenty of customers, many of them obviously regulars, were enjoying the pub's spirits and atmosphere, along with live fiddle music provided by a grizzled old Irish guy who was apparently a fixture at the place. Baird had staked out a place at the bar, where she was slowly nursing a single beer. She was on-duty, as it were, so she was watching her intake as well as the clientele.

"Popular place," she observed to Bridget, who was busy behind the bar, where Stone had pitched in to help out, bartending being among his many unexpected talents, while Baird and Ezekiel staked out the scene. There had been no banshee sightings yet, but the night was young.

"Just wait until Thursday!" Bridget drew a pint of stout from a tap—slowly, to give it a proper head of foam—and handed it to a waiting customer. "Saint Patrick's Day is always our biggest day of the year, not to mention our most profitable."

Baird could believe it. "So I guess lying low until we sort out this whole banshee business is not an option?"

"Not if I want to stay in business," Bridget said, wiping her brow. "Saint Pat's Day is a big deal here in Chicago: parades, parties—they even dye the river green for the occasion. I can't afford to miss out on the festivities." She leaned toward Baird, lowering her voice in order to avoid being overheard. "Plus, how do you hide out from a banshee anyway?"

"Good question," Baird conceded. As far as she knew, there wasn't a Banshee Victim Protection Program.

"Personally, I'm looking forward to checking out the scene Thursday," Ezekiel said. By amazing coincidence, he had taken a seat at the bar right where the magic gold coin was displayed. "Saint Patrick's Day is one of my favorite holidays."

"Funny," Stone commented from the other side of the bar, "you don't look Irish."

"Haven't you heard?" Ezekiel said, grinning. "Everyone is Irish on Saint Patrick's Day. And what with all the green beer and tipsy people not paying close attention to their personal belongings . . . it's better than Christmas."

Baird rolled her eyes. *Once a thief, always a thief. . . .*

"Don't even think about it," she warned him. "We're here on Library business, remember."

"Gotta admit, though," Stone said, "there are probably worse ways to spend Saint Patrick's Day than camping out at an Irish pub."

I suppose, Baird thought, although she hoped they wouldn't have to stake out the pub for two more days. In theory, they were on hand to see if the banshee made an appearance to-night, while also keeping an eye on Bridget to protect her from whatever life-threatening jeopardy the banshee might be warning her about, be that the Serpent Brotherhood, her dam-aged heart, or something else altogether. *Too bad the banshee couldn't be more specific about what sort of danger we should be looking out for.*

Baird shifted restlessly atop the barstool. As much as she

liked and sympathized with Bridget, she still wasn't entirely convinced that this was the best use of the Librarians' time. Who knew what the Serpent Brotherhood was up to while they were stuck here, cooling their heels in an admittedly cozy bar, waiting for a crybaby fairy to show up?

Here's hoping Jenkins and Cassandra are making more progress on their end of the investigation . . .

Applause rippled across the pub as the fiddler wrapped up his set.

"Thank ye kindly." He doffed his cap in acknowledgment as he carefully laid his fiddle and bow down on a stool. "I'll be taking a wee break now if ye don't mind. Ye wouldn't think it, but fiddling's thirsty work, so it is."

Leaving his instrument behind, he wandered over to the bar, where Bridget had a glass of amber whiskey waiting for him. "Here you go, old man. Jameson's, neat, just how you like it."

"Ah, thank ye, Bridget, me darling. Ye're an angel, ye are."

The fiddler certainly looked the part, as though he'd stepped out of some old Hollywood movie set in a colorful Irish village. He was a lanky fellow with bright eyes and a jovial expression, whose bushy eyebrows and scraggly beard had long ago surrendered to the gray. A well-worn paddy cap rested atop his head, while his rumpled tweed jacket was patched at the elbows. Calluses on his palm and index fingers were flushed from fiddling.

He raised his glass to toast all present. *"Slainte!"*

"Right back at you." Baird lifted her glass. "I enjoyed your music, by the way."

"Pleased I am to hear that, truly." The fiddler sat down at the bar next to her. "And who might ye be?"

Bridget stepped in to provide introductions. "This is Eve

Baird, who is visiting from Oregon, along with her friends." She gestured toward Stone and Ezekiel. "Eve, meet Grady, a devilish old rascal if ever there was one, and one of the best Irish fiddlers in Chicago."

"Och, ye're just saying that 'cause I'll play for spirits," Grady said, pausing to imbibe some of his liquid compensation. "Not that I have any objections to the arrangement, mind ye."

"So I can count on you Thursday night?" Bridget asked.

"And where else would I be?" Grady answered. "This fine establishment is me home away from home away from me old home." He sighed wistfully. "If I can't be back in the Auld Sod for the sainted Patrick's day, this be the next best thing, so it is."

Baird picked up on the homesickness in his voice. "You miss Ireland, do you?"

"Every blessed day," Grady confessed, "but . . . well, let's just say that it would be unwise to return in this lifetime, no matter how fiercely my poor heart yearns to look upon Erin's emerald shores once more."

"That's too bad." Baird assumed that the old man's self-imposed exile had something to do with "The Troubles" of years past, but didn't feel obliged to press him for the details. "Still, Ireland's loss is Chicago's gain."

"A fine attitude," Grady said, his mood lifting along with his glass. "So how do ye and yer friends come to know our Bridget?"

'We're librarians," Stone said, joining the conversation. "Doing a research project on the Irish-American experience." He wiped down the counter with a damp rag. "Hands-on research, obviously."

"Fascinating," Grady said, "and a worthy project to be sure. Ireland is famous for its scholars and libraries, so it is." He eyed Baird carefully. "Still, I would not have pegged ye as a librarian."

"Well, *they're* librarians," she confessed. "I'm more like . . . security."

"Is that so?" Grady raised an eyebrow. "Who knew librarians needed security these days?" He polished off his whiskey and looked to Bridget for a refill. "Bridget, me darling . . . ?"

"Way ahead of you." She began to refill Grady's glass from a bottle of Jameson's, only to suddenly freeze mid-pour. Her face went pale and she stared in shock at something beyond the bar. "No, not now, not here. . . ."

"Steady, me girl." Grady gently raised her arm as the glass overflowed, spilling whiskey onto the bar. "Ye don't want to be wasting that."

Baird was more worried about what Bridget was reacting to. She immediately kicked into high-alert mode, as did her Librarians. Stone and Ezekiel both dropped what they were doing and put their game faces on.

"What is it?" Baird asked, softly but urgently.

"That woman, there in the corner," Bridget said, her voice quavering. Her eyes remained fixed on the sight. "I swear, she wasn't there a moment ago."

Turning, Baird followed Bridget's gaze to see what had alarmed her. She strained to see past the other customers milling about, but quickly located the woman in question: a solitary figure wearing a hooded gray cape, sitting alone at a table in the far corner of the pub. The woman's head was bowed, staring into an empty glass, so Baird couldn't make out her face. Looking closer, however, she saw that the woman's body seemed to be quaking beneath her thick woolen cloak, as though she was sobbing.

A weeping woman in gray?

Baird's brain made the connection. "Is that . . . her?" The banshee?

"Maybe. I'm not sure," Bridget whispered. "She doesn't always look the same. . . ."

Right, Baird recalled. *Maiden, mother, crone, and all that.*

Bridget was visibly trembling. Stone prudently took the whiskey bottle from her shaky hand as the redheaded bartender whimpered in fear.

"She . . . she's never come inside before. . . ."

Baird hopped off the stool to investigate. To be honest, part of her was relieved to be finally getting down to business. They had come to Chicago to deal with a banshee, so she was anxious to get on with it. She just hoped this wasn't a false alarm.

"Leave her be, miss." Grady placed his hand on Baird's arm to restrain her. "No good will come of this."

"Sorry," Baird said, not entirely sure where he was coming from or what exactly he thought this was about. "That's not how I roll."

Shaking off his grip, she glanced back at her team. "Stone, you stay close to Bridget. Make sure nothing happens to her."

"And I'll guard the magic gold," Ezekiel volunteered. "What?" he said off her look. "Somebody needs to keep an eye on it."

Baird started to roll her eyes, then realized he had a point. The Serpent Brotherhood *had* been chasing after that leprechaun's gold back in the day, and the Librarians had established a possible link between the gold coins and the banshee haunting.

"Just keep an eye on the door, too," she ordered. If this was their banshee, Baird didn't want her getting away before they could get some answers at last. "Stay sharp, people."

She made her away across the crowded pub. Given the number of unsuspecting civilians around, she figured it was probably just as well that the whole team wasn't ganging up on the mystery woman; Baird didn't want to cause a scene if she could avoid one. She quietly approached the suspect, going in smooth and easy. As she drew nearer to the table, she definitely thought she heard, over the general hubbub, low sobs coming from the hooded stranger. Just somebody crying into their beer after a very bad day, Baird wondered, or something more sinister? The sobbing started to attract concerned and/or annoyed looks from nearby customers, a few of whom looked relieved to see Baird walk right up to the woman. No doubt they preferred to let somebody else deal with her.

"Excuse me," Baird said. "Do you mind if I join you?"

Without waiting for an answer, she sat down opposite the woman in gray, who kept her face turned down toward the table as she wrung her hands in seeming despair. The hands appeared smooth and unblemished and youngish.

Maiden, then, Baird concluded.

If the seemingly young woman noticed Baird's arrival, she did not acknowledge it. Instead she began moaning, a low keening that tugged at Baird's sympathy even as it sent a chill down her spine. She wished again that there weren't so many civilians present.

"Is something wrong?" Baird asked softly. "Do you want to talk about it, maybe somewhere more private?"

She reached out and laid a gentle hand on the woman's arm, only to be shocked by how cold it felt to the touch. There was no human warmth there, only the cold of a bleak winter night . . . or the grave.

But Baird's touch provoked a reaction. Sitting up abruptly, the woman threw back her hood to reveal the corpse-white, tear-streaked face of a young woman with hypoxic blue lips, wild brown hair, and blank white eyes with no visible pupils or irises.

Uh-oh, Baird thought. *Little Orphan Annie eyes are* never *a good sign.*

The woman's mouth opened, her bottom jaw falling farther than humanly possible, revealing a bottomless chasm from which emerged a hellish, high-pitched, high-decibel keening that instantly drowned all other sounds as its pitch and volume rocketed upward at a deafening rate.

In short, the banshee screamed.

Baird instinctively clamped her hands over her ears. Glasses shattered all across the pub, spraying beer and whiskey everywhere. Lightbulbs in the hanging lamps exploded, causing sparks to rain down on startled customers. Alarmed, Baird glanced back at Bridget and saw Stone playing bodyguard, shielding Bridget with his body and pulling her down behind the bar as whiskey bottles went off like firecrackers. The mirror behind the bar cracked down the middle, as Ezekiel and Grady and others dived for cover behind stools and tables. Ezekiel had his hands over his ears, grimacing in discomfort along with everyone else in the pub. Flickering lights created a strobe effect as panicked customers bolted for the exits, knocking over the furniture and each other in their frantic attempts to escape the chaos and the din. Baird assumed that people were shrieking and shouting and swearing, but couldn't hear them over the ear-piercing cry of the banshee.

That's right, she silently urged the fleeing civilians. *Get far away from here, pronto.*

The banshee, on the other hand, was not going anywhere, if Baird had anything to say about it. Risking her hearing, Baird tore her hands from her ears and lunged for the banshee, determined to silence and apprehend her, preferably in that order. Her hands seized the woman's wool cloak, her fingers sinking into the freezing fabric. She was ready to shake some answers out of the banshee if necessary.

"That's enough!" Baird shouted at the top of her lungs, still unable to hear herself regardless. "Stop wailing and start talking! What's this all about?!!"

Lights sparked and sputtered overhead. Baird tugged hard on the cape, which went limp in her grasp. She blinked in surprise as she suddenly found herself holding an empty cloak that had held a woman inside it only a heartbeat before. She looked around in confusion, but the weeping woman/maiden/banshee was gone, vanished into thin air.

Yet her wail lingered, echoing in Baird's ears for several long moments before finally fading away along with the cloak, which dissolved into a cold, damp mist before dissipating entirely.

"Crap," Baird said.

She was reassured to hear her own voice again, but there was little else to celebrate. Blowing on her chilled fingers to warm them, she took in the messy aftermath of the banshee's visit. The pub was trashed: tables and chairs overturned, broken glass and spilled booze everywhere. Bridget was going to have a hell of a job getting the place put back together in time for business tomorrow, if she was even interested in re-opening at this point. The panicky exodus had emptied the pub of customers, but nobody seemed to have been seriously hurt in the stampede, at least as far as Baird could see.

"Everyone okay?" she called.

Murmured assents came from the few people remaining: Bridget, Stone, Ezekiel, and even Grady, who had apparently stuck around when everyone else had run for the hills. Baird remembered her earlier suspicions about his involvement in The Troubles decades ago and figured that he'd probably seen worse than a stray banshee or two; he'd been through the wars in his time.

"My ears are killing me," Ezekiel said, "but don't worry: I saved the gold!"

Sure enough, the glass sheet over the gold coin had shattered as well, but the coin rested safely in the thief's outstretched palm. Baird was genuinely relieved to see that nobody had absconded with the magical gold in the tumult. That possibility hadn't even occurred to her until this moment.

"Good job, Jones," she said. "Just remember, you don't get to keep it."

"Party pooper," he said, smirking.

Stone and Bridget leaned against the bar, which they had taken shelter behind earlier. Stone had his arm around Bridget, who was understandably shaken. She trembled uncontrollably, looking nearly as pale as the banshee. Baird hoped her bad heart was up to the stress.

"You all saw her?" Bridget asked. "Heard her? It wasn't just me this time?"

"Oh, we heard her all right." Baird's ears were still ringing. "It's official: we've definitely got a banshee on our hands."

And the situation seems to be escalating, she added silently.

"That it's then," Bridget moaned. "I'm doomed. I think part of me was still kinda hoping you'd prove me wrong, that this was all in my head, after all, but now that we know for sure . . . I'm as good as dead."

"Nay, don't say that." Grady tried to comfort her. "Ye mustn't lose heart, me fine girl."

"But don't you know who that was?" she said. "*What* that was?"

"The *bean-sidhe*," he said somberly, sounding none too surprised by proof of a banshee's existence, as though he had always taken it for granted. "But ye can't be sure that it's truly ye she's keening for. It may be the death-coach is coming for another."

"Who?" she demanded tearfully. "Who else could it be?"

Grady shook his head sadly. "That I cannot say."

Because Bridget is the obvious target, Baird thought. She appreciated Grady's attempt to console the woman, but he was offering false hope at best—not that Baird had anything better to offer at the moment. Still, she no longer regretted involving the Librarians in Bridget's case. This was exactly the kind of spooky, supernatural terrorism the Library was meant to protect people from, and Bridget was an innocent victim who needed their help. Baird wasn't about to abandon her now, even if that meant putting the Serpent Brotherhood on the back burner for the time being.

Speaking of whom, Baird thought, *I wonder what Cassandra and Jenkins have learned by now—and why we haven't heard from them yet.*

17

The map of Pittsburgh had been rolled up and put away, replaced by the map of the USA, which was once more spread out atop a table. The first light of dawn streamed through Coral's magic prism, transforming into a rainbow that arced above the table before diving like a dowsing rod toward a specific spot on the map, somewhere in the middle of the country.

"There we go," Max said.

He moved quickly to mark the spot, hoping as always that this would be the last time they performed this ritual. Pittsburgh had proven to be yet another disappointment, despite the consolation prize of the cobbler's pot of gold. Max was tired of wasting time on false leads. The Pot was waiting for him . . . somewhere.

"Do you have it?" Coral asked eagerly. "Where to this time?"

Max consulted the marked map. "Illinois. Chicago, to be exact."

"Ooh!" Coral lowered the prism as the rainbow dissolved back into plain white light. "I've never been to Chicago."

"Pack your bags," Max replied. Although he always left

Coral behind when he actually went to claim a pot of gold from an unwilling leprechaun, he preferred to keep her close at hand no matter where he traveled. He was going to need her when he found the Pot, after all.

He was already texting the jet crew to alert them to their next destination. By his calculations, they could be in Chicago with hours—and ready to summon the rainbow again at noon. Glancing at the date, he was amused to note that Saint Patrick's Day was only a day away.

An omen of sorts?

The irony appealed to him. Centuries ago, a certain Padraic had helped keep the Serpent Brotherhood from obtaining the Pot the first time around. It would be perversely amusing if they finally found it again on or around the saint's own day.

"This is it," Coral said, ever the optimist. "I feel it in my bones."

Max glanced over at Lady Sibella's skull, waiting patiently atop the aluminum reliquary containing the rest of her remains.

If only those bones could talk as well. . . .

18

"I can't believe we're stuck here," Cassandra vented for the umpteenth time. She paced back and forth across the archives chamber. "What does MacDonagh think? That the Serpent Brotherhood is going to slither right in the minute we try to slip out?"

Hours had passed since Mill Ends had gone into lockdown. She and Jenkins had been left alone in the archives so that Jenkins could at least continue his research in the interim, while MacDonagh had departed to personally see to the colony's security in the wake of the Pittsburgh attack. Brigid had slipped away as well, no doubt embarrassed by the whole situation.

"That we know the way in and out of Mill Ends is surely also a consideration," Jenkins said. A hefty tome rested open in his lap as he bided his time in the comfy chair MacDonagh had vacated. "Under the present circumstances, MacDonagh no doubt prefers to keep that information confined, lest the Serpent Brotherhood somehow attempt to use us to gain access to Otherworld."

Jenkins shifted his weight in the chair. Cassandra was

surprised that he could remain so calm in captivity, but she imagined that immortality taught one patience over time. It took a lot to make Jenkins lose his cool.

"That being said," he added, "this forced confinement comes at a very inconvenient time." He closed the book on his lap. "I believe I've learned all we need to know here. The sooner we can return to the Library, so I can embark on some judicious cross-referencing, the better."

Cassandra wondered if Baird and the others had missed them yet. "Any chance that our friends will be coming to liberate us?"

"Eventually, perhaps," Jenkins said. "Certainly, Mister Carsen might have some ideas and options should it come to that, if and when he returns from undersea, but there's no way of knowing what might be occupying our compatriots at the moment. They may well be preoccupied with a hostile banshee as we speak. Or even, conceivably, the latest incarnation of the Serpent Brotherhood."

"Right," Cassandra said glumly. "For all we know, they're counting on us to come to *their* rescue."

Her stomach grumbled, reminding her that she had not eaten since departing the Annex a good while ago. A tempting repast, provided by their apologetic "hosts," sat uneaten on a desk nearby. A bowl of Irish stew, accompanied by generous plates of bread and cheese, called out to her, despite Jenkins's warnings earlier.

"So, anyway," she said, "about the whole food-and-drink thing . . ."

Jenkins contemplated the enticing Irish cuisine. "Traditionally, accepting refreshments in any sort of underworld is not a good idea if you don't want to end up losing any desire or ability to leave, but given that we're all already under house arrest as it were, we may have to compromise on that front eventually." His own stomach rumbled audibly. "Mind you, I once fasted for more than a year during a prolonged stay in Lyonesse. . . ."

Cassandra was about to point out that she probably couldn't hold out that long when Brigid quietly slipped back into the grotto.

"Brigid?" she said. "I was wondering what happened to—"

"Hush!" Brigid held a finger to her lips. She glanced around the library to confirm that they were alone before continuing in a low voice. "If I show ye a way out of Mill Ends, will ye take me with youse? I'm ever so longing to see the world I came from . . . and this other Bridget who ye say could be my double."

Once again, Cassandra was struck by how much Brigid resembled her twin back in the real world. It dawned on her that, distracted by the new murder and its aftermath, she and Jenkins had yet to figure out what the story was there. What was it Jenkins had said about "changelings" before?

"We would be delighted to show you our world," Jenkins said, quick to seize the opportunity Brigid held out to them, "if there is indeed a path open to us."

"Sure and there is," she said. "I keep my eyes and ears open, which is how I heard tell of a secret escape route back to the world. In truth, I've oft been tempted to dare the path on me own, but I've never had the courage, since there's also said to be cunning traps and lures along the way." Her emerald eyes gleamed with excitement. "Yet with yer help, perhaps we can all take leave of this place?"

"That's the best offer I've heard all day," Cassandra said. "Jenkins?"

"Do not expect that this will be easy," Jenkins warned, "despite our new friend's timely assistance. Nevertheless, we would be fools to let this chance pass by." He rose from the chair and gestured toward the exit. "Please lead on, Miss Brigid."

"Come," she said, sounding both tense and relieved. "But tread softly while the Fair Folk sleep."

They slipped out into the hall, where they found the sentry slumped against the wall, snoring loudly. A jug rested in his lap, while his shillelagh had slipped from his fingers onto the floor.

"Drinking on the job?" Cassandra said. "For shame."

"Do not judge him too harshly," Brigid said. "It may be that a powerful sleeping draught came with the wee bit of refreshment I offered him ever so thoughtfully." She shrugged. "'Twill do him no harm, although his head may feel like the very divil come morning, by which time we shall be well away from here, if the fates be with us."

Cassandra was impressed. "Crafty!"

"One doesn't grow up among the Folk without learning a thing or two about shenanigans," Brigid said with a smirk. "But let's not tarry. Time is a-wasting!"

"Sound advice." Jenkins helped himself to the drugged leprechaun's shillelagh and hefted it in his grip. "Shall we be on our way?"

Brigid led them through a bewildering maze of underground passages and side-tunnels, which were quieter and more dimly lit than before. The stillness reminded Cassandra of the graveyard shift at some of the hospitals she'd spent too much time in back in her pre-Librarian days. She pushed aside the memory; that was not her life anymore.

"Where is everybody?" she asked.

"Sleeping off this evening's hooley," Brigid explained, "or else locked away in their chambers, fearing for their lives and gold."

Cassandra couldn't blame them on that latter score, especially if the Serpent Brotherhood was involved. They were scary enough to drive anybody to hide behind closed doors.

"With any luck," Brigid said, "our way will be clear."

Cassandra didn't like relying on luck. *Too bad they took our four-leaf clovers.*

Brigid stuck with unfrequented back corridors until they had to take a necessary shortcut through the ballroom Cassandra had visited earlier. The festivities were long over, however, with many an exhausted celebrant passed out atop oversize mushrooms, mossy boulders, and each other. The fiddler was catching forty winks as well, so the only music came from one off-key leprechaun butchering "Danny Boy" in his sleep. Jenkins winced, with reason.

"Looks like quite a blowout," Cassandra whispered as they tiptoed carefully around the slumbering partyers. "Is it Celtic New Year's Eve or something?"

"'Tisn't," Brigid answered. "Why do you ask?"

"Never mind," Cassandra said, concluding that leprechauns simply knew how to have a good time. It occurred to her that Saint Patrick's Day was getting close, at least by Real World Time. She wasn't sure whether to be relieved or disappointed that they'd be missing that bash here in Mill Ends. *Assuming we can even find our way out of here.*

Somehow they made it across the ballroom without waking anyone. Cassandra started to relax, only to spot a pair of green-clad guards heading toward them. Short woolen capes held on by a broach, along with surly expressions, differentiated the soldiers from the other leprechauns. She froze, briefly tempted to double back the way they'd come, but it was too late for that. The guards had already spotted them.

"Oh-oh," she murmured.

Jenkins began to raise his borrowed shillelagh, but Brigid discreetly shook her head. "Follow me lead," she whispered before falling back between Jenkins and Cassandra and throwing her arms around their waists. She giggled loudly and added a drunken list to her gait as she tottered toward the approaching men.

"How's she cutting, me fine boys!"

"Brigid?" one of the men said, seemingly puzzled to bump into this unlikely trio. "What are ye about at this unseemly hour of the morning? 'Tis fierce late to be roaming so, and in such company."

"So ye say, Fergus O'Toole!" she exclaimed merrily, slurring her words somewhat. "Sure the night is young, and don't ye be telling me any different!"

The other guard regarded Jenkins and Cassandra suspiciously. "And what are ye doing with these two?"

"And what business be that of yours, me man?" she shot back, giggling some more. She pulled both Jenkins and Cassandra in closer to her. "MacDonagh himself did request that we make our guests feel quite at home, so ye'll pardon me for doing just that!"

Cassandra blushed in embarrassment, while Jenkins stared resolutely at the ceiling, striving to maintain his dignity as best he could.

"I see," O'Toole said. "Is that what you're calling it then?" The guards exchanged knowing looks before stepping aside to let them pass. "Very well then. Away with you. Some of us have more serious duties to attend to, like protecting the Folk from those who would do us ill."

"And don't we all appreciate it?" Brigid slurred, leading the other two mortals past the smirking guards. "Eyes sharp, me lads!"

She staggered unsteadily between Jenkins and Cassandra until the guards were out of view, then released her hold on her partners-in-crime. A chuckle betrayed her pride in her own cleverness.

"So much for me reputation," she said, "but 'tis a small price to pay to finally see the world above."

Jenkins sighed. "Was that performance truly necessary?"

"Ye would have preferred to trade blows with those buck eejits?"

"Possibly," Jenkins said. "Probably."

Cassandra changed the subject. "How much farther to the escape route?"

"Just a short ways," Brigid promised.

True to her word, they soon reached a dead end of sorts: a gaping chasm in the earth that was, oddly enough, guarded by a particularly tough-looking leprechaun, which was not a description that would have ever occurred to Cassandra before. Surly eyes glowered above a shaggy red beard. A curved hunting horn hung from his belt. He gripped a heavy wooden club and stood nearly as tall as Jenkins himself. A boxer's nose and cauliflower ears suggested that he was no stranger to brawling.

"That's far enough," the looming leprechaun said gruffly. "Turn around and go back the way ye came."

Cassandra got the distinct impression that this guy wasn't going to fall for Brigid's giggly party-girl routine. His very presence, however, begged a pertinent question: Why position a sentry in front of a bottomless ravine?

Unless appearances were again deceptive?

"Is this it?" she asked Brigid. "What we're looking for?"

"'Tis." The other woman nodded. "Or so they say."

"And none too soon." Jenkins strode forward. "Remind me to think twice the next time I feel inclined to go calling on the Wee Folk."

"Go no farther!" The sentry raised his club in a menacing manner. "I'm warning ye."

Jenkins was undaunted. Flipping his shillelagh in his hand, he grasped the heavy end of the cudgel as though it were the hilt of a sword. He swung it about, testing its balance.

"Not exactly Excalibur," he observed, "but it will have to do."

The sentry gulped. Still brandishing his own weapon, he reached for the horn on his belt to sound an alarm.

"Come no closer! Ye don't know who ye're trifling with."

"I believe that's *my* line," Jenkins said.

He lunged forward with both speed and power. The tip of the shillelagh jabbed the guard's wrist before he even saw the attack coming. The horn flew from the leprechaun's fingers and went flying off into the chasm, and his jaw dropped as his gaze swung back and forth between his suddenly empty hand and Jenkins, who barely seemed to have broken a sweat.

"I'd advise you to let us pass," the caretaker said, "although I suppose I can use the exercise after sitting at a desk all day."

"Blackguard! Mortal swine!"

"Mortal?" Jenkins said. "Not exactly."

The guard charged at Jenkins, swinging his club, but he was no match for a former knight of the Round Table. Jenkins nimbly sidestepped the attack, ducking beneath the guard's truncheon, and pivoted to bring his shillelagh squarely across the back of the leprechaun's skull with a satisfying thunk. The big little man fell forward, face-planting at Cassandra's feet. She hurriedly stamped her foot on the hand holding the club, just in case he still had some fight in him, but it turned out he was down for the count. She kicked the club into the chasm anyway.

"Och!" Brigid exclaimed. "Yer man's a right corker, he is!"

"Don't I know it?" Cassandra beamed at Jenkins. "Mac-Donagh was right about you, you know."

"Oh," he said. "And how is that, Miss Cillian?"

"You *are* still a knight."

"Nonsense. I'm merely a caretaker in a hurry to get back to his work." He turned away from his fallen foe to contemplate the chasm gaping before them. "Although this does rather remind me of a bottomless pit I once encountered while in pursuit of a certain grail."

Cassandra and Brigid joined him at the brink of the chasm. Peering into the gulf, Cassandra saw nothing but a long fall into inky, impenetrable darkness. It took plenty of nerve not to back away from the precipice.

"That's it?" she asked uncertainly. "The way out?"

"Why else post a sentry before it?" Jenkins said, echoing her own earlier thoughts. "And falling down to go back up to the surface world? That's just the sort of trickiness you'd expect from a leprechaun." He stared into the abyss. "I must say, however, that if this is an illusion, it's quite the convincing one."

"Too convincing." Cassandra fingered the buttonhole that had once held the protective four-leaf clover. "This would be easier if we could see past any magic tricks."

"I cannot disagree," Jenkins said. "Still, we've come this far, so I'm not inclined to turn back now."

"In for a penny, in for a pound," Brigid said. "Or so they say."

Cassandra looked back the way they came. The vanquished guard was still sprawled on the ground but he was bound to come to eventually.

"MacDonagh's not going to be happy about this," she said.

"All the more reason not to delay our departure." Jenkins stepped up to the edge of the chasm. "Ordinarily, I would say 'Ladies first,' but in this instance perhaps you had best permit me to take the lead."

"No," Cassandra said decisively. "We're doing this together or not at all."

"But—" Jenkins started to protest.

"No buts," she said, pulling rank. "You may be immortal, but I'm not, and you're not leaving me alone here for who knows how long." She glanced over at Brigid. "No offense."

"None taken," the other woman said.

"It's decided then," Cassandra said. "On my count . . . three, two, one . . . *Erin go Bragh!*"

They jumped together into the abyss. Gravity seized her, and as she found herself with nothing but empty air beneath her, Cassandra had time enough to wonder if maybe she should have taken Jenkins up on his offer to go first, after all, but then bright golden sunlight replaced the darkness and she

landed in the midst of a seemingly endless field of clover somewhere beneath a bright blue sky. A warm, gentle breeze felt like
summer.

Come again?

Cassandra took a moment to appreciate that she wasn't
splattered at the bottom of a ravine, then looked around.
Jenkins and Brigid, who had also landed safely in the meadow,
did the same. The vast field of clover appeared to stretch in
all directions, for as far as the eye could see. They clearly
weren't underground anymore, and yet . . .

"This doesn't look like Portland," she said.

"And what does Portland look like?" Brigid asked.

The unseasonal weather worried Cassandra. How long had
they spent in Otherworld anyway, relative to the real world?

"This isn't Ireland, is it?" she asked.

"I think not," Jenkins replied, a dour look on his face. He
bent to pluck a shamrock from the acres of clover surrounding them. "More likely it is another illusion hiding the actual
exit from Otherworld. One of the traps and snares our guide
alluded to earlier."

Cassandra turned around and around, seeing nothing resembling a path to follow. "So which way do we go now?"

Jenkins gestured at the sprawling carpet of clover. "The
only way to see through the glamour is to find another four-
leaf clover . . . which could take a while, given that only one
in ten thousand clovers have four leaves instead of three."

"Och!" Brigid gasped at the enormity of the task. "Finding
one lucky clover amidst a sea of shamrocks . . . sure and it will
take forever!"

"Well, not forever," Jenkins said, "but at least long enough
for MacDonagh and his men to catch up with us."

Brigid dropped to the ground and began sorting through the shamrocks, one by one.

"Wait!" Cassandra said. "We don't have time for that. There may be a better way."

Brigid looked confused. "How is that?"

"Wait and see." Jenkins nodded at Cassandra. "Wait and see."

Cassandra took a deep breath, not letting the seemingly infinite number of clovers intimidate her. Her senses mingled and merged as she put her magic brain to work. The gentle rustling of the shamrocks turned into a symphony of shimmering numbers and equations that tinkled like calculus and tasted like geometry.

"It's all about the math," she murmured, mostly to herself. "If one in ten thousand clovers has four leafs, and"—she took a moment to listen to the colors and watch the sounds rising from the field—"there's roughly two hundred clovers per every nine square inches of the field, then we can expect, on an average, one four-leaf clover"—the calculations shimmered before her eyes—"in every thirteen square feet of shamrocks."

That was a much more manageable area to search than the entire field, but she was just getting warmed up. Her brain superimposed a hallucinatory grid, about the size of a standard office desk, on one thirteen-square-foot patch of clover. She then proceeded to break down that grid into smaller and smaller grids, while applying basic geometry to the problem. If ordinary three-leafed shamrocks were basically triangles, but four-leaf shamrocks were squares, then all she had to do was eliminate the triangles, which were now outlined in pink in her mind's eye, and . . .

"There we go!"

A single green square flashed within the grid. It chimed like a harp and smelled like marshmallows. Grinning in triumph, Cassandra plucked a perfect four-leaf clover from the surrounding shamrock. The imaginary grid popped out of existence as her brain ramped back down again. It occurred to her that there was something almost mathematically elegant about using a hallucination to beat an illusion. Like two opposing factors canceling each other out.

"So swiftly?" Brigid looked up in surprise from where she had been scouring for a lucky clover on her own. "Are ye a sorceress?"

"More like a mathemagician," Cassandra explained, sort of. She was still determined to make that word a thing. "But don't be too impressed until we see if this works."

Closing her eyes, she affixed the four-leaf clover to her sweater.

Here goes nothing, she thought.

She opened her eyes to a whole new scene. The endless clover was gone, vanished like a mirage, and instead she found herself in a subterranean grotto, facing a stone stairway leading up to . . . freedom?

"Oh my goodness," she exclaimed. "I can see it! The way out!"

"Where?" Brigid asked, looking about in bewilderment. She and Jenkins were still seeing the illusory field of clover, Cassandra realized. "I believe ye, truly, but me poor eyes see only what they see."

"Trust me," Cassandra said. Magic brain or not, she wasn't about to waste time finding two more four-leaf clovers for her companions. "You got us this far. Let me guide us the rest of the way."

Jenkins took her hand and offered his other to Brigid, form-ing a chain with Cassandra at the front. "With pleasure, Miss Cillian."

"Good." She started toward the stairs. A damp, earthy smell, like a forest, wafted down from above. "Now close your eyes and follow me."

She couldn't wait to get back to the Library—and find out what was happening with the rest of the team.

19

❋ *Chicago* ❋

Despite the tumult of the night before, which they were officially blaming on "a crazed opera singer on drugs," the pub had drawn a decent post-lunch crowd. Ezekiel yawned as he shared a table with Baird, consuming a coffee of the non-Irish variety. They had spent most of the night and the better part of the morning helping Bridget clean up after the banshee vandalism and had even managed to put some Saint Patrick's Day decorations up as well, in anticipation of the festivities tomorrow. A large plastic pot of fake gold pieces sat by the fireplace, not far from where Grady was softly playing his fiddle. Stone was again behind the bar, assisting Bridget, who was still recovering from last night's haunting, which had been a little too up close and personal for comfort.

"Still no word from Cassandra or Jenkins." Baird stared worriedly at her phone. "I don't like this. How long can it take to talk to some leprechauns?"

"Depends on whether you're after their Lucky Charms or not," Ezekiel joked. "Seriously, what's keeping them? Don't they realize we're stranded here until Jenkins gets back to the Annex and can open a Magic Door for us?"

"Well, we're not exactly 'stranded,'" Baird said. "There are still such things as cars and planes, you know."

Ezekiel shrugged. "What can I say? The Magic Door has spoiled me. Who wants to spend hours in transit when you can just—"

Baird's phone chimed, interrupting him. She hushed him as she checked her messages. A sigh of relief escaped her lips. "About time."

Ezekiel leaned forward. "Is it—?"

"It's Cassandra," Baird stated. "She and Jenkins are back . . . and they have news."

———

"The Pot O' Gold," Max observed, amused and intrigued by the pub's name. He trusted that Coral's magic prism had not been deceived by a bit of not-so-clever marketing. "A bit on the nose, don't you think?"

Owens grunted as they entered the pub.

Max glanced around the establishment, noting with annoyance that the number of customers present precluded any immediate action. He would have to be content to case the establishment at present and return later, perhaps after closing, to actually procure whatever genuine pot of gold must be hiding in the vicinity, behind the usual tavern trappings and the festive paper shamrocks strung about here and there. He wondered what the late, unlamented Padraic would make of the tawdry holiday decorations festooned in his name.

A shame he didn't end up on Lady Sibella's altar instead.

A nudge from Owens called Max's attention to a patently fake pot of gold on display by a stone hearth. Max briefly considered the possibility that their prize might be hiding in plain sight, a la Poe's purloined letter, but suspected that he was overthinking matters. Chances were the holiday decoration was nothing more than that. The real Pot would not be so readily on display.

It was too valuable to play games with.

A more promising clue presented itself as the men approached the bar and ordered a couple of pints to blend in. Taking a seat, Max admired what appeared to be an authentic gold coin, boasting the unmistakable image of a certain pagan deity, before reading a plaque that identified the coin as coming from an actual leprechaun's pot.

"An audacious claim," he said to the bartender, a weary-looking redhead who mustered a welcoming smile as she served their drinks. Max couched his query as polite conversation. "How much truth is there to it?"

"That's the story," she said glibly, having no doubt been asked the same question more times than she could count, "passed down through my family from one generation to the next. You can believe it as much as you like, although I find it goes down easier after a drink or two."

"Your family, you say?" Max suddenly found the bartender much more interesting. "So the Pot O' Gold belongs to you?"

"Such as it is," she said. "Bridget O'Neill, at your service, and this pub's been in my family for six generations."

"Fascinating." He found it hard to imagine that she was actually a leprechaun in disguise, but maybe she had a silent partner? Max found himself growing increasingly optimistic regarding this expedition. It was possible, he supposed, that the prism had merely steered him to a single piece of authentic fairy gold, but where there was one lucky coin, there might well be a pot as well, perhaps even *the* Pot. "And how did your illustrious ancestors earn the goodwill and beneficence of one of the Little People?"

"Nobody really knows," she replied, "or if they did, nobody passed that part of the story along. I have to admit that I've sometimes wondered that myself."

"Got some fresh ice," a gruff voice interrupted as a second bartender emerged from a back room, bearing a heavy tub of crushed ice, which he dumped into a trough behind the bar. Max glanced briefly at the man, then paused and looked again. The bartender's rugged American features looked vaguely familiar, but Max couldn't immediately place him—until Bridget addressed the newcomer by name.

"Thanks, Stone! We were running low."

Stone? Max managed to maintain a poker face. *As in Jacob Stone?*

He suddenly realized where he knew the other bartender's face from. Max had never personally crossed paths with the Librarians before, but as a high-ranking member of the Serpent Brotherhood he had naturally familiarized himself with the Library's current agents. Turning away from the bar, he covertly surveyed the pub—and quickly spotted Ezekiel Jones and Colonel Eve Baird sitting at a nearby table, busily engaged with their phones. He chided himself for not noticing them earlier.

Two Librarians and their Guardian, Max counted. Notably missing were Flynn Carsen and Cassandra Cillian, leading him to wonder where exactly those two personages were at the moment. Carsen had a reputation for flying solo, but Cillian was reported to be more of a team player. Max gave Bridget a second look, just to confirm that, yes, she was indeed a different redhead

This unexpected complication left Max conflicted as to his next move. The Librarians seemed unaware of his identity, so he was tempted to discreetly slip away without engaging the enemy. On the other hand, what did it mean that the Librarians were here? Did they know something he didn't about this particular Pot O' Gold? The very presence of the Brotherhood's ancestral foes made this site all the more promising. Perhaps he had finally tracked down the Pot at last?

He weighed his options. He was not about to cede the prize to the opposition, not if he had truly struck the mother lode, but he had to be considerably more circumspect now that the Librarians were involved. Perhaps it *would* be wiser to retreat, regroup, and come back after closing time with a larger force at his disposal. Owens was formidable, but he and Max were undeniably outnumbered at present, and Max knew better than to underestimate the Librarians. Dulaque had made that mistake, and Edward Wilde before him; Max liked to think he was smart enough to learn from history.

"Come," he instructed Owens. "We're going."

He was leaving a few bills on the bar to settle their tab when a clumsy customer accidentally knocked over a glass behind them, causing it to crash onto the floor. All heads turned toward the crash, including Owens's blocklike cranium, so that the back of his head, with its shaved-in serpent design, was reflected in the cracked mirror behind the bar. Max frowned at the sight, suddenly questioning the wisdom of such ostentatious markings. Was it possible Stone wouldn't notice?

Not a chance.

The undercover Librarian stiffened behind the bar as he glimpsed the back of Owens's head. His alert gaze darted toward Max, who moved to cover his telltale Ouroboros ring, a second too late.

Oh well, Max thought. *So much for a stealthy retreat.*

———

"Nice ring," Stone said, looking the stranger in the eye. It occurred to him that he had first encountered the Serpent
Brotherhood in a tavern, while chatting up a woman with a
serpentine tattoo who had turned out to be one of the Brotherhood's top assassins. Funny how history sometimes repeated
itself.

"Nice of you to notice," the stranger said in a posh British
accent. He uncovered the ring, clearly realizing that there was
no point in trying to hide it anymore. His arch tone implied
that he knew that his cover was blown and he knew that Stone
knew that he knew. "In retrospect, possibly a bit too conspicuous, but there's something to be said for maintaining the old
traditions, don't you think?"

Stone pegged the Englishman as the brains of the operation
and his scowling, thick-necked companion as the muscle.
Stone's own sinews tensed as he rapidly assessed the situation. He glanced over at Baird and Ezekiel, who had not yet
registered the brewing situation at the bar. How could he
alert them to the Serpents without endangering the pub's unsuspecting clientele? Heck, how could he warn Bridget that
their new customers were big-time bad guys?

"Some traditions are better off dead and buried," Stone
said, with enough of an edge to his voice that Bridget picked
up that something was amiss, as did the big guy with the crew
cut. She cast a worried look at Stone, who kept his eyes on
the Serpents. "If you know what I mean, Mister . . . ?"

"Call me Max," the man said, without volunteering a surname. "And I think we both know what you mean, Librarian."

Crew Cut got off his stool and loomed behind Max, shielding
his boss from view as the Englishman discreetly drew a pistol

from beneath his jacket and aimed it at Stone, who was surprised to find himself on the business end of so mundane a threat. Poison darts, lightning bolts, hellfire, and ninja stars were the kinds of weapons he'd gotten used to facing.

"A gun, really?"

"Don't try anything rash, Mr. Stone," the man said, laying his cards on the table. "We wouldn't want to raise a ruckus with all these nice people about. There's no need for any collateral damage." Keeping his voice low, he addressed Bridget, who had frozen at the sight of the pistol. "And please don't go anywhere, Miss O'Neill. I'm most interested in learning more about your family's curious history."

Crew Cut cracked his knuckles for emphasis.

Stone fumed inwardly, his fists clenching at his sides. "What are you after anyway?"

"To be honest, I *had* been planning to slink away unnoticed, the better to preserve the element of surprise, but it seems matters have come to a head prematurely." He indicated the coin under the glass. "I'll have this intriguing souvenir, if you don't mind. And, please, don't make me ask twice."

Bridget swallowed hard. Her hand went to her chest in a way that worried Stone despite the recent repairs to her heart. Surgery or no surgery, she'd already had one heart attack—and that was before all this new stress. Stone wasn't sure how much her troubled ticker could take.

"Fine." Stone wasn't going to risk Bridget's health or safety over the coin. From behind the bar, he was able to slide out the glass pane over the coin, allowing Max to pocket it. "But don't think you're going to be able to get the drop on me again."

"Pleased to make your acquaintance as well," Max said sardonically. "Now then, we'll be leaving with the gold . . . and its lovely owner."

Bridget gasped. "This is it," she murmured. "My doom . . . just like the banshee warned!"

"Leave her alone," Stone snarled. "What do you want with her?"

"Simply to have a discussion regarding a literal pot of gold, albeit at a somewhat less public location."

There you have it, Stone thought. The Serpents *were* after a pot of gold, just like back in the fifth century. And this time Saint Patrick wasn't on hand to chase them away.

But Stone did have a Guardian and another Librarian on his side. Ignoring the gun pointed at his chest, he peered past Max and his goon to see Baird and Ezekiel rising to their feet on the other side of the pub. Wary expressions indicated that they had belatedly noticed that there was a situation of sorts playing out at the bar. They started making their way toward Stone, who suddenly hit on a way to bring them up to speed. Pouring a random bottle into a pair of empty glasses, he called out in his best bartender's voice.

"Two Snakes in the Shamrocks! Who ordered the Snakes in the Shamrocks?"

Confused patrons shook their head, no doubt wondering what kind of exotic concoction that was, but Baird and Ezekiel surely got the message: there were Serpents in their midst.

"That's enough," Max snapped, unamused. "Owens, watch my back. Miss O'Neill, please step lively and come out from behind—"

"Excuse me, sir, would ye mind holding me fiddle for a minute." Grady squeezed up to the bar, having somehow slipped past Owens. The fiddler seemed oblivious to the abduction-in-progress. "I'm powerful thirsty, so I am."

"Let me alone, you old fool," Max said curtly. "Make your-self scarce."

"Och, don't be like that." He thrust the fiddle at Max. "It's just a wee favor I'm asking."

"I told you, leave me alone or—"

Max's jaw dropped as he found himself grasping the neck of the fiddle instead of the gun, which was now somehow in Grady's grip instead. He blinked in surprise at the unexpected switcheroo.

"How the devil . . . ?"

Stone was equally dumbfounded. He couldn't tell how it had happened, but now Max had the fiddle and Grady had the gun, all in the blink of an eye.

That's some sleight of hand, Stone thought.

Before Stone could figure it out, Max angrily swung the fiddle at Grady, knocking the gun out of the old man's grip. The dislodged firearm flew over the bar, causing Bridget to duck in alarm. It crashed to the floor somewhere behind the bar—or possibly in the ice trough?

Stone saw his chance. No longer being held at gunpoint, he vaulted over the bar to confront the Serpents. He didn't bother scrambling for the gun; hand-to-hand combat was more his speed anyway, experienced as he was in both bar-room brawling *and* the martial arts. At the same time, he saw Baird charging at Owens, whose telltale haircut made it clear whose team he was playing for. Grunting, the bruiser snatched a bottle of malt vinegar off a table and smashed it against the edge of the table, turning it into a jagged weapon—and throw-ing the whole pub into a panic again.

For the second time in less than twenty-four hours, custom-ers bolted from their seats and tables to get away, jamming the exits. Fleeing bodies jostled Stone as he faced off against Max, who looked more vexed than worried by the escalating conflict. Stone figured Baird could handle the big guy on her own, which left the head Serpent to him.

Fine by me, Stone thought. "I'd offer you the chance to give up now, but, honestly, I'd rather teach you a lesson first."

He threw a right at Max's goateed chin, aiming to knock him out with one punch, but Max expertly blocked the blow with his forearm, revealing good reflexes and no little training, while countering with an open-handed palm strike at Stone, who dodged it with a split second to spare. Impressed, Stone tried to sweep Max's legs out from beneath him with a roundhouse kick, but Max leapt high above the kick, landing nimbly atop the bar, where he kicked an empty glass at Stone, who spun sideways to avoid being beaned by the missile.

"It appears I have the higher ground," Max gloated, not even winded.

"Says who?" Stone sprang onto the bar as well, where he adopted a fighting stance taught to him by none other than the Monkey King himself. Upset drinks crashed onto the floor. "Bring it on, snake-boy."

"If you insist."

Fighting atop the bar, the men engaged in a rapid-fire exchange of strikes, jabs, snaps, kicks, feints, blocks, parries, and old-fashioned haymakers that proved them all too evenly matched. Stone quickly realized that Max had serious skills; he was going to have to bring his A game if he wanted to squash this Serpent.

Okay, he thought, *if that's what it takes.*

"Nice technique." Max asked as he tested Stone's defenses by combining a driving punch with a right-reverse kick. "You've studied in Shangri-La, I take it?"

"From the best." Stone parried Max's attacks and retaliated with a sideways elbow strike that Max somersaulted backward to avoid. The man's fighting style reminded Stone of Lamia, a top-flight Serpent operative he had tussled with a few times before karma caught up with her. He wondered if she and Max had studied under some of the same teachers. "You?"

"Two years at the Midnight Dojo in Jigoku." Max sprang back onto his feet before launching a flurry of ridge-handed chops at Stone's head and throat. "Plus a supplementary course in dirty tricks from an exclusive fight club in Manchester."

"Bet that came natural." Stone flipped over Max's head to land on the bar behind his smirking opponent. A backward kick targeted the Serpent's lower back, but Max spun around in time to grab Stone's leg and swing him off the bar onto the floor, which was now strewn with broken glass and spilled booze. Stone grimaced as he hit the ground hard, just as Max hopped off the bar after him. Stone rolled out of the way— and was nearly flattened by the big thug fighting Baird, who came flying through the air at him.

———

A few moments earlier:

Snakes in the Shamrocks? Baird thought. *Seriously?*

Not that she didn't appreciate the heads-up where the Serpent Brotherhood was involved; it had been a few years since the Librarians had last tangled with them, but she hadn't forgotten how dangerous they could be. She should've known they'd show their slimy faces eventually, but what were they doing here at Bridget's pub?

She'd have to figure that out later, she realized. Right now she had a muscle-bound goon with a bad attitude and a broken bottle to deal with. The belligerent bodybuilder had a few

inches and several pounds on Baird, but that wasn't enough
to intimidate her. Compared with the banshee the night before, taking on some hired muscle was right in Baird's wheel-
house.

Thugs she knew how to handle. Banshees not so much.

"Growing your snakes big these days," she said, wanting to
keep the goon's attention on her while the civilians made a
break for it and Ezekiel scrambled under and around the tables
to get to Stone and Bridget. Her eyes tracked the jagged
glass bottle in the thug's hand, on guard for any sudden movements on the goon's part. "But not any prettier, apparently."

The thug growled in response.

"Guess we're not doing the banter thing." Baird shrugged.
"Works for me."

She grabbed the back of a wooden chair and swung it at the
goon like a club. Reacting faster than she expected, he turned
sideways to absorb the impact as the cheap pine chair crashed
against his linebacker's shoulder, which felt as solid as a slab
of meat. The blow elicited a grunt from him, but failed to
knock him off his feet. Snarling, he seized the bottom half of
the chair and yanked it out of Baird's grip, flinging it across
the pub. It slammed into the bogus pot of gold, sending fake
plastic coins everywhere.

"Nice try," he said smugly.

"How about that?" Baird said. "It speaks."

He lunged forward, the broken bottle slashing through the
air at her, but Baird was ready. Relying on her training, she
darted toward him, inside the path of the weapon. His thick
neck presented a perfect target, so she rammed her palm into
the vulnerable nerve cluster just above the clavicle, delivering a textbook brachial stun that would have dropped a less

cement-like opponent. Even still, the man spasmed as though zapped with a Taser. His eyes rolled in their sockets as he tottered unsteadily, not quite falling down.

Geez, she thought. *He's not making this easy for me.*

She took full advantage of his dazed state. Without a single wasted motion, she grabbed the back of his neck with one hand and the wrist of his weapon hand with the other, shoving the arm holding the broken bottle away from her body while simultaneous yanking his head down into her knee, which shot up to meet his face with as much force as she could muster. The collision kept the goon on the ropes as she pivoted to one side, wrenching his arm until he let go of the bottle, which shattered as it hit the floor.

Damn it, Baird thought. *We just swept up this place!*

Baird released the goon's wrist as he stumbled backward, clutching his nose. His brutish face flushed with anger, showing that he still didn't know when to give up. He charged at her like an angry boar or minotaur, both of which she had some experience with. All he'd have needed to complete the picture was steam billowing from his nostrils.

Baird smiled.

I like it when they're too mad to think straight, she thought. *Makes them sloppy.*

Employing some basic jujitsu, she turned his weight against him, throwing him over her shoulder so that he went flying across the pub—where he nearly landed on Stone, who looked like he was having some trouble with the other Serpent. The goon crashed into the bar only a few inches away from Stone's head.

"Oops!" she blurted. "Sorry about that."

———

Grady tugged on Bridget's arm as they crouched behind the bar, hiding out from the violence that had erupted in her pub. Her heart pounded recklessly in her chest.

"Come along, me girl," the fiddler urged her. "We need to get ye safely away from here, while yer new friends keep those blackguards occupied."

Bridget hesitated. "But we can't just desert them!"

"Don't ye worry about them! It's ye those greedy Sassenachs are after!"

"But why?" Bridget had no idea what was happening. What did any of this have to do with the banshee?

Unless, she reminded herself, this was the doom the spirit had foretold.

———

"No problem!" Stone said after Baird nearly nailed him with Crew Cut. "Just watch where you're throwing that guy!"

Meanwhile, Max was moving in for the kill. Stone tried to scramble to his feet before the Englishman could exploit his vulnerable position on the floor, but the wet, slippery tiles, not to mention the broken glass all around, made that more difficult than Stone would have liked. He was still trying to stand when Max seized a metal barstool to throw at the fallen Librarian. Stone threw up his arms to defend himself, but doubted it would do much good against the heavy object. He was about to be battered.

"Pleasant dreams, Librarian." Max raised the stool high. "Seems you needed a few more lessons at Shangri-La. . . ."

"Or maybe he just needs a little backup!"

Ezekiel sprang out from beneath a table to tackle Max before he could take Stone out. They slammed into the bar as they grappled, the stool crashing harmlessly to the floor instead of ramming into Stone, who backed away from the falling bar furniture in time.

"Watch out, Jones!" Stone finally made it to his feet, grateful for the save, but worried about his friend. Ezekiel was a thief, not a master fighter, and no match for somebody like Max. "He's got major moves!"

His warning proved superfluous, however, as Max proved his point by effortlessly breaking Ezekiel's hold and spinning the plucky-but-outclassed Librarian around so that Max could seize him from behind. In a heartbeat, Ezekiel went from rescuer to hostage and human shield as Max twisted the Librarian's arm behind his back while placing a single finger against his temple in a way that made Stone's blood run cold.

Crap, he thought. *This isn't good.*

Max smirked at Stone from behind Ezekiel's shoulder. "Ah, I see you recognize this clever little move."

"The Yucatan Death Touch," Stone said grimly. "A technique forbidden by every honorable fighting system."

"Honor is subjective," Max said with a shrug. "In any event, you understand why this pointless, if invigorating, donnybrook is over. The time has come, I think, to remove ourselves from this increasingly chaotic situation before your fellow Librarians can arrive to further complicate matters. I'll thank you not to interfere with my departure . . . for Mr. Jones's sake."

Baird hesitated. "Stone?"

"He's got us over a barrel," Stone confirmed. "For now."

Max nodded. "Listen to your esteemed colleague. He knows whereof he speaks." He called out to his recovering bodyguard, who looked ready for another round with Baird. His bruised face had seen better days. Blood trickled from a squashed nose. "Owens, get the door."

Glowering at Baird, the bruiser nevertheless did as in-structed. Max backed across the pub toward the open door, dragging his hostage with him. Stone watched in frustra-tion, unable to keep the Serpents from absconding with his friend, who was looking distinctly unhappy about the way things were going.

"Hang on!" Ezekiel protested. "What exactly is this Yucatan Death Touch thingie anyway?"

"Trust me," Stone said. "You don't want to know."

"That doesn't make me feel any better!" Ezekiel said.

"Get the car ready," Max ordered Owens, who exited the pub ahead of his boss. Max paused before the doorway to get his gloat on. "Don't feel too bad, Librarians, Guardian. You can't win all the time."

A shot rang out, stealing Max's thunder.

All heads turned toward the bar, where Bridget stood grip-ping Max's lost pistol with two shaking hands. Her face was pale but resolute as she pointed the gun at Max.

"Let Ezekiel go," she ordered. "You hurt him and you're not going anywhere except six feet under!"

Max blanched at the sight of the gun, but held on to his composure, as well as his hostage. "I hardly think you're in a position to dictate—"

Bridget fired again. The sharp report of the gun startled Max, distracting him long enough for Ezekiel to demonstrate that he had some moves of his own. Twisting his head toward Max's lethal finger, he bit down hard on the deadly digit while simultaneously driving his foot into Max's ankle, causing the Serpent leader to cry out for two reasons at once.

"Blast it!"

Choosing the better part of valor, Max angrily shoved Eze-kiel away from him, with enough force that Ezekiel fell forward onto the floor. The Englishman cradled his injured hand as he dashed out the door.

Stone hesitated, torn between chasing after Max and checking on Ezekiel.

"I'm fine!" Ezekiel said, lifting his face from the tiles. "Follow that snake!"

That was good enough for Stone. He started after Max, but got only a few steps before he heard Bridget gasp behind him. Spinning around, he saw her slumping against the bar, looking like she could barely stand up. She dropped the gun onto the bar as she gasped for breath. Her face had gone as pale as the banshee's and her head reeled atop her neck as though she was on the verge of blacking out.

Her heart?

"What is it?" Baird asked urgently, obviously sharing Stone's concern. Pursuing Max suddenly came in second to making sure Bridget was okay. Baird got her phone out. "Should I call 911?"

"Not yet," Bridget said unconvincingly. Short of breath, she barely managed to get the words out as she tottered unsteadily. "Just need my pills."

She fumbled with a vial of prescription medication, spilling a handful of small white pills into her palm before tossing one into her mouth. Popping up behind her, Grady poured her a glass of water to wash the pill down.

"Thanks," she said.

Stone kept a close watch on Bridget as he helped Ezekiel to his feet. The pill seemed to do the trick; within a few minutes her color returned and she began breathing easier. Working together, Baird and Grady assisted her to a chair so she could rest her legs as she recovered from the shock of the attack.

"Oh, God," Bridget said. "What just happened? Who were those men?"

"The competition," Baird said succinctly. "They're called the Serpent Brotherhood . . . and they're serious bad news."

That's putting it mildly, Stone thought. He scowled at the open doorway, figuring Max and his flunky were long gone by now. "And they just got away with your lucky gold coin."

"Did they?" Ezekiel opened his palm to reveal the supposedly purloined coin. "Then what's this?"

"Hang on," Stone said. "You picked his pocket?"

"Naturally," Ezekiel said. "You don't think I let him capture me by accident? I'm Ezekiel Jones. Getting caught is against my religion."

Stone wondered if his friend knew just how close he'd come to having his brain turned to yogurt. "Nervy move, pal. Just saying."

"We're Librarians," Ezekiel reminded him. "Since when do we play it safe?"

Fair enough, Stone thought.

"But what were they doing here?" Bridget asked. "Why were they after that coin . . . and me?"

"Funny you should ask that," Baird said. "Right before the craziness started, I heard from Jenkins and Cassandra. They're back from their own investigation . . . and they may have some answers for us."

20

❀ *The Annex* ❀

"It's like looking in a mirror, so!"

Brigid met Bridget as the Librarians reconvened at the Annex, bringing their two new charges with them for safekeeping. Cassandra was struck again by the startling resemblance between the two women, which was all the more obvious now that they were standing across from each other. Only their hair, clothing, and accents differentiated them; Bridget was a modern American, while Brigid still looked like she'd stepped out of Ye Olde Ireland.

The escape route from Mill Ends had led Cassandra, Jenkins, and Brigid to an abandoned stone cabin in Forest Park, a wooded area about ten minutes west of downtown Portland. From there they had simply taken a Lyft back to the Annex, with Brigid gaping wide-eyed at the modern world the whole way. Cassandra figured that Portland was just as exotic to Brigid as Mill Ends had been to her. There weren't many Starbucks or traffic jams in Otherworld.

"But I don't understand," the other Bridget said, noticeably more distraught than her double. She was not on a grand adventure; she was being terrorized by a banshee and would-be abductors. "Who is this woman? How can she look just like me?"

Cassandra let Jenkins explain his theory, which he'd already shared with her and Brigid on the way back to the Annex. She didn't want to step on his lines.

"I have been developing a possible solution to that mystery," the caretaker began as Cassandra and her teammates milled about the main office, digging into the card catalog and bookshelves in search of reference material on leprechauns, banshees, and Serpents. "Tell me, Miss O'Neill, are you familiar with the concept of changelings?"

"A little," Bridget said. "That's when the fairies supposedly steal a mortal baby and leave a fairy child in its place."

"Precisely." Jenkins plucked a book from a shelf and opened it to an old woodcut of a gnomish fairy stealing away from a cradle with a mortal infant in his hands. Another, even creepier illustration showed a fairy baby, with tapered ears and suspiciously pointy teeth, resting in a cradle. "Changelings can be found in the folklore of many nations, including Ireland."

"Wait," Ezekiel said. "I thought changelings were shapeshifters?"

"Only in comic books and science fiction," Jenkins said. "Your classic changeling, from myth and history, is a fairy swapped for a mortal child in infancy, although, admittedly, magic is sometimes employed to make the substitute appear identical to the original child, the better to pull off the switch."

Bridget stared at him in disbelief. "What are you saying? That we were switched at birth . . . and that this Brigid is the real one? And that I'm just a changeling, made to look like her?"

"Not quite," Jenkins assured her. "The chronology argues against that. Granted, time flows differently in Otherworld, but Brigid appears to have resided with the leprechauns for centuries at least, when by all accounts you were born only twenty-plus years ago?"

"That's right," Bridget said. "In 1996."

"Far after Brigid's time," Jenkins stressed, "unlike your family's connection to the leprechauns, which began long before your birth. Furthermore, Miss O'Neill, you give no indication of being a fairy in disguise."

"Are we sure about that?" Stone asked. "No offense."

"Close enough for Library work," Jenkins said. "Still, perhaps Miss Cillian can confirm my assessment?"

Cassandra was still wearing the magic four-leaf clover she had found in Otherworld. She had previously determined that Brigid was fully human, just as she'd claimed. Now Cassandra looked closely at Bridget, on the lookout for any magical shenanigans.

"I'm not seeing any obvious glamours," she reported after a minute. "If I squint a little, maybe there's something a teensy bit off about her ears and eyes, but it's so subtle that it could be just my imagination."

Bridget nervously fingered an ear. "So what does that mean?"

"My current theory," Jenkins said, "which I stress is still a work-in-progress, is that you are in fact *descended* from a changeling, who replaced the real Brigid at some point in the distant past."

"The fifth century?" Stone wondered aloud. "In Saint Patrick's time?"

Cassandra suddenly made a connection. "The baby in the old story! The one the leprechaun ran away with." She looked with excitement at Bridget. "You said the leprechauns took you in because you were an orphan!"

"So they say," Bridget said. "But refresh me memory. What old story again?"

"I'll catch you up soon," Cassandra promised. "What do you think, Jenkins? Could Brigid be the baby that was rescued from the Serpent Brotherhood years ago?"

"Possibly," Jenkins said, "but only possibly. We should not jump to that conclusion before it is confirmed. The actual identity of the nameless child has yet to be verified."

"Hang on," Bridget said. "I'm still trying to sort this out. If I'm not a changeling, why do we look alike?"

"My guess is that magic was employed to make the original changeling—your distant ancestor—a perfect twin of little baby Brigid. And that spell caused the resemblance to be passed down through your family, after the false Brigid grew up, married, had children, and otherwise lived out a mortal life, possibly not ever knowing her true origins." Jenkins closed the book on changelings. "In short, Miss O'Neill, while you are not a changeling yourself, you may well have one in your family tree."

Stone nodded. "That would explain why you have a leprechaun looking after your family and sharing his gold with you. A relative from the faerie side of the family, watching out over his mortal descendants?"

"And the banshee?" Bridget asked.

"Still not sure where she fits in," Stone confessed.

Aside from the fact that Bridget is obviously in jeopardy, Cassandra added silently, *for more reasons than one.*

"Can we talk about the Serpents now?" Baird said, perhaps worrying about the imminent threat to Bridget as well. "A magical switched-at-birth scenario fifteen hundred years ago is intriguing, but I'm honestly more concerned with what the Serpents are up to at the moment, especially after what happened at the pub."

The reunited Librarians had already compared notes on

their respective expeditions to Chicago and Mill Ends. Cassandra had been surprised to discover that more than a day had passed in the real world while she and Jenkins had been visiting the leprechaun colony. She wished again that there was some sort of reliable mathemagical equation for calculating the time-dilation effect when crossing back and forth between mortal and faerie realms. Maybe something to look into after the current crisis was resolved?

"Well, we know one thing for sure now," Stone said. "The Brotherhood is definitely after pots of gold again, just like in the olden days. And according to what Jenkins and Cassandra learned down in Otherworld, that business at the pub is only the most recent incident. They've been going after leprechauns and their pots in a big way."

"Bloody-handed gobshites," Brigid said. "Preying on the Wee Folk for their treasure!"

"I can't imagine that this is simply about gold." Jenkins stepped away from his desk, which now held the gold coin from Bridget's pub. "The Brotherhood has always been more concerned with accumulating power—in particular, magic power—than riches. I suspect there is far more here than meets the eye."

"For sure," Ezekiel agreed. "If gold is all you're after, why run around the world hunting for leprechauns? Just rob Fort Knox like a normal person."

Bridget blinked. "Come again?"

"Let it go," Cassandra advised her. "That's what we usually do."

Baird kept them focused on the task at hand. "We have any idea who this Max guy is?" She looked to Jenkins, who knew more about the Library's ancient rivals than the rest of them combined. "Jenkins?"

"Not on my radar, Colonel," he replied. "And I'm afraid the Serpent Brotherhood guards its membership roster even more zealously than certain politicians hide their tax returns." He sighed heavily. "Sadly, there have always been ruthless and ambitious individuals prepared to step into any open slots in the Brotherhood's upper leadership. Evil abhors a vacuum."

Cassandra wished she had been present to get a look at this "Max" character, if only to commit his face to her eidetic memory. "Any security camera footage from the pub?"

Bridget shook her head. "The only camera was taken out by the banshee's scream the night before. That was one thing we hadn't managed to replace yet."

"What about the stolen gold?" Baird asked. "Follow the money, remember? If the Brotherhood is accumulating large quantities of leprechaun gold, any way we can scour the financials to trace the gold back to them? Maybe look for large, irregular deposits into shady accounts or signs of magical money laundering?"

"Easy peasy." Ezekiel opened his laptop, cracked his knuckles, and got to work. "Just give me a little time to prowl the Dark Web and work some of my old underworld contacts. No way anyone can move around that much gold without some chatter on the Net."

Bridget turned to Cassandra and whispered, "Just to be clear, he's a criminal, right?"

"He's a Librarian," Cassandra assured her. "That's what matters." She glanced at her own computer, tempted to join in the search, but no, this was Ezekiel's natural habitat. If anyone could track down the stolen gold, it was Ezekiel Jones. "Let him at it."

In the interim, Brigid remained fascinated by her double. "So what are we to each other? Twins? Sisters?"

"From the sound of it," Bridget said, "I'm more like a fifth-generation copy—and something of a defective printing to boot."

Cassandra assumed that Bridget's weak heart came from her mortal side, not from the faerie blood way back in her genealogy. The scientist in Cassandra wondered whether the magic behind Bridget's resemblance to Brigid extended all the way down to her DNA. Would it fool genetic testing?

"You're not defective," Cassandra told Bridget. "You have a medical condition, that's all."

"And a banshee haunting me and some sort of evil 'brotherhood' stalking me." Bridget slumped down into a chair at the conference table. "I'm sorry if I'm coming off as a buzzkill, and not more excited about meeting you, Brigid, but it's all too much. It feels like the whole world is out to get me, up to and including my own bum ticker."

"Och, no need to apologize," Brigid said. "From what I've heard, ye've had a fierce hard time of it lately. None can blame ye for not being fully yerself just now." She sat down beside her twin and patted her hand. "'Twill be time enough for us to get better acquainted, once the danger's passed." She eyed Bridget's hair and clothing. "Perhaps ye can help me fit into this brave new world of yers."

Bridget managed a smile. "I'd like that."

Time passed as they left Ezekiel to his work. Jenkins settled in at his desk to do some research, while Baird tried and failed to get ahold of Flynn, who was presumably still unruffling the scales of feuding fish-people somewhere at the bottom of the briny deep. Stone munched on a sandwich as he brushed up on his ancient ogham. Cassandra briefly considered offering their guests a tour of the Library, but realized that Jenkins would never allow that. She chatted with the women, taking part as they briefed each other on where they'd each come from.

"So there's actually an honest-to-goodness leprechaun colony—underneath Portland, of all places?" Bridget marveled. "Who knew?"

"Just saw it with my own eyes," Cassandra said. "A bit easier to enter than leave, mind you, but it was still a neat place to visit."

"Wow," Bridget said. "I admit I'd like to see that at least once before I . . ." Her voice trailed off, leaving the final bit unspoken.

"Och, it's a grand place," Brigid said. "But I can't wait to visit this Chicago of yers . . . and to toast yer health at that fine pub ye speak of. Sure and it must be a grand place at that."

Cassandra was looking forward to checking out the Pot O' Gold herself, preferably without any banshees or barroom brawls to spoil the visit. As she understood it, the pub had been closed for business since the kidnapping attempt, although Bridget still wanted to reopen in time for Saint Patrick's Day tomorrow.

"Flawless victory!" Ezekiel exclaimed, pumping his fist. He leaned back in his chair, looking even more pleased with himself than usual. "I know, I know, you're blown away by how fast that was, but what can I say? I really am that good."

"We'll get you an applause sign later," Stone said. He and the others hurried over to the conference table to see what Ezekiel had turned up, with only Jenkins waiting patiently for Ezekiel to elaborate. They peered over his shoulders at his laptop. "What have you got?"

Ezekiel beamed as he explained. "I did some poking under

some of my favorite rocks. Turns out there's a new player on the scene, who has been trading in ancient gold coins on a no-questions-asked basis. Old *Irish* coins, to be exact—and did I mention that the guy goes by the handle 'Ophidian'?"

"As in Serpent," Baird said. "Good work, Jones. Always pays to have friends in low places."

"Well, I wouldn't exactly call some of them 'friends'. . . ."

Cassandra was excited by his breakthrough. "What now? Can we find out where they're hiding?"

"Way ahead of you," Ezekiel bragged. "Posing as a fence with big pockets, I managed to get a link to a secure site where people can do business with Ophidian. Once he answers my query, I should be able to track his reply back to a physical address."

"Ooh," Cassandra blurted. "I can help you with that!"

Crime was Ezekiel's bailiwick, but cracking encrypted security measures and tracing a signal through a maze of servers and networks was something Cassandra's brain could do faster than most computer programs.

"Works for me," Ezekiel said. "Two hackers are better than one."

"Way to go, people," Baird encouraged them. "With any luck, we can get out ahead of this situation instead of playing catch-up. I don't know about you, but I'm tired of the Serpents knowing more than we do."

"Tell me about it," Stone agreed. "And when we find out where they're skulking these days . . . ?"

"Preemptive strike," Baird said decisively. "We go in hard and fast, we get some answers, and we shut down whatever hostile action the Serpents are cooking up this time." A determined smile promised trouble for any two-legged snakes that got in her way. "I gotta say, I like the idea of being one step ahead of the bad guys for once."

"You and me both, Colonel," Jenkins said.

Cassandra hoped things worked out that way, but she had been tricked by the Serpent Brotherhood before. You never knew when and where they might strike.

21

Eden Manor was a mansion on the outskirts of Chicago. Max had converted its attic into a war room of sorts, complete with large bulletin and dry-erase boards mounted on easels. Surveillance photos of the current Librarians and their Guardian were pinned to one such board, above capsule biographies summarizing whatever intel the Brotherhood had been able to glean regarding the opposition. Maps and time lines traced Max's tireless pursuit of the Pot, while Lady Sibella's skull and reliquary provided inspiration to continue the quest. Tall dormer windows offered views of the surrounding grounds, which included a helipad, tennis court, private cemetery, and moat. Max had not planned to linger near Chicago quite so long, but he had to admit that this particular Brotherhood safe house was more than adequate for his needs.

"Here it comes!" Coral exclaimed as she captured the last ray of the setting sun with her prism. The resulting rainbow swerved above the map table before dipping toward the left side of a map of the continental United States. "Where'd it land?"

"Portland, Oregon," Max said with a scowl. Now home to

the Library, one of the most secure repositories on the face of the Earth. The Brotherhood had been aware of the Annex's location for some time, but that didn't make it any more accessible. The Brotherhood had required a weak link on the inside to break into the Library last time—Max glanced at the surveillance photo of Cassandra Cillian—but it was unlikely that they could work that angle again. "The Library, no doubt."

"Oh, no!" Coral said, alarmed. "Does this mean they have the Pot?"

Max didn't want to think that. "Let's not jump to worst-case scenarios. Your prism might simply still be locked onto the gold from the pub, which may well be in our adversaries' hands at the moment, but that does not necessarily mean they've claimed the Pot itself."

His fingers fiddled with the fake gold piece he'd found in his pocket after retreating from the pub, which he'd kept as a reminder never to underestimate a Librarian. His blood pressure rose slightly as he recalled his dismay at discovering that Ezekiel Jones must have switched out the coins at some point. The counterfeit "coin" taunted and challenged Max, tangible proof that the real coin had eluded him.

For the time being, he thought.

The attic grew darker with the sinking sun. "Echidna, lights please."

"*Lights on*," the house's voice-activated digital assistant responded, raising the attic's interior lights. "*You're welcome*."

The illumination failed to dispel Coral's anxiety. "But what if the Librarians do have the Pot already?" she fretted. "Can't we just tell them what we want it for? Maybe we can work *with* them instead of against them?"

"An admirably idealistic notion," Max said, "but entirely impossible. The Librarians are all about hoarding magic, not using it. That's why the Brotherhood parted company with them in the first place, millennia ago. They're not going to see the light now, not after all this time."

"But maybe if we actually *talked* to them for once?" Coral persisted.

Max shook his head. "Snakes may shed their skins, but the Library never changes. What we seek is anathema to them. No reconciliation is possible, even if there weren't also generations of bitter conflict between the Brotherhood and the Library. Too much bad blood has passed under the bridge as it were."

And there are too many old scores to be settled, he added silently.

His gaze drifted from the remains of Lady Sibella to the profiles of their enemies pinned up on the boards. He rolled the bogus coin back and forth across his knuckles as he contemplated his all-too-resourceful adversaries—and wondered what they were up to at this very minute.

————

The private cemetery behind the mansion attracted few visitors, particularly after dark, so no one noticed when the entrance to the mausoleum was lit by a bright white flash.

Or at least Baird hoped nobody noticed.

She and the Librarians lingered furtively in the shadow of the mausoleum, getting their bearings while waiting for night to descend completely. Once Ezekiel and Cassandra had managed to trace "Ophidian" to a gated estate on the outskirts of Chicago, the Librarians had been able to scope out the premises via Google Earth and a few less public surveillance systems—and had zeroed in on the mausoleum as a possible weak spot in the estate's defenses. If the estate was indeed

a Brotherhood stronghold, it was surely locked up tight, but
Baird had gambled that the mausoleum entrance was one door
that probably wasn't being heavily guarded.

So far, so good, she thought.

The whole team was on hand for the mission aside from
Jenkins, who was babysitting Bridget and Brigid back at the
Annex, where they'd kicked their own security measures up
a notch now that they knew for sure that the Serpent Brother-
hood was back again. Baird counted on Jenkins to keep the
Library safe while they took the fight to the enemy.

"Welcome to Eden," she said. "Complete with serpents."

She contemplated the looming stone mansion, comparing
it with the exterior views she had studied earlier. Eden Manor
was an imposing stone edifice with four floors, a turret, and
a drawbridge. Gargoyles and gutters fashioned in the sinuous
shape of snakes adorned its brooding gray façade. Stone had
managed to dig up some history on the estate; apparently it
had been constructed in 1913 by one Rupert Eden, a wealthy
robber baron, who had eventually vanished on an expedition
to find the actual Garden of Eden, never to be seen again. At
the risk of unfairly profiling the man, Baird guessed that Rupert had been a Serpent himself back in the day, whose quest
had ended badly for him, but whose property still belonged
to the Brotherhood.

"Not exactly my idea of paradise," she added, "but . . ."

"Like you aren't totally in your element right now," Stone
teased her. "Leading a covert raid on an enemy compound,
just like back in your counterterrorism days."

"Busted," she said. "This does feel a bit like old times . . .
in a good way."

Part of her wished, in fact, that she had a full squad of
special-forces commandos and Navy SEALs backing her up

on this mission; but then again, they were dealing with an ancient secret society in pursuit of magical treasure, so conventional military assets were unlikely to be enough. If there was one thing she had learned as a Guardian, it was that some operations required Librarians, not soldiers.

"At least they're not hiding out in some creepy old cave or catacomb," Cassandra observed. "Have I mentioned that I'm kinda over caves?"

"I'm impressed, actually," Ezekiel said. "A pile like that just screams old money and expensive tastes. Probably lots of pricey artwork and antiques."

"Just remember the plan," Baird stressed, "and our priorities. We want Max, actionable intel, and the stolen pots of gold . . . in that order."

Max and his underlings could hardly be charged with hunting leprechauns in conventional courts, so she hoped to turn them over to Mill Ends for justice, after she and her Librarians uncovered and shut down whatever nefarious master plan the Brotherhood was pursuing this time around, beyond simply stealing oodles of faerie gold. Maybe tonight they could finally find out what Max and Company were *really* up to?

"Too bad we couldn't enlist some Little People for backup," she said. "Since this is their fight, too."

"You heard what Jenkins said," Cassandra reminded her. "Leprechauns are more homebodies than soldiers. They may defend their own territory if they have to, but they're not going to charge into battle. They prefer to deal in mischief and, in extreme cases, curses."

"What kind of curses?" Baird asked.

"Funny you should ask that," Stone said. "I've been digging deeper into Irish myths and folklore, and right before we left I stumbled onto some obscure old accounts, written in ancient

Gaelic, of faerie royalty sometimes punishing those who wronged them by siccing a banshee on them . . . as a curse."

Despite the urgency of their mission, Baird was intrigued. "How exactly did that work?"

"I gather the idea is that the banshee would hunt and hound the guilty party to their death . . . or something like that."

"You think that could be Bridget's problem?" Cassandra wondered aloud. "Somebody cursed one of her ancestors with a banshee?"

"Would have to be somebody with some clout," Stone said. "Banshees are potent spirits in their own right. Your average sprite or leprechaun wouldn't be able to command one."

"Makes you wonder what you'd have to do to get cursed with a banshee," Ezekiel said. "We've been assuming that Bridget's gold came from a leprechaun, but did we ever wonder *who* the leprechaun got it from in the first place? Maybe she's accidentally passed some 'hot' faerie gold?"

"Which attracted the wrong king of attention from a very persistent banshee?" Baird said. "Like accidentally passing a marked bill from an old bank robbery or hijacking?"

"The banshee *did* show up when Bridget used the gold to pay her medical bills," Stone pointed out. "There could be some sort of ancient curse attached to the gold."

"It's a workable theory," Baird said, "but maybe we ought to put a pin in it until after we finish raiding the bad guy's headquarters? We need our heads in the game right now." She decided it was dark enough to get going. "Remember, Max is our main objective. Any smaller fish are gravy."

"Isn't that kind of a mixed metaphor?" Cassandra asked. "Is there such a thing as fish gravy?"

"Depends on how you define 'gravy,'" Stone said. "There are fish sauces."

"But those go *on* the fish," Ezekiel nitpicked. "They're not *made* of fish."

Baird rolled her eyes. *Librarians . . .*

"Focus, people. We're moving out."

Night-vision goggles, requisitioned from General Rockwell at DOSA, assisted Baird and her Librarians as they crept toward the mansion, sticking to the shadows and skirting any lighted windows or porches. Baird took notice of the helipad as they snuck past it, registering the copter as an alternative escape route if things went south; Lord knew it wouldn't be the first time she'd had to hot-wire an aircraft in a hurry, like that one time in Kandahar.

As they approached the house from behind, Baird saw lights come on in the attic.

Looks like we've got a full house, she thought. *Top to bottom.*

The Magic Door and the mausoleum had got them past the iron gates and security cameras guarding the perimeter of the estate. Beating the next obstacle was going to be trickier, not to mention damp.

"A moat?" Ezekiel scoffed. "Seriously? Who does moats anymore?"

"Don't knock it," Stone said. "Moats have been used for defense since the Bronze Age at least, as far back as Twelfth Dynasty Egypt. We're talking time-tested old-school security."

Cassandra eyed the still, black waters uncertainly. "What if there are . . . things . . . just beneath the surface?"

"Like?" Ezekiel prompted her.

"Alligators? Anacondas? You know, scaly things."

"In Chicago?" Stone asked. "In March?"

Baird saw his point. Even before the sun had gone down, the climate and season weren't exactly hospitable to cold-blooded critters—unless the Brotherhood had sprung for a *heated* moat? That struck Baird as both far-fetched and extravagant.

"Never mind." Cassandra shivered in anticipation. "This is going to be cold, isn't it?"

Baird shrugged. "Why do you think we're wearing wet suits?"

The matte-black rubber suits were another gift from DOSA, donned in anticipation of just this crossing. Baird took a moment to savor how prepared they were for this mission; given a choice, she preferred a well-planned operation to winging it, which was what they usually ended up doing.

If only all their missions allowed for this kind of prep work!

One by one, they slid quietly into the moat, which turned out to be far from heated, as well as deep enough that Baird couldn't feel the bottom of the trench. They swam stealthily across, being careful not to splash noisily, until they reached the base of a side wall, around the corner from the front gate and drawbridge. A narrow fringe of rocky soil separated the moat from the mansion, providing just enough room for the team to huddle together on dry land. Baird gazed up at the mortared stone wall rising up before them. A darkened window on the second floor looked promising.

"Ezekiel?" she said.

"Leave it to me." He flashed a cocky grin. "I love old stonework. Plenty of handholds."

Stripping off his wet suit to reveal some equally dark skulking clothes, he scrambled up the side of the building as nimbly as any experienced cat burglar. There was a reason, Baird recalled, why burglars were sometimes called "second-story men," and Ezekiel was demonstrating that reason at that very moment, and without any suction cups or grappling hooks. She and the others barely had time to shed their wet suits and stow them in the dark before a nylon climbing rope dropped down from the window. Snagging it with her hand, she tested it to make sure it was secure.

"Nice work, Jones," she said, although he was out of earshot. "Up we go."

They scaled the wall after Jones, with Baird going first just in case they ran into any opposition at the top. Stone took up the rear, ready to catch Cassandra if she slipped. The petite mathematician gulped as she pulled herself up, bracing her sneakers against the wall. This sort of stunt work was slightly beyond her comfort zone.

"Refresh my memory," she said. "When exactly did I become Batgirl?"

"Remind me to take you rock-climbing at the gym," Baird said, "when this case is over."

"Oh, boy," Cassandra said. "Something to look forward to."

Despite her discomfort, the trio made it to the second floor, where they were met by Ezekiel, who helped them climb through the window into an apparently empty hallway lined with framed oil paintings, many of them inspired by a certain garden known for its highly persuasive snake.

"Sorry for the delay," Ezekiel said, as though he hadn't carried out his task in record time. "Had to de-alarm the window first."

"No complaints here." Baird scanned the corridor, but detected no immediate threats. "What have you been able to scope out so far?"

Although they'd been able to study the mansion's exterior in advance, they were flying blind now. Baird was on high alert and assumed the rest of the team was too. Adrenaline kept her sharp.

"Managed to do a little scouting." Ezekiel nodded toward a nearby door. "This way."

They followed him into—what else?—a stately, well-appointed library, which appeared to be unoccupied at present. Baird wondered if it was worth examining the bookshelves in hopes of finding out what the Brotherhood liked in the way of reading material.

"Figured we'd be less exposed here than in the hall," Ezekiel explained. "While we work out our next move."

"That's where the science comes in." Cassandra sounded much more excited than she had been about crossing the moat or scaling the wall. This part was more her speed. "Finally."

She unzipped a waterproof bag to access a handheld magic detector, while Baird did the same. Bringing a backup sensor had seemed like a good idea when heading straight into the mouth of the Serpent, as it were. With any luck, the detector would lead them to the stolen pots of gold, and possibly to Max as well. With any luck, the Brotherhood's new Big Bad wouldn't be too far from his ill-gotten gains.

"Don't forget to set the detectors on mute," Baird reminded everyone. "The last thing we need is beeping gadgets giving away our locations."

"Right!" Cassandra switched on her device. "Okay, I'm already picking up magical vibrations from somewhere upstairs." Her brow furrowed as she peered at the digital display. "Hmm. There's something odd about these readings. I've never quite seen etheric harmonics like these before. . . ."

"That's funny," Baird said, after activating her own sensor. "I'm detecting some concentrated mojo downstairs."

"The Serpent Brotherhood collects magical objects the same way we do," Stone observed. "No surprise there's more than one spike registering on our gadgets."

Baird made a strategic decision. "Guess we're splitting up then. Stone and Cassandra, you check out those odd vibrations from upstairs. Ezekiel and I will find out what's downstairs."

Her reasoning behind the pairings was considered; she wanted one topflight fighter on each team, plus she was inclined to keep an eye on Ezekiel, just in case the old mansion offered too many tempting distractions to the thief, who was possibly more likely to lead her to Max and the purloined pots anyway.

Set a thief to catch a thief. . . .

"Keep frosty, people, and don't be afraid to call for help if you need it. If things get too hairy, we'll rendezvous back at the Library."

"Sounds good," Stone said. "Watch yourselves."

Baird handed the detector to Ezekiel to free up her hands. "You, too," she said. "Think like a Librarian, but keep on your toes. We're behind enemy lines here."

22

"You know, we make a good team," Ezekiel said as they made their way downstairs. "I take out the locks. You take out the bad guys."

Baird crammed an unconscious goon into a broom closet; a serpent tattoo on his neck suggested that she had not just decked an innocent homeowner or houseguest. Caught by surprise, the unlucky lug hadn't known what hit him. The speed and efficiency with which Baird had dealt with him before he could even sound an alarm reminded Ezekiel once again why he was so glad that he and Baird were on the same side. You really didn't want to get on her bad side.

"Sounds like a plan," she said, keeping her voice low.

More henchmen could be heard watching TV a few rooms away. Consulting the detector, Ezekiel saw that the source of the magic was apparently coming from the basement one floor down. He could live with that; chances were the cellar was a less popular hangout, provided they didn't stumble onto any secret dungeons or torture chambers.

He hated when that happened.

A cellar door just off the kitchen led down to a dusty basement that, at first glance, appeared mercifully free of armed guards, death traps, or iron maidens. Scanning the scene,

Ezekiel saw only the usual basement stuff: a furnace, a water heater, low-hanging ductwork, and, oh yeah, a huge stainless-steel bank vault built into one wall.

"Bingo!" he said gleefully. "Come to poppa."

Baird glanced behind them to make sure nobody had followed while Ezekiel gave his full attention to the vault, which looked big enough to hold any number of enticing treasures, including several pots of gold. The thief felt like a kid on Christmas morning with a humongous present just waiting to be unwrapped. He made a beeline for the vault.

"What do you think?" Baird asked. "Can you open it?"

He looked at her incredulously. "Did you seriously just ask me that?"

"What was I thinking?" She stepped back to let him work, while keeping one eye on the basement stairs. "Go to it, maestro."

The vault was a deluxe Glenn-Rieder X-3000, circa 2017. Constructed of ninety tons of reinforced steel and compressed concrete, it was state-of-the-art and all but impregnable—unless, like Ezekiel, you knew and had memorized the electronic back doors and cheat codes for pretty much every model of safe and security system in circulation. A digital keypad guarded access to the vault, but instead of trying to crack the password, he simply did a forced reset and changed the codes altogether. He paused only a second before picking out a new password:

PWNED

A red light on the keypad clicked over to green, locks and backup locks disengaged, and the heavy vault door slid open without so much as a squeak. Ezekiel beamed triumphantly.

"You were saying?" he asked.

"Sorry for doubting you," Baird said. "Let's see what we have here."

The vault was big enough to hold both of them, as well as shelves of neatly stacked gold coins, along with various other golden valuables: jewelry, goblets, plates, utensils, candlesticks, scepters, and ingots. Ezekiel didn't need an assayer to guess that all that glittered was indeed solid gold. He whistled softly in appreciation; he hadn't seen this much gold in one place since the last time he'd browsed the Midas collection at the Library.

"Gotta hand it to them," he said. "They've been busy."

Baird glanced around. "I don't see any pots. Must have discarded them after they got the gold."

"Stands to reason," Ezekiel said. "Who needs a rusty old pot when you've got a beauty of a bank vault?"

"I guess this confirms that it is the Brotherhood who has been hunting leprechauns for their gold, as if we hadn't already suspected that. But that still begs the question: Where is Max and what else is he up to?"

Ezekiel shrugged. "Well, we had to leave something for Stone and Cassandra to discover. . . ."

———

"Follow me," Stone said to Cassandra. "A manor this size would have a separate stairway for the servants that would be smaller and out of the way. Probably nobody's using it at the moment."

She trusted Stone's judgment when it came to navigating rambling old houses. Her magic detector indicated that the unusual emanations were coming from the attic, so she trailed Stone up a narrow, winding staircase that thankfully didn't creak too much under her delicate tread. She winced, however, every time her soggy sneakers squished.

I'm with Ezekiel, she thought. *Moats are a pain.*

The Librarians tiptoed up the stairs until they were at eye level with the topmost landing. Peering over the edge of the floor through the gaps in the railing, they spied a pair of bored-looking sentries posted before a closed door at the end of a hallway. Stone shot her an inquiring look and she nodded back at him. According to her sensor, the signal was coming from behind the door ahead.

But how were they going to get past the guards?

She was trying to figure that out when, to her alarm, she heard voices and footsteps coming from the bottom of the stairs, heading toward them.

"Oh, no!" she whispered to Stone. "I thought you said only servants took these stairs."

"Well, guards *are* servants," he said sheepishly. "Sorta."

The footsteps were getting louder and closer, leaving the two of them trapped between the guards above and the newcomers below. There was no way they could avoid being caught, unless . . .

Cassandra closed her eyes and concentrated on Baird, who was just a few floors away by now. Her one hope was a new ability, unlocked by her recent surgery, that she was only recently beginning to understand and control. Squeezing her eyes, she projected a single thought as hard as she could:

Help! We need a distraction . . . now!

Down in the basement, Baird's eyes widened as an urgent thought landed in the in-box of her mind.

"Cassandra and Stone!" she blurted. "They need a distraction, pronto!"

Ezekiel looked confused for a second, but caught on right away. "Oh, you just received a PM straight from Cassandra's magic brain."

"Got it in one," Baird said. Glancing around the vault, she saw only one option available. "We have to set off the alarm."

"You can't be serious!" Ezekiel protested, appalled at the very notion. "I'm Ezekiel Jones. I don't do alarms!"

"First time for everything." Baird spotted another keypad on the inside of the vault. Darting over to it, she spotted a red panic button on the console. A bell icon on the button advertised its function. "Cover your ears."

She poked the button, setting off a high-pitched klaxon that echoed painfully off the walls of the walk-in safe. Red-alert lights flashed as the door of the vault suddenly slammed shut, locking Baird and Ezekiel inside.

"Was that part of the plan?" Ezekiel asked.

"What plan?" Baird said. "I'm improvising."

For her team's sake.

————

The blaring alarm came in the nick of time, at least as far as Stone was concerned. The footsteps ascending the stairs toward him and Cassandra suddenly did an about-face and rushed back down the steps in response to the alarm. Stone, who had been bracing himself for a knockdown fight, sighed in relief. Maybe they weren't up a creek just yet.

"Thank you, Eve," Cassandra said softly, opening her eyes.

Stone realized that she must have telepathically alerted Baird to their plight, using her peculiar new gift. He hoped Baird and Ezekiel hadn't put themselves in too much jeopardy as a result, but had to trust that they could take care of themselves, as they had so many times in the past. They knew what they were doing . . . mostly.

In the meantime, the two goons guarding the door also scrambled to investigate the alarm. Taking the main stairway, they exited the attic, leaving the door at the end of the hall undefended. Stone wasn't going to waste the opportunity his friends had just provided.

"Let's go," he said tersely. "You with me?"

Cassandra held on tightly to her detector. "Right behind you."

They charged down the hall to the door. Stone was prepared to batter his way in with his shoulder if necessary, but the unlocked door opened readily. The Librarians barged into a spacious, well-lit chamber, where they found Max and a pink-haired woman Stone didn't recognize. An array of mounted charts and maps and bulletin boards suggested that they had found the nerve center of the Serpent Brotherhood's current operation.

Looks like upstairs was the way to go, Stone thought. *Baird's going to kick herself for going the other way.*

"Mister Stone, Miss Cillian," Max addressed them with his customary aplomb. He and the woman appeared to be getting ready to make a rapid departure in light of the alarm. Max was shredding a file, while his bespectacled companion was frantically gathering up some papers. He looked up at the Librarians' arrival. "Breaking and entering—really? How ill-mannered of you."

"You're one to talk." Stone spotted a polished skull sitting atop what appeared to be a portable aluminum reliquary. "Looks to me like you've been doing a little grave-robbing on the side. Off the coast of Ireland, maybe?"

"Simply reclaiming what one of your predecessors hid from us," Max stated. "Although I'm flattered that you're so abreast of my activities."

"Don't be," Stone said.

He clenched his fists.

———

Cassandra scanned the attic chamber with her detector, which rapidly zeroed in on a crystal prism dangling on a chain around the unknown woman's neck. The magic radiating from it was a new variety that didn't fit any of the standard patterns or wavelengths.

"That prism of hers," she told Stone. "That's where that weird signal is coming from."

The woman's eyes bulged behind her glasses. She looked to be about Cassandra's age and was dressed far less elegantly than Max, as though she'd just thrown on a rumpled sweatshirt and jeans that had never seen an iron. She was nondescript in appearance, actually; only her candy-colored hair would stand out in a crowd.

"Whoa!" she exclaimed. "Is that an actual magic-detecting device? What does it measure? Differential resonances between metaphysical strata, or transcendental quantum signatures?"

"The latter mostly," Cassandra said, pleasantly surprised to find someone who spoke her language, even if the other woman was presumably one of the bad guys, "although it can also be calibrated to detect fluctuations along the ectoplasmic spectrum and volitional ripples in the space-time-spirit continuum. But what kind of magic object is that prism? Where did you find it?"

"I didn't find it." The woman's accent pegged her as an American. "I *made* it."

"You created a brand-new magical object?" Cassandra was impressed despite herself. She'd known that this was theoretically possible, given the rebirth of wild magic; the Library had recently started collecting new magic objects that had been generated spontaneously throughout the world, but she'd never known anyone to create one from scratch. "On purpose?"

The woman grinned, pleased to have her achievement recognized.

"It wasn't easy," she said. "You have to find a way to alchemically fuse the raw magic with an object symbolically suited to achieve the desired effect, which means taking into account both mind *and* matter, along with deleting the uncertainty from the uncertainty principle by—"

"Not now, Coral," Max interrupted.

Stone had to agree. Now was no time for a symposium on the science of magic and/or the magic of science. Cassandra could get her geek-girl on *after* they'd taken Max and his brainy accomplice into custody—and delivered them to the Library via the nearest Magic Door.

"You're coming with me," he told Max, dropping into a fighting stance. Stone was ready for a rematch and confident of the outcome, now that he knew what to expect from Max and didn't have to worry about any innocent bystanders getting hurt. A fighter's true strength came from his heart and soul, Stone had been taught, and he'd put his soul up against a Serpent's any day. He beckoned Max with the universal hand gesture for bringing it on. "On your feet or off them, your choice."

Max declined the challenge. "If it's all the same to you, I think I'll delegate this time around." He raised his voice to address an unseen presence. "Echidna, reinforcements if you please."

A computerized voice replied via a public-address system. "*Understood. Alerting security.*"

"Hang on," Stone said, taken aback. "Did you just order up more muscle via Alexa or Siri or something?"

"The name is Echidna, and she's quite a time-saver." Max smirked at Stone. "See for yourself."

A door slammed open behind Max and three more guards stormed in from an adjacent room. They rushed to defend Max and Coral, wielding a truncheon, a switchblade, and brass knuckles, respectively. They looked annoyed at having their downtime interrupted and more than willing to bust some overstuffed Librarian skulls.

"Wait a second!" Cassandra protested. "Where'd these guys come from?"

"Beats me." Stone suddenly found himself facing off against three new opponents instead of the guy he really wanted to spar with. He took up a defensive position between the men and Cassandra. "I thought that was a closet door!"

"But you're the architecture guy!" she said. "You're supposed to know about old houses and stuff!"

"Every old house is different." He ducked and weaved, staying constantly in motion so the henchmen couldn't catch him in a squeeze play. The trick with fighting multiple opponents was to keep them in each other's way. Seizing the offensive was also key to overcoming a number disadvantage. "That's what makes them so fascinating. They're not all standard-issue, like today's cookie-cutter McMansions. They have character, individuality—"

"I get the point," she said. "Less lecturing, more kung fu!"

"But I was just getting warmed up." Stone dodged a knife-thrust by executing a flawless Flying Armadillo spin taught to him by the Monkey King himself. The move worked better with a prehensile tail, but, combined with a reverse Yeti punch and a triple Swaying Bamboo counterattack, Stone managed to throw the Knife Guy into the path of the other two thugs, causing Baton Guy to trip over Knuckles, who knocked over a dry-erase board, setting off a chain reaction that caused the other boards to tumble like dominoes. "Although, yeah, I'm wasting my breath on these lunkheads."

What was worse, the goons were just dangerous enough to keep him too busy to go after Max, who didn't seem inclined to stick around for the end of the bout. Keeping clear of the fight, Max called out to Coral, who was waging a tug-of-war with Cassandra over a marked-up map of the United States that had been stretched atop a table. The map tore down the middle, causing both women to stumble backward, each clutching half of the map.

"I fear our privacy has been compromised," Max told Coral. "Prudence suggests we seek a change of address." He collected the skull and the reliquary, lifting the latter by its handle while tucking the former in the crook of his arm. "Echidna, initiate extraction procedure . . . with all due haste."

"*Understood*," the digital helper replied. "*Your lift is en route.*"

Stone heard the helicopter revving up outside.

Crap, he's making a break for it, while I'm tied up with the hired help!

Ducking beneath a swinging truncheon while delivering a gut-punch to Baton Guy, Stone watched in frustration as Max headed for the balcony overlooking the backyard. Cassandra tried to chase after them, but was hampered by the four-way brawl between her and the balcony. She tossed her half of the map over Knife Guy's head to mess with his vision, then scrambled backward to keep from being stabbed, clubbed, or punched.

"Come along, Coral," Max said. "Our ride awaits."

The pink-haired alchemist hesitated. "But the maps, the gold . . ."

"Leave them," Max said forcefully. "We can't let your prism fall into the hands of the Library, who will lock it away for all time."

Coral blanched at the prospect. "I'm coming!"

Stone fumed in frustration as the goons covered their boss's escape. Caught up in the brawl, the two-fisted Librarian could only watch out of the corner of his eye as the helicopter came whirring into view, hovering parallel to the balcony. The wash from its spinning rotors invaded the attic, blowing loose papers around like chaff. Max put down the skull and reliquary long enough to help Coral over the railing and into the passenger compartment of the copter before turning to take his leave. Reaching into his pocket, he took out a fake gold coin and lobbed it toward his embattled foes.

"Good-bye, Librarians!" Max shouted over the whir of the rotors. "Rest assured I *will* possess the Pot, no matter where it is hiding!" He reclaimed the skull and reliquary, gripping the grinning skull like a bowling ball with his fingers in its empty eye sockets. "But first: Echidna, execute Gomorrah Protocol."

"Understood. Five minutes to detonation."

"Detonation?"

Stone knew a self-destruct sequence when he heard one.

Max was cutting his losses—and he didn't want to leave any incriminating evidence behind.

"You hear that, dudes?" Stone barked at the henchmen. "Your boss just left you to blow up with the premises. You going to keep tussling with me . . . or get the hell out of Dodge?"

The thugs paused and looked at each other. Black eyes, split lips, and a busted nose indicated where Stone had managed to get his licks in. Beyond the balcony, Max and the helicopter were already taking off without them.

"Four minutes to detonation," Echidna reported.

"Screw this," Knuckles said. "I'm saving my own skin."

Abandoning the fight, he bolted for the stairs, with his buddies close behind him. Stone let them go; he had bigger things on his plate than chasing after these small fry.

Staying alive, for one thing.

"We gotta go," he told Cassandra.

"Hang on." She was sorting through the overturned boards and scattered papers, trying to absorb as much intel as she could. Avid eyes scanned the contents of the war room. "Just give me a few more moments."

Stone dragged her away from the debris. "There's no time for that. This whole place is going to blow!"

"Wait!" she said. "I can make sense of this. I know I can!"

"Not if you're blown to smithereens." Stone was worried about Baird and Ezekiel, too, but had to hope that they were already making their own escape. "We need you more than we need any secret info!"

"Three minutes to detonation."

Racing the countdown, Stone ran through their options at lightning speed. Fighting their way down three flights of stairs, possibly encountering various hostile Serpents, was going to take too long. He tried calling Jenkins, but got a busy signal. He hoped that meant Jenkins was occupied firing up a Magic Door for the rest of the team.

"Two minutes to detonation."

There was no time to waste. They were going to have to go for the quickest route out of danger. Hustling Cassandra onto the balcony, he scowled at the sight of Max's helicopter vanishing into the cloudy night sky, then peered over the railing at the moat several stories below.

"Wonder just how deep that is."

Cassandra looked aghast. "Please tell me you're not thinking what I think you're thinking."

"You ever see *Butch Cassidy and the Sundance Kid*?"

"Don't they die in the end?"

"Not from the fall."

Lifting all one-hundred-plus pounds of her, he hurled her over the railing. A descending scream terminated in a loud splash.

"One minute to detonation."

That was as close as he wanted to call it. Vaulting over the rail, he plunged toward the chilly black water below, counting on gravity to save him. Accelerating faster than the bomb could count down, he hit the water feetfirst and sank below the surface, discovering to his relief that the moat was deep enough to keep him from slamming into the bottom. He kicked to the surface in search of air and Cassandra, not necessarily in that order, and found her treading water in the shadow of the mansion, which he figured had to be going boom any second now.

"Dive!" he shouted. "As deep as you can!"

They submerged themselves with only a heartbeat to spare.

A massive explosion shook the moat, the deafening blast and shock wave only slightly muffled by the water. Chunks of shattered masonry rained down on them, falling past Stone and Cassandra as they swam underwater toward the opposite side of the moat.

One good thing, Stone thought. *If there is any nasty creature dwelling in the moat, it's gotta be hiding now.*

Starving lungs drove them back to the surface. Panting, they crawled onto the grounds behind where the mansion used to be. Cold and wet and pumped with adrenaline, Stone looked back at the conflagration they had narrowly escaped. Eden Manor was nothing but flaming rubble. Thick plumes of smoke and ash rose toward the heavens, taking with them whatever useful clues the team might have salvaged otherwise. Max had burned his bridges behind him—in a big way.

Cassandra gaped at the destruction. "Baird and Ezekiel must have gotten out in time, right?" She hugged herself to keep from shivering. "There's no way they were trapped in there?"

"I don't know, Cassie. I wish I could be sure of that."

"This is why I hate alarms," Ezekiel said.

He and Baird were pinned down in the underground vault while angry Serpents, locked out of the safe, did their damnedest to force their way in. So far the two of them had heard automatic weapons fire and sledgehammers pound against the other side of the thick steel door. Ezekiel figured power drills and welding torches were only a matter of time.

"How long until they get in?" Baird asked.

"Not soon," he replied. "This vault is rock-solid. We're going to run out of air long before anybody breaks in here."

"Why don't I find that reassuring?"

Ezekiel couldn't figure out a way to put a positive spin on suffocation, so he started stuffing his pockets with precious gold coins instead. He couldn't carry off the entire contents of the vault, but he'd never forgive himself if he didn't at least make a dent in it.

"Seriously?" Baird asked him. "At a time like this?"

He shrugged. "It's evidence, right? Minus a small finder's fee, that is."

"That's what you're thinking about right now—?"

An automated voice, blaring over a public-address system, intruded on the conversation:

"Attention! Gomorrah Protocol in effect. Five minutes to detonation."

The pounding on the door halted abruptly, leaving them alone in the vault with an unexpected complication.

"Detonation?" Ezekiel echoed.

"Gomorrah?" Baird said. "As in fire and brimstone? That doesn't sound good."

Ezekiel had to agree. In his experience, secret bases and headquarters had an unfortunate tendency to go up in flames when compromised. He could only assume that the Serpent Brotherhood believed in covering its tracks as well.

"On the bright side," he observed, "it sounds like the bad guys have given up trying to get to us."

"Because they know better than to stick around for the fireworks." Baird surveyed their surroundings. "What do you think? Can this vault survive a big blast?"

"Hard to say without knowing what kind of explosion we're talking about," Ezekiel replied. "Personally, I don't want to take my chances." He nodded at the sealed vault entrance. "That counts as a door, right?"

Baird's face lit up. "You bet it does!"

"Of course, we'll have to risk opening it," he pointed, "without knowing who or what is waiting on the other side."

"*Four minutes to detonation*," a voice updated them.

Baird took out her phone. "Do it."

Grabbing a solid-gold candlestick just in case, Ezekiel worked the keypad on the inside of the vault. Overriding the emergency lockdown was child's play, but it wasn't until after he hit the final key that it occurred to him that the whole self-destruct countdown might be just a ploy to trick them into opening the vault from the inside. Ezekiel held his breath as the door slid open.

He was going to feel really stupid if he got shot right now.

But the open door revealed only an empty basement, which meant that the countdown was no joke. "Baird?"

"I'm on it." She stepped outside of the vault to get a better signal before dialing the Annex. "Jenkins! We need an extraction, ASAP." She took a picture of the vault entrance. "I'm sending you a photo and the precise GPS coordinates now."

Ezekiel couldn't hear the other end of the conversation, but he could imagine Jenkins hurrying over to the tricked-out globe that operated the Magic Door. He mentally spurred the ageless caretaker on.

"*Three minutes to detonation.*"

Pilfered gold weighed down Ezekiel's pockets as he waited tensely for their escape route. He wished he had time to load up on some more treasure, but knew better than to ask Baird to grab an armful, particularly when she was trying to save their lives.

A bright white light filled the doorway, rewarding her efforts.

"Right on time," she said. "Thank you, Jenkins."

"Hold on," Ezekiel said. "What about Stone and Cassandra?"

"We'll meet them on the other side," Baird said. "Just like we planned."

"And if they're not there?"

"They'll be there," she stated.

"But how do you know that?"

"Because they're Librarians."

23

"Max said that he was after *the* Pot," Stone said. "Not *a* pot, or *pots*, but *the* Pot, as in one particular pot of gold he hasn't found yet."

The team had converged back at the Annex to dissect what they'd learned from the raid on Eden Manor. Stone had been relieved to find Baird and Ezekiel waiting for them after he and Cassandra had taken a return trip through the mausoleum door. Dry clothes and hot coffee had helped put the moat behind them, although Stone's hair still smelled of smoke and ash. Bridget and Brigid were also on hand, anxious to get the scoop on what was happening.

"And he didn't seem all that concerned about leaving that other gold behind," Cassandra added. She was seated at the conference table along with the others, all except for Jenkins, who preferred the privacy of his own desk. "From what I could gather from the charts and notes I glimpsed, he's all about locating a specific pot."

"Belonging to one particular leprechaun?" Baird speculated. "And he's been hunting leprechauns in general just to find the right one?"

"Sucks to be one of the wrong leprechauns, I guess." Ezekiel had his feet up on the table. "Too bad we don't know who the real target is."

"I may be able to remedy that." Jenkins rose to address the room. "While you've been bearding the enemy in their lair, I've been cross-referencing the Library archives with the leprechaun census reports I acquired from Mill Ends. It took considerable time and effort, but I've determined that a particular leprechaun, one Finbar O'Gradaigh, completely fell off the grid nearly sixteen hundred years ago, around the same time as a certain incident on Saint Patrick's mountain, almost as though he has been in hiding ever since."

"So what are we thinking?" Baird asked. "That this Finbar character is the leprechaun who ran afoul of the Serpent Brotherhood way back when? And that they're still after his personal pot of gold for some reason?"

"MacDonagh said that the bad guys were targeting hermits and loners," Cassandra recalled. "If Finbar has been lying low since the fifth century, he could be the one they're really after."

"But what's so special about his pot of gold?" Ezekiel asked.

"That, Mister Jones, remains a mystery," Jenkins said, "although I'm hopeful that more research will shed some light in that direction."

The leprechaun's name tugged at Stone's memory. "'O'Gradaigh,'" he repeated. "As in 'Grady'?"

"My Grady?" Bridget blurted. "From the pub?"

"'Grady' would be a modern derivation of 'O'Gradaigh,'" Jenkins noted.

"Indeed, 'tis a fine old Irish name," Brigid said. "Among both mortals and the Wee Folk alike."

Jenkins looked at the other Bridget. "How much do you know about this individual's background, Miss O'Neill?"

"Nothing really," she admitted. "He just showed up a while back, offering to play his fiddle at the pub in exchange for free drinks. Seemed like a fair exchange at the time."

"He implied he couldn't return to Ireland because of some unspecified issue," Baird said. "I just assumed he was alluding to The Troubles, not to some close encounter with the Serpent Brotherhood centuries ago."

Stone recalled the switcheroo Grady had pulled on Max back at the pub, trading his fiddle for Max's pistol. Stone never had figured out exactly how Grady had pulled off that magic trick. . . .

"Whoa!" Bridget said. "Grady's a crafty old devil, to be sure, but are you seriously suggesting that he's actually a leprechaun?"

Cassandra took a book down from a shelf. She gently opened it to reveal a four-leaf clover pressed between its pages.

"Only one way to find out," she said.

24

※ *Chicago* ※

The Pot O' Gold was packed. It seemed that not even the disturbances of the past few days could keep Chicagoans away from an Irish pub on Saint Patrick's Day. Festive folk, dead-set on getting their Irish on, crammed into the pub, which had been spruced up just in time for the holiday. Green was the color du jour, proudly displayed via sweaters, bandannas, feather boas, plastic bowler hats, novelty eyeglass frames, tiaras, wigs, sequins, and beads, while green beer flowed as freely as the Chicago River, which had also been dyed for the occasion. Cassandra, who was visiting the pub for the first time, saw why Bridget couldn't afford to close her doors today, no matter the various menaces stalking her. Not opening on Saint Patrick's Day would be akin to, well, throwing away a pot of gold.

Good for her, Cassandra thought. *I know all about getting on with life despite a threat hanging over your head.*

Bogus leprechauns, sporting fake red beards, store-bought costumes, and exaggerated "Oirish" accents, mingled with the other customers, but Cassandra had yet to spot anything resembling the real thing from her stool at the bar. The four-leaf clover she'd found in Otherworld was threaded through a buttonhole in her warm woolen sweater. Green leggings and a glass of emerald beer kept up appearances as well.

"What's keeping Grady?" she asked Bridget, who was busy behind the bar, assisted by Brigid, whom they were passing off as a visiting "cousin" from Dublin. Cassandra struggled to keep watch over the giddy crowds streaming in and out of the pub. "Has he showed up yet? Did I miss him?"

It didn't help that, unlike the other Librarians, she hadn't met Grady yet.

"No sign of him," Bridget said, a puzzled look on her face. "I don't understand it. I can't imagine he'd skip today of all days."

Unless, Cassandra fretted, he'd been scared off by the banshee or the Brotherhood, or both. She hoped that she and the others were not wasting their time staking out the pub, waiting for somebody who had already made himself scarce. What if O'Gradaigh—if that's who Grady truly was—dropped out of sight for another fifteen-hundred-plus years?

The rest of the team was positioned strategically throughout the pub, ready for anything, or so they hoped. Like Cassandra, they'd dressed to blend in with the crowd. Baird was sporting a green turtleneck sweater and a shamrock tattoo on her cheek, Stone had on a green flannel shirt and a miniature bowler hat, while Ezekiel was cheekily flaunting an oversized "Kiss Me, I'm Irish!" button. Bridget's gold coin, which Max had already made a play for, remained safely tucked away in the Annex under Jenkins's watchful eye. None of the rowdy pub-crawlers appeared to notice its absence.

"Och," Brigid said as she served up another pitcher of green beer. She couldn't operate a modern cash register, but she could pour and serve drinks with the best of them. With her long hair tied up in the back, she resembled her double more than ever. She wiped her brow with the back of her hand. "And here I thought the Fair Folk knew how to make merry!"

"Love your accent!" a tipsy celebrant enthused. "Is it for real?"

Cassandra chuckled. *You have no idea*, she thought.

Amused by the exchange, she almost missed it when a grizzled old fellow sat down at the bar a few seats away, a well-worn fiddle tucked under his arm. He tipped his paddy cap at the redhead tending the bar.

"Forgive me tardiness, me fine girl. 'Tis packed the streets and sidewalks are. A soul can barely make one's way through the crush and all."

"Och," Brigid said. "I think ye've mistaken me for me cousin."

"Cousin?" The fiddler's eyes bulged. Confusion gave way to what looked like genuine consternation on his weathered features. "Nay, it cannot be. . . ."

"Me name is Brigid," she said, "and I'm pleased to meet ye."

"Bridget and Brigid?" A frown deepened the creases on his face. "Is this a trick ye're playing on me?"

His perturbed reaction caught the actual Bridget's attention.

"That's him!" She reached across the bar to nudge Cassandra, and whispered as she walked over to Grady, "Talking to Brigid!"

Grady?

Cassandra placed her hand over the magic four-leaf clover and closed her eyes for a moment. Reopening them, she gasped as the seemingly ordinary fiddler rippled like a mirage—or a faerie glamour dissolving. All at once, "Grady" was replaced by an honest-to-goodness leprechaun straight out of the storybooks, dressed entirely in green, from his cocked hat to his breeches. A bushy red beard spouted from nowhere, while Grady lost at least three feet in height perched atop his bar-stool. His fiddle shrank in size as well. Brass buckles gleamed upon his shoes.

Leprechaun in the house, Cassandra thought. *I call that a positive ID.*

She signaled the others by raising her glass and loudly toasting in a prearranged code word.

"Slainte!"

Nearby revelers joined in the toast, so the rest of the team couldn't possibly miss it. Baird and the guys began to quietly converge on Grady, squeezing their way across the crowded pub. Cassandra hopped off her stool and approached Grady, who was too preoccupied by the twin Bs to notice. The leprechaun looked anxiously back and forth between the two women, trying to make sense of it. More than just puzzled, he appeared genuinely distressed. He shook his head unhappily.

"Both of youse in one place? Sure, this can't be happening. . . ."

Bridget played it cool. "About time you got here, you old rapscallion. Let me guess—you want a wee nip before playing?" She stalled until Cassandra could join them. "Say, have you met my friend Cassandra? I was telling her all about you."

"Is that so?" The leprechaun turned toward Cassandra, then froze at the sight of the genuine four-leaf clover on her sweater. Their eyes met and a flicker of alarm crossed his face, as though he could see his true reflection in her eyes. He swallowed hard. "Pleased to meet ye, miss, but I must be going—"

Cassandra grabbed him by the wrist. "Finbar O'Gradaigh, I presume?"

The leprechaun tried to tug his arm free, but she'd caught

him fair and square. She kept her gazed fixed on him while waiting for the rest of the team to make it to the bar. The general hullabaloo of the pub drowned out Grady's protests.

"Unhand me, ye cunning jezebel!"

"Not until we find out what's so special about your pot of gold, and why the Serpent Brotherhood wants it so much."

His ruddy face went pale. "Ye don't know what ye're asking!"

"Explain it to me then. What are you so afraid of?"

Before he could answer, a mournful cry rang out across the pub. Cassandra turned to see a middle-aged, rather matronly woman emerge from the crowd, which nervously parted to let her through. Hints of white infiltrated her dark brown hair. A tattered gray shawl was draped over her shoulders. Her mouth hung open as she wailed in anguish. Her eyes were red from weeping. Tears stained her cheeks. She wrung her hands as the other customers stared at her in shock and confusion. A few crossed themselves.

"No, no," Bridget murmured, clutching her chest. "Not tonight, not now—"

"*The bean-sidhe!*" Brigid said. "She's come, just as ye said— but for whom?"

Understandably distracted by the banshee, Cassandra lost her grip on the leprechaun, who slipped free and bounded off the barstool onto the floor. Nobody else noticed the sprite making his escape, and Cassandra reminded herself that she was the only one who could see past the glamour disguising the leprechaun. Everyone else still saw only a rumpled old fiddler.

A leprechaun and *a banshee*, she marveled, *on Saint Patrick's Day no less! Talk about getting in touch with my Irish roots!*

Cassandra hesitated, torn between pursuing Grady and

shielding Bridget from the banshee. According to Jenkins, a banshee only warned of impending doom; she didn't actually attack people. But could the ominous specter scare Bridget to death if it got too close, what with her weak heart and all?

Cassandra's own pulse was certainly racing.

The banshee approached the bar. Her woeful gaze swept back and forth between Bridget and Brigid, as though momentarily confused as to whom she was haunting. Her keening acquired a quizzical note; you could practically hear the question mark.

"Keep away from them!" The leprechaun bounced onto the bar between the banshee and her targets. Wide eyes and startled gasps came from the other customers as Cassandra realized that he had just revealed his true form to the banshee—and everyone else. The little man shook his tiny fist defiantly. "'Tis meself ye've been searching for, isn't it? All these many years?"

The banshee threw back her head and wailed at the top of her lungs. Unclasping her hands, she pointed an accusing finger at O'Gradaigh. Glasses and lightbulbs shattered, panicking the other customers. Tables and chairs were knocked over by the frightened crowd, forcing Baird to go to the rescue of a toppled senior citizen who was in danger of being trampled, even as the banshee lunged toward the leprechaun with outstretched arms and grasping claws.

"Uh-uh!" Stone shouted above the keening. "Find your own leprechaun!"

"You tell her!" Ezekiel said. "And tell her to dial down the volume, too!"

Shoving their way through the panicky crowd, the Librarians converged on the banshee from both left and right. They tackled her simultaneously, but she dissolved into a gray mist, causing Stone and Ezekiel to collide instead. They ended up sprawled on the floor, grappling with each other.

"Son of a gun!" Stone growled. "Where she'd go?"

"Don't ask me!" Ezekiel said. "I'm still trying to figure out where she came from!"

Baird helped the fallen oldster to his feet. "Forget the banshee for now!" she shouted from across the pub. "Grab that leprechaun!"

But Grady had another idea.

"Many thanks for coming to me rescue, lads!" he called to the guys as they clumsily untangled themselves. "Pardon me if I don't stick around to buy ye a pint or two!"

He dashed down the length of the bar and out the front door.

"Oh, no!" Cassandra said. "You're not getting away from me! I caught you once and I can catch you again!"

She sprinted out of the pub—into a raucous green madhouse.

Saint Patrick's Day had taken over downtown Chicago, possibly even more so than inside the pub. One of several parades was progressing down the street, while the sidewalks were overflowing with spectators and merrymakers. Bagpipes and drum corps competed with the general din of the celebration. Mobs of seasonally Irish partyers jostled Cassandra as she suddenly grasped the challenge before her: trying not to lose a leprechaun on Saint Patrick's Day was like trying to keep track of a zombie on Halloween or a Harley Quinn at a comic-book convention. She checked to make sure her fourleaf clover was secure.

I'm going to need all the luck I can get.

The brisk temperature came as a jolt after the toasty comfort of the pub. Several feet ahead, O'Gradaigh wove through a procession of Irish dancers river-dancing their way through an intersection. Cassandra ran into the street, barely dodging a pungent puddle of lime-green puke, only to be greeted by squealing brakes as a holiday float, crafted to resemble an enormous pot of gold, nearly flattened her. Fake leprechauns and local beauty queens, tossing green beads and foil-wrapped chocolate coins, shouted at her to get out of the way.

"Sorry!" Cassandra yelled back sheepishly. "Excuse me!"

Crossing the street in front of the parade despite the jeers of onlookers, she momentarily lost sight of O'Gradaigh, then spotted him strutting down the sidewalk, heading away from her. She raced forward and, bending low, grabbed him from behind.

"Told you!" she said. "You're not getting away from me that easily!"

"Hey, you want me, babe, you got me!"

Her prisoner twisted around to reveal the leering face of a different little person, of the strictly mortal variety. His bristly red beard was held on by an elastic band and was about as real as his rubber pointed ears. His breath reeked of whiskey as he puckered up expectantly. "Lay it on me, baby!"

Cassandra yanked back her arms.

"Sorry! Wrong leprechaun!"

"Hey, where you going, Red?" he objected as she pulled away from him. "You know what they say, big things come in small packages!"

Ignoring the disappointed "leprechaun," she frantically scanned the crowd for the real O'Gradaigh, but was stymied by the overpopulated festivities all around her. It was like trying to find the four-leaf clover in acres of shamrocks all over again!

"Where is he?" Baird asked as the team caught up with her. "Did he get away?"

"I don't know!" Cassandra shivered in the wintry weather, hugging herself to stay warm. "Maybe."

"He's gotta be here somewhere," Stone said. "He can't have just disappeared."

"You mean, like the banshee did?" Ezekiel pointed out.

Cassandra didn't think O'Gradaigh could just go invisible, at least not while she was wearing her four-leaf clover, but she feared that he had given them the slip the old-fashioned way, aided and abetted by the celebrations in the streets. It occurred to her that, in a sense, the leprechaun had been rescued by Saint Patrick a second time. . . .

Or had he?

Wailing like a police siren, the banshee reappeared, flying low over the Librarians' heads. Startled bystanders oohed and aahed and pointed in amazement, evidently thinking that the airborne wraith was part of the parade. Marching horses reared up in fright, almost throwing their riders. A chill passed through Cassandra in the banshee's wake, along with a sudden revelation.

"She's after Grady . . . Finbar . . . whatever!" With any luck, the relentless specter was on the leprechaun's trail and could lead them straight to him, if they could just keep up with her. "Follow that banshee!"

———

The jig was up, Grady feared.

After years of hiding far from his native land, his worst fear had come to pass: the banshee had found him at last. He should've known better than to show his face at the pub again, and indeed had almost chosen to stay well clear of the place tonight, but, in the end, he had not been able to leave sweet Bridget unattended, not while she was beset by evils from his own guilty past.

She's a fine, brave girl, she is. She shouldn't have to pay for me crimes.

Had that been the banshee's intent all along? he wondered. To terrorize Bridget in hopes of flushing him out of hiding? If so, the devious campaign had worked all too well.

He dashed through the teeming streets, feeling like a fox pursued by hounds, even as he tried to make sense of how all his craft and cunning had failed him, bringing him to this sorry pass. No doubt that she-devil, Sibella, would say that sentiment was his undoing in the end, but she'd had no heart, that one. She'd never understand that some ties could stretch across the centuries, all the way to a New World across the ocean.

And what of that other Brigid back at the pub? That was no "cousin," to be sure; Grady knew full well who that flame-haired beauty was, even though he had not laid eyes on her since she was a wee babe many hundreds of years ago, when he'd filched her from her cradle, leaving a changeling in her place, in order to hide that other child from the Serpents after that close call on the mountain. The real Brigid had been given to the Fair Folk to raise, but when and how she had come to these shores he'd no way of knowing.

And what was she doing in these parts, here and now?

The questions dogged him as he ran for his life, frustrated by the jubilant mobs clogging the city. The ruckus in the streets provided welcome cover, but also impeded his flight to a worrisome degree. His present dwelling was hidden beneath a venerable oak tree in Lincoln Park, but could he reach the park before his various pursuers caught up with him? That was the question, wasn't it?

A fearsome keening chased after him, proving beyond a doubt that he had not run far or fast enough. Glancing back over his shoulder, he saw the banshee, in her guise as a mourning mother, gliding over the heads of mortal merrymakers, with the Librarians in hot pursuit as well. The implacable wraith was gaining on him, her greedy hands reaching out for him. Her pale gray shroud trailed behind her like the tail of a comet, yet another omen of ill fortune. Grady felt an old curse breathing down his neck, reawakened by all the wild new magic at loose in the world. Alas, when he had shared that old gold with Bridget, he had failed to grasp just how powerfully the coins would call out to the banshee now that the ley lines were flowing stronger than they had in centuries.

"Make way!" Grady shouted at the laggards blocking his escape. "Let me through!"

"What's your hurry, old man?" a drunken lout mocked him. Green face paint and a ridiculous felt hat made a mockery of Erin's ancient mysteries, prompting Grady to wish that he had brought a shillelagh instead of a fiddle to the pub this night. Cheap beer slopped from the eejit's bottle as he spied the banshee drawing near. "Whoa, check out the spooky special effects!"

The banshee dipped toward Grady, who feared his goose was as good as cooked, but the spirit's descent brought her within reach of Cassandra, who sprang upward and grabbed the banshee by the hem of her flowing gown.

"Leave him alone!" the plucky colleen shouted. "I caught him first!"

The banshee shrieked in anger, causing people up and down the block to cover their ears, but Cassandra, who was obviously a Librarian, did not let go of the spirit's garb even as it yanked her off her feet into the air.

"Yikes!"

The girl weighed down the banshee, who was solid enough when materialized, keeping her from climbing more than a story or so. Howling, the specter glared furiously at Cassandra before vanishing from sight, leaving the Librarian clutching nothing but a wisp of mist. Cassandra screamed, almost as loudly as the banshee had, as she plunged toward the crowded sidewalk below. Grady's heart quailed at the sight.

Not another paying for me sins!

"Here she comes!" Baird shouted. She and Stone and Ezekiel rushed to catch Cassandra, getting beneath her just in time. A few brave passersby joined in the effort as well, forming a human net to cushion Cassandra's fall and keep her from striking the pavement. She landed with a muffled thump in the arms of her rescuers, including Baird's. "Got you!"

Cassandra gasped as she was gently lowered back onto her feet. "Remind me not to hitch a ride on a banshee again!"

"'Cause that situation comes up so often," Baird joked.

Ezekiel shrugged. "Pretty sure we're not done with that banshee."

"I wish!" Stone said. "My ears could use a break—and so could Bridget."

Grady watched the Librarians warily. Glad as he was to see that Cassandra had survived her reckless tangle with the banshee, the leprechaun knew better than to stick around. While the Librarians and their Guardian paused to assure themselves that Cassandra had only had the breath knocked out of her, Grady took advantage of his reprieve to resume his desperate attempt to evade his pursuers, both mortal and otherwise. The ceaseless crowds made him feel like the fabled Salmon of Knowledge, swimming upstream against the current, so he took off down a narrow alley instead, hoping for a clearer path to safety.

Yet the Librarians proved almost as persistent as the banshee. Marking his dodge, they raced into the alley after him, no more willing to give up their quest than Erasmus and Deidre and the pious Padraic had been so many centuries ago. Grady felt as though history was repeating itself, with himself caught between the Librarians and the Serpent Brotherhood once more, and a vengeful banshee now added to the stew he was boiling in.

"Come back here, Grady!" Baird hollered. "We just want to talk to you!"

Grady couldn't chance it. The Librarians meant well, no doubt, but they had their own agenda and no idea what was truly at stake. They could not guarantee his safety from either the banshee or the Brotherhood, so he could not risk being detained by them. Running and hiding was what had kept him safe for centuries, ever since he'd stolen that damnable Pot. . . .

Flight was a fugitive's sole recourse.

The frantic chase was taking its toll on him, however. He was breathing hard, and a stitch stabbed his side with every step. The mortals' long legs gave them an unfair advantage as they ate up the distance between them and him. But the end of the alley beckoned, urging him on.

"Leave me be!" he pleaded. "For mercy's sake!"

"Not a chance!" Stone shouted. "This is all about you somehow . . . and your Pot!"

Not me *Pot*, Grady thought. *Not at first.*

Now was hardly the moment, though, to share that woeful tale, not with all the world closing in on him, or so it seemed. Breaking from the alley just ahead of the Librarians, he looked up and down the sidewalk, weighing his options. To his dismay, the walks appeared nearly as crowded as the parade route. No clear path to freedom presented itself.

If only he could wish himself a wee bit of luck!

An all-too-familiar wail came from above. Looking up in alarm, Grady saw the banshee swooping down at him yet again. Weary of being chased and hunted, the leprechaun briefly flirted with the notion of letting the banshee call the death-coach for him at last. At least he could finally stop looking over his shoulder . . . and perhaps the banshee would then leave poor Bridget alone?

Suddenly a sleek black limousine pulled up sharply to the curb. A passenger door flew open and a woman with fluorescent-green hair called out to him.

"In here! Hurry!"

Grady hesitated only a moment, all thought of surrender abruptly exorcised by the tantalizing prospect of seeing another morn. *Any port in a storm, so they say . . .*

He sprang into the back of the limo, landing on a black leather seat beside his nameless savior, who yanked the door shut behind him. Overhead, the banshee howled in frustration as the vehicle accelerated away from the curb and sped down the street, leaving the malignant specter behind. Grady gasped in relief as her blood-chilling wail receded into the distance.

"Many thanks, miss," he said. "Ye're a lifesaver, whoever ye may be. I'm right grateful to—"

His voice broke off as he saw who was sitting opposite them: Max the Serpent and his brutish bodyguard.

"Wait now!" Grady yelled as, too late, he grasped that he had jumped from the frying pan into the fire. Scrambling, he groped for the door, only to feel something cold and metallic click shut around his wrist. Silver cuffs bound him as surely as the silver wire Lady Sibella and her minions had twisted about his wrists on a bleak, moonlit night many centuries ago. And this time there would be no Librarian to free him, because they, too, had been left behind—and every moment was taking him farther away from his only hope of rescue.

Where is Saint Patrick now that I need him again?

The limo sped through the night. Grady's heart sank.

"We meet again, Mister O'Gradaigh." Max smirked in triumph. "My apologies for not recognizing you earlier, but your glamour fooled even me."

The woman removed her green wig to reveal hair an equally unnatural shade of pink. "Sorry we have to restrain you," she apologized, "but you wouldn't believe how long we've been looking for you."

"And me Pot," Grady said bitterly.

"But of course," Max said. "And now you're going to tell us exactly where you've hidden it."

25

"And then the limo pulled away," Cassandra said, "taking the leprechaun with it."

"Oh dear," Jenkins said, troubled by the news from Chicago. The Librarians and their Guardian had returned to the Annex to report the ominous turn of events. "I fear we must assume that Mister O'Gradaigh has indeed fallen into the hands of the Serpent Brotherhood, which puts them one step closer to obtaining his pot of gold, if they have not already done so."

"But what's the big deal about this one particular pot?" Stone asked. He paced restlessly about the Annex, understandably frustrated at losing the leprechaun to their foes. "What makes it so important?"

"That remains a puzzlement," Jenkins said. Stacks of tomes and scrolls from the Library's Hibernian Collection were now piled on his desk. "Although I am continuing to investigate the matter."

"At least the stakeout wasn't a total loss," Baird said. "We know for sure now that Grady is O'Gradaigh, who is presumably the same leprechaun who ran afoul of the Serpents way back in Saint Patrick's time."

"And we also learned that the banshee seems way more interested in Grady than in Bridget," Ezekiel pointed out. He fiddled with his phone in the way of most folks these days. "It forgot all about her to go chasing after Grady once he blew his cover."

Both Bridget and Brigid had chosen to remain back at the pub to cope with the holiday rush, which not even the banshee's reappearance had put a dent in; if anything, curious crowds had been drawn to the Pot O' Gold by spreading talk of actual leprechaun and banshee sightings. Despite the tumult, Bridget was looking to have her most profitable Saint Patrick's Day ever, while the existence of the Magic Door ensured that the Librarians were only a phone call away from rushing back to Chicago should the need arise, although Jenkins rather suspected that the Brotherhood would leave Bridget alone now that they'd acquired O'Gradaigh himself. They had what they were really after, at least in part.

And as for the banshee . . .

"From what you say," Jenkins said, "it does sound as though the banshee's primary target is the elusive Mister O'Gradaigh."

"I'm guessing somebody sicced that banshee on Grady long ago," Stone said. "Cursing him because of something to do with that pot the Brotherhood is after."

Ezekiel snickered. "Sorry. Just realized how funny that sounds if you take it the wrong way."

"Would that the Brotherhood were merely in pursuit of recreational herbs," Jenkins said. "But they would not be so intent on obtaining their prize if it didn't further some larger, undoubtedly malevolent purpose."

"Maybe the gold in that pot is special somehow, with unique magic powers?" Baird speculated. "Or points toward some more powerful magic object hidden somewhere in the world?"

"Both are plausible scenarios," Jenkins said, "although we should be careful not to be led astray by red herrings and false trails."

"So where does that leave us?" Cassandra asked anxiously. "The Brotherhood has Grady, which means they probably have his pot, too. Do we have to start preparing for some kind of Irish apocalypse or something?"

"Maybe," Baird said, "but we don't know for certain that they have the Pot already. Perhaps Grady can stall or resist them long enough for us to get to the Pot first? That's what we do, right? Find magical objects before the bad guys do?"

Jenkins admired her gumption and never-say-die attitude. *We could have used her in Camelot back in the day*, he thought. *Things might have turned out differently with a Colonel Baird to keep the Round Table in line.*

"Traditionally, there are only two ways to claim a lepre-chaun's pot of gold: capture the leprechaun or find the pot at the end of the rainbow. Given that the competition has already beaten us to the former, that leaves us with the latter."

"But rainbows don't actually have an end," Cassandra pro-tested. "They're simply sunlight refracted through water droplets in the sky. It's an optical phenomenon that occurs when the sun shines through a departing weather pattern at just the right angle. As it happens, Ireland gets more rainbows than most other countries because it gets lots of intermittent showers due to low-pressure systems in the North Atlantic, and because its distance from the equator means that it gets more sunlight coming in from no more than fifty-three de-grees above the horizon, significantly increasing the chance of the rainbows. But rainbows don't really touch down on the ground anywhere. There's no such thing as the end of the rainbow."

She paused as a contemplative look came over her face. "Unless . . ."

Jenkins could practically see the wheels spinning in her remarkable brain. "Yes, Miss Cillian?"

"Just a crazy idea," she said, "which might be worth trying once we have a better idea of where and how to find the right rainbow."

Curious, Jenkins was about to press her on the matter, when Stone cut to the chase instead.

"So it's a race," he said gruffly. "We need to find Grady's pot before Max does, if the Brotherhood hasn't already gotten their hands on it—which, of course, they've only been looking for since the fifth century."

Ezekiel snickered again.

"I'm sorry," he said, collapsing into giggles. "I can't help it!"

❈ *High above America* ❈

The silver handcuffs chafed Grady's wrists as the private jet whisked him away from Chicago and liberty. His short legs dangled over the floor as he sat across from Max and Coral in the aircraft's luxurious passenger cabin. The sleek interior of the cabin, which was all polished steel and plush black leather seats, was a far cry from the cozy ambience of Bridget's pub.

"Be a dear," he entreated Coral, holding out his cuffed hands, "and loosen me bonds a wee bit, for mercy's sake."

The woman, who struck Grady as having a slightly gentler nature than her cohorts, put down the energy drink she'd been sipping. She looked to her leader for his blessing. "Max?"

"Not for a moment," he said firmly as he meticulously

buffed his nails with a file. "We've searched for the Pot for too long to take any unnecessary chances now."

Grady scowled at the villain. "And where would I go, soaring high above the world as we are? Is it wings you expect me to sprout, so that I can flap me way to freedom? I'm a leprechaun, not a member of the heavenly host!"

"That may well be," Max conceded, "but your kind is notorious for its slippery ways. You'll remain bound until you've led us to the Pot, period."

"And then?" Grady asked.

"Well, that depends on how cooperative you are, I suppose," Max said. "But I've had enough experience with your trickery to want to keep you on a tight leash, as I'm certain you can understand."

Coral offered him a pained smile. "I'm sorry, Mister O'Gradaigh, but Max is right. There's too much at stake."

"And don't I know it," Grady said bleakly. "More's the pity."

"Déjà vu" was not an Irish expression, but Grady was feeling it now. His gaze fell upon a bleached skull resting upon a padded divan near the front of the cabin. Many mortal lifetimes had passed, and her lustrous black hair and ivory skin were long gone, but Grady recognized the late Lady Sibella from the viperish fangs that added bite to the skull's sinister grin. He shuddered as he remembered how close those fangs had come to slaying a certain Librarian ever so long ago. It seemed that even immigrating to the New World, along with so many others of his kin and countrymen, had not been enough to keep his past from catching up with him at last. History was repeating itself.

"A word of advice," he said to Max. "Ye might be wise to reconsider the path ye're taking." He nodded at the grisly relic.

"Sure it is that this quest did not end well for she who went before youse."

"I'll take my chances," Max said smugly. "The Serpent Brotherhood has not endured for millennia by giving up after a setback or two, even if it takes over fifteen centuries to finish what we started long ago."

Grady glowered at his captor. "Ye're just as reckless and arrogant as she was, no rest to her blackened soul."

Coral flinched at his harsh words and tone, but Max merely smirked.

"I'll take that as a compliment," he said, "while you had best hope that you are not wasting my valuable time with this transatlantic excursion." Ice entered his voice as his true colors showed through his polished manners. "It will not go well with you if this proves to be a wild-goose chase."

"'Tis nothing of the sort," Grady said. "I'm bound, in more ways than one, to take ye to me treasure for as long as you hold me captive. The Pot is back in blessed Eire, hidden away from the likes of youse . . . or so I had hoped it would remain."

He was not lying. When he'd finally departed Ireland back in 1850, taking only a decent store of gold to save for a rainy day, he'd left the Pot behind, safely stowed away, where none had ever found it in all the years since that fateful night on Patrick's mountain. He had hoped that it would remain there, undisturbed, until the crack of doom.

"But why leave such a treasure behind?" Coral asked. "I still don't understand."

"Why?" Grady echoed. "Because I wanted nothing to do with that cursed Pot, which has brought me naught but woe since your Lady Sibella forced me to steal it for her centuries ago. Better that it remained locked away from mortal and immortal alike than risk transporting it across the seas along with the rest of me meager possessions."

Max filed his nails. "If it's truly such a burden to you, we'll be delighted to take it off your hands."

"Ye'd like that, wouldn't ye, ye preening bashtoon?"

"But can't you just magically whisk it here?" Coral persisted. "Or transport us all to Ireland with a wish?"

"Across the vast ocean and halfway around the world?" Grady chuckled bitterly. "Ye flatter me, miss, if ye think me that powerful. I'm a humble fiddler, not one of the high-and-mighty Tuatha Dé Danann. And would I have endured that long sea voyage in steerage to reach America's welcoming shores all those years ago if I could just magic my way across the globe in the wink of an eye?" He shook his head. "If youse want that wretched Pot, ye'll have to go to where this long, doleful tale began: the green hills and valleys of Erin."

"Apt enough," Max conceded, "if deucedly inconvenient as well. Still, I suppose a touch of jet lag is a small price to pay for claiming the Pot after all this time." He sighed in resignation as he settled back into his seat in anticipation of the long flight ahead. "Congratulations, little man. Seems as though you're going home at last."

Grady wished that prospect brought him more joy than dread.

26

❊ *The Annex* ❊

"We need a clue," Stone said. "Just one clue to point us toward Grady's pot of gold."

He roamed impatiently around the office, all too aware that the Serpent Brotherhood had a head start on them—if Max and Company hadn't in fact already acquired the Pot. Baird was right that finding hidden magical artifacts was a big part of what being a Librarian was all about, but they still needed somewhere to start. The world was a big place, and even bigger than most people realized when you counted all the lost kingdoms and secret tombs. For all they knew, the Pot could be anywhere.

"What about that coin from the pub?" Ezekiel asked. "The one I cleverly filched back from Max? That's supposed to have come straight from Grady's pot." He fought back a giggle. "Sorry. Can't unhear that anymore."

"Try harder," Baird said. "But that's a good thought." She turned toward Jenkins, who had taken custody of the coin earlier. "Jenkins?"

"As you wish, Colonel."

He retrieved the gleaming gold coin from a locked drawer

in his desk and turned it over to the Librarians, who passed it back and forth as they took turns inspecting it.

"It's real gold all right," Ezekiel confirmed after biting down on it. "I'd know a counterfeit if I saw one."

Cassandra wiped the coin off with a tissue before scanning it with her favorite magic detector, which whirred and beeped in response.

"There's definitely some magic radiating from the gold, but nothing that tells me where the coin came from or where the rest of the Pot might be now."

She handed it to Stone, who contemplated the crowned god or king embossed on its surface. "Well, the art is definitely Celtic in origin, so it was presumably minted in Ireland, sometime before the fifth century, which is the last reported sighting of the Pot."

"When O'Gradaigh vanished with it and went into hiding," Baird said, nodding. "Anything else?"

"Not that I can see," Stone grumbled. "Too bad there's not any sort of written inscription."

"Are we sure of that?" Baird asked. "That old language—ogham—didn't you say that it was typically written on the *edges* of objects?"

"That's right!" Stone ran a callused finger along the thin edge of the coin, which had to be less than two millimeters thick. Was it just his imagination, or could he feel tiny notches scratched into the side of the coin? His pulse quickened in excitement. "Somebody get me a magnifying glass!"

"Right here!"

Cassandra procured a handheld magnifier from an antique desk and rushed it over to Stone. She and the others peered over his shoulder as he took a much closer look at the edge of the coin, where, sure enough, he saw what was unmistakably

ogham etched into it. The inscription was too small to be read
by the naked eye . . . but just small enough to have been written by one of the Little People?

"You called it!" he said. "There's something written here."

"By Grady?" Ezekiel wondered. "As a clue to where the rest
of the gold is?"

"Here's hoping," Baird said. "What does it say?"

"Give me a minute." Stone slowly rotated the coin as he attempted to translate the message. "I just need to figure out
where the inscription begins."

Jenkins stepped forward. "If I can be of assistance . . ."

"Thanks," Stone said, appreciating the offer, "but I've been
boning up on ogham ever since our trip to Ireland. I think I've
got it." He mentally double-checked his translation before
reading the inscription aloud:

*"I arise today through the strength of heaven . . . through the
firmness of rock."*

"Come again?" Ezekiel scratched his head. "Why do hidden messages always have to be so cryptic? Would it have
killed those old-school treasure hiders to make their clues
more user-friendly? Like maybe some convenient GPS coordinates for once?"

"I think that would defeat the point," Cassandra said.
"They're supposed to be tests, puzzles that only the wisest
and most worthy can solve, so that just anybody can't walk
off with the treasure."

"Whatever," Ezekiel said, unconvinced. He plopped down
in a chair. "I still think that Ye Olde Folk had too much time
on their hands, probably because TV and computer games
hadn't been invented yet."

"Focus, people," Baird said. "'The strength of heaven, the
firmness of rock'—what do we think that's all about?"

"That one's easy," Stone said. He had recognized the quote as he was translating it. "Those lines are part of a famous Irish prayer traditionally attributed to Saint Patrick . . . and used to ward off black magic and sorcery."

"As well as the Serpents?" Baird speculated.

Ezekiel shrugged. "Is there a difference?"

"Not as it matters," Jenkins said. "Any magic employed by the Brotherhood will surely be put to the blackest of ends."

Stone heard centuries of dire experience in the ageless caretaker's tone. He wondered exactly how many times Jenkins had seen the Serpents rear their venomous heads and how many souls had been lost in the ceaseless conflict between the Library and the Brotherhood. As Stone understood it, Flynn's own immediate predecessor, Edward Wilde, had been corrupted by the Serpents and had turned against the Library— with tragic results.

"Saint Patrick again," Baird noted. "Maybe the Pot is hidden somewhere associated with the historical Patrick?"

"Well, that certainly narrows it down," Jenkins said dryly. "In Ireland alone, there's no shortage of sites and shrines said to be linked to the legendary Patrick. Indeed, back in the days of pilgrims and pilgrimages, any Irish monastery or chapel worth its salt was going to claim Patrick as its founder, not unlike the way every Ray's Pizza in New York City bills itself as the Original Ray's."

"Well, we don't have time to search all of Ireland looking for the Pot." She wagged a finger at Ezekiel preemptively. "No more snickering."

Nodding, he clenched his jaw to maintain a poker face.

"Maybe there's another angle of approach here," Cassandra said, contemplating the globe by the back door. "We know that Grady, aka O'Gradaigh, seems to have been looking out for Bridget's family for generations. Family lore has it that a leprechaun provided the gold to open the pub in Chicago back in the day, and that he stepped up again with more gold when the pub and Bridget were in trouble."

"Plus, Grady protected Bridget from first Max, then the banshee," Stone recalled. "Even blowing his cover to lure the banshee away from Bridget."

"Because she's descended from a changeling," Cassandra reminded them, "and therefore has some leprechaun blood in her. Chances are, Bridget and Grady are related in some fashion."

"Makes sense," Baird said. "But how does this help us find the Pot?"

"By working the family connection and tracing Bridget's roots," Cassandra suggested. "If we can find out exactly where in Ireland her family immigrated from, then cross-reference that with historical sites associated with Saint Patrick, we'll have a place to start looking for the Pot."

"It's a slim lead," Stone said, "but it's our best shot. I'll get in touch with Bridget and start tracing her family's roots back to Ireland. With any luck, she knows some specifics about where her family came from: the name of a town or village, the port they sailed from, the names of some distant relations back in the Auld Sod. In fact, I think I remember seeing a framed black-and-white photo of a small Irish village back at the pub in Chicago, on a wall behind the bar. Some sort of family heirloom, maybe?"

Baird nodded in approval. "Sounds like a plan. I just wish the Serpents didn't have a head start on us."

"Do they?" Jenkins asked. "Don't forget, Colonel, we have one thing they don't have: a Magic Door that cuts down on the travel time to Ireland considerably. That advantage may allow you to catch up with our adversaries . . . and perhaps even pull ahead of them."

"So what are waiting for?" Baird said. "Get the Magic Door ready, Jenkins. We're heading back to Ireland."

27

The abandoned monastery lay in ruins atop a craggy hilltop overlooking a small rural village that looked reasonably quaint and cozy if you liked that sort of thing. Ezekiel would have preferred some place hipper and more exciting, but what were you going to do—magical relics tended to be hidden in the middle of nowhere, and this desolate locale certainly fit the bill. Crumbling stone walls and tombstones littered the damp, grassy landscape. Dawn was still a few hours away in this part of the world, so the ruins were dark and cold and dank. Flashlight beams supplemented a meager amount of moonlight.

"Wow." Stone eyed the glorified rubble as though it were the Taj Mahal. "You can still see remnants of the old cathedral and refectories and such. And look at that authentic High Cross over there, still standing after centuries." He gestured at a distinctly Celtic stone monument and whistled appreciatively. "Just imagine how this place must have looked back in the Dark Ages, when it was still an active monastic community, attracting devout scholars and scribes from all over. It's been said that Irish monks helped save Western civilization by preserving and copying countless books and manuscripts that might otherwise have been lost after the fall of Rome. . . ."

"Whatever, mate," Ezekiel said, unimpressed. Boring old ruins and statues were Stone's thing. Ezekiel just wanted to find the Pot and get back to someplace that actually had indoor plumbing, nightlife, and pizza. *Two trips to Ireland,* he thought, *and we still haven't come anywhere near an actual city.*

Baird surveyed their surroundings. "No sign of Serpents." She glanced up at the cloudy night sky. "Or rainbows, unfortunately. Are we sure this is the right place?"

"It's our best bet." Stone indicated the sleeping village below, which was located in the Midlands of Ireland. "After picking Bridget's brain regarding her family history, I did some homework back at the Library. It took some digging, but not only is Ballycarrick the ancestral birthplace of Bridget's ancestors, but these ruins are indeed associated with Saint Patrick, who is said to have founded this monastery back in the fifth century. Indeed, legend has it that this is where he baptized an early Irish chieftain who was one of the very first O'Neills."

Turning around, Stone pointed out the arched stone doorway the Librarians had just stepped through to reach the ruins. The door was all that remained of a collapsed gatehouse at the southwest fringe of the site. A robed figure bearing a shamrock was carved above the doorway, a stone halo circling his tonsured head.

"That's Patrick up there," Stone said. "You can tell by the shamrock, which he used to explain the concept of the Holy Trinity to the pagan Irish. Three leafs, but one flower— get it?"

"I'll take your word for it," Ezekiel said, "but doesn't pretty much every church, cemetery, pond, or wishing well in Ireland claim a connection to Saint Pat? Kind of like 'George Washington Slept Here' back in the States?"

"To a degree," Stone conceded, "but if you put Bridget, the inscription on the gold coin, and Saint Patrick together, this is where you wind up. Unless you've got a better idea?"

"Nope," Ezekiel said. "Just trying to keep us honest, as funny as that sounds coming from me."

"Somebody has to play devil's advocate," Cassandra said. "Might as well be your turn." A bulging backpack held some special gear she'd brought along from the Annex. She sighed as she gazed out over the extensive ruins, which covered several acres at least. "But where do you think the Pot is?"

Good question, Ezekiel thought. Looking around, he spied a slew of crumbling and collapsed structures left over from the monastery's medieval heyday, before centuries of war and invasions had reduced the place to rubble. In some cases, a single standing wall or archway was all that was left of what used to be a storehouse or a library or a chapel or whatever else your average old-school monastery needed. A gutted cathedral had long ago lost its roof and was now just a decrepit stone shell. A field of weathered tombstones and slabs marked the final resting places of generations of monks, who had shed their earthly woes well before Ezekiel's native Australia was colonized by convicts back in the day. A cylindrical watchtower loomed over the site, but Ezekiel doubted that anybody was on the lookout for would-be pillagers anymore.

From the sorry state of the ruins, the monastery had been well and thoroughly sacked a long, long time ago. Anything worth stealing had been carried off by Vikings or whomever . . . except, perhaps, for a certain pot of gold?

"You got me," Ezekiel replied to Cassandra. "There's way too many places to hide or bury an old pot. I don't even know where to start looking."

"The tower," Stone said confidently, striding forward. "Irish fortifications of that sort are often traditionally referred to as 'rocks,' as in the Rock of Cashel or the Rock of Dunamase. That particular tower? Known hereabouts as the Rock of Bally-carrick."

Baird made the connection. "*I arise today through the strength of heaven . . . through the firmness of rock.*"

"Bingo. A 'rock' climbing to heaven at a religious site founded by Saint Patrick." Stone led the way toward the tower. "Plus, round towers like this were specifically built to protect price-less relics and manuscripts from raiders. They're where the monks would hide their most valuable treasures in the event of an attack."

"Valuable treasures," Ezekiel echoed. "Like maybe a very special pot of gold?"

"That's what I'm thinking," Stone said, "although I still wish we knew what makes this Pot so special."

"First things first," Baird said. "Jenkins is hitting the books to figure that out, but job one is getting the Pot before Grady can lead Max and the Brotherhood to it. We can figure out *why* they want it later, hopefully."

Cassandra peered up at the tower, which looked to be about a hundred feet tall. "Still seems like an awfully big place to search. I assume we're talking a secret compartment or a hid-den passageway, with maybe a death trap or two?"

"Probably," Stone said. "The outer walls are at least a meter thick, which gives you plenty of room to hide a pot, and who knows what could be buried in the foundation?"

GREG COX

"You don't say?" Grinning, Ezekiel rubbed his palms to-gether. "Hidden treasure vaults waiting to be cracked? Things are definitely looking up."

They arrived at the base of the tower, where a series of well-worn stone steps led up to the open front entrance, which was located more than ten feet above the ground. The Librarians paused at the bottom of the steps.

"Why so high up?" Ezekiel asked.

"Couple of reasons," Stone explained. "Structurally, you put the opening higher up in order to avoid weakening the foundation of the tower. Defensively, it made it harder for raiders to gain access since—"

Ezekiel kicked himself for giving Stone another opportu-nity to lecture on old-timey architecture. At this rate, they'd never find the Pot.

"Just watch me gain access," he interrupted as he darted up the steps into the murky interior of the tower, which was missing its roof as well. He'd expected to find more steps inside the tower, but instead he found himself at the bottom of a tall circular shaft that reminded him of an aban-doned missile silo he'd broken into a few years ago during his short-lived career with MI6. The tower was just a big empty tube.

"Seriously?" he said as the others joined him inside the tower. "There's no way up?"

"Doesn't look like it," Stone said. "The original wooden floors have either burned or rotted away sometime over the centuries. And instead of stairs, Irish round towers typically had wooden ladders that could be drawn up to foil invaders. In fact, come to think of it . . ."

Stone's eyes lit up. Ezekiel could practically see a lightbulb flashing above his friend's tousled head. Stone dashed out of the tower and back down the steps, which now had his full attention. The other Librarians scurried to keep up.

"What is it?" Baird asked.

"These steps," Stone said. "They're all wrong. They shouldn't be here. You entered a round tower like this via a wooden ladder that could be drawn up in emergencies, just like inside. Having actual stone steps defeats the purpose . . . unless maybe they serve an entirely different purpose?"

Ezekiel saw where Stone was going with this. "That inscription again. Rising, blah, blah, through the firmness of rock." He nodded at the apparently incongruous steps. "How else do you rise on this rock except by these firm stone steps? As written in Olde Irish on the side of a coin from the Pot."

An exciting possibility occurred to Ezekiel. He trotted up and down the steps, tapping on each step one by one while listening carefully to the sounds of his footsteps. *Not that one, not this one, maybe the next one. . . .*

Baird looked on in puzzlement. "Are you . . . tap-dancing?"

"Sssh!" He held a finger to his lips. "A little quiet, if you don't mind. A maestro is at work."

A hint of an echo reached Ezekiel's ears as he stomped on the topmost step, right before the tower's entrance. He got down and placed his ear against the cold, rough stone, wishing that he had thought to bring a stethoscope. He held out an open palm.

"A rock, please?"

"You got it." Stone secured a fist-sized stone from the general debris and ran it up to Ezekiel. "You find something?"

"Was there ever any doubt?" He rapped the rock against the top step and was greeted by a definite echo. "You hear that? There's a hollow compartment under this step."

"Good work, Jones," Baird said. "So how do we open it?"

"Working on that." Ezekiel felt around the step, probing for the camouflaged switch that had to be hiding there. Finding secret latches was second nature to him at this point. No doubt there were ancient counterweights just waiting to be triggered. "Any moment now . . ."

Expert fingers explored every edge, corner, and crack, but came up empty, much to his growing frustration. He was Ezekiel Jones; no old monk or leprechaun could outsmart him. If he could crack the state-of-the-art, top-of-the-line vault back at the Brotherhood's mansion, he could surely beat a secret hatchway built long before lasers, motion detectors, and biometrics changed the game.

But . . .

"Having trouble?" Stone asked.

"A little," Ezekiel admitted in embarrassment. "There must be some way to open this thing, but I can't find it." He tugged on the heavy stone step, resorting to brute strength, but the bloody thing didn't budge. Giving up for the moment, he rose to his feet. "I don't suppose anybody packed a jackhammer?"

"'Fraid not." Baird stepped back from the steps. "Maybe this isn't the end of the rainbow, after all?"

"We'll see about that." Cassandra shrugged off her backpack and started fishing around in its contents. "It occurred to me earlier that there may be another way to interpret that bit about the end of the rainbow. A rainbow is basically the visible spectrum from red to violet, right? So you can argue that, scientifically, the very end of the rainbow is the violet . . . or maybe ultraviolet?"

She removed a portable black-light projector from the backpack. "I borrowed this from Jenkins's workshop back at the Annex. It's not a jackhammer, but maybe if we bring the end of the rainbow to the rock of heaven . . . ?"

Ezekiel hurried down the steps to get out of the way as, flicking a switch, Cassandra turned on the projector and directed it toward the top step. A cool purple radiance lit up the stone. Ezekiel held his breath, not entirely sure what he was waiting for. A secret hatch to open? A hidden message to be revealed?

But nothing happened.

"Oh, well," Ezekiel said. "It was worth a try, I guess."

"Hang on," Stone said. "Anything hidden on the top of the stone would have been worn away by the tread of centuries, but what about the front of the step?"

"Let me see." Cassandra tilted the projector downward so that the light fell upon the vertical face of the step instead. She gasped out loud as an embossed four-leaf clover was revealed, as well as lines of scratch marks that Ezekiel now recognized as ogham. Cassandra beamed along with her beam. "Oh my goodness, it worked! It's the end of the rainbow!"

"Talk about thinking outside the box," Baird said. "Give that magic brain of yours a star."

"I don't get it," Ezekiel said, pouting just a little. "How come I didn't feel any of that with my fingers?"

"Magic?" Baird guessed. She turned to Stone. "What's written there?"

Stone peered at the newly exposed clue. It took him only a minute to translate the ogham into English.

"'*Luck will bring you treasure,*'" he read aloud.

"All right!" Ezekiel said. "That's my kind of fortune cookie. A four-leaf clover equals luck, so maybe we just press here. . . ."

Darting back up the steps, he reached for the carved clover, but Stone chased after him and grabbed him from behind before Ezekiel could touch the glowing step. He seized Ezekiel's outstretched arm.

"Not so fast, man," Stone cautioned. "You know the drill. We got to watch out for booby traps and stuff. You want to bring this whole tower down on top of us?"

Ezekiel considered the tons of ancient masonry looming over them.

"Good point, mate." He withdrew his hand. "You're the expert on this Dark Ages stuff. What do you suggest?"

Stone let go of Ezekiel. He scratched his chin as he pondered the problem.

"Let's see. Traditionally, the four leaves of the clover stand for Faith, Hope, Love, and Luck, in that order. So if Luck will bring us fortune . . ."

"Got it." Ezekiel approached the step more cautiously. "Mind if I do the honors?"

"Knock yourself out, pal."

Taking a deep breath, Ezekiel reached forward and pressed the *fourth* leaf, which sank into the stone with a satisfying click. Ancient gears creaked back to life as the top of the step slid beneath the inner floor of the tower to reveal a hidden cubbyhole.

And the Pot.

A large bronze pot rested in the niche. Celtic art adorned the exterior of the empty pot, which was big enough to hold a king's ransom in gold—in theory. Ezekiel noticed at once that something was missing.

"Hey!" he said. "Where's the gold?"

28

❈ *The Annex* ❈

"It's not about the gold," Jenkins realized. "It was never about the gold. It's about the Pot."

Jumper cables linked a vintage rotary phone to the magic mirror, allowing him to FaceTime with Baird and the Librarians without any of those newfangled smartphones, which were far too easy to tap into or hack, in his considered opinion. His jury-rigged apparatus was infinitely more secure, while still allowing him to inspect the Pot at long distance—and without any roaming charges.

"What about the Pot?" Baird asked. Behind her, the exhumed Pot rested at the foot of the steps leading up to the tower. "Explain."

A voluminous tome on Irish myths and legends lay open upon Jenkins's desk, revealing a portrait of a particular Celtic deity that matched the image on the gold coin from Bridget's pub. The same visage—of a crowned and bearded god-king—was embossed on the exterior of the Pot. Jenkins silently castigated himself for not identifying the god in question earlier. The problem with immortality was that one's memory tended to get overstuffed, making it harder to retrieve any relevant arcana without an excess of rummaging around first.

"That not just any pot," he said. "That's the Cauldron of Dagda, one of the four great treasures of ancient Ireland."

"An empty pot is a treasure?" Ezekiel asked. "Seriously?"

Baird stayed on point. "What's the story there?"

"Legend has it," Jenkins said, "that when the Tuatha Dé Danann first came to Ireland, in the misty days of yore, they brought with them four powerful magical objects from the mystic islands from which they hailed: a stone, a spear, a sword . . . and a cauldron."

"Which is basically just a fancy word for a cooking pot," Baird said, "like witches use to brew their potions."

"And druids," Jenkins said. "In fact, the Dagda—whose visage is emblazoned on the Pot—was among the mighty leaders of the Tuatha Dé Danann. He was a god of fertility, magic, and druidry. It's said that his bountiful pot, which was forged by one of the oldest and wisest of druids, could feed multitudes without running dry, so that none ever went away from it unsatisfied."

"So it's a magical all-you-can-eat cooking pot?" Cassandra said, sounding puzzled. "That doesn't sound terribly bad or dangerous."

"On the surface, perhaps," Jenkins said, "but if you dig deeper, there are far darker legends concerning the Cauldron."

Baird sighed, as though expecting as much. "How deep and how dark?"

"Human sacrifice and necromancy, to be exact." Jenkins flipped over a page in the book to reveal a pair of rather more ominous illustrations. The left-hand page depicted writhing human forms being cast into the Cauldron, while the facing page showed living skeletons arising from the depths of the

Pot. "According to some old tales, those sacrificed to the Cauldron would rise again as unstoppable undead creatures, under the sway of whoever controlled the Pot."

Stone nodded in the mirror. "Kinda like the Children of the Dragon's Teeth in Greek mythology. The ones Jason and his Argonauts ran across."

"A very similar motif and magic," Jenkins agreed, "but let us not digress, given that the Serpent's Teeth were filed down by an earlier Librarian back in the eighteen-fifties." He pushed that long-closed case out of his mind to focus on the discovery at hand. "Like the Dagda himself, the Cauldron embodies both abundance and destruction, the eternal cycle of birth, death, and resurrection. In the wrong hands, this power could be put to terrible ends."

"Which is where the Serpent Brotherhood comes in," Baird said, grasping the threat with commendable speed. "In theory, they could use the Cauldron to create an army of unkillable zombie soldiers."

Jenkins nodded gravely. "In a nutshell, Colonel."

"Whoa!" Stone said. "No wonder the Serpents have been after the Pot for centuries. It all makes sense now."

"Except," Cassandra pointed out, "how did O'Gradaigh get his hands on the Cauldron in the first place?"

29

❋ Ireland, 441 A.D. ❋

O'Gradaigh fled from the forbidding mountain, grateful for his liberty and life, but by no means confident of preserving either. Testing gravity's patience, he bounded across the sleeping countryside despite being weighed down by two precious burdens, traversing misty fields and bogs in his desperate haste to elude whoever and whatever might be pursuing him. The stolen Cauldron dangled from the crook of his left arm, while he clutched the wee babe to his chest with his other arm, holding the infant so that it was draped over his shoulder as well. A gentle enchantment had soothed the baby to sleep, so that her cries would not draw unwelcome attention. Only a peaceful gurgle disturbed the night.

The child's name was Siofra, and her innocent mewling tugged at the leprechaun's racing heart. This was not just any helpless baby, after all; she was his own flesh and blood, conceived three seasons past on a warm Beltane night, when bonfires blazed across Eire, welcoming summer back after its long absence. Poignant memories tormented O'Gradaigh as he recalled Siofra's poor mother, a lonely young widow who had caught him beneath a spreading hawthorn tree when his guard was down. Caring nothing of gold, she had wished for one thing only—a child—and, in the spirit of the season, it had been his pleasure to oblige her.

Alas, the widow's happiness had been short-lived. It was not uncommon for Beltane babies to be born nine months later, but somehow rumors of Siofra's unique parentage reached the ears of the Serpent Brotherhood and its vast network of spies, and so it was that Lady Sibella and her bloody-handed lackeys saw fit to slay the young mother and capture the child, all to force O'Gradaigh to do their bidding . . . and steal the fabled Cauldron of Dagda.

An owl hooted in the night, startling him. He glanced back nervously over his shoulder as he raced through murky woods, clinging to the shadows wherever possible. Guilt and grief chased after him, along with the memory of his crime. . . .

'Twas during a great feast in Tír na nÓg, the otherworldly realm of the *sidhe*, hidden away from the mortal world beneath sacred mounds dating back to the coming of the Tuatha Dé Danann, that he had done what he must. Light, music, and merriment had filled the sprawling, palatial caverns, drawing Fair Folk of every station from all across the land. High lords and ladies of the Unseelie Court were in attendance in all their glittering finery, along with common leprechauns, sprites, pookas, and pixies, coming together to mark the night with drinking, dancing, and gaiety. This particular feast was consecrated to the Dagda, so his legendary Cauldron was on full display on this night of all nights, as opposed to being locked away in the hidden treasure vaults of the Tuatha Dé Danann, as it usually was. The Cauldron occupied a high stone altar

strewn with gifts and offerings to the god—and was protected by a fearsome curse.

O'Gradaigh had come to the feast bearing both his fiddle
and a hidden purpose. That night he'd played as never before,
with his infant daughter's life at stake. Winning a fiddle con-
test through the passion of his playing, he was awarded a pot
of gold by the lord of the feast, but that was not the prize he
truly sought. The Cauldron was what he was after, despite the
curse. To steal the ancient treasure was punishable by death,
but O'Gradaigh had no choice, not if he wished to ransom his
child from the Serpents.

So he had bided his time, waiting anxiously through the
festivities until drink and revelry provided cover enough for
him to risk a bold deception, employing a clever illusion to
switch his own pot for the Cauldron, while hoping against
hope that the trick would go unmarked long enough for him
to deliver the Cauldron to Lady Sibella in exchange for her
precious hostage.

But matters had not gone as planned, thanks to the Librarian and his allies.

Now Sibella was no more, but O'Gradaigh was still being
hunted. A wind wailed through the treetops, or was it a banshee already in pursuit of him who stole the Cauldron? There
could be no forgiveness for his crime, the leprechaun realized;
he was a fugitive, doomed to run and hide until the end of
days. Holding his daughter close, he longed to keep her with
him always, but knew too well that she would never be safe
in his company. He needed to find a new home and family
for her, where his enemies could never find her.

Fortunately, he knew just the place.

A thatched cottage provided a home to a family of simple

farmers. Smoke from the hearth rose from the chimney, but no candles or lanterns could be glimpsed through the windows, suggesting that the family had well and truly retired for the night, just as the leprechaun had hoped. He slipped through a gap in the fence around the farm, taking care not to disturb the livestock, and hid the Cauldron beneath a haystack, where he prayed it would remain undisturbed until he had finished his business here.

Cradling Siofra in his arms, he entered the cottage through the window and crept stealthily across the floor until he reached a cradle holding another tiny red-haired infant. Born during the festival of Imbolc, only a few weeks past, the little girl had been named after the patron goddess of the season: Brigid, who, O'Gradaigh remembered uncomfortably, just happened to be the daughter of the Dagda. Still, little Brigid was roughly the same size and age as Siofra.

Aye, he thought. *Ye will do the trick, so.*

While Brigid's parents slept nearby, the leprechaun gently laid Siofra in the cradle beside the mortal child. Speaking softly so as not to rouse the household, O'Gradaigh whispered ancient words of power to weave a powerful magic. An emerald glow briefly filled the cradle, the light swiftly fading to reveal that little Siofra was now the mirror image of Brigid, the resemblance so complete that not even Brigid's own mother would be able to tell the babes apart.

Or so O'Gradaigh devoutly wished.

Gasping, the leprechaun sagged against the cradle, exhausted by the potent spell he had just cast. This was no mere illusion; the transformation needed to last a lifetime and beyond for the sake of Siofra and all her future offspring. Disguised as Brigid, the changeling could live out a normal life as a mortal, her true nature unknown even to herself. In time, fate and fortune willing, she would have children and grand-children and so on down the generations, all secretly de-scended from O'Gradaigh, who vowed then and there to keep a watchful eye over Siofra and her line no matter where they might roam. He owed Siofra's poor mother that much at least.

I failed to protect ye, he thought guiltily, *but I'll watch over our family, I promise ye that.*

And as for the real Brigid? Well, he still had friends in Other-world who would welcome an "orphaned" mortal babe with no questions asked. Brigid would grow up hale and happy in the timeless realm of Faerie, from which O'Gradaigh was now forever exiled. Time being as flexible as it was in Other-world, it might well be that the real Brigid would outlive them all.

A fair compensation, he rationalized, *for letting Siofra be "Brigid" for the rest of her life.*

Leaving the changeling in the cradle, he claimed Brigid for the Fair Folk per the ancient tradition. He knew he needed to be on his way, lest his enemies catch up with him, yet he lingered longer than he should have, reluctant to leave his dear, sweet daughter behind. Tears welled in his eyes as he bid her good-bye.

Ye will not know me, he thought, *but I will never be far from ye.*

The wind howled again, reminding him of the vengeful wraith pursuing him. The night was growing older and one more burden still awaited his attention.

The Cauldron.

He could not return the treasure without condemning him-self to death, but neither could he let the Cauldron fall into evil hands, as it so nearly had. All he could do now was hide it away where it could never tempt or trouble any soul again. The Cauldron would become a lost treasure, forever sought after but never found.

Much like me own poor self, he hoped.

30

✳ *Ireland, today* ✳

"I can't believe we got this before the Serpents did," Baird said as she and the Librarians hustled across the moonlit ruins to reach the gateway they had used earlier. Stone lugged the empty Cauldron, which was lighter than it looked. Baird hurried the others along, anxious to get the Pot back to the Library before the leprechaun led Max and his henchmen to its former hiding place. "Let's get a move on, people."

"But what about Grady?" Cassandra asked.

"I don't know," Baird admitted. She didn't like the idea of the sly old fiddler being in the Brotherhood's clutches either. "Hopefully we can rescue him later, after we make sure the Cauldron is locked up tight." She checked in with Jenkins via her phone. "Heading your way. Got a door waiting for us?"

"Raring to go, Colonel," he answered. "I look forward to your timely return."

"Me, too." She spied the archway up ahead, where the gatehouse used to be. Heaps of rubble and fragments of bygone walls and buildings rose from the grounds of the derelict monastery. Baird was already anticipating the successful completion of their mission, not to mention being warm and dry again. "Portland, here we come!"

"I wouldn't count your cauldrons before they're collected," an unwanted voice intruded as Max stepped out from behind the remains of a crumbling chapel, accompanied by his hulking bodyguard, as well as a female companion who matched the description of the woman Stone and Cassandra had encountered at the Serpents' safe house. The former carried an aluminum carrying case, while the latter had Grady, in his true guise, on a leash. The leprechaun's hands were cuffed before him. Gunmetal glinted in the moonlight as Max held his firearm on Baird and the Librarians. "It appears we arrived at this godforsaken location just in time."

"Later would have been better," Baird said coldly. She glanced around, weighing their chances, even as more henchmen emerged from the scattered ruins, surrounding them. Baird counted at least four additional hostiles. "Brought plenty of backup this time, I see."

"A prudent precaution," Max said, "given how Librarians are multiplying these days." He surveyed the opposition. "I take it Mister Flynn is still otherwise occupied?"

"Lucky for you," Baird said.

"Oh, I doubt his presence would significantly alter the equation," Max argued. "I have the upper hand . . . and a hostage, to boot. I'm certain you wouldn't want any harm to come to Mister O'Gradaigh here."

"Forgive me, me friends," the leprechaun said forlornly. His shoulders slumped in defeat. "'Twas never me desire that ye should be caught up in me sorrows."

"We're Librarians," Ezekiel assured him. "Filing evil under history is kind of what we do."

"Not for much longer," Max said smugly. "It's high time that the eternal war between the Brotherhood and the Library ends in a decisive victory . . . and not for your side, I'm afraid."

He nodded at Owens, who put down the case in order to frisk Baird and the Librarians while the other henchmen stood guard. Baird scowled, but she wasn't ready to cry uncle just yet. The Librarians' best weapons were their brains, so she still had an arsenal at her disposal. If anybody could think their way out of this predicament, it was her team. Preferably before Max made off with the Cauldron.

"Colonel?" Jenkins's voice emerged from her phone. "What is it? What's happening?"

Snarling, Owens snatched Baird's phone from her hand. His surly expression made it clear that he hadn't forgotten Baird kicking his butt back at the pub in Chicago, as did the bandage taped over his busted nose. He took obvious pleasure in snapping the phone in half with his bare hands and hurling the pieces in her face before disposing of the other team members' phones as well.

"Now then," Max said, "onto our main objective."

Owens smirked as he claimed the Cauldron from Stone, earning him a dirty look from the unhappy Librarian. At Max's direction, Owens placed the relic atop an aboveground stone tomb that bore an unpleasant resemblance to an altar. Max admired the Cauldron as he took a moment to savor his triumph.

"Magnificent," he pronounced. "And mine at last."

Coral looked equally thrilled. "We've found it, just like you always said we would!"

"Aye," Grady said bitterly. "Ye have what ye asked for. Now will youse let me free?"

Coral looked hopefully at her boss. "Max?"

"Not yet, Coral," he stated. "If nothing else, he still makes a valuable hostage."

"Oh, right. I forgot about that." She regarded the Librarians warily before apologizing to the leprechaun. "I'm sorry, Mister O'Gradaigh, but it's for the greater good. . . ."

"Sure it is," Baird scoffed. "Nothing like human sacrifice and turning people into zombies to make the world a better place."

"What are you talking about?" Coral gave Baird a puzzled look. "We're going to use the Cauldron to feed the world, eliminate want and hunger."

She sounded utterly sincere to Baird, who almost felt sorry for her. "So I'm guessing your boss left out the part about the Cauldron being able to bring the dead back to life—and not in a good way?"

"No, you've got it all wrong." Coral turned to Max for reassurance. "Tell her, Max. Tell her that's not what we're about."

Max smirked at her distress. "Well, to tell the truth, I may have indeed kept you in the dark regarding certain aspects of our operation. The Cauldron is far too powerful a relic to waste on charitable enterprises and, personally, I have little interest in overseeing a magical soup kitchen."

"But . . . but I thought we wanted to help people."

"Aside from all the leprechauns you murdered to steal their pots?" Cassandra challenged her. "Both in Ireland and America?"

"Murdered? We never . . ."

Max chuckled. "You were better off not knowing, my dear."

Coral's face fell. She clutched the prism dangling around her throat as she backed away from Max. "This can't be true. I would never have helped you if had known. . . ."

"Which is precisely why I never told you." Max nodded at his bodyguard. "Owens, please relieve Coral of her precious brainchild."

The pink-haired woman quailed as the looming thug took the prism from her and thrust it into his pocket. Stepping behind her, he claimed the leash holding Grady as well. Tears ran down Coral's face as the betrayal sunk in. Guilt rattled her voice.

"I'm such an idiot. I should have known you were just using me. I'm never going to be able to live with myself. . . ."

Max shrugged. "Allow us to relieve you of that difficulty."

He nodded at Owens, who was now standing behind Coral. Before Baird or the others could even think about intervening, Coral gasped and toppled face-forward onto the ground, exposing the bloody stiletto in the bodyguard's hand. Crimson drops fell from the blade.

"Ye cold-blooded devil!" Grady raged. "That poor colleen had a trace of a heart in her, unlike the rest of youse. Ye didn't need to do that!"

"I beg to differ," Max said. "A sacrifice was required, per the old ways, so Coral had one last role to play in these proceedings. Behold."

He beckoned to Owens, who handed Grady's leash over to Max before lobbing the bloody knife into the waiting Cauldron, which reacted immediately to the grisly offering. Steam rose from the Pot as its bowl filled with a bubbling, sickly green brew that smelled like a bonfire. The brew fumed and foamed as though it were cooking over hot coals. An eerie glow lit up the Cauldron from the inside, illuminating the Celtic art adorning the outside of the Pot. A wild wind came out of nowhere, whipping up the grass and weeds around the ad hoc altar. The temperature seemed to drop several degrees in a matter of moments. Baird felt goosebumps breaking out across her flesh.

"Uh-oh," Cassandra murmured. "This can't be good."

"Not one bit," Stone exposited, filling in for Jenkins. "The blood sacrifice has brought out the Cauldron's darker nature."

"So, no all-you-can-eat deal?" Ezekiel sighed. "I knew I should have grabbed a snack on the way."

Max procured the aluminum case. "Keep watching, Librarians. You don't want to miss this part."

Cracking open the case to reveal a human skull with matching bones, he carefully fed the osseous remains into the Cauldron, saving the skull for last. The bleached death's head appeared to grin in anticipation, flaunting a pair of curved fangs that struck Baird as distinctly serpentine in nature. The fangs reminded her of Jenkins's account of how an earlier Guardian had decapitated a female Serpent centuries ago— and of the looted grave they'd found beneath that overturned monument a few days ago. How had that inscription on the megalith gone again?

"Here lieth the bones of that foul serpent which once infested our shores. Let no hand disturb these unholy remains, on peril of your soul."

Baird feared she saw where this was going. . . .

With a dramatic flourish, Max cast the fanged skull into the bubbling Cauldron, then stepped back to await the results of his conjuring. Thick black fumes billowed from the Pot, obscuring its contents. Flashes of eldritch energy could be glimpsed through the smoke, like lightning glimpsed through churning storm clouds. The brew bubbled furiously. Bones clattered loudly before falling ominously silent. Thunder rumbled overhead. Dark clouds grew darker still even as the eerie glow of the Cauldron got brighter.

"Wait for it," Max said.

A figure rose sinuously from the Cauldron, like a cobra called forth from a wicker basket by a snake charmer. The swirling mists dissipated to reveal a tall, raven-haired woman clad in a silvery sheath that glittered like the scales of a serpent. Her pale skin had a faintly iridescent sheen.

"Lady Sibella," Max greeted his reborn predecessor. "Welcome back to the world of the living."

I knew it, Baird thought. *He's literally brought the Serpent back to Ireland.*

"Wait," Ezekiel asked. "Where did her dress come from?"

Cassandra gave him a look. "Seriously, that's what you're worrying about now? It's magic, okay?"

"Whatever," Ezekiel said. "Excuse me for asking."

Sibella stretched her arms above her head, luxuriating in her unholy resurrection, before stepping gracefully out of the Cauldron and onto the damp, grassy earth. Slitted yellow eyes surveyed the desolate surroundings.

"And you are?" she asked Max.

"Maximillian Lambton," he replied. "Current heir to the glory of the Serpent Brotherhood."

Lambton, huh? Baird filed Max's surname away for reference. However, that he had openly divulged it in front of her and the Librarians spoke volumes about his intentions regarding them. *He's not planning to let us go.*

"I see," Sibella said sibilantly. "I take it I have you to thank for my rebirth?"

"You're quite welcome," Max said, laying on the charm. "And with you at my right hand, my leadership of the Brotherhood will be unquestioned, as we finally achieve our greatest goals."

Baird remembered what Jenkins had said about revenants

being under the control of whomever brought them back to life. She assumed that Max was diplomatically reminding Lady Sibella who was in charge now.

"In that case, I'm at your disposal," Sibella replied, getting the message. Her expression hardened as her reptilian gaze shifted to Grady, whom Max still had on a leash. Venom dripped from her voice. "We meet again, little man."

Grady glared back at her. "I don't suppose ye're inclined to let bygones be bygones?"

"Hardly," she said. "We have unfinished business, you and I. Time has been kinder to you than I shall be."

Baird piped up to keep her from taking any steps against Grady right away. "Spoken like a Serpent. Still holding a grudge after fifteen hundred years."

Sibella turned her attention to the captives, crossing the churchyard to inspect them. Her nose wrinkled in distaste.

"I know your kind. You reek of the Library." Her smooth brow furrowed as she swept her gaze over Baird and the others. "But . . . more than a single Librarian in this age?"

"That's right," Baird said. "We've expanded the franchise. Try to keep up."

"Ah, you must be their Guardian." Sibella's hand went to her throat, as though to reassure herself that it was intact once more. "One of yours cost me my head in days gone by. Dear Deidre is doubtless dust by now, so I'll have to settle our account with you."

Baird had faced down terrorists, demons, and the Egyptian god of chaos. She wasn't going to let this slinky snake-woman intimidate her.

"Do your worst. The Library outlived you before and it will again. Even if you kill me, there will be another Guardian to squash you Serpents, as many times as it takes."

"Ah, but now we have the Cauldron," Sibella pointed out. "And you and your companions are at our mercy, so it will be a simple matter to sacrifice each of you to the Cauldron, one after another, and thereby transform you all into thralls serving the Serpent Brotherhood. Under our command, you will grant us admittance to the Library, bypassing its myriad fortifications, so that we may lay claim to its treasures and secrets . . . before finally destroying it once and for all time!" She glanced at Max. "With your permission, of course."

"By all means," he consented. "I applaud your initiative, Lady Sibella. We are indeed of like minds."

Baird fought to maintain a poker face. She wasn't sure what dismayed her more, being killed in cold blood or personally letting the Serpents penetrate the Library's defenses.

That last one, she decided. *Definitely.*

"Hang on there!" she said. "I hate to break it to you, toots, but human sacrifice has gone out of fashion since your day. Maybe you need to update your act?"

Her argument carried no weight with Max. "What can I say?" he quipped. "We're traditionalists at heart." He smiled at Sibella. "Would you care to do the honors, milady?"

"It will be my pleasure." She eyed Baird with vindictive glee. A forked tongue licked her lips. "You first, Guardian."

A cold hand grabbed Baird's arm, locking onto it like a vise, and began dragging Baird toward the waiting Cauldron. Baird fought back with all her strength and skill, punching and kicking expertly, but, just as Jenkins had warned, Sibella had returned from the grave inhumanly strong and indestructible; she shrugged off Baird's blows as though she were being swatted with a feather. Baird dug in her heels, but succeeded only in leaving two deep grooves in the ground behind her.

"Let go of me, you witch!"

Her Librarians shouted in protest as well. They tried to go to her rescue, but were held back by Max's goons, not to mention the gun aimed in their direction.

"Stop it!" Cassandra yelled at Max. "You can't do this! It's barbaric!"

"Patience," he counseled her. "Your turn will come soon enough." He glanced down at Coral's lifeless form. "A shame I can't resurrect an even more cooperative version of Coral, but her sacrifice was required to bring Lady Sibella back to life after all this time."

Grady buried his face in his hands. "May the fates forgive me. This is all my doing. . . ."

"Please," Max said. "Give me a little credit as well."

"You son of a bitch!" Stone snarled. "You better hope that Cauldron works as advertised or I'm coming for you, man!"

"What he said!" Ezekiel added.

Baird overheard the heated exchange as, despite her furious efforts, she arrived at the makeshift altar bearing the Cauldron. Her fists pounded uselessly against Sibella's immaculate visage as the undead aristocrat gripped Baird's shoulders with both hands and bent her backward against the brim of the Cauldron, which was still bubbling and boiling. Baird felt the heat of the scalding brew against the back of her neck. A bitter aroma filled her nose and lungs.

"Say your prayers, Guardian," Sibella said. "And give my regards to Deidre during your ever-so-brief stint in the underworld."

Sibella's jaws opened wider than was anatomically possible, baring twin fangs that absolutely had to be venomous as all get-out. Baird refused to cringe, but she flinched inwardly at the thought of Sibella's fangs plunging into her neck . . . as well as the horrors that would come afterward.

I'd rather stay dead than become a Serpent. . . .

Before Sibella could strike, however, a bell rang out across the ruins.

The serpent-woman winced at the sound. She hissed angrily, forgetting Baird for the moment, although the Guardian remained caught in Sibella's unbreakable grip. Sibella glared balefully in the direction of the ringing, as did everyone else.

"No!" she cried out. "Not that damnable bell again!"

Twisting her neck around to see what was happening, Baird saw Jenkins striding toward them across the ruins, ringing a plain iron bell.

And not just any bell.

"Ohmigosh," Cassandra blurted. "It's Saint Patrick's Bell!"

Straight from the Library, Baird guessed. "Seriously, I'm actually being saved by the bell?"

The sight of the Bell enraged Sibella, who flung Baird away in order to charge at Jenkins with frightening speed. Screeching more in anger than in pain, she tore the Bell from the ageless caretaker's grasp, then struck him with a backhanded blow that sent Jenkins smashing through a decrepit stone wall, leaving him sprawled on his back amidst the debris. He blinked and shook his head, looking dazed by the impact.

"*Saint* Patrick?" Sibella said furiously. "That was his reward for hindering me?"

"Narcissistic much?" Jenkins sat up slowly, recovering from her attack. "Not everything is about you, Lady Sibella. I regret to inform you, but you're little more than a footnote in some dusty old archives these days."

Sibella hissed and flashed her fangs at him. "No matter! I am stronger and more invincible than I ever was before. This irksome relic is a mere annoyance now." She crushed the iron bell with her bare hand, the metal crumpling loudly. "Did you truly think I feared its ugly pealing now that I am reborn?"

Jenkins brushed pulverized stone from his suit as though it were dandruff. "Who said I was ringing the Bell for you?"

A mournful wail echoed across the ruins, sending a chill down Baird's spine.

The banshee had found them again.

31

The banshee appeared high above the ruins, provoking gasps from those below. No longer a tearful young woman or a weeping matron, she now manifested as a spectral, white-haired crone clad in a tattered gray shroud. Grief contorted her wizened countenance, while her ceaseless keening echoed across the landscape. A bony finger pointed accusingly at Grady.

"You want him?" Max let go of Grady's leash and shoved the leprechaun away from him, clearly vexed by the interruption. "He's all yours."

"It's not that simple." Jenkins winced as he rose slowly to his feet. Immortal though he was, being tossed through a stone wall by a super-strong revenant was enough to take the wind out of anybody's sails. He felt as though he'd been unhorsed by a lance during a particularly hard-fought joust back when knighthood was in flower. "No doubt the banshee has come for the Cauldron as well."

Max blanched at the prospect of losing the Pot. "Never! The Pot is mine, I tell you. Mine!"

He opened fire at the soaring wraith, but his shots had little effect on the banshee, who simply dematerialized each time she was shot, only to reappear a heartbeat later. She misted in and out of visibility, barely missing a note in her keening, much to Max's distress.

"Begone, you bloody hag! You'll not take the Cauldron from me!"

"Don't think she's listening to you, mate," Ezekiel jeered from the sidelines, where he was still being restrained by Max's underlings. "Tough luck."

In the commotion, Jenkins remained focused on the object of the quest. Sibella stood between him and the Cauldron, but Baird had a clear path to the prize now that Sibella had cast her aside.

"Colonel!" he shouted urgently. "The Cauldron!"

Scrambling to her feet, Baird dashed back toward the frothing relic. "On it!"

"Owens!" Max called out in response. "Secure the Pot!"

The muscle-bound lackey charged toward the Cauldron, but Baird got there first. Seeing Owens lunging for her, she kicked over the Pot, spilling its fuming contents in the thug's direction. The noxious flood washed Owens off his feet, causing him to tumble backward onto the rocky soil. He sputtered furiously as the foul brew drenched him, even as Baird seized the now-empty Cauldron.

"I'll take this, if you don't mind."

Baird's capture of the Pot did not go unnoticed by Sibella. Abruptly remembering what truly mattered, she discarded the crumpled Bell and hurried back toward Baird, leaving Jenkins behind.

"Unhand the Cauldron!" Sibella demanded.

"Or what? You won't play nice this time?" Baird took off across the ruins, carrying the Pot. "Come and get it, witch!"

———

Things started happening very fast.

With all eyes on the banshee and the ensuing chaos, Stone saw his chance to take out the goons restraining him and the other Librarians. Moving quickly, he rammed the back of his head into the face of the thug behind him, causing the man to stagger backward, clutching his nose. Stone wheeled about to deliver a hard left hook to the man's jaw, followed by a knockout blow to his chin that left the stunned henchman flat on his back. Fists clenched and ready, Stone wasn't going to waste time dancing with Max's flunkies.

One down, he thought. *Who's next?*

The guards holding Cassandra and Ezekiel barely had time to register what was happening. Combining kung fu with his best bare-knuckle bar-fight moves, Stone laid into the surprised henchmen like an Oklahoma tornado, all whirling limbs and sudden impacts. Moving quickly, never staying still for a moment, he took on both men at once, kicking one while punching the other, and then the other way around. Max's men didn't know what had hit them; they were tough guys, to be sure, but Stone had fought ninjas and come out on top.

You messed with the wrong Librarian, he thought.

The other Librarians broke free from their besieged captors. Ezekiel and Cassandra scurried away from the fracas, then looked back to see if Stone needed any reinforcements.

As if, he thought.

"Don't worry about me!" he hollered. "I can handle these bruisers." With Baird busy keeping the Cauldron away from Sibella, Stone shouted out instructions to his teammates. "Ezekiel, help Grady!"

"Way ahead of you, mate!"

Keeping his head down, the thief raced across the graveyard toward the bound and powerless leprechaun. Stone trusted Ezekiel to see to Grady's safety while he finished off Max's goons.

"Cassandra . . ."

"Sorry," she blurted, bolting from the scene. "I'll be right back!"

Huh? In between trading blows, Stone watched in confusion as Cassandra sprinted toward the waiting gateway back to the Annex. For a fraction of an instant, he feared that she was deserting them, but swiftly rejected that notion. Cassandra was a Librarian; she knew what she was doing, even if Stone couldn't guess what she had in mind.

And he was too busy fighting to give it much thought.

"Where were we again?"

A palm-elbow-knee haymaker combo left Stone the last man standing. *So much for the hired muscle*, he thought. His eyes zeroed in on Max, who was still shooting at the flying banshee, and he cracked his knuckles.

"Your turn, dude," he muttered. "Just like I promised."

———

"Saints preserve me!" Grady moaned. "'Tis doomed I am!"

The leprechaun cowered on the ground, shrinking from Max, Sibella, and the banshee. Silver handcuffs trapped him in his true guise, while depriving him of his magic. Racing toward the pint-sized sprite, who looked as though he'd stepped right off a Saint Paddy's Day greeting card, Ezekiel still found it hard to wrap his head around the fact that the leprechaun and Grady were one and the same.

"No worries, mate!" Ezekiel dropped to his knees so that he was more or less eye level with the shackled leprechaun. "We'll get you out of those shiny bracelets in a jiffy."

Plucking one of his favorite picks from his back pocket, Ezekiel got to work on the handcuffs, which, to his slight disappointment, posed no challenge whatsoever. As it turned out, the only thing remarkable about the cuffs was that they were made of silver; the locking mechanism itself was boringly standard-issue, requiring only a few deft motions to circumvent. First one cuff, then the other clicked open, releasing Grady's wrists.

"See?" Ezekiel pocketed the pricey restraints. "Child's play."

"Ye're a wizard at locks, so ye are!" Grady rubbed his chafed wrists to restore their circulation. "A thousand thanks to ye!"

"Hold that thought." Ezekiel wondered how much gold a leprechaun's gratitude might be worth, but decided that would have to wait until after he'd saved the world in his usual inimitable fashion. "In the meantime, we could use your help to—"

Grady vanished from sight before Ezekiel could even finish his sentence. The Librarian sighed and shook his head in exasperation, even as he realized that he really should have seen this coming. The leprechaun had flown the coop again.

"Figures!"

———————

Cassandra ran for the stone archway, hoping that Jenkins had left the Door open so that they wouldn't end up stranded in Ireland. She hated to leave the others behind, but between the Serpent Brotherhood, the indestructible Sibella, and the banshee, they were going to need every advantage they could get. Fortunately, she knew just where to look. . . .

White light flashed in the gateway as she left the Emerald Isle behind.

"Leave us alone, you blasted wraith!"

Max's polished hauteur unraveled as his triumph dissolved into chaos. He emptied his gun at the banshee, then paused to reload. Stone had the distraught Serpent in his sights as he rushed across the ruins, darting from one crumbling monument to another on his way toward his armed adversary. Max had already gotten away from Stone twice; the angry Librarian wasn't about to let the murderous schemer hurt anyone else.

"Give it up, Max!" Stone said. "You're in over your head here . . . and the *sidhe* is hitting the fan!"

"Never!" Max swung his gun back and forth wildly, uncertain who to target. He fired at Stone, who sought cover behind a sturdy stone cross. "I will restore the Serpent Brotherhood to greatness. I will succeed where Wilde and Dulaque failed!"

Bullets chipped away at the ancient monument shielding Stone.

"Don't kid yourself, Max," Stone retorted. "I knew Dulaque, I fought Dulaque, and, dude, you are no Dulaque!"

"We'll see about that." Max shifted position to try to get a clean shot at Stone. "Did Dulaque ever blow your head off, you impertinent cowboy?"

Stone moved to keep the bullet-ridden cross between them. If nothing else, he was drawing Max's fire away from his friends, but it was only a matter of time before Max got the drop on him again unless Stone caught a lucky break. Where was that four-leaf clover now that he needed it?

"Max?"

A plaintive voice came from an unexpected source. Stone blinked in surprise as, impossibly, Coral approached Max from behind, despite having died several minutes ago. A hasty glance revealed that her body was no longer lying where it had fallen. Hurt and betrayal filled her face and voice.

"Why, Max? How could you do this to me? I trusted you!"

"Coral?" Max wheeled about to confront his victim. "I don't understand. You're gone. I killed you. . . ."

"Why, Max? Why?"

Stone didn't understand either, but he wasn't about to look a gift ghost in the mouth. Snatching a fist-sized rock from the scattered debris, he flung it at Max, zonking him squarely in the back of the head. Max staggered forward, his gun arm sagging, as Stone tackled him from behind, knocking him to the ground. Pinning Max down with his knees, Stone slammed the dazed Serpent's wrist against the stony earth until he let go of the gun. He jabbed a key pressure point to render Max unconscious.

"Say good night, Max."

Max went limp. Satisfied that the mastermind was down for the count, Stone rose to his feet to face Coral, whose anguished expression gave way to a mischievous grin. The "ghost" shimmered like a mirage before transforming into . . . a miniature figure clad in green?

"Grady?"

"None other," the leprechaun replied. "Ye didn't truly think I'd abandoned youse all, did ye?"

"Well . . ."

"Fair enough," Grady conceded. "'Twas a time when I would've made meself scarce if the opportunity arose, but no more. I've let you Librarians fight me battles for too long."

"Good thing," Stone said. "'Cause this battle ain't over yet."

———

Baird held on tightly to the Cauldron as she scrambled across the ruins, anxious to keep the relic away from Sibella and the other Serpents. She darted in and around the crumbling remains of abandoned buildings and monuments, hurdling over scattered heaps of rubble as though running an obstacle course, but without any clear destination in mind. The last thing she wanted to do was lead Sibella back to the Annex.

You're not getting anywhere near the Library, Baird thought, *or this damn Pot.*

But Sibella was not the only supernatural being in pursuit of the Cauldron. Still wailing at the top of her lungs, the banshee swooped down from the sky, chasing after Baird. Her withered arms stretched out before her, reaching for the Pot. Glancing back over her shoulder, while trying not to run headlong into some random heap of debris, Baird saw the banshee gaining on her. The wraith's ear-piercing shriek sounded like the screeching horn of a semitruck bearing down on her. Baird could practically feel the banshee's icy fingers grabbing onto her shoulders any second now.

"Leave her, crone! That Guardian—and the Cauldron—are mine!"

Sibella pounced on the low-flying banshee, attempting to sink her venomous fangs into the spirit's neck, but the banshee vanished before she could bite her, so that Sibella hit the ground instead, skidding to a halt after sliding across a stretch of rocks and grass. Frustrated, she sprang to her feet in order to keep after Baird, who suddenly found herself much more popular than she would have preferred.

Seriously? I've got both Sibella and the banshee hot on my heels?

Baird allowed herself to hope that her pursuers would keep getting in each other's way, but knew that wasn't a long-term solution. Her heart sank as the banshee abruptly rematerialized in her path, even as Sibella closed in on her once more. Ruined walls and derelict structures hemmed Baird in, trapping her between the vengeful Serpent and the implacable wraith. She had nowhere to run, which left her with only one choice.

"Yo, Celtic Woman!" she shouted. "The Pot's all yours, courtesy of the Library!"

She lobbed the Cauldron over to the banshee, who caught it greedily. A flicker of a smile crossed her wrinkled face as she halted her incessant wailing, if only for the moment. She clutched the Pot to her bosom.

"No!" Sibella froze in dismay. Consternation marred her exquisite features. "You fool!" she screamed at Baird. "What have you done?"

"Better her than the Brotherhood," Baird said, convinced she had made the right decision. "As I understand it, she's just trying to reclaim some stolen property. I can respect that."

Keening once more, the banshee rose into the sky, taking the Cauldron with her. She dissolved into thin air, but her strident wail lingered behind her, only gradually fading away . . . to be supplanted by the sound of pounding hooves coming from somewhere deep beneath the earth:

Clop, clop, clop, clop . . .

"What the heck?" Baird said. "Please tell me I'm not the only one hearing that!"

"Would that were so!" Grady's ruddy complexion paled. "'Tis the *Coiste Bodhar* . . . the death-coach! Summoned by the banshee to carry out the curse upon me!"

Tremors shook the ground beneath Baird's feet, threatening her balance. Serpents and Librarians alike backed away from the ominous clippity-clopping, which grew louder and closer by the moment.

"Great," Baird muttered. "We've got another party-crasher!"

32

A gaping chasm suddenly opened up in the ancient church-yard, swallowing centuries-old grave markers and debris. A funereal black coach, drawn by four black horses, burst from the underworld onto the grounds of the defunct monastery. Fire spurted from the horses' nostrils while sparks flew from the wheels of the ebony coach. Silver sconces mounted outside the carriage held tapered black candles topped by flickering orange flames. Opaque black curtains concealed the carriage's interior.

You've got to be kidding me, Baird thought. *When did Saint Patrick's Day turn into Halloween?*

The unearthly carriage was spooky enough even before you took into account its driver: a headless coachman wielding a human spine as a whip. Vertebrae rattled loudly as he cracked the grisly whip above his snorting steeds, urging them on. Although missing from his shoulders, his severed head was mounted on a spike protruding from the coach's dashboard. Black eyes gleamed with demonic animation above a fiendish grin that stretched from ear to rotting ear. Moldering flesh had the bluish-green tint of rotting cheese—and, judging from a sickening odor being carried on the night breeze, smelled like it, too.

"The Dullahan," Jenkins ID'd the coachman. "Come to carry his fated passenger off to the land of the dead."

The ghastly apparition, along with its shocking entrance, was enough to convince Max's henchmen that they had better places to be, especially with their victory slipping away. Already battered by the fray, Owens and the other men abandoned their fallen leader to flee the ruins as fast as their bruised bodies could carry them.

Good riddance, Baird thought. *We've got enough on our plate right now.*

Such as Lady Sibella, who was not so easily discouraged by the untimely arrival of the death-coach. She hissed at the interloper, baring her fangs. Clearly, she wasn't about to let a little thing like a headless coachman and fire-snorting demon horses get between her and her revenge.

Unless . . .

An idea occurred to Baird. It was risky, but if she could just keep Sibella good and mad at her, maybe she could use the snake-woman's vengeful nature against her?

"Hey, Scales!" she taunted. "You forget about me? We've got unfinished business, remember?"

Sibella wheeled about, her reptilian gaze shifting from the oncoming coach to Baird. Fury made her look even more demonic. "Guardian!"

"That's right. I took your Pot, just like Deidre took your head. Guess that makes you a two-time loser!"

Overcome with rage, she charged at Baird, who turned and ran—directly into the path of the speeding death-coach. Sibella chased her, heeding only the call of vengeance.

"That the best you've got, Sibby? No wonder Deidre made short work of you back in the day!"

Sibella was right on Baird's heels. The timing was going to be tricky, Baird realized, but if she got it right . . .

She threw herself forward, out of the way of the coach.

Sibella wasn't so lucky.

The coach ran the other woman down, trampling her beneath the sparking hooves of the horses. Sibella let out an unusually sibilant scream as she fell beneath the wheels of the coach. Would this be enough to send her back to whatever hell she had escaped from?

We should be so lucky, Baird thought.

Trapped beneath the coach's wheels, at least for the moment, Sibella hissed and squirmed and vowed bloody vengeance on all present.

"To Hades with every one of you! You will pay for this indignity. No power on Earth can protect you from—"

The Dullahan's bony whip disputed that claim. Seated behind the reins of the coach, he lashed Sibella to quiet her as he attended to his fatal business. The door of the coach opened of its own accord, revealing a beckoning emptiness as black as death. The spiked head swiveled toward Grady. Its moldy lips uttered a single word:

"O'Gradaigh."

"No way," Stone said. He stepped between the coach and the leprechaun, adopting a protective stance. Ezekiel and Baird hurried to join him. "You might as well turn around and go back where you came from, bud. We're not letting you take Grady," Ezekiel yelled at the driver.

Baird felt the same way. The fiddler was a crafty one all right, but he obviously had a good heart, as proven by the way he had watched over Bridget and her family all these years. Curse or no curse, she couldn't just stand by and let the coachman take him, not without a fight.

The Dullahan's head scowled. He cracked his whip in warning.

"Nay, me brave friends." Grady slipped past the Librarians. "Sure and I appreciate youse standing up for me, but I won't have youse risking yerselves on me account." The leprechaun sighed wearily, seemingly resigned to his fate. "I'm tired of running and hiding. 'Tis time I finally pay the piper. Maybe then sweet Bridget will be left alone. . . ."

"But I gave the Cauldron to the banshee," Baird said. "Isn't that enough?"

Grady shook his head. "Me sentence was passed centuries ago, after I stole the Cauldron to ransom me precious daughter from Sibella. There can be no reprieve for me." He looked away from the extinct monastery to contemplate the sleeping village and countryside below. "At least I got to set foot on me beloved Ireland one last time."

He took a step toward the waiting coach.

———

"Wait! Don't give up!"

Cassandra came rushing back onto the scene, breathless and flushed. Before anyone could stop her, she dashed between Grady and the coach.

"Excuse me, Mister Dullahan, sir? If I can have a moment of your time?"

The coachman's head turned toward her. His headless body raised its skeletal whip.

Gulping, Cassandra backed off, but only physically. She raised her voice to be heard over the impatient hooves and snorting of the horses and spoke with as much confidence as she could muster under the circumstances.

"I, Cassandra Cillian, a true daughter of Erin, appeal for

mercy on behalf of Finbar O'Gradaigh, who has surely been punished enough for a crime committed many mortal lifetimes ago. He's spent more than fifteen hundred years in exile from the land he loves. Can't we write that off as time served?"

The Dullahan smirked, unmoved by her plea. He cracked his whip, which miraculously extended in length as it snapped past Cassandra to wrap itself around Grady, binding his arms to his sides. The coachman tugged on the whip, dragging Grady toward the open door of the death-coach.

"No! Wait!" Cassandra pleaded. "You have to listen to me. I'm not finished yet!"

Baird, Stone, and Ezekiel grabbed Grady, trying to keep him from being reeled in by the Dullahan. Cassandra could see her teammates straining, but the pull of the whip was too strong. They looked like they were losing a life-or-death game of tug-of-war. Despite their best efforts to dig in, they were surrendering inch after inch as they were pulled across the grounds toward the carriage.

"Don't let go!" Baird said. "We can do this . . . maybe!"

"I'm trying," Stone said, grunting in exertion. "But it's sucking us in like a black hole!"

"Nah," Ezekiel said. "We've escaped a black hole. This is tougher!"

Grady squirmed in their grasp, struggling to free himself from his would-be protectors, but he was held tight by the three of them.

"Let me go, I beg ye! Save yer selves!"

"Forget it," Baird said. "Haven't you heard? You never let go of a leprechaun until you get your wish, and right now I'm wishing for a happy ending . . . for everyone!"

But the Librarians were losing ground by the moment.

Jenkins joined the tug-of-war, but even his immortal vitality was no match for the Dullahan and the ancient curse empowering the coachman. Cassandra realized it was up to her to get Grady's sentence commuted, if only the right words came to her.

"Hear me, please. You can't do this. It's not just."

"Ye're wasting yer breath, lass," Grady said. "This is Ireland. The old ways, the ancient traditions, are too strong. Ye cannot change them!"

"But what of forgiveness and mercy? Those too are Irish traditions, dating all the way back to Saint Patrick at least! Did you know that Patricus first came to Ireland as a prisoner, captured by Irish raiders and taken by force from his home in Britain? He spent six years of his life laboring as a slave before finally escaping back to Britain. After all that, you'd think that he'd never forgive the Irish people, let alone want to set foot on this emerald isle again, but instead he felt a calling to return to Ireland to minister to its people for the rest of his life, even coming to the rescue of O'Gradaigh when the Serpent Brotherhood brought their evil here. If Saint Patrick could find it in his heart to forgive and forget, surely the Fair Folk can do the same for one of their own . . . for mercy's sake?"

The Dullahan's smirk faded as his disembodied head listened to Cassandra, his ghoulish leer replaced by a more thoughtful expression. The bony whip slackened to a degree, slowing Grady's inexorable progress toward the death-coach.

"It's working!" Baird cheered Cassandra on. "Keep it up! You're getting through to him!"

"Not possible!" Grady said. "Once the Dullahan has been summoned, he cannot return empty-handed!"

"This is true," Jenkins confirmed, while lending his shoulders to the task nonetheless. He strained with the others to keep Grady from the coach. "The lore is quite clear on this point."

"But does it have to be Grady?" Cassandra asked. "Or can it be someone else, like maybe—"

"Librarians!"

Sibella finally slithered out from beneath the coach's wheels. Mud defiled her ivory skin and scaly attire. With the Dullahan's whip wrapped around Grady, she was no longer deterred by the coachman's lash. Spittle sprayed from her lips as she flashed her fangs, reminding Cassandra of the half-woman, half-snake creature in Bram Stoker's old novel. Hadn't Jenkins said something about that book being more fact than fiction?

The female Serpent rose slowly to her feet. "You have incurred my wrath for the last time. You will writhe in agony as my venom consumes you from within, until you beg for the sweet release of death!"

"Yeah, speaking of that," Cassandra said hastily, "what about her?" She pointed out the undead snake-woman. "She's the one who wanted the Cauldron in the first place, and the one who shouldn't even be alive right now. She was dead and buried for centuries until the Serpent Brotherhood cheated death by bringing her back from the grave. If anybody here needs a one-way trip back to the Other Side, it's her."

"Who are you to condemn me?" Sibella gave Cassandra the evil eye. "No, truly, who are you again?"

"It's not about me," Cassandra said. "It's about making things right." She looked up at the attentive coachman. "Don't you think?"

The head spun on its spike to contemplate Sibella. Its fiendish grin returned as it fixed its baleful gaze on the female
Serpent. The decapitated coachman wagged its finger in her
direction. The bodiless head spoke again:

"Sibella."

"No!" Her face contorted in fear. "She's a mere mortal. You
can't listen to her!"

With a flip of his wrist, the Dullahan released Grady from
the whip. The spine cracked loudly as he lashed out at Sibella,
trapping her in its embrace so that it looked as though she was
caught in the coils of a skeletal python. He yanked her off her
feet and toward the gaping abyss inside the carriage as she
writhed and wriggled in vain.

"You cannot do this! I'm alive . . . alive!"

"Actually, you died in 441 A.D.," Jenkins corrected her
as, along with the rest of the team, he let go of Grady. "Look
it up."

Screaming almost as loudly as a banshee, Sibella was flung
into the coach. An ebony door slammed shut behind her. Her
anguished face could be glimpsed briefly through a window
as she tore the curtains asunder, but then the Dullahan
cracked the spine like a whip once more, more violently than
any mortal chiropractor ever had, and the horses sprang into
motion, kicking up fiery sparks with their racing hooves. The
coach dived back into the bottomless chasm from which it
had emerged, vanishing from view even as the earth closed
up behind it. Within moments, no trace of the coach—or
Lady Sibella—remained.

"Whoa." Ezekiel clasped the silver handcuffs on Max's unconscious form. "Did we just drive the snakes out of Ireland
again?"

"So it appears, Mister Jones." Jenkins straightened his tie.

"And saved the Library from being looted by the Brotherhood as well. Not a bad night's work."

"But what about the Pot?" Stone asked.

"Returned to Tír na nÓg, where it belongs, or so I assume." Jenkins sighed wistfully. "A pity, really. It would have made a lovely addition to the Hibernian Collection."

Grady patted himself to confirm that he was still among the living. "Can it be?" he asked, as though barely able to believe it. "I'm truly reprieved, after all these years?"

"Looks like it." Baird beamed at Cassandra. "Great job, Red. I can't believe you actually talked that thing into sparing Grady."

"Well, it wasn't all me," Cassandra confessed. "I may have had an ace up my sleeve, as it were."

Jenkins figured it out. "The Blarney Stone?"

"That's right," Cassandra said. "While the rest of you were fighting, I ran back to the Library to kiss the Stone." She made a face and wiped her lips, which still tasted of grit. "I figured I could use the gift of the gab if I wanted to convince the banshee to leave Grady and his descendants alone."

"Thus granting you uncommon powers of persuasion, if only for a time." Jenkins tipped his head to Cassandra. "An elegant solution, Miss Cillian, and, if I may say so, an appropriately Irish one. Your forebears would be proud."

Cassandra liked hearing that.

"'Tis a wonder such as I never dreamed of," Grady said, choking up. He appeared overcome with emotion. "I'm a fugitive no longer . . . and home at last." Misty eyes sought out the Librarians. "However can I thank youse?"

Ezekiel's face lit up. "Well, about your gold—?"

Baird elbowed him. "Uh-uh. We're not going there."

"As it happens," Jenkins said, "it *would* be helpful if you could fill in a few blanks regarding what transpired back in the fifth century, simply for the record."

Grady grinned at the prospect.

"Och, if it's a tale ye're wanting, it will be me pleasure to oblige you . . . perhaps over a pint or two?"

33

※ *Chicago* ※

"Slainte!"

The Librarians toasted their victory (and continued survival) with foaming pints of green beer, left over from Saint Patrick's Day. Bridget, Brigid, and Grady were also on hand to join in the celebration. The Pot O' Gold was closed for the night, which meant that Stone and the rest had the pub to themselves. Sipping his beer, Stone surveyed the scene from a stool at the bar with a sense of deep and abiding satisfaction. After the damp desolation of the ruined monastery, the cozy pub, along with the good company, was just what he needed.

And he was pretty sure the others felt the same way.

"So we've worked it all out," Bridget said, her arm around her twin. "Brigid and I have decided to switch places. She's eager to explore the mortal world, after being cooped up in Otherworld for centuries, while I can't wait to see Mill Ends with my own eyes, especially now that I know that I'm part leprechaun, no less."

"So ye are," Grady assured her. Since he was among friends,

the leprechaun had dispensed with his mortal guise. He perched atop a barstool, the better to be at eye level with everyone else. "And the Fair Folk will be happy to welcome ye back into the fold."

"Are you sure about this?" Baird asked, enjoying a pint by the fireplace, across from Cassandra and Ezekiel. "It's a pretty big switch . . . for both of you."

"Och," Brigid said. "'Tis a fine adventure it will be, and fitting, too. I was born to live a mortal life, so I was, and it's high time I get on with it." She was practically glowing in anticipation. "What's more, I hear tell that this brave new world holds many an exotic marvel I'm yearning to discover for meself, including something called . . . bubble tea?"

"And pizza," Ezekiel said. "You got to check out pizza."

"Ooh." Brigid's eyes widened. "Tell me more. . . ."

Stone considered the other Bridget. "What about your heart?" he asked her. "Are you going to be okay in leprechaun land, considering?"

"Don't ye be worrying about that, Jake Stone," Grady said. "Time and mortal ailments cannot touch her where she's going. Years will pass like days, granting her a long and merry life."

"That's part of it," Bridget admitted. "But I'm also excited about finding out what it really means to be descended from an honest-to-goodness changeling. I grew up in and around this pub, hearing all the old stories and legends and wishing they were real. Can you imagine what it feels like to find out that the magic of old Ireland is literally in my blood . . . and waiting for me?"

"You want to explore your roots, without your illness hanging over you," Cassandra said. "I totally get that."

"I'm sold, too," Stone said. "You're both going back where you belong, just like the Cauldron." He raised his glass. "To fond farewells and new beginnings!"

※ The Annex ※
A short time later

Saint Patrick's bell was in less than mint condition.

"Oh dear." Jenkins examined the crumpled hunk of iron, which now looked like nothing more than a fist-sized piece of scrap metal. Glancing over from her desk, Baird could actually see where Sibella's super-strong fingers had dug into the metal.

"Can you fix it?" she asked.

"It may be salvageable," the caretaker said, sighing heavily. "Although a proper restoration will be neither quick nor easy."

"Good thing you've got plenty of time then," Ezekiel quipped. He and the other Librarians were taking it easy after their Irish adventure. "What with being immortal and all."

"There is that," Jenkins conceded. "In any event, it was a small price to pay to keep the Cauldron out of the hands of the Serpent Brotherhood."

"So what's the story with Max?" Stone asked, looking up from a hefty volume on Toltec burial chambers. "The local leprechauns happy to have him under lock and key?"

"I have been in touch with Connall MacDonagh at Mill Ends," Jenkins reported as he put aside the crushed bell for the moment. "He assures me that the odious Mister Lambton will indeed face justice for his crimes against the Fair Folk, as committed both here and overseas. I don't imagine that he will be troubling us—or anyone else—again."

"Glad to hear it." Baird always liked knowing that a dangerous character had been taken out of circulation for good. "Guess the Serpents are headless again, at least for the time being."

"Can we not mention headless things?" Cassandra asked. She shivered as she amused herself with a particularly devious sudoku. "That coachman was way too creepy for comfort."

Baird was about to point out that Lady Sibella was the stuff of nightmares as well when the back door of the Annex swung open and, soaking wet, Flynn Carsen sloshed in through a curtain of white light. Seaweed clung to his head and shoulders as he dripped onto the floor. He peeled a stray strand off his lapel even as Jenkins frowned at the puddle forming beneath him.

"So," Flynn asked, "what did I miss?"

ABOUT THE AUTHOR

GREG COX is the author of two previous Librarians novels: *The Librarians and the Lost Lamp* and *The Librarians and the Mother Goose Chase*. He has also written the official movie novelizations of such films as *Daredevil, Ghost Rider, The Dark Knight Rises, Man of Steel, Godzilla, War for the Planet of the Apes*, and the first three Underworld movies. In addition, he has written books and short stories based on such popular series as *Alias, Buffy the Vampire Slayer, CSI: Crime Scene Investigation, Farscape, The 4400, Leverage, Riese: Kingdom Falling, Roswell, Star Trek, Terminator, Warehouse 13, The X-Files*, and *Xena: Warrior Princess*. He is also a consulting editor for Tor Books.

www.gregcox-author.com